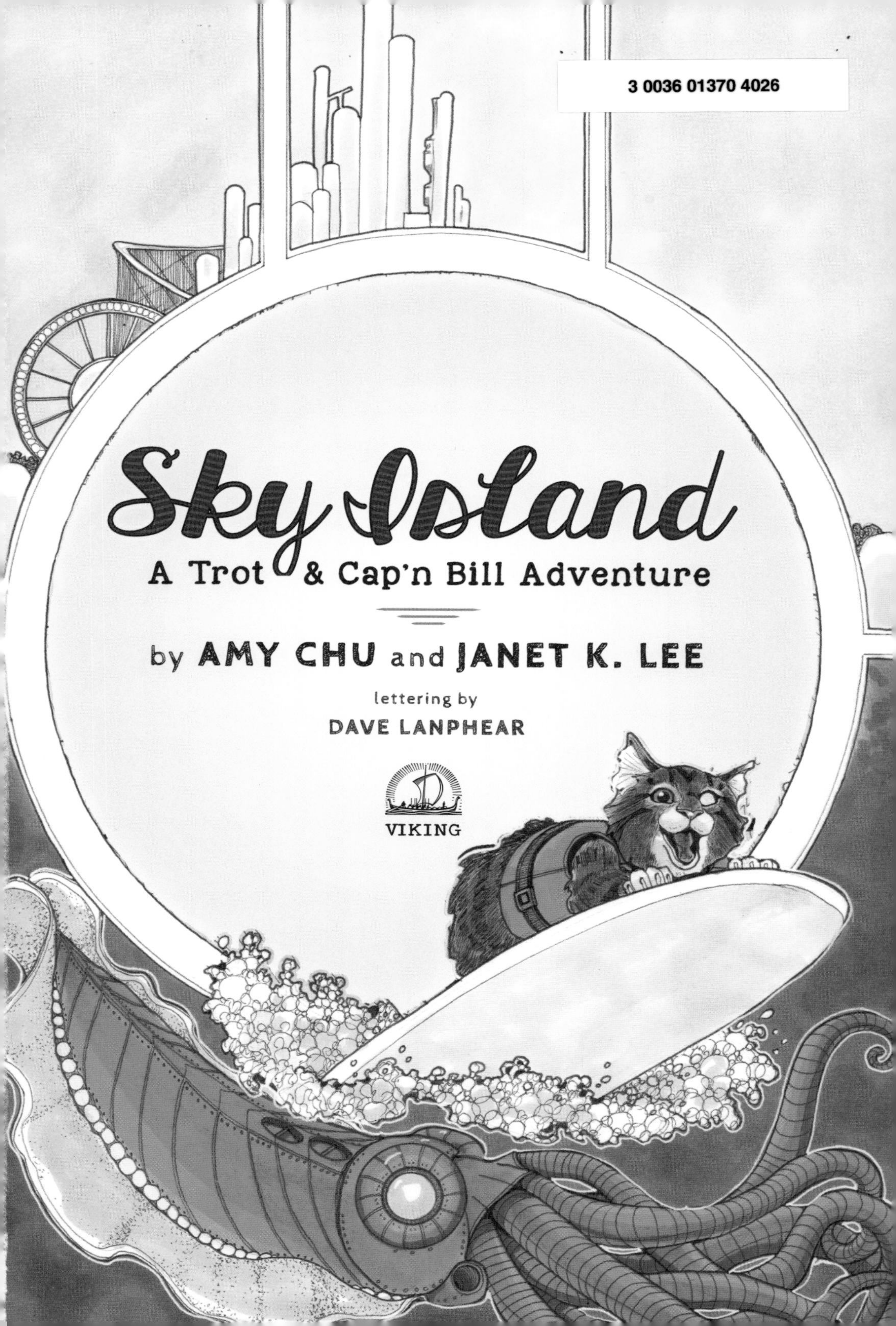

Sky Island

A Trot & Cap'n Bill Adventure

by **AMY CHU** and **JANET K. LEE**

lettering by
DAVE LANPHEAR

VIKING

VIKING

An imprint of Penguin Random House LLC, New York

First published in the United States of America by Viking,
an imprint of Penguin Random House LLC, 2020

Visit us online at penguinrandomhouse.com

LIBRARY OF CONGRESS CATALOGING-IN-PUBLICATION DATA IS AVAILABLE.
ISBN 9780451480231 (hardcover)
ISBN 9780451480248 (paperback)

Manufactured in China   Book design by Nancy Brennan
1 3 5 7 9 10 8 6 4 2

Contents

To my boys. You are the best. —A.C.

....

For Mike, who did all the chores

and wrangled all the cats so that I could draw.

—J.K.L.

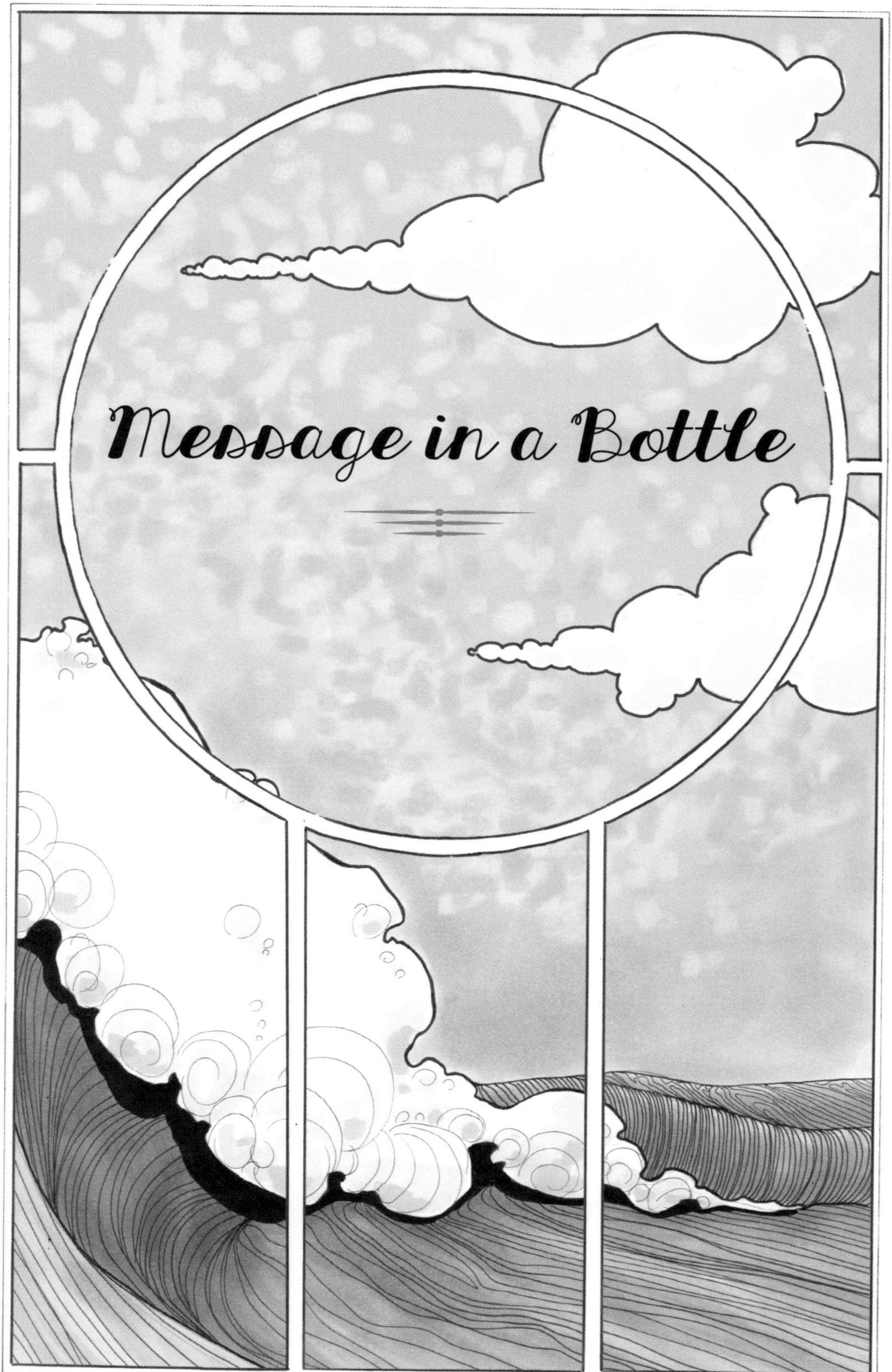
Message in a Bottle

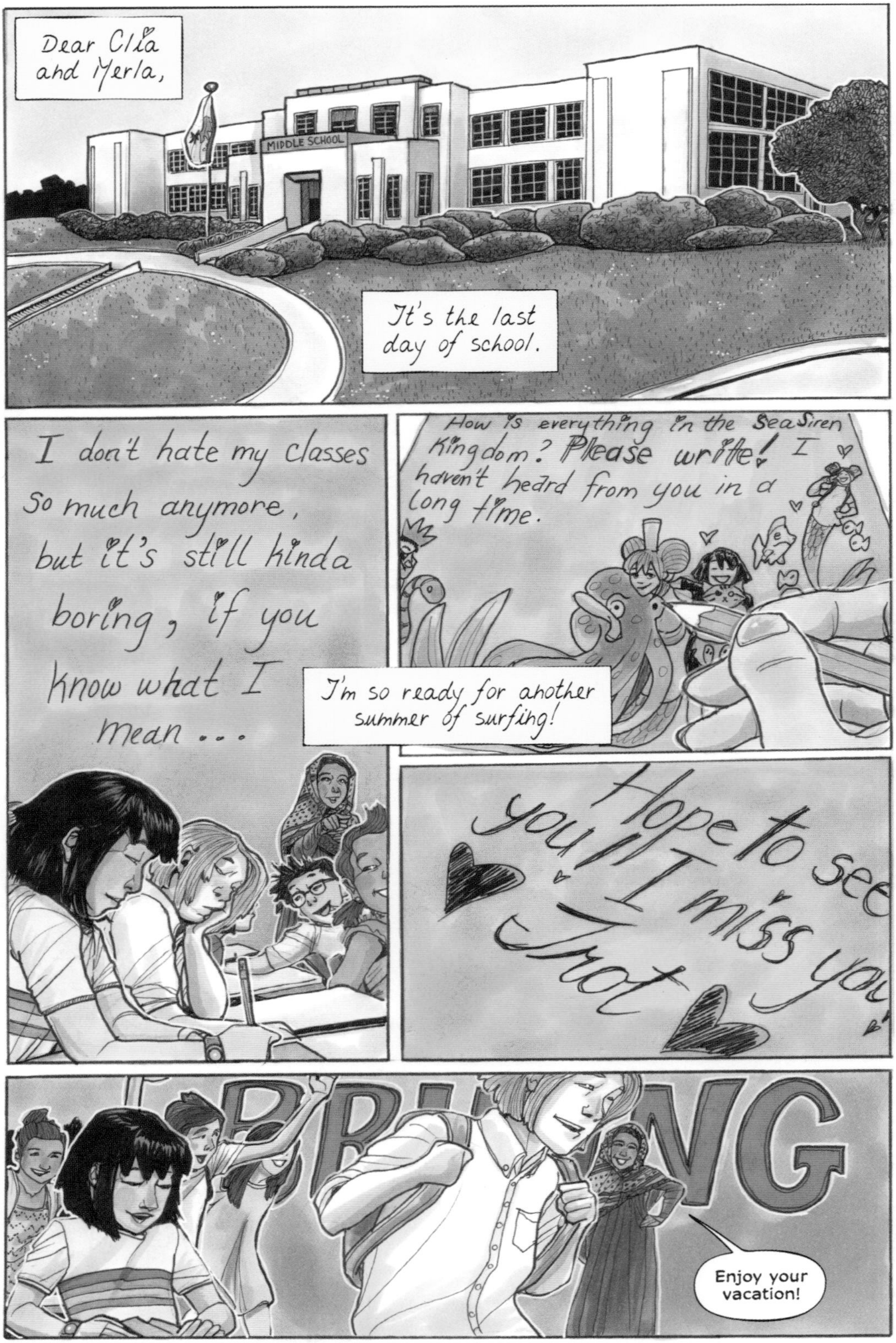
Dear Clia and Merla,
MIDDLE SCHOOL
It's the last day of school.
I don't hate my classes so much anymore, but it's still kinda boring, if you know what I mean ...
How is everything in the Sea Siren Kingdom? Please write! I haven't heard from you in a long time.
I'm so ready for another summer of surfing!
Hope to see you!! I miss you
Trot
Enjoy your vacation!

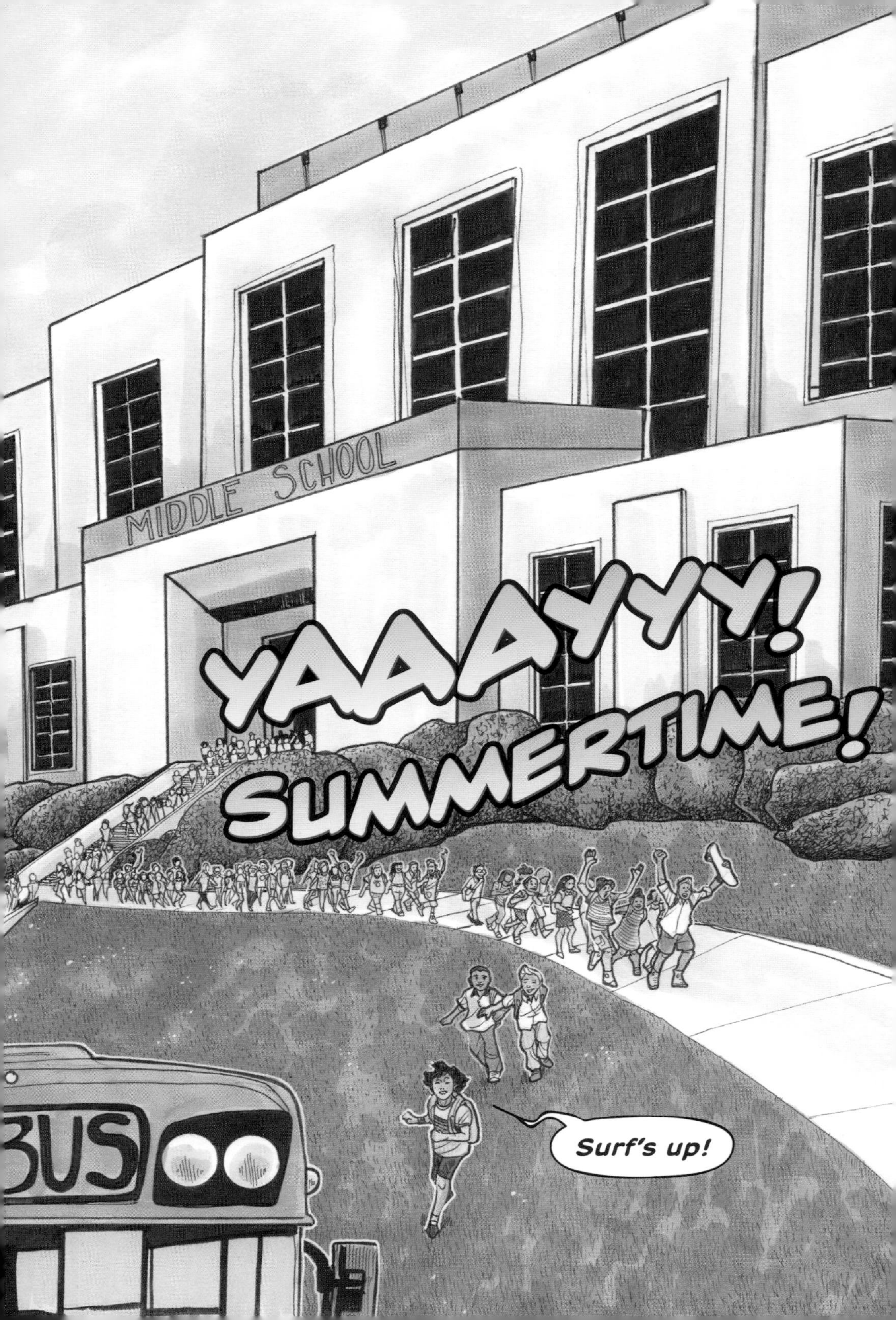
MIDDLE SCHOOL
YAAAYYY! SUMMERTIME!
BUS
Surf's up!

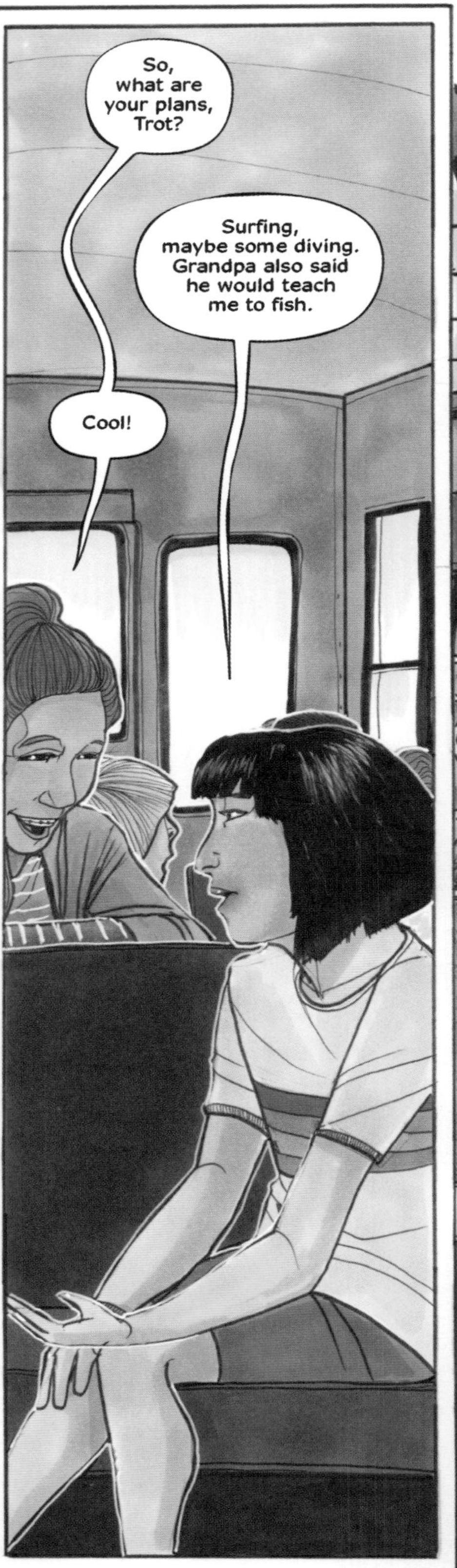
So, what are your plans, Trot?
Surfing, maybe some diving. Grandpa also said he would teach me to fish.
Cool!

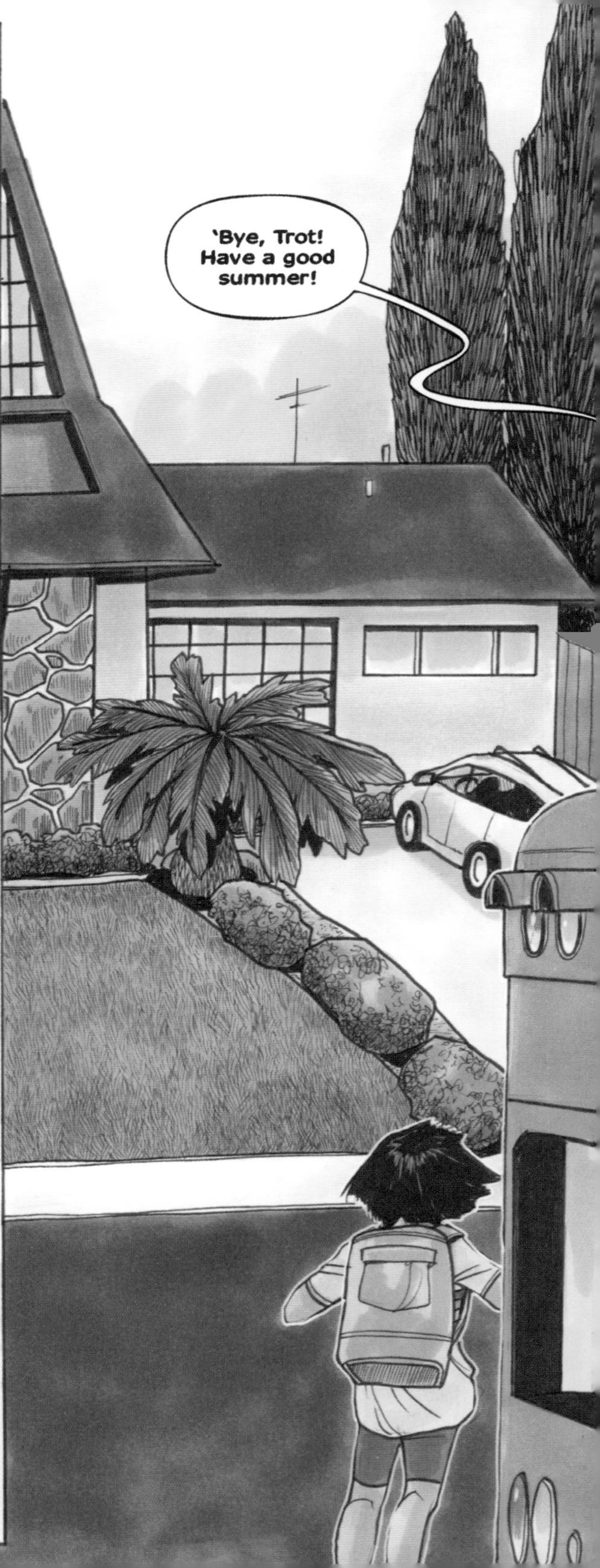
'Bye, Trot! Have a good summer!

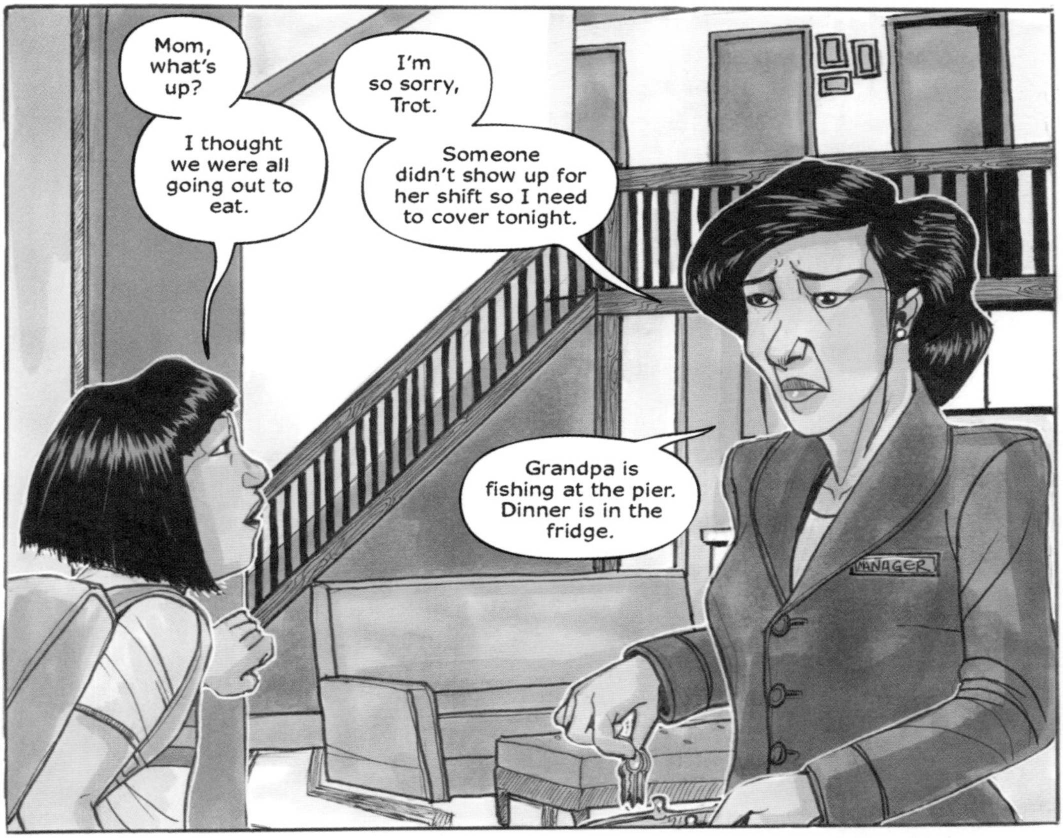
Mom, what's up?
I thought we were all going out to eat.
I'm so sorry, Trot.
Someone didn't show up for her shift so I need to cover tonight.
Grandpa is fishing at the pier. Dinner is in the fridge.
MANAGER

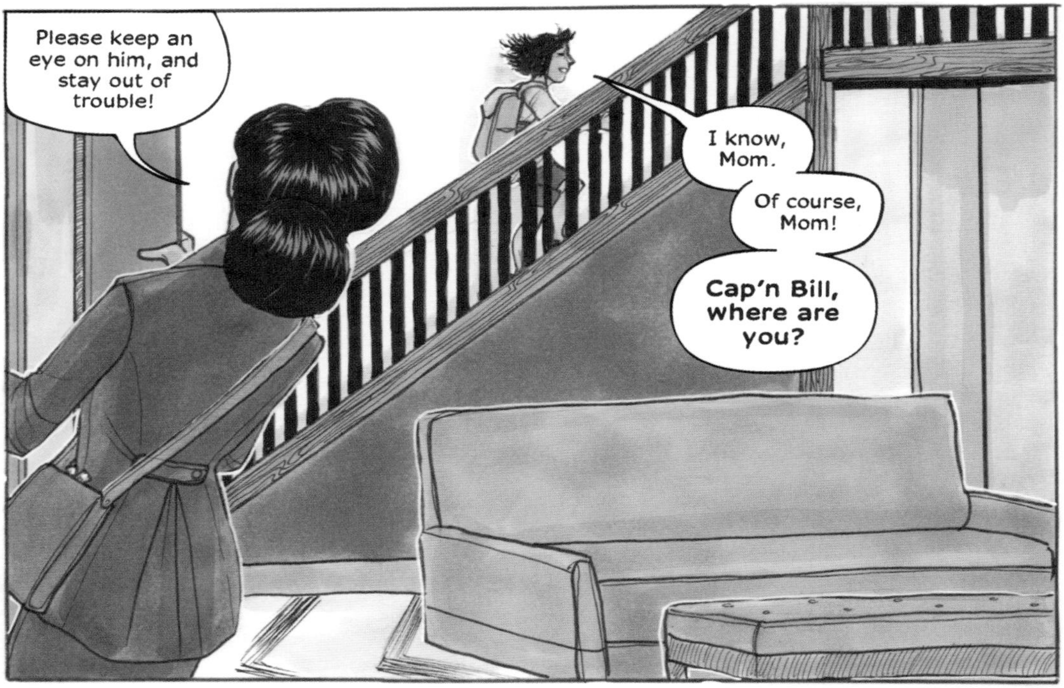
Please keep an eye on him, and stay out of trouble!
I know, Mom.
Of course, Mom!
Cap'n Bill, where are you?

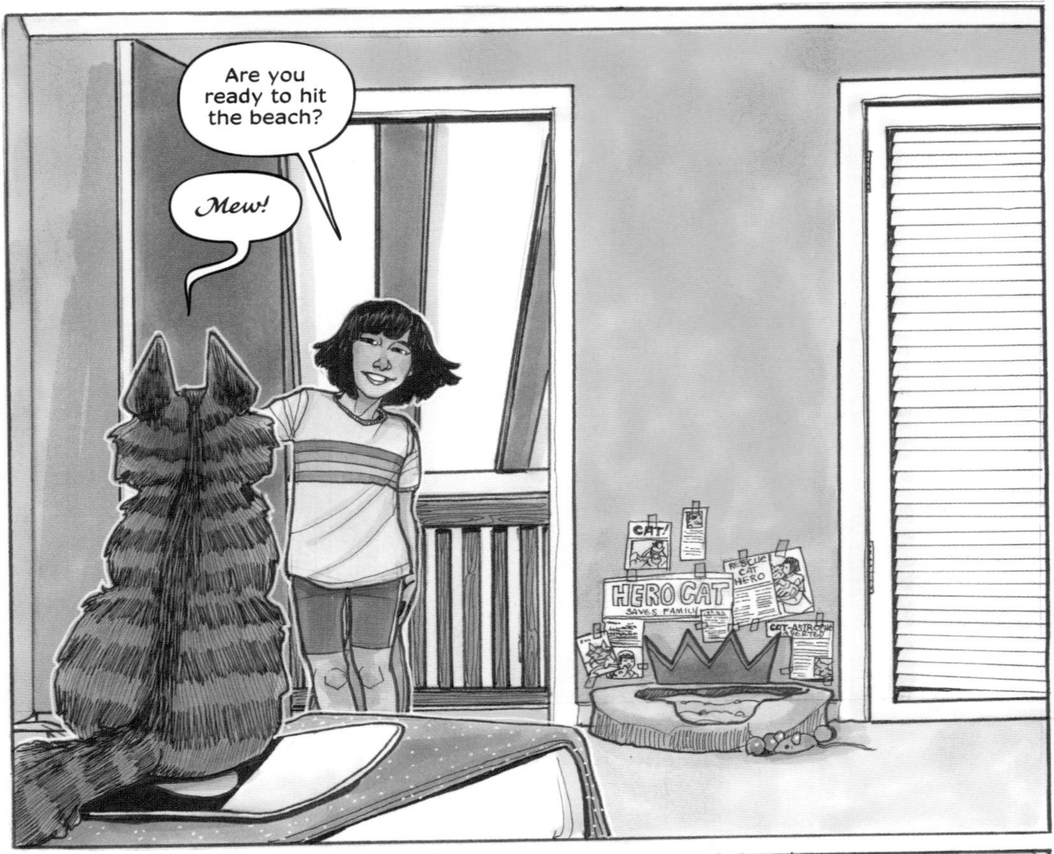
Are you ready to hit the beach?
Mew!
CAT!
HERO CAT
SAVES FAMILY
RESCUE CAT HERO

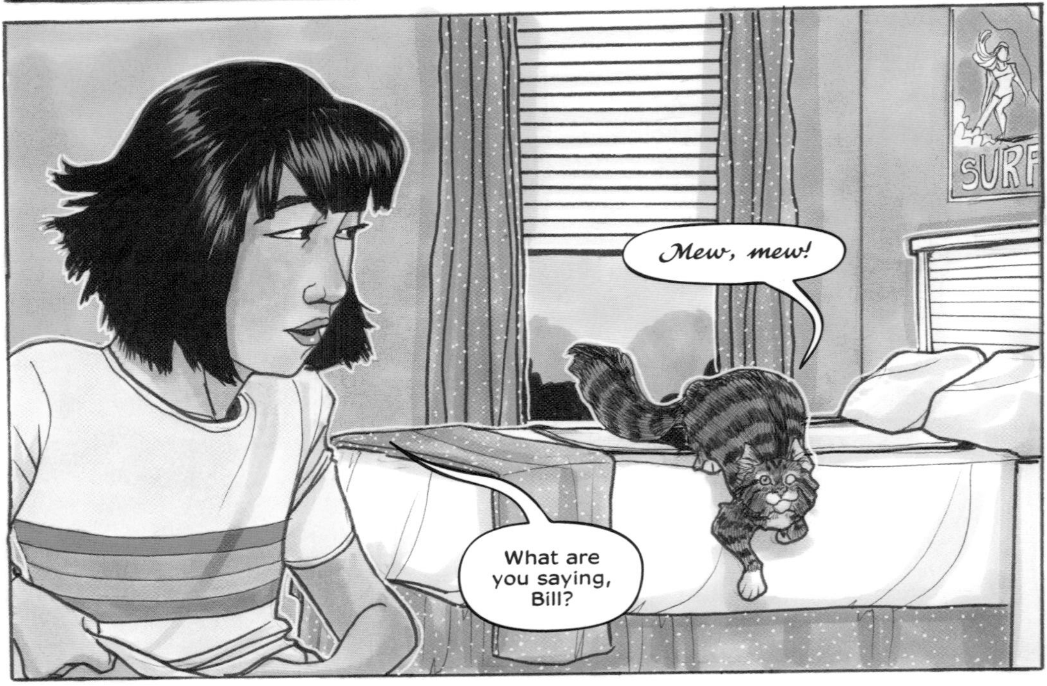
SURF
Mew, mew!
What are you saying, Bill?

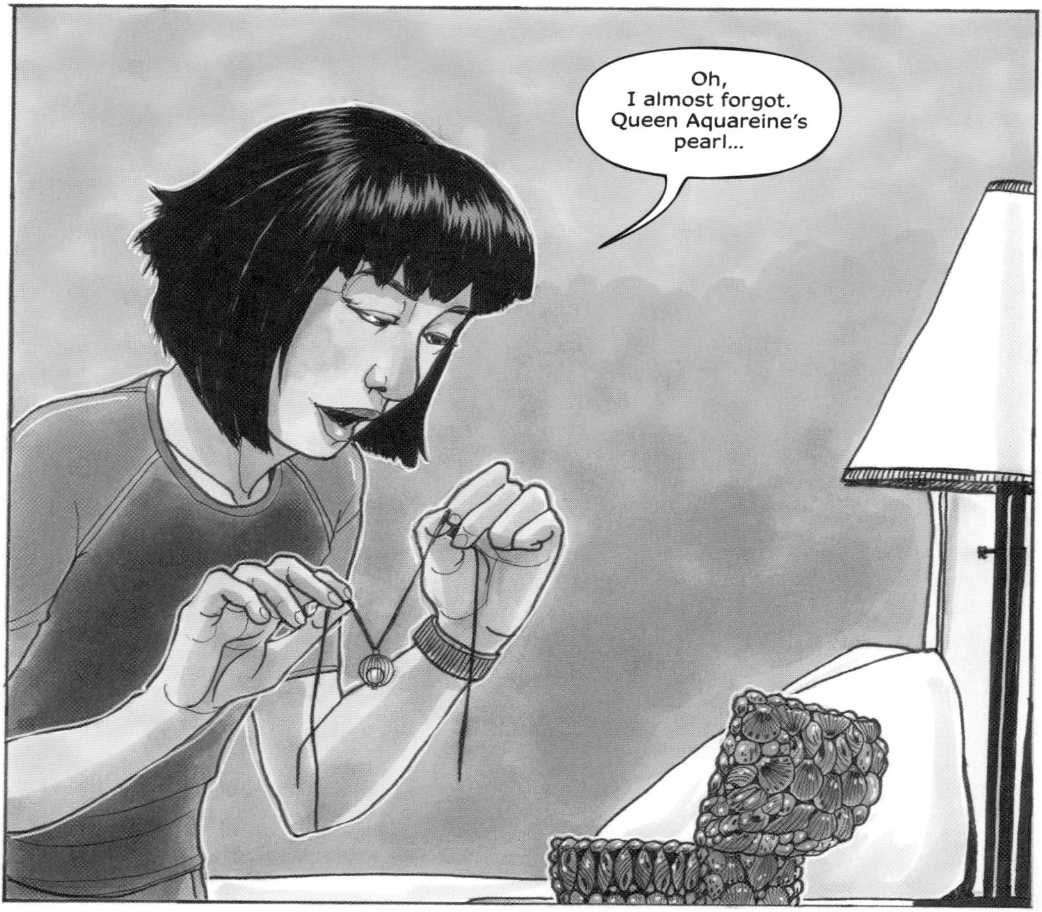
Oh, I almost forgot. Queen Aquareine's pearl...

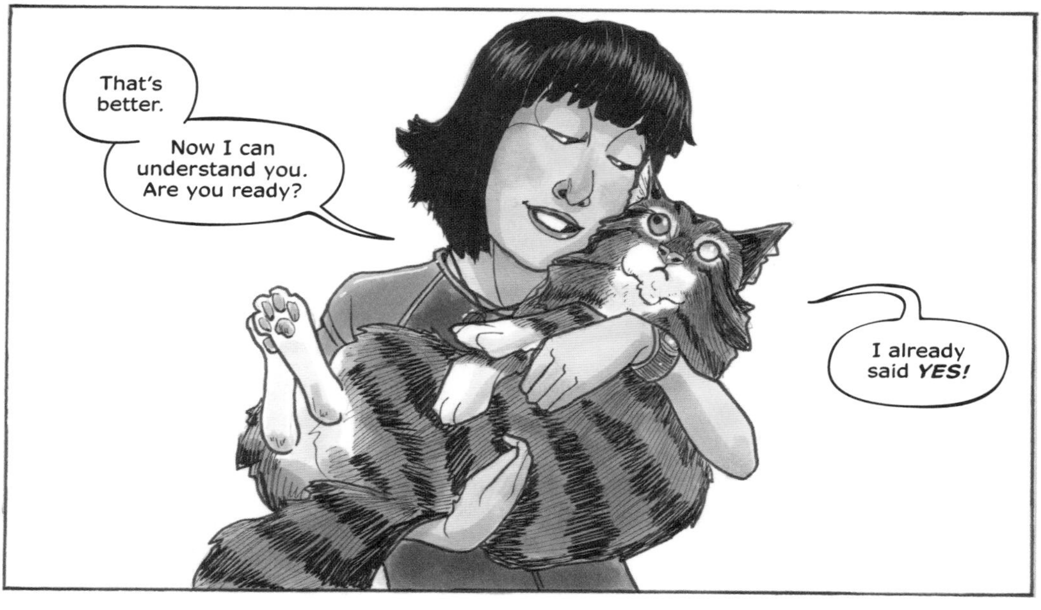
That's better.
Now I can understand you. Are you ready?
I already said ***YES!***

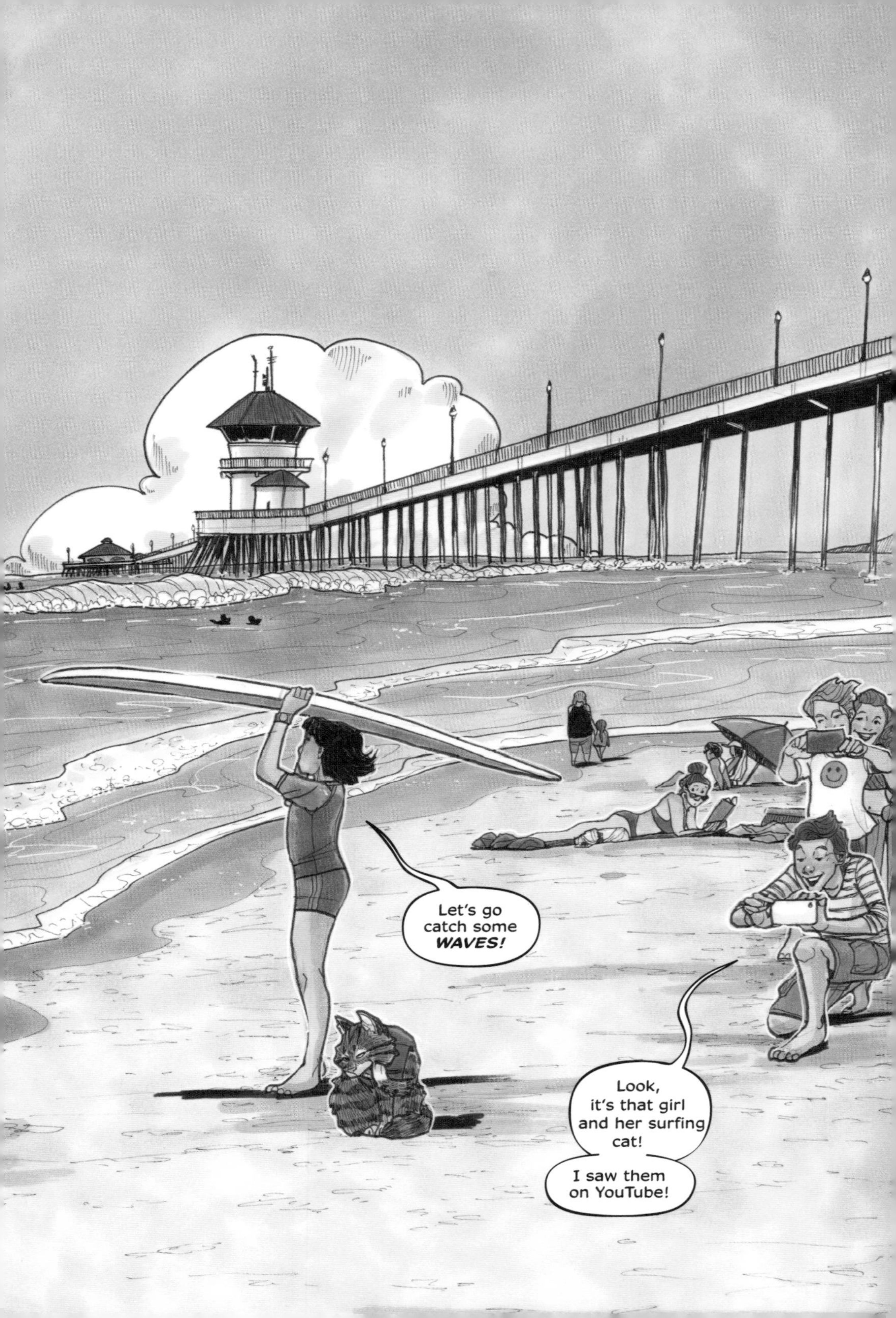
Let's go catch some ***WAVES!***
Look, it's that girl and her surfing cat!
I saw them on YouTube!

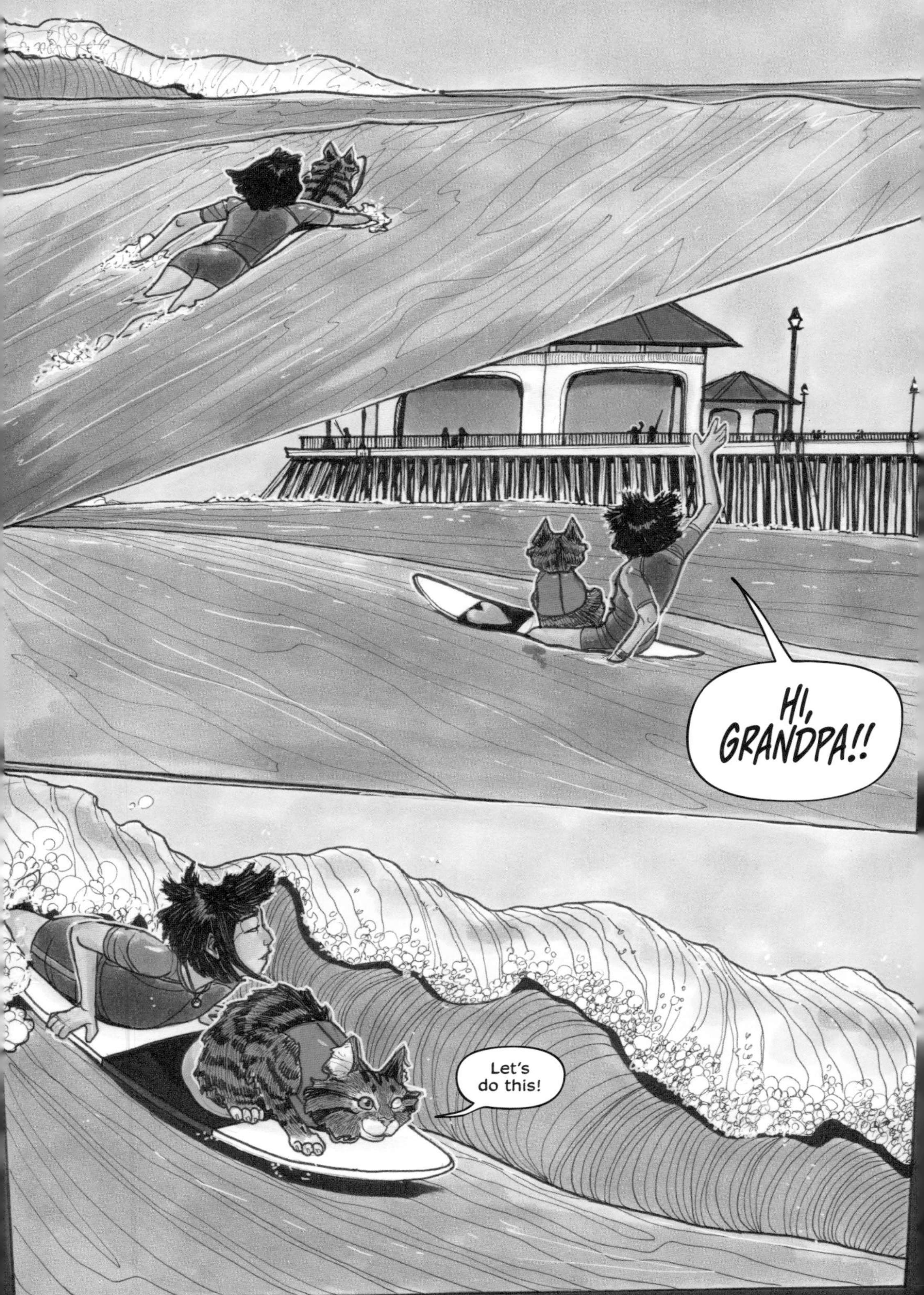
HI, GRANDPA!!
Let's do this!

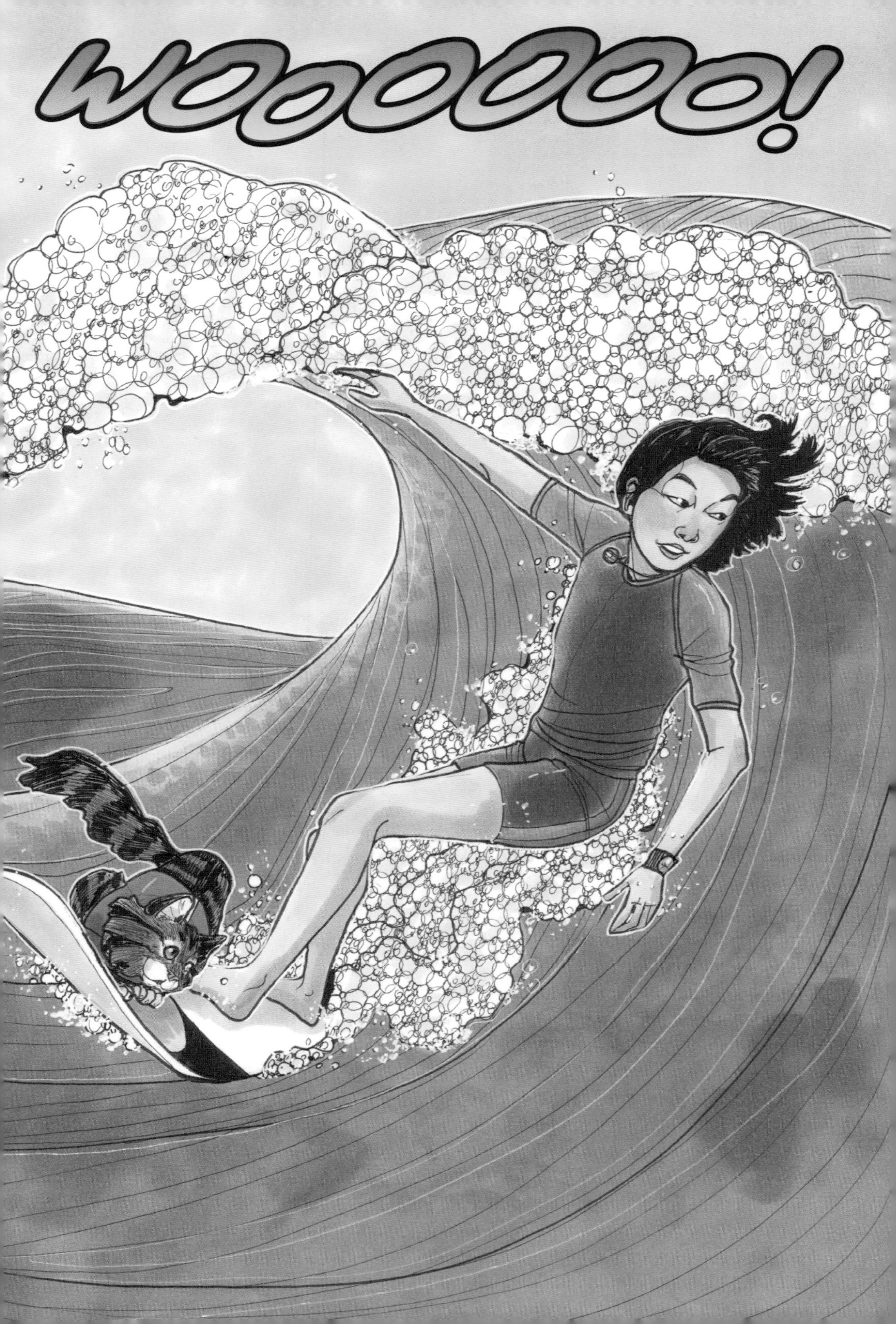
WOOOOOO!

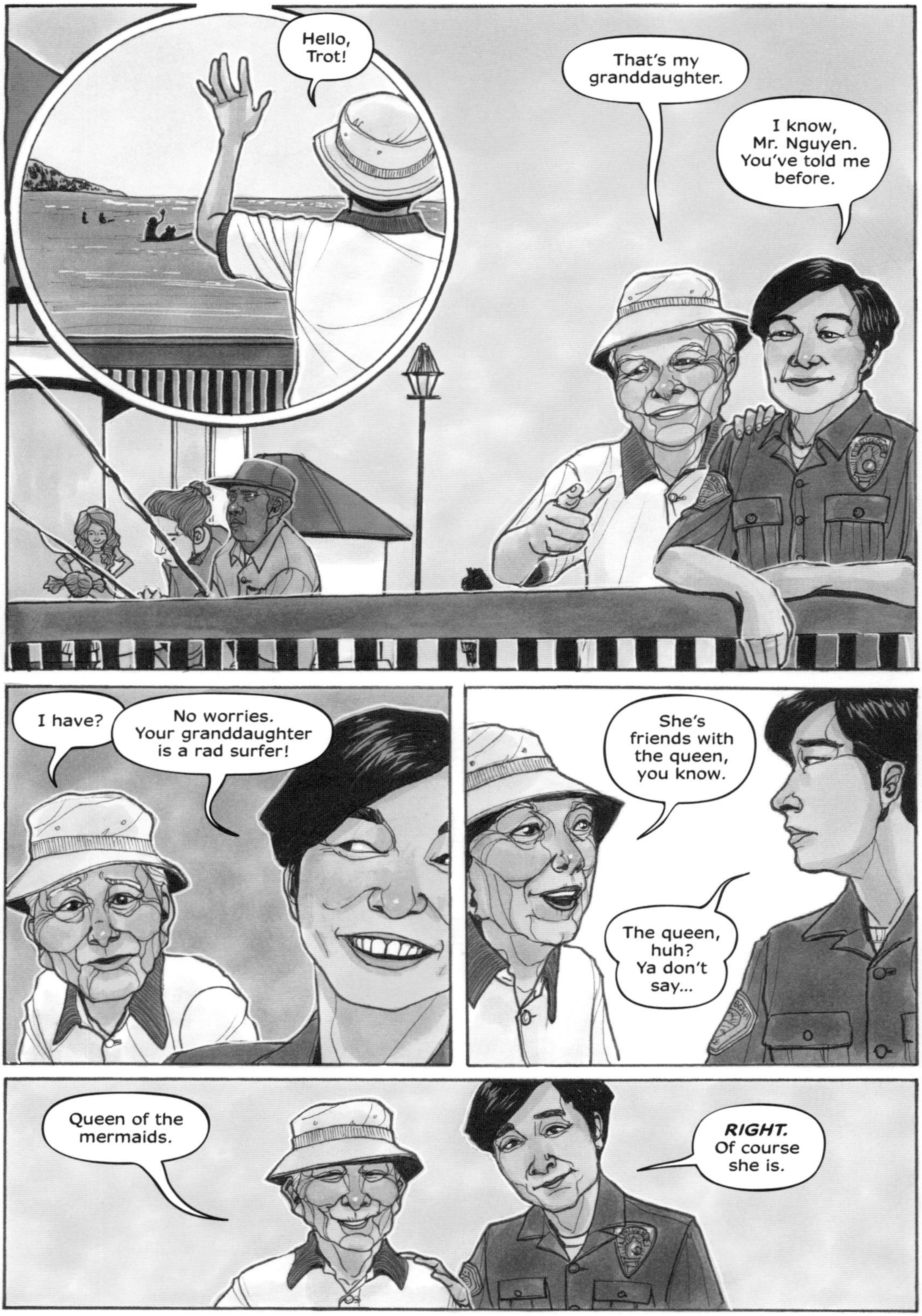
Hello, Trot!
That's my granddaughter.
I know, Mr. Nguyen. You've told me before.
I have?
No worries. Your granddaughter is a rad surfer!
She's friends with the queen, you know.
The queen, huh? Ya don't say...
Queen of the mermaids.
RIGHT. Of course she is.

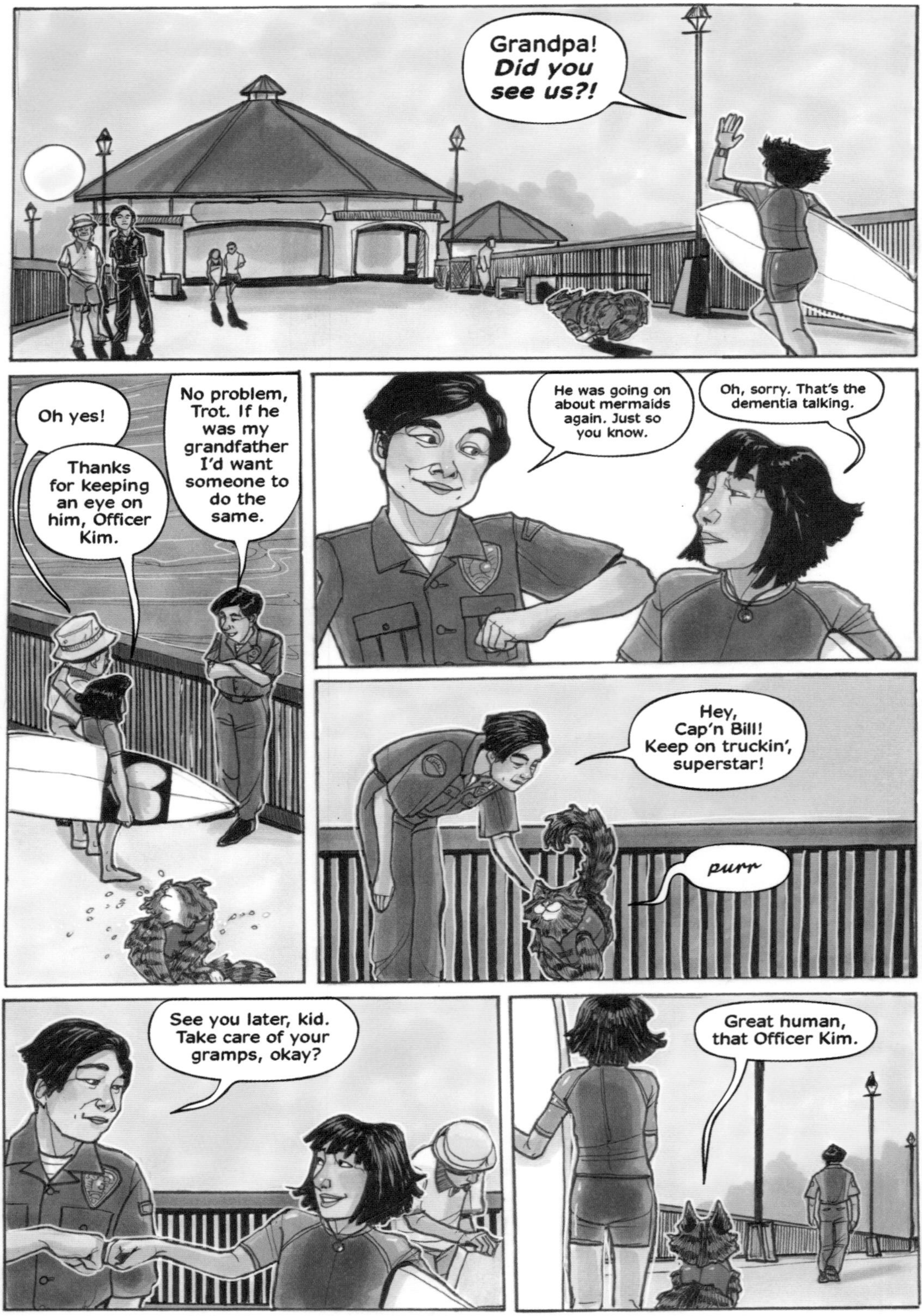

Grandpa! *Did you see us?!*
Oh yes!
Thanks for keeping an eye on him, Officer Kim.
No problem, Trot. If he was my grandfather I'd want someone to do the same.
He was going on about mermaids again. Just so you know.
Oh, sorry. That's the dementia talking.
Hey, Cap'n Bill! Keep on truckin', superstar!
purr
See you later, kid. Take care of your gramps, okay?
Great human, that Officer Kim.

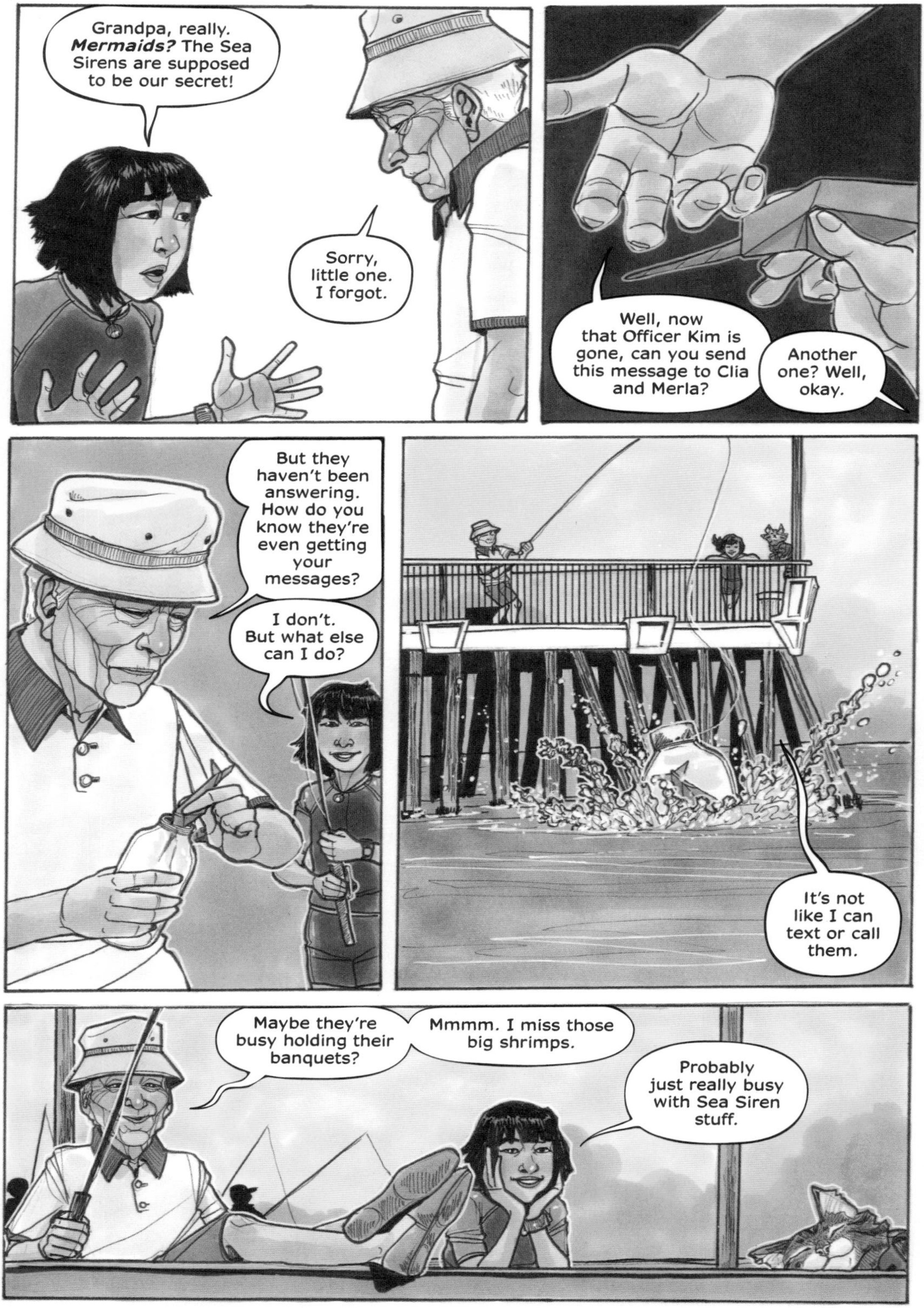

Grandpa, really. *Mermaids?* The Sea Sirens are supposed to be our secret!
Sorry, little one. I forgot.
Well, now that Officer Kim is gone, can you send this message to Clia and Merla?
Another one? Well, okay.
But they haven't been answering. How do you know they're even getting your messages?
I don't. But what else can I do?
It's not like I can text or call them.
Maybe they're busy holding their banquets?
Mmmm. I miss those big shrimps.
Probably just really busy with Sea Siren stuff.

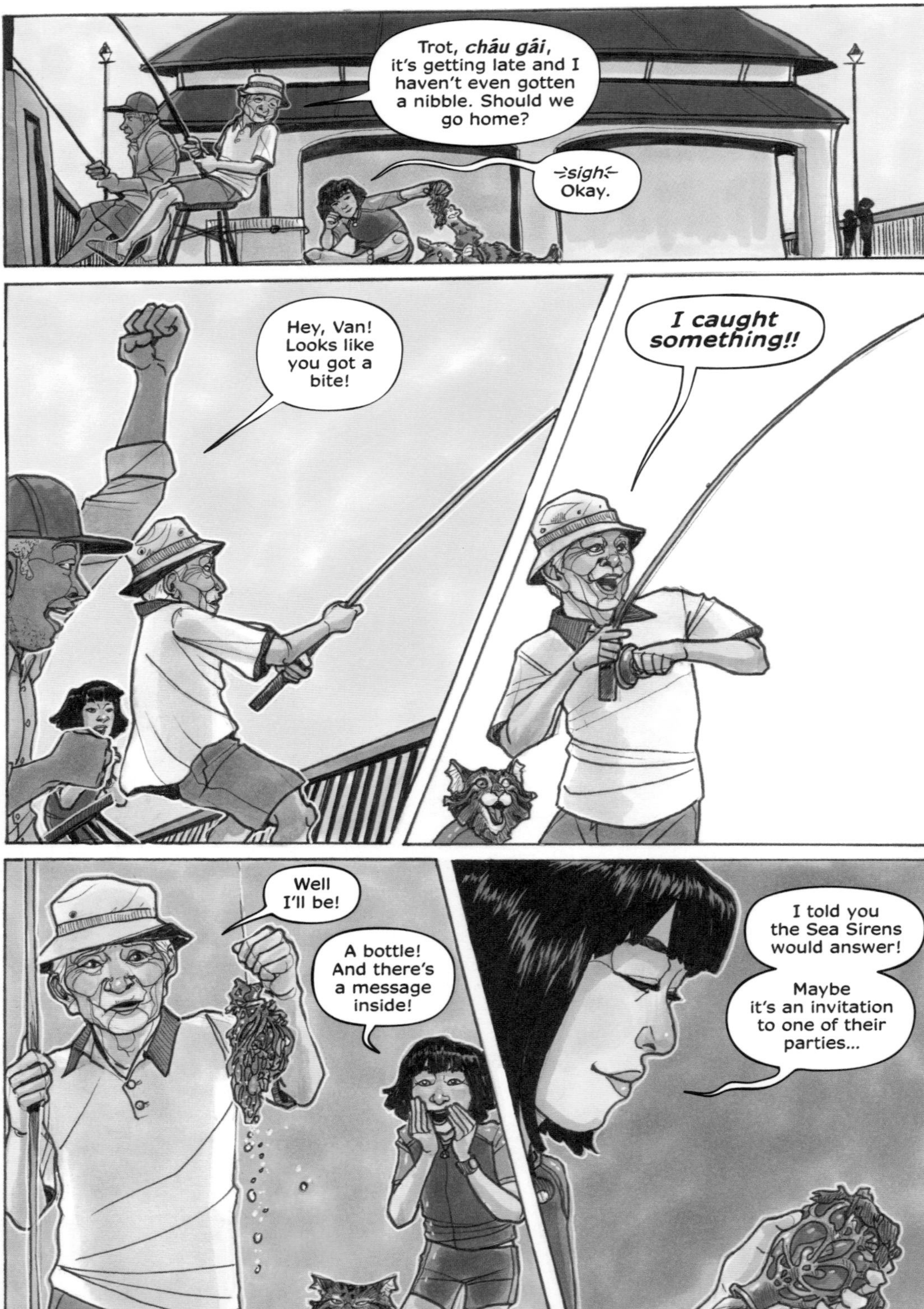
Trot, *cháu gái*, it's getting late and I haven't even gotten a nibble. Should we go home?
-sigh- Okay.
Hey, Van! Looks like you got a bite!
I caught something!!
Well I'll be!
A bottle! And there's a message inside!
I told you the Sea Sirens would answer!
Maybe it's an invitation to one of their parties...

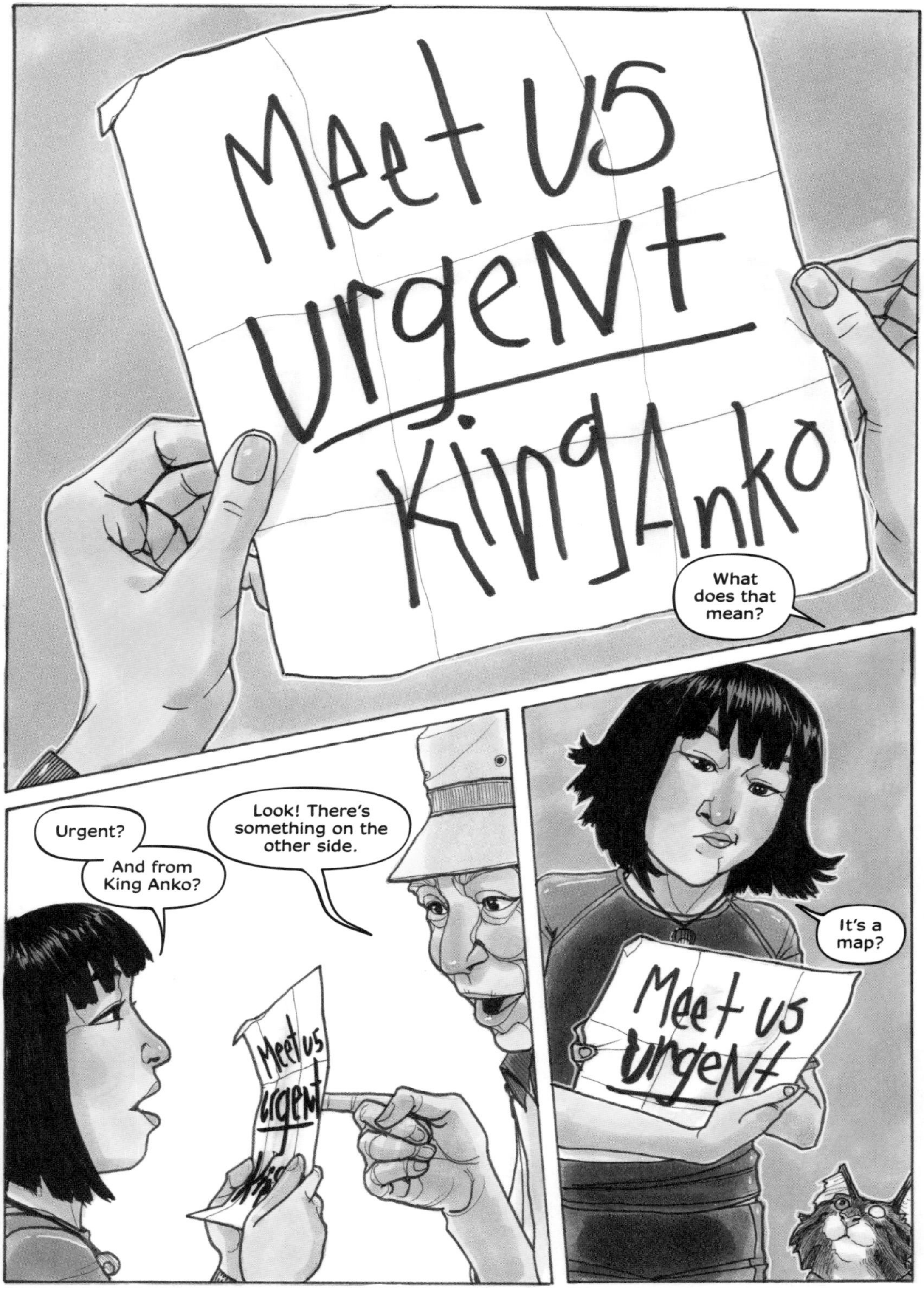
Meet us
urgent
King Anko
What does that mean?
Urgent?
And from King Anko?
Look! There's something on the other side.
Meet us
urgent
It's a map?
Meet us
urgent

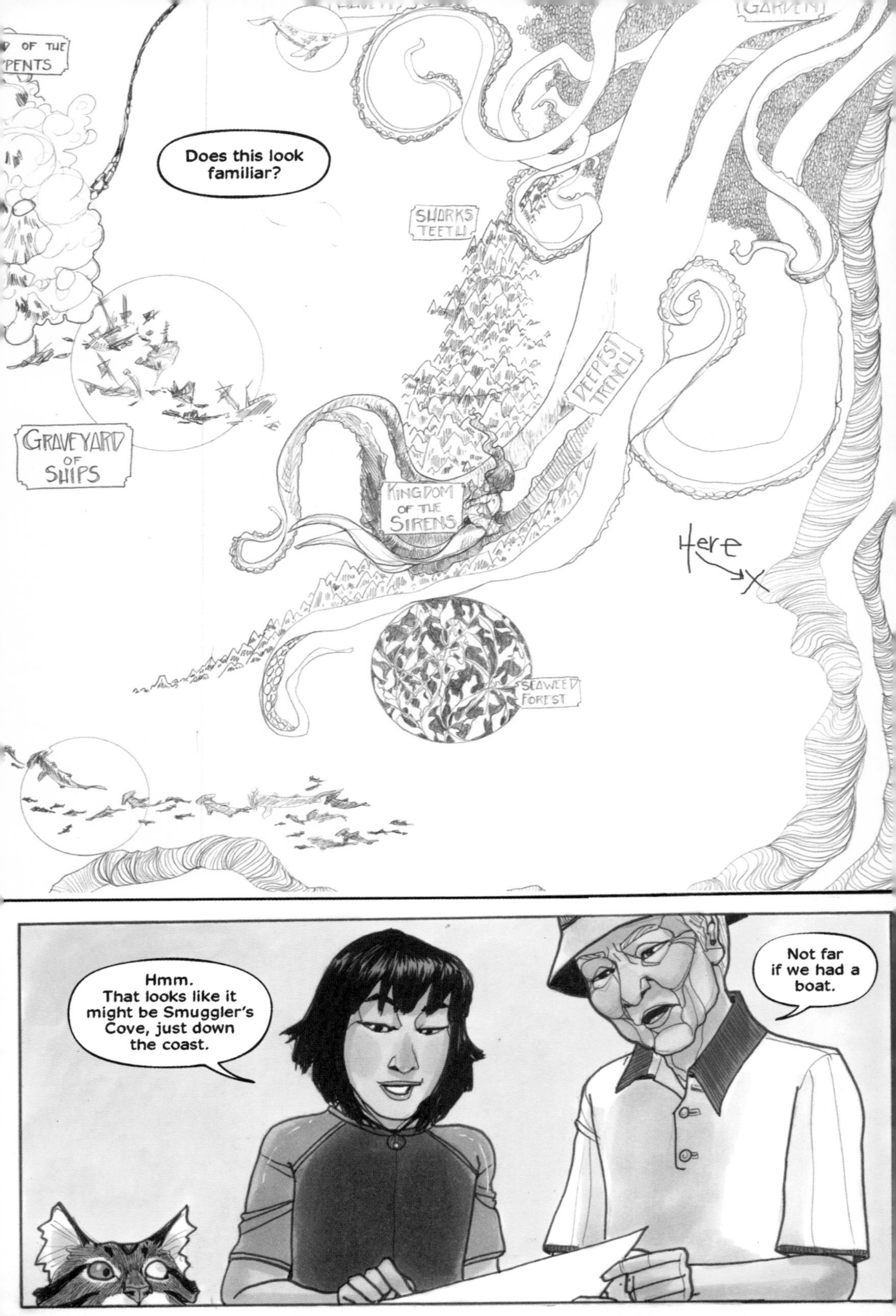
Does this look familiar?
SHARKS TEETH
DEEPEST TRENCH
GRAVEYARD OF SHIPS
KINGDOM OF THE SIRENS
Here
SEAWEED FOREST
Hmm. That looks like it might be Smuggler's Cove, just down the coast.
Not far if we had a boat.

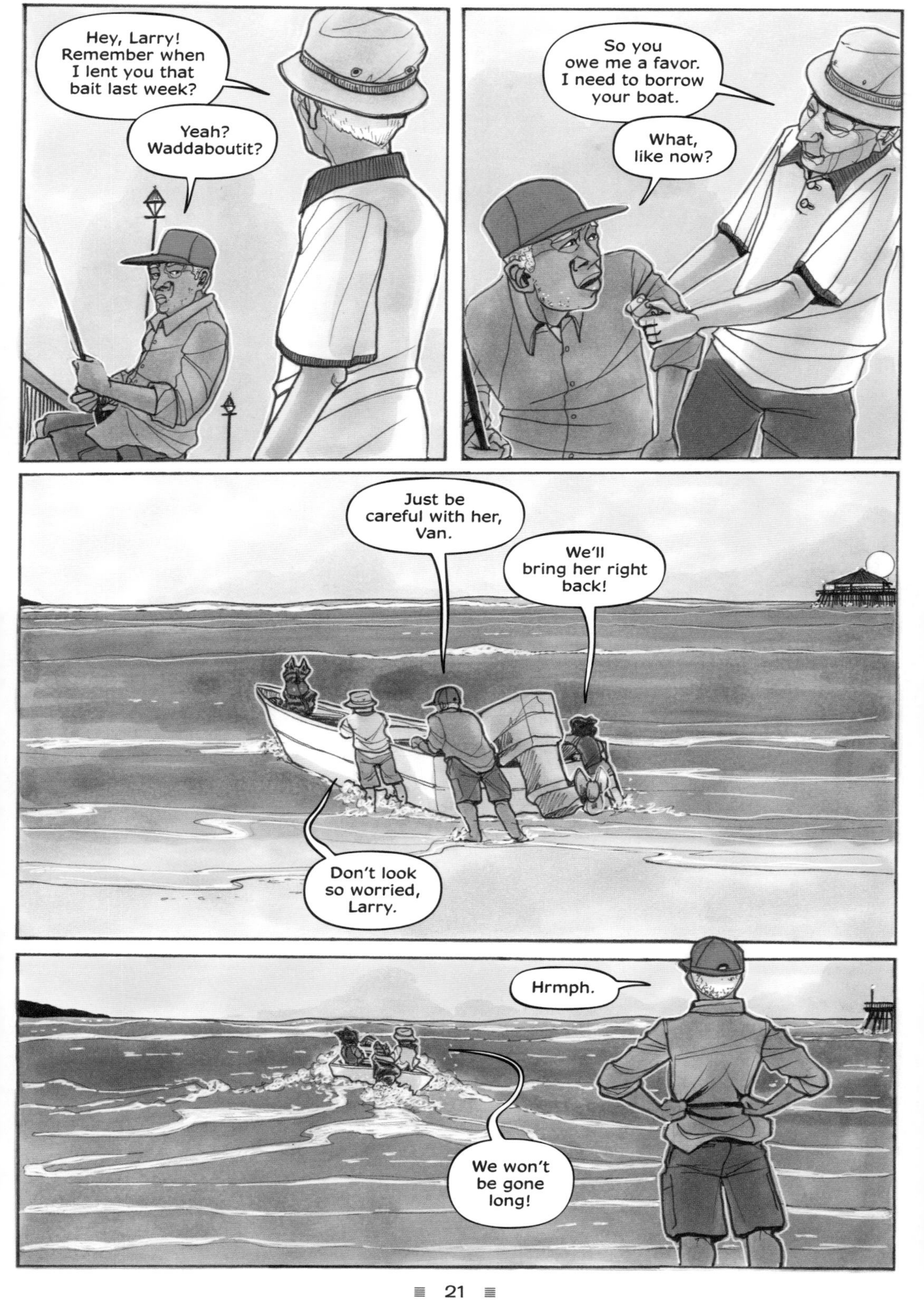

Hey, Larry! Remember when I lent you that bait last week?
Yeah? Waddaboutit?
So you owe me a favor. I need to borrow your boat.
What, like now?
Just be careful with her, Van.
We'll bring her right back!
Don't look so worried, Larry.
Hrmph.
We won't be gone long!

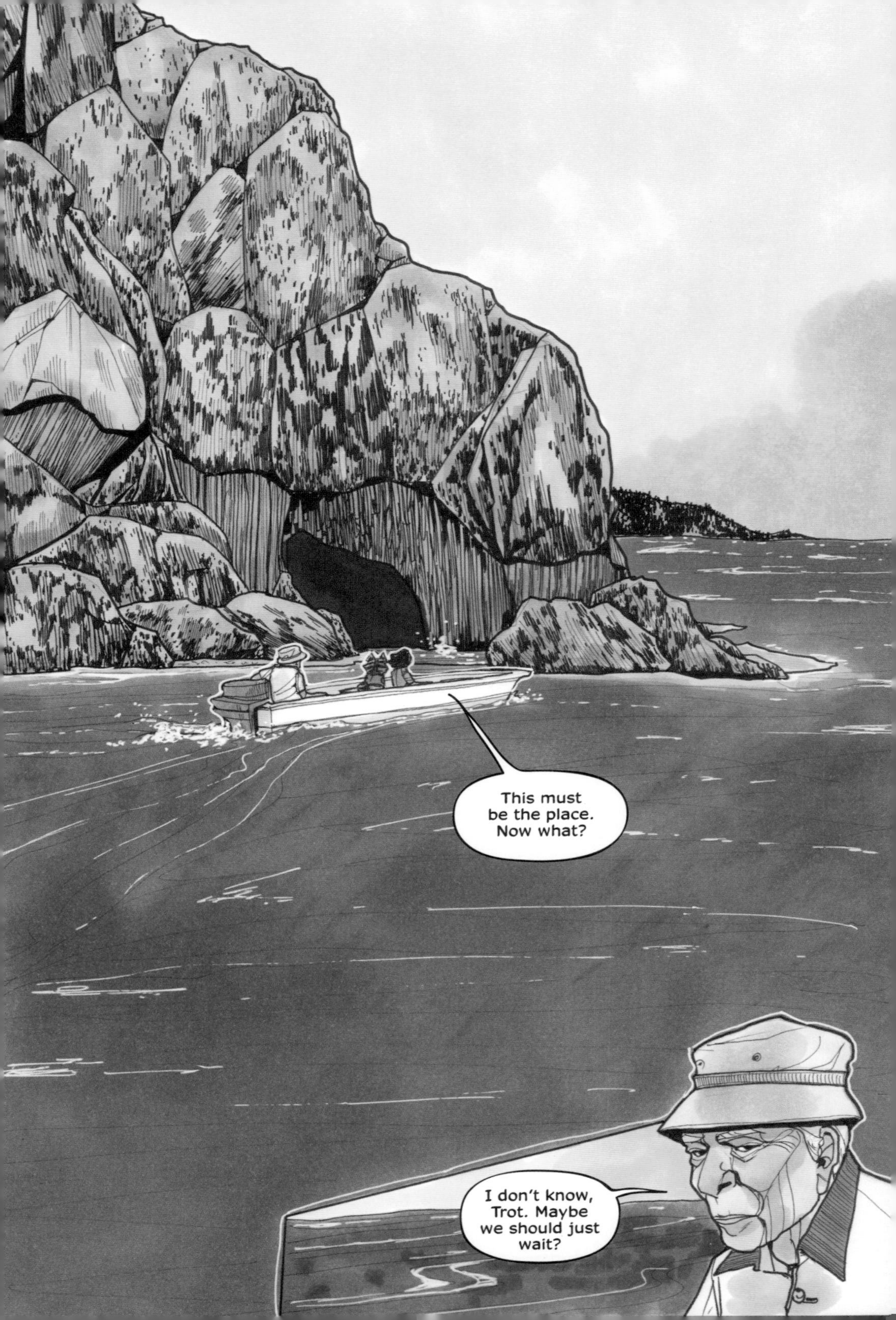
This must be the place. Now what?
I don't know, Trot. Maybe we should just wait?

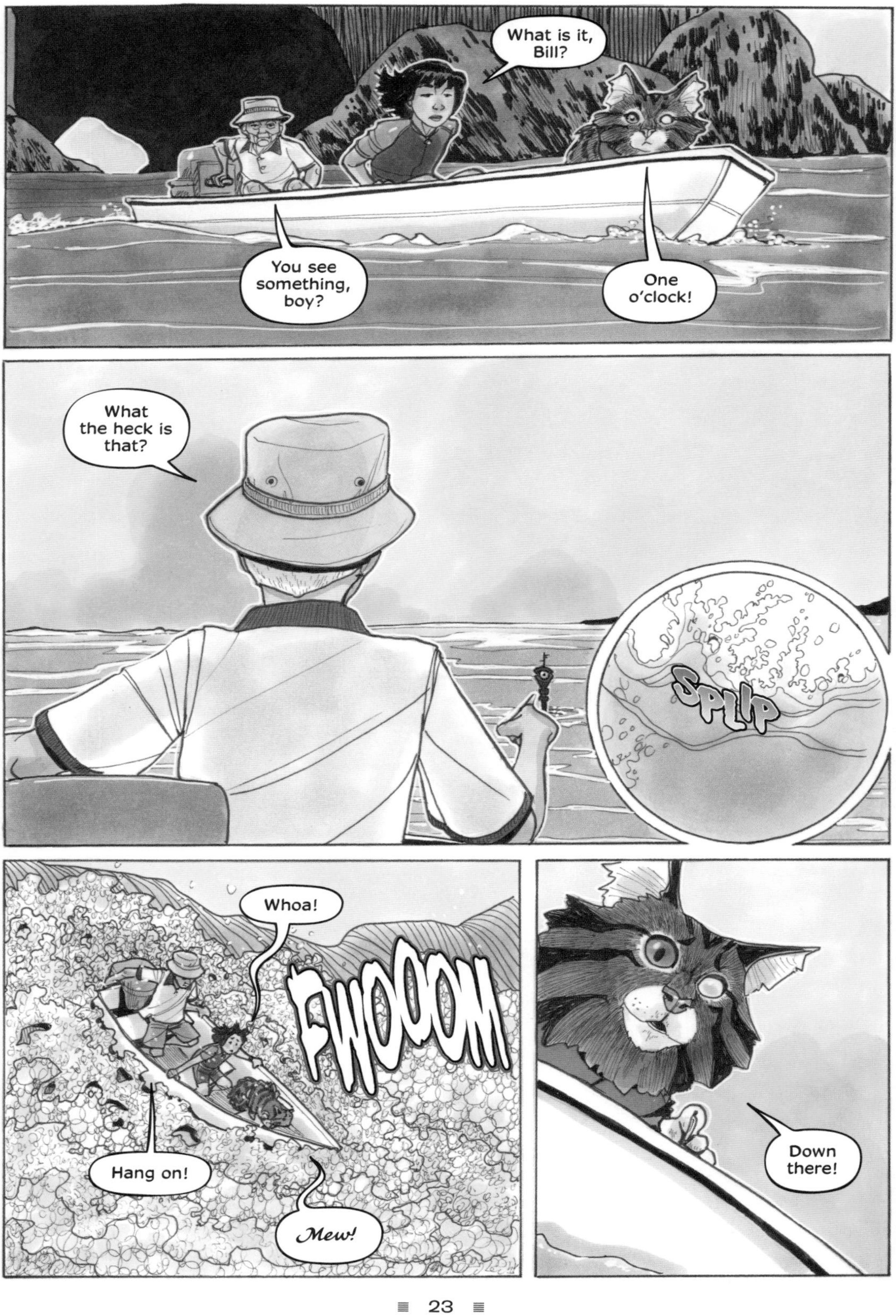
What is it, Bill?
You see something, boy?
One o'clock!
What the heck is that?
SPLIP
Whoa!
FWOOOM
Hang on!
Mew!
Down there!

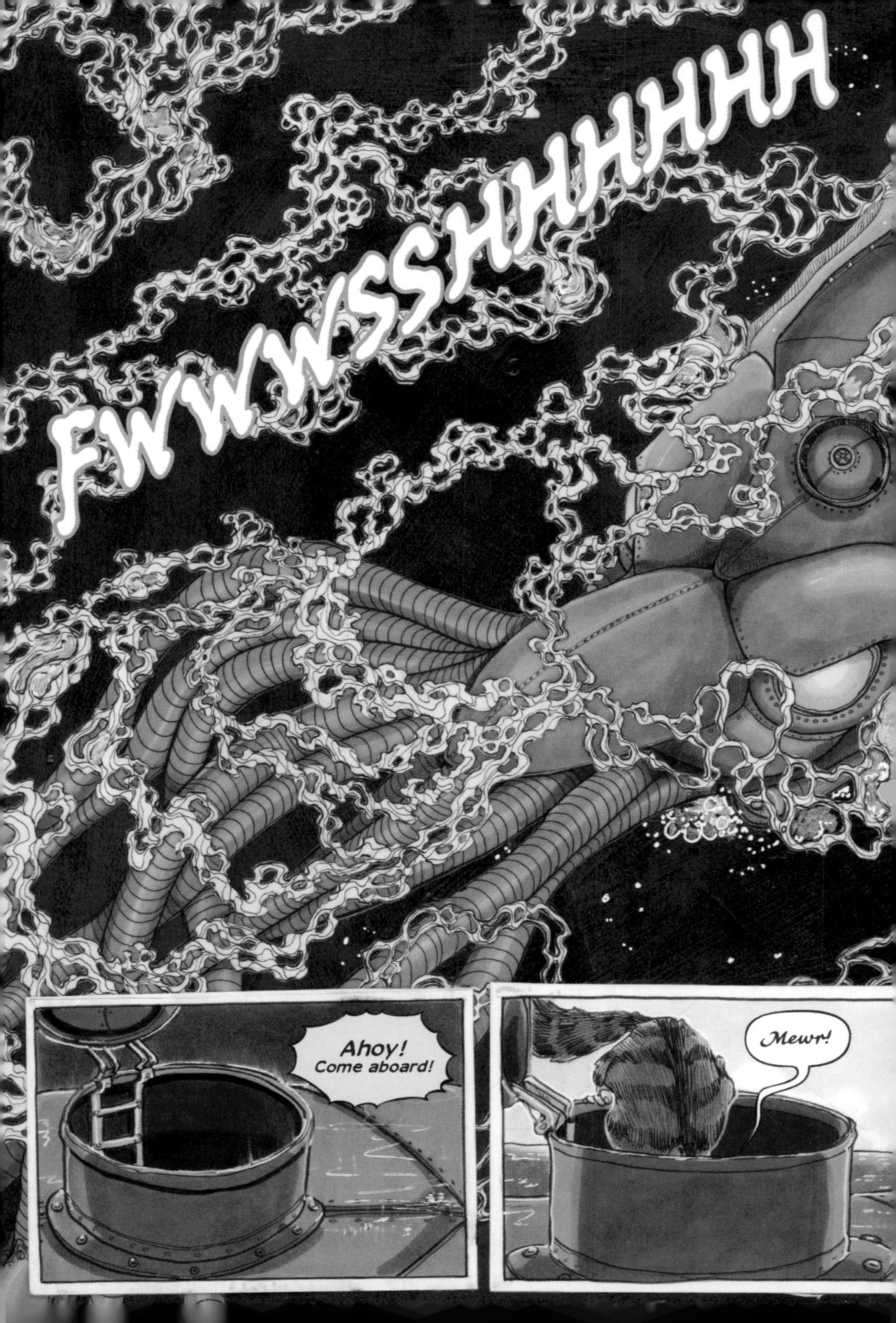
FWWWSSHHHHHH
Ahoy! Come aboard!
Mewr!

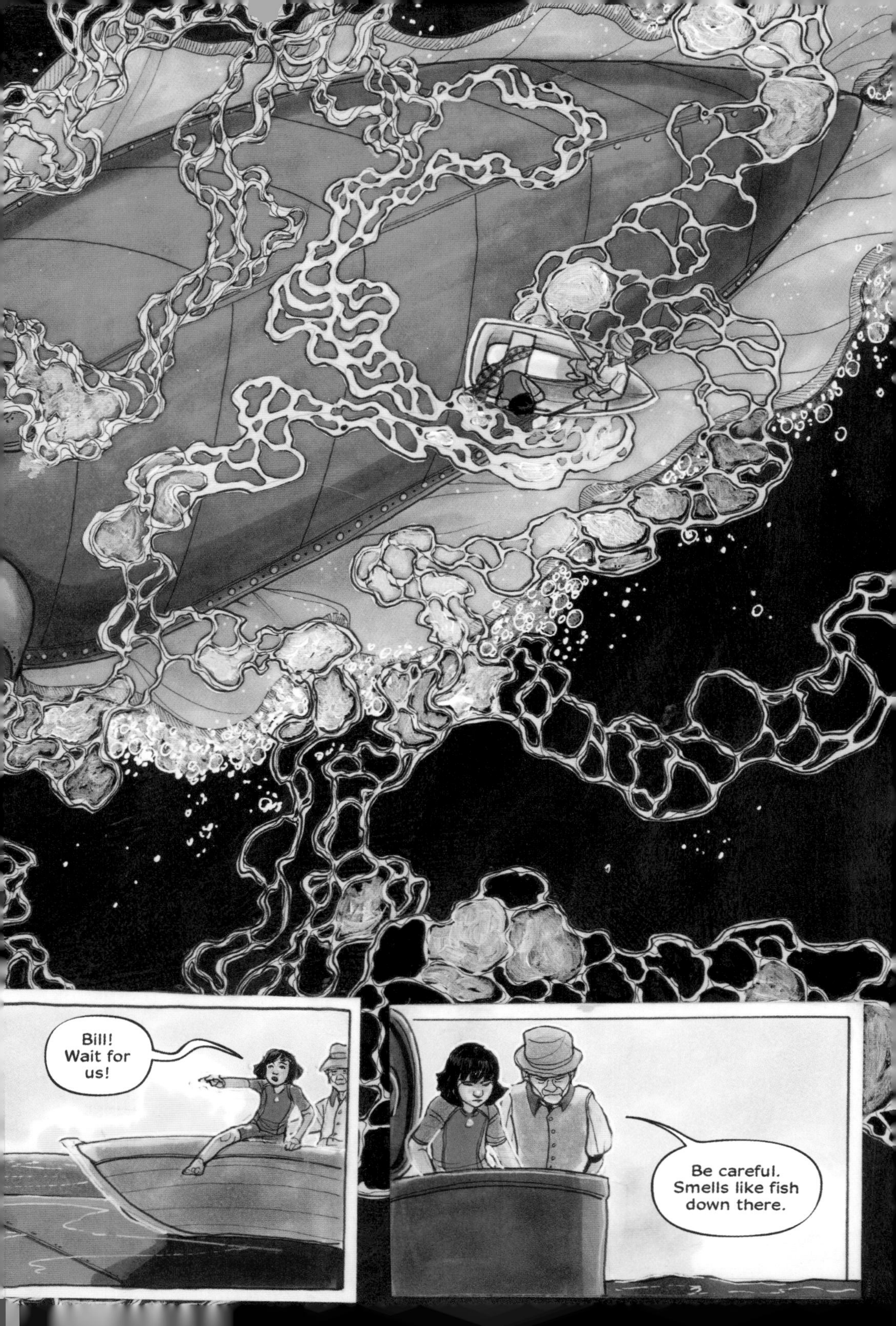
Bill! Wait for us!
Be careful. Smells like fish down there.

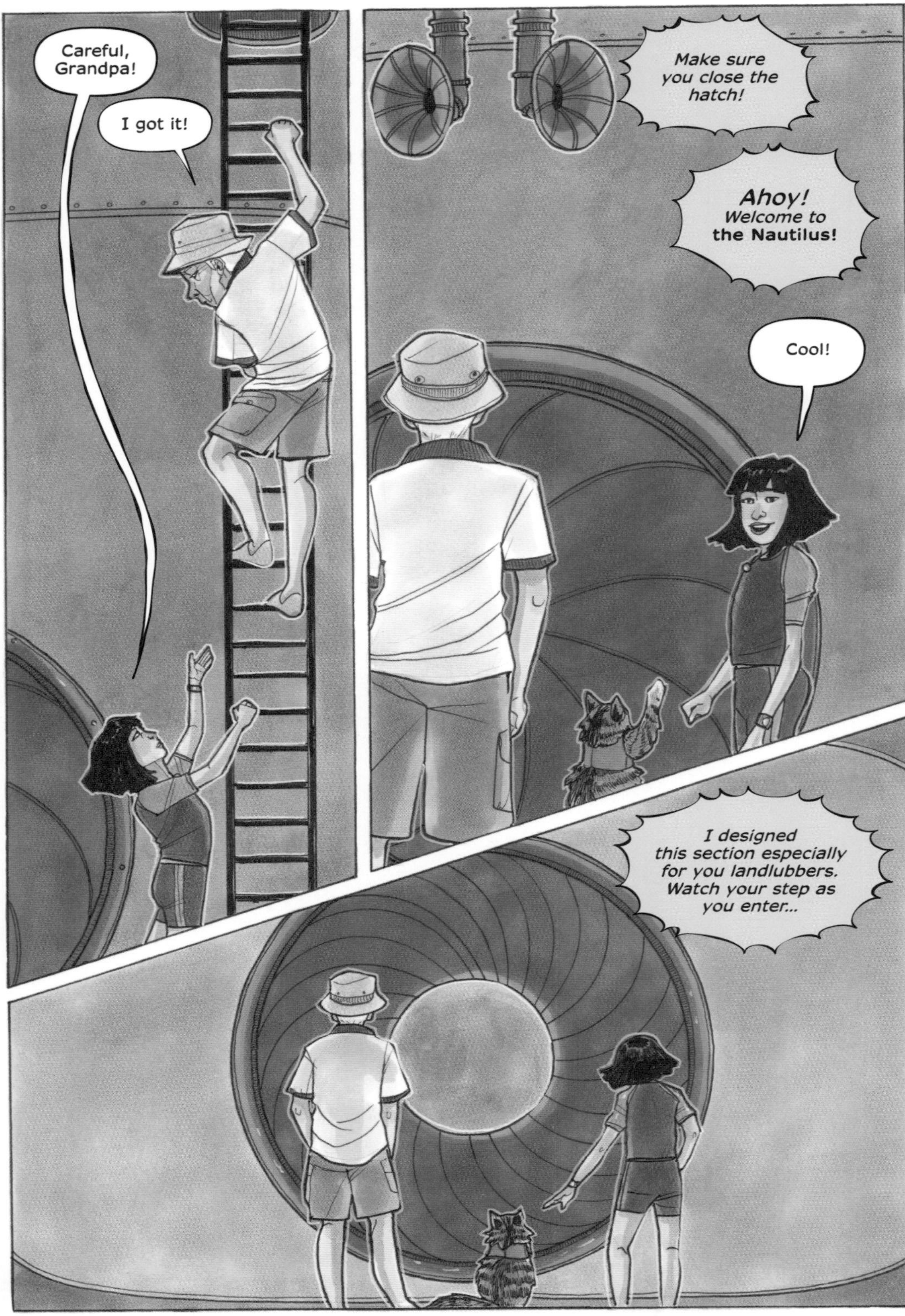
Careful, Grandpa!
I got it!
Make sure you close the hatch!
Ahoy! Welcome to the Nautilus!
Cool!
I designed this section especially for you landlubbers. Watch your step as you enter...

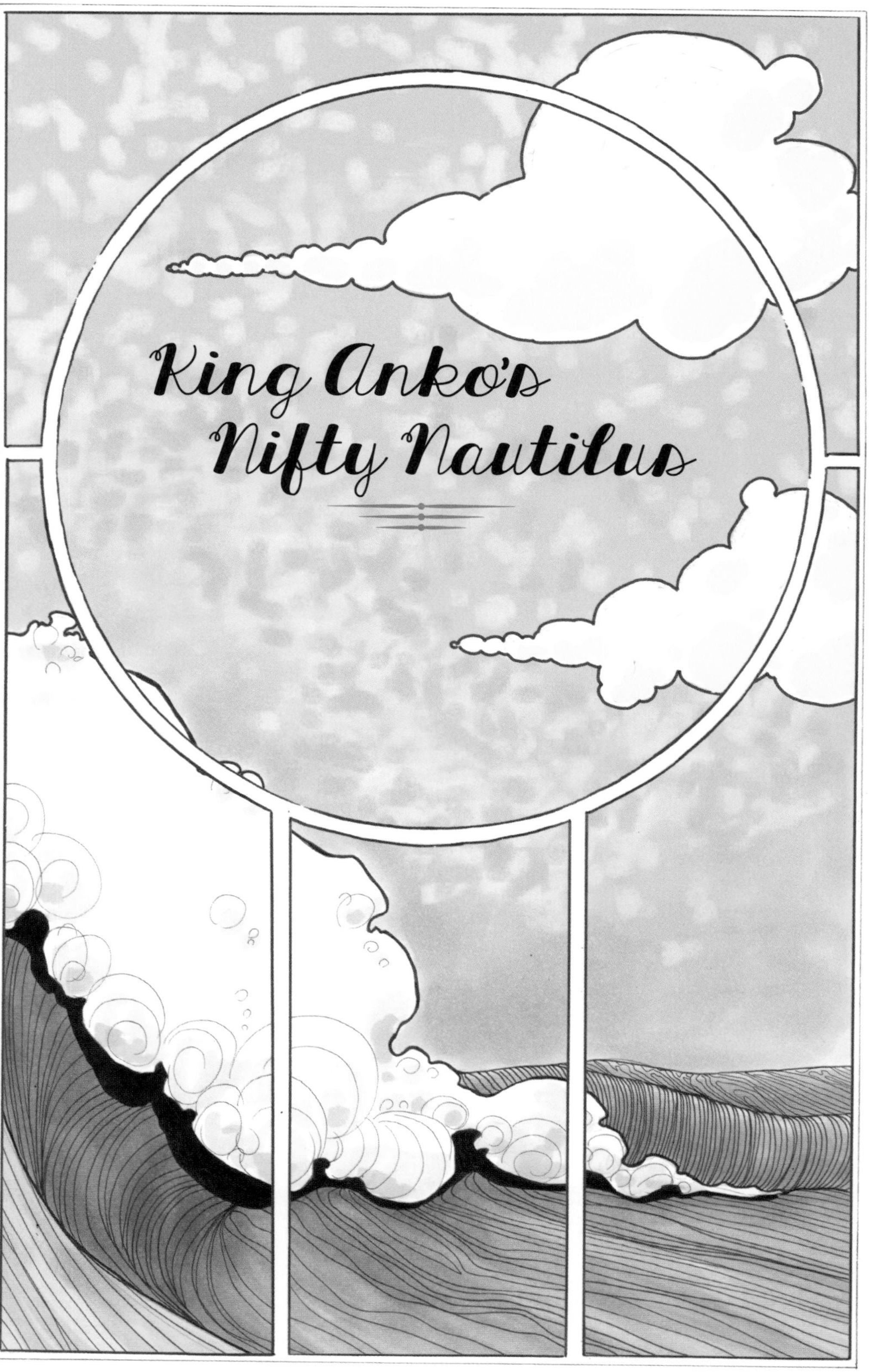
King Anko's
Nifty Nautilus

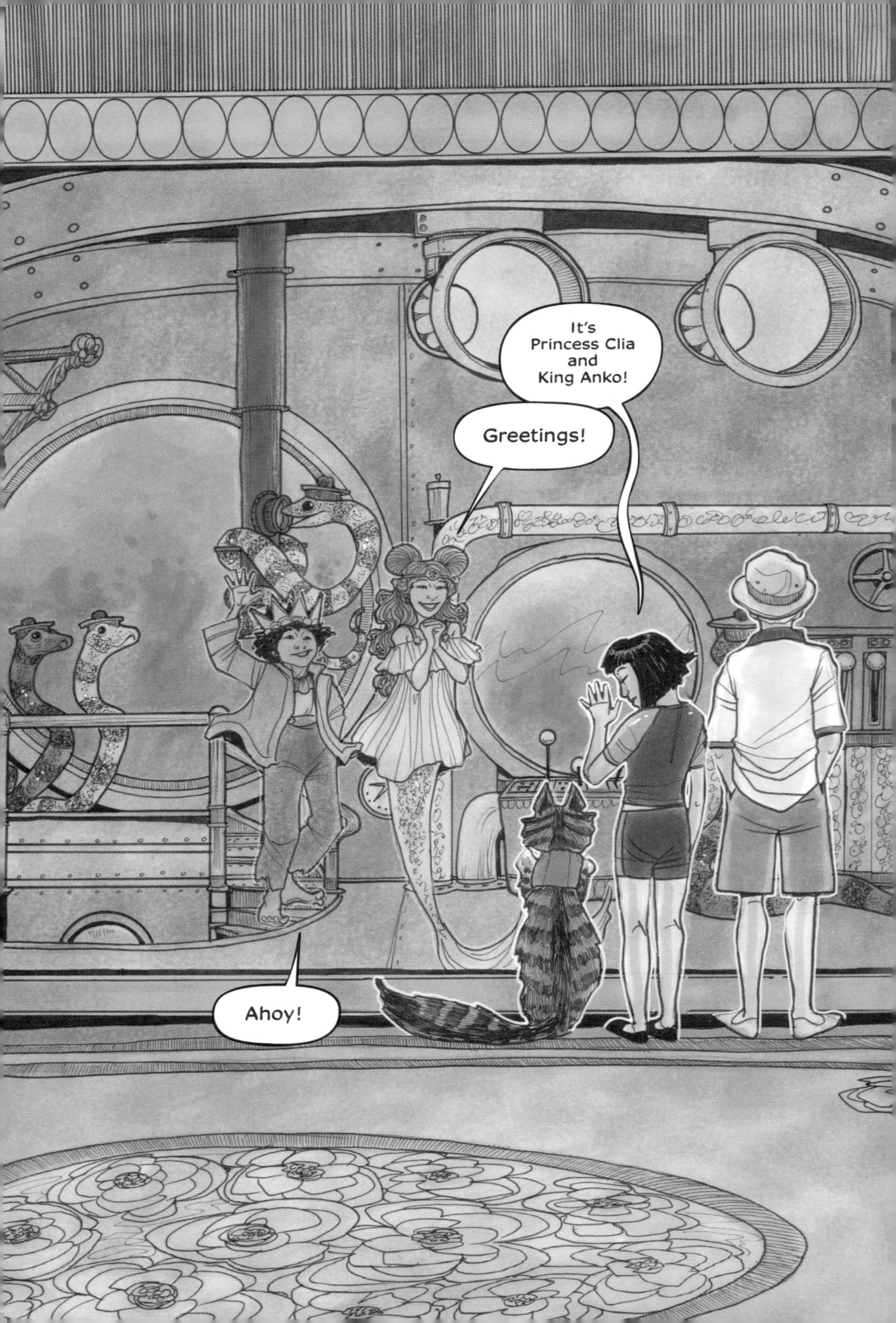

It's Princess Clia and King Anko!
Greetings!
Ahoy!

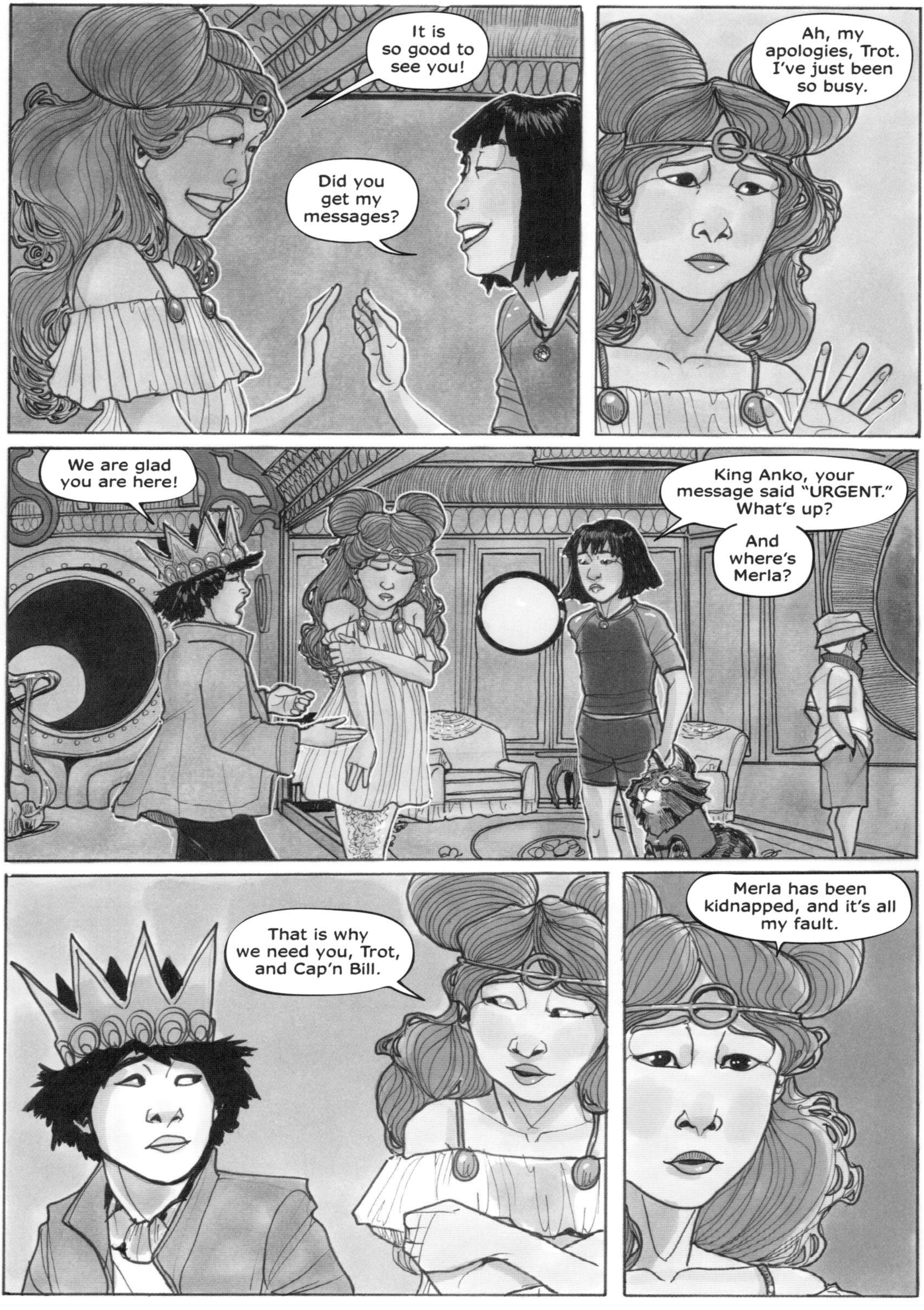
It is so good to see you!
Did you get my messages?
Ah, my apologies, Trot. I've just been so busy.
We are glad you are here!
King Anko, your message said "URGENT." What's up?
And where's Merla?
That is why we need you, Trot, and Cap'n Bill.
Merla has been kidnapped, and it's all my fault.

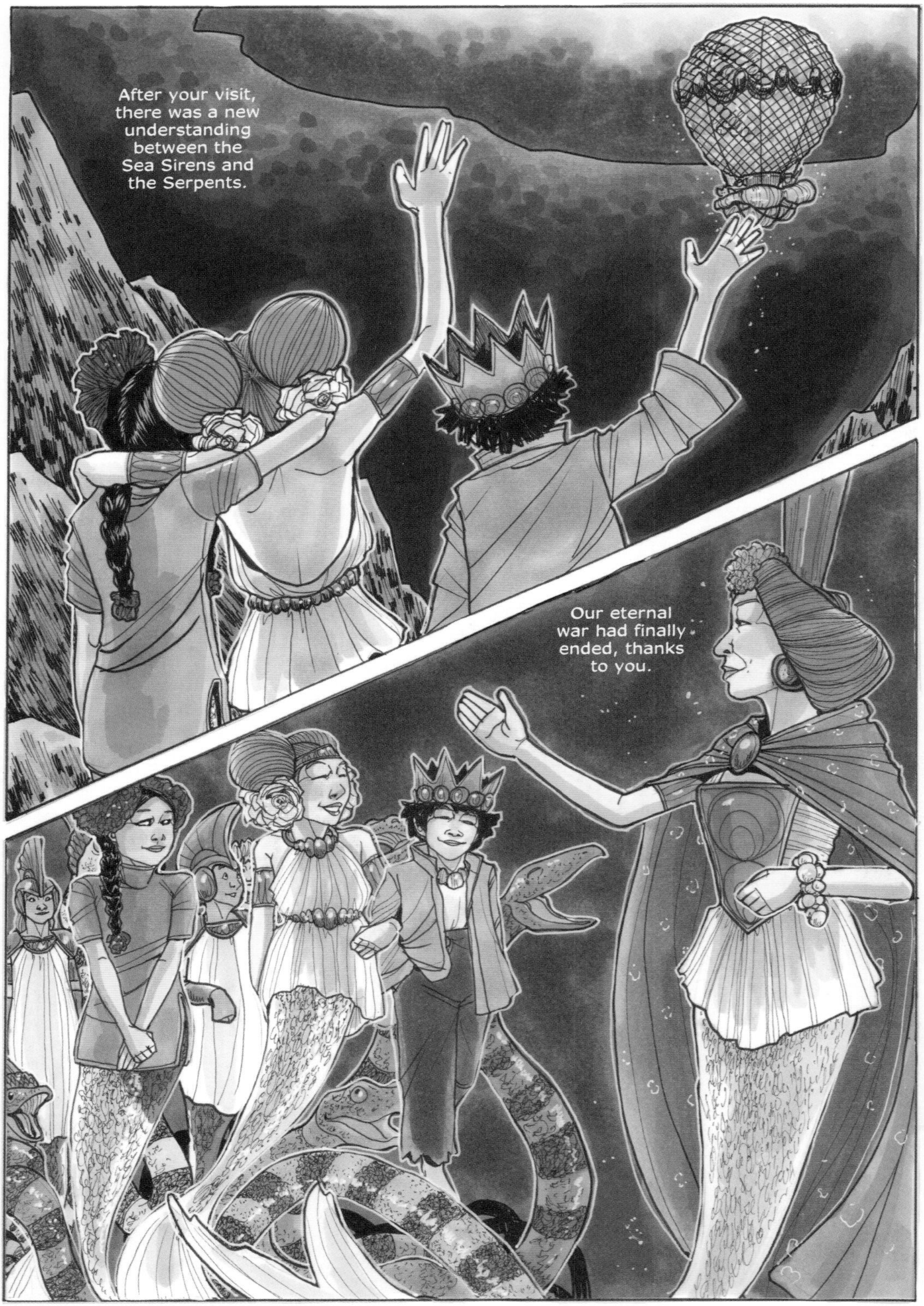
After your visit, there was a new understanding between the Sea Sirens and the Serpents.
Our eternal war had finally ended, thanks to you.

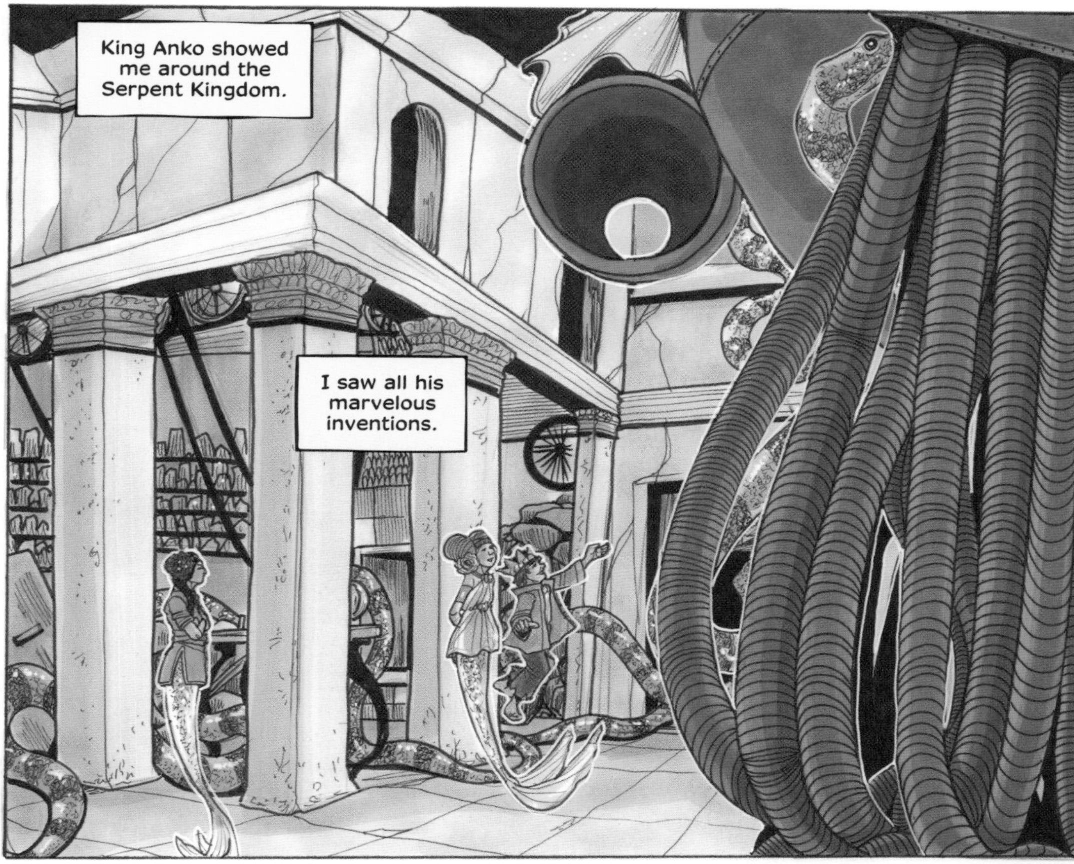
King Anko showed me around the Serpent Kingdom.
I saw all his marvelous inventions.

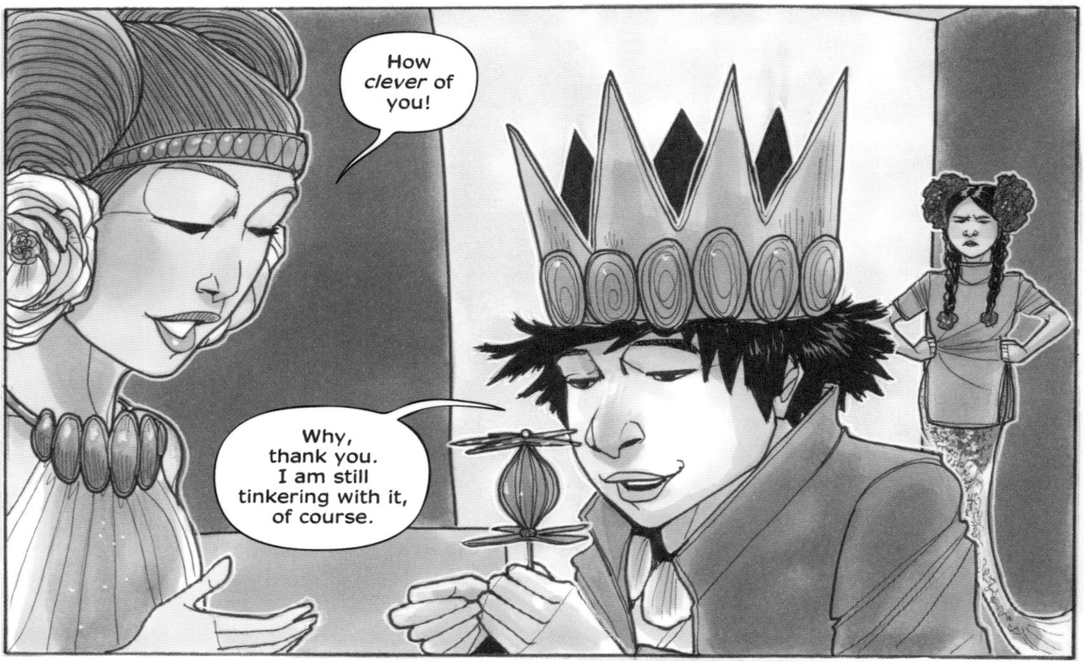
How *clever* of you!
Why, thank you. I am still tinkering with it, of course.

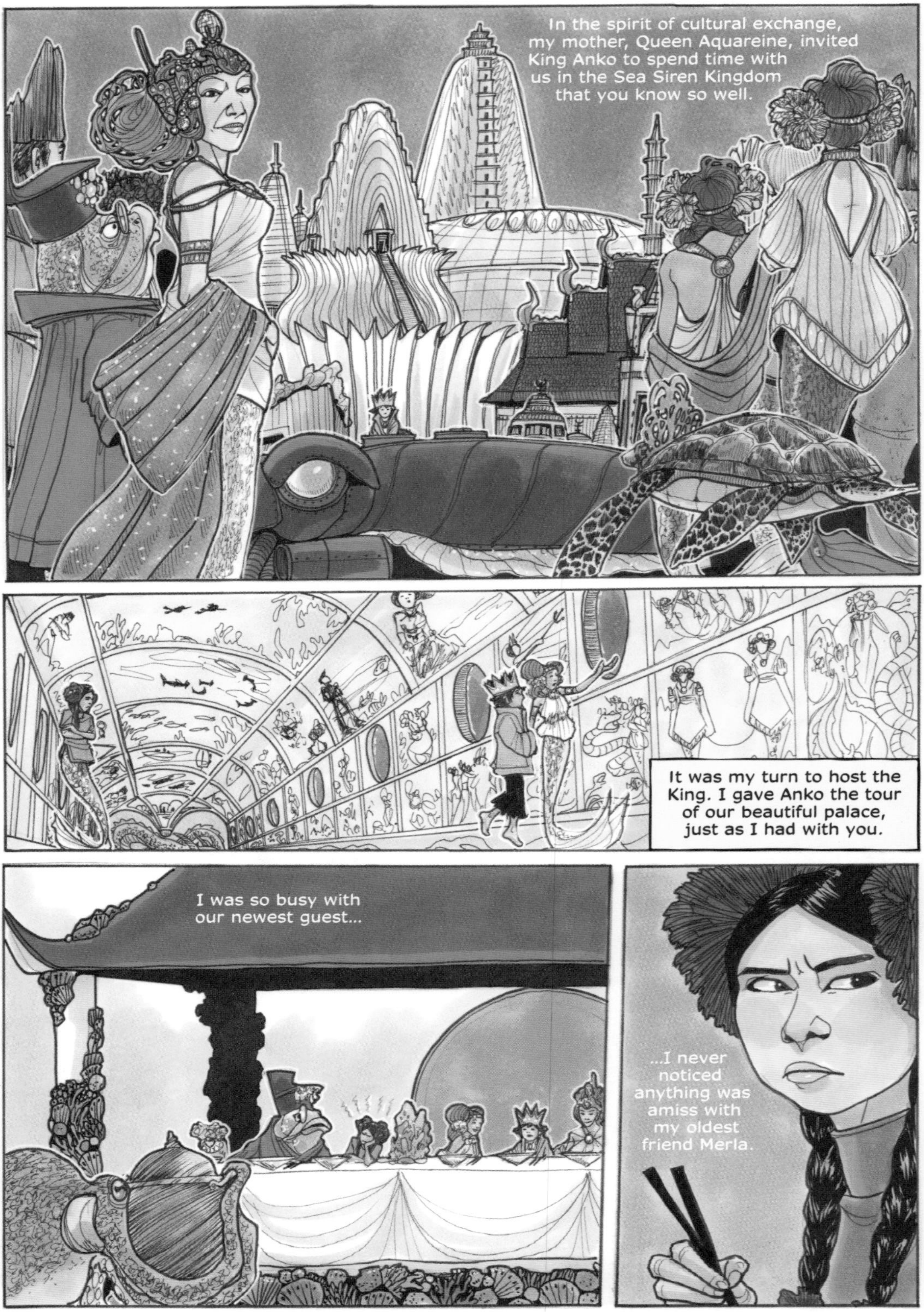
In the spirit of cultural exchange, my mother, Queen Aquareine, invited King Anko to spend time with us in the Sea Siren Kingdom that you know so well.
It was my turn to host the King. I gave Anko the tour of our beautiful palace, just as I had with you.
I was so busy with our newest guest...
...I never noticed anything was amiss with my oldest friend Merla.

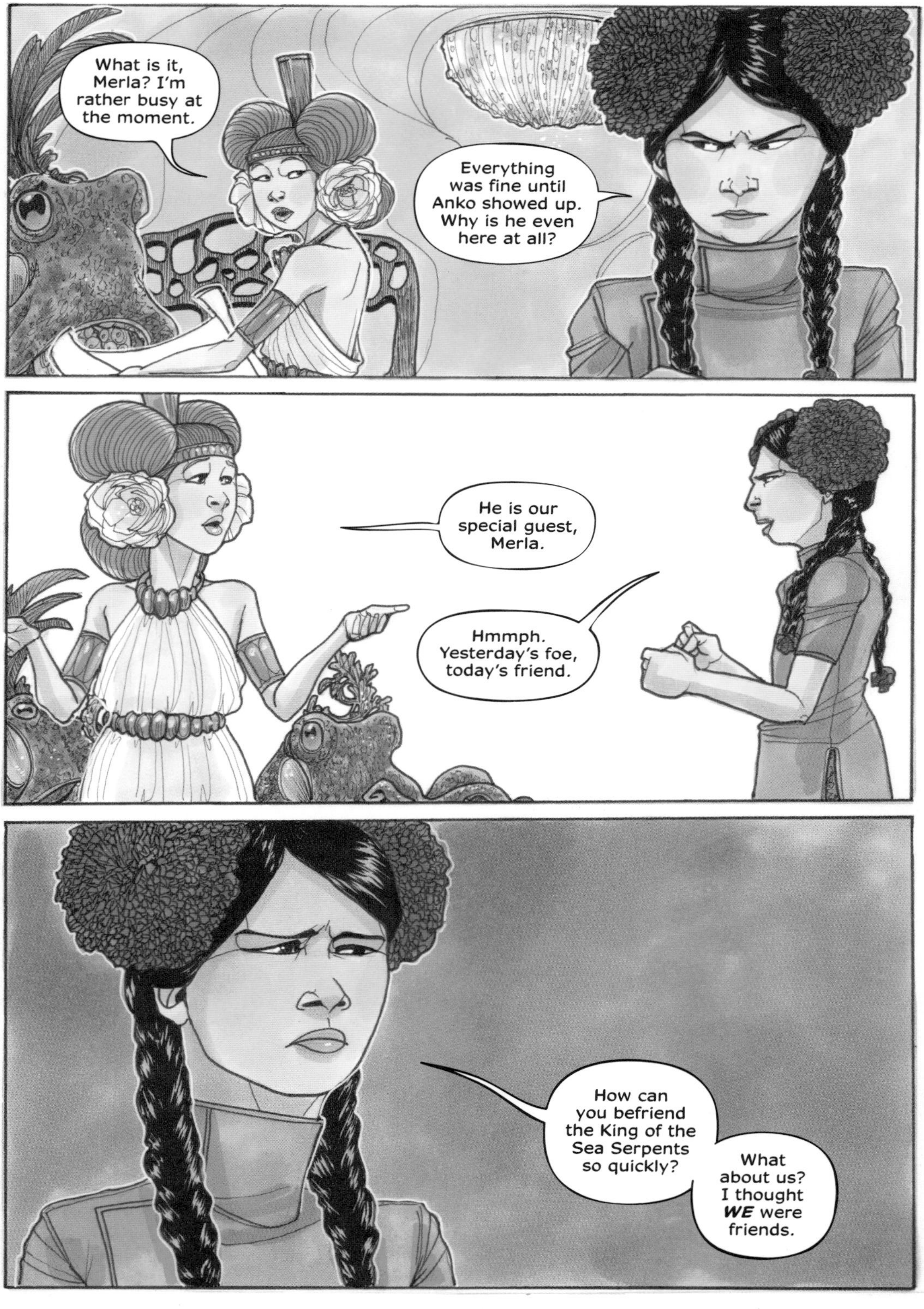
What is it, Merla? I'm rather busy at the moment.
Everything was fine until Anko showed up. Why is he even here at all?
He is our special guest, Merla.
Hmmph. Yesterday's foe, today's friend.
How can you befriend the King of the Sea Serpents so quickly?
What about us? I thought *WE* were friends.

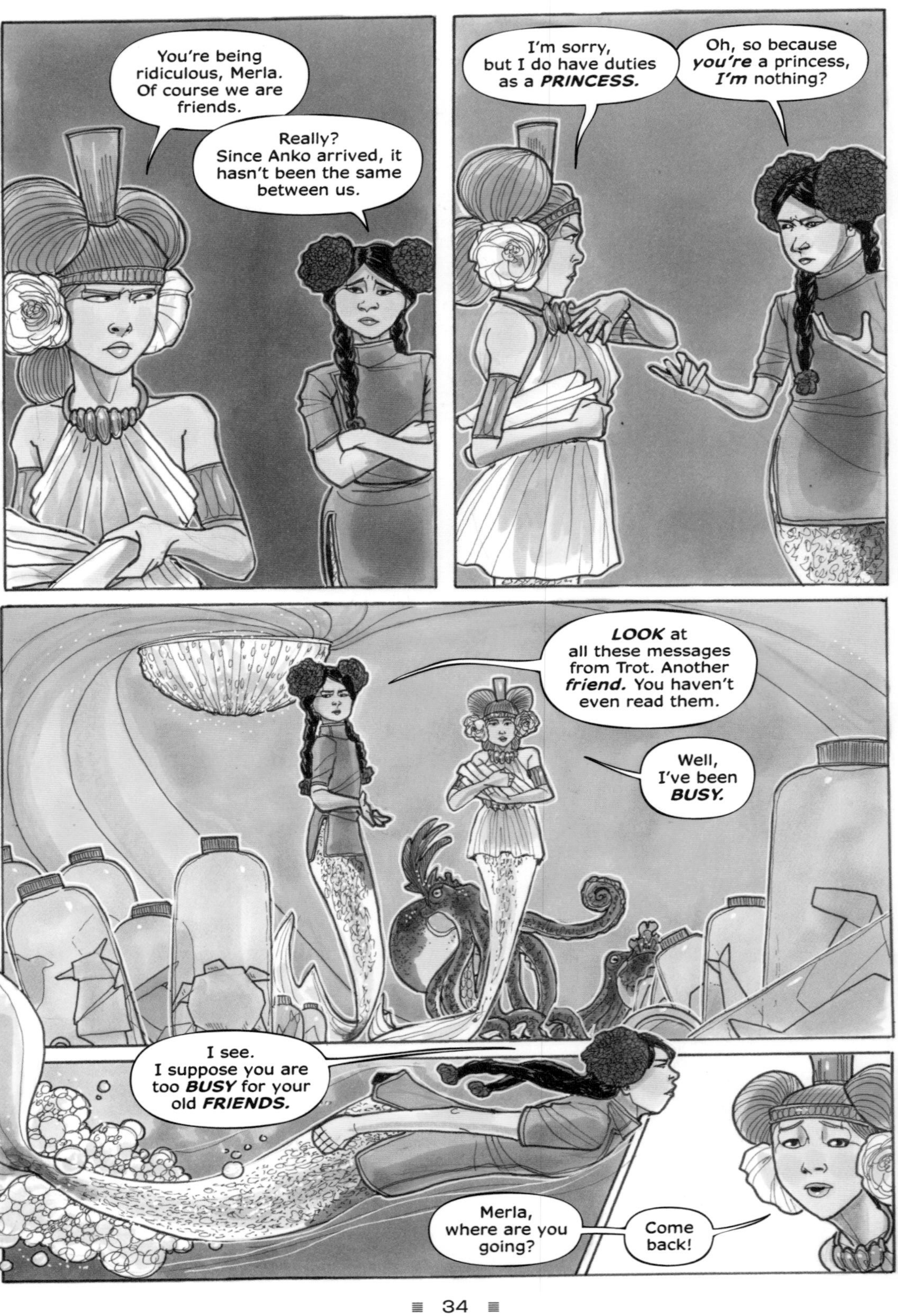
You're being ridiculous, Merla. Of course we are friends.
Really? Since Anko arrived, it hasn't been the same between us.
I'm sorry, but I do have duties as a **PRINCESS.**
Oh, so because ***you're*** a princess, ***I'm*** nothing?
LOOK at all these messages from Trot. Another ***friend.*** You haven't even read them.
Well, I've been ***BUSY.***
I see. I suppose you are too ***BUSY*** for your old ***FRIENDS.***
Merla, where are you going?
Come back!

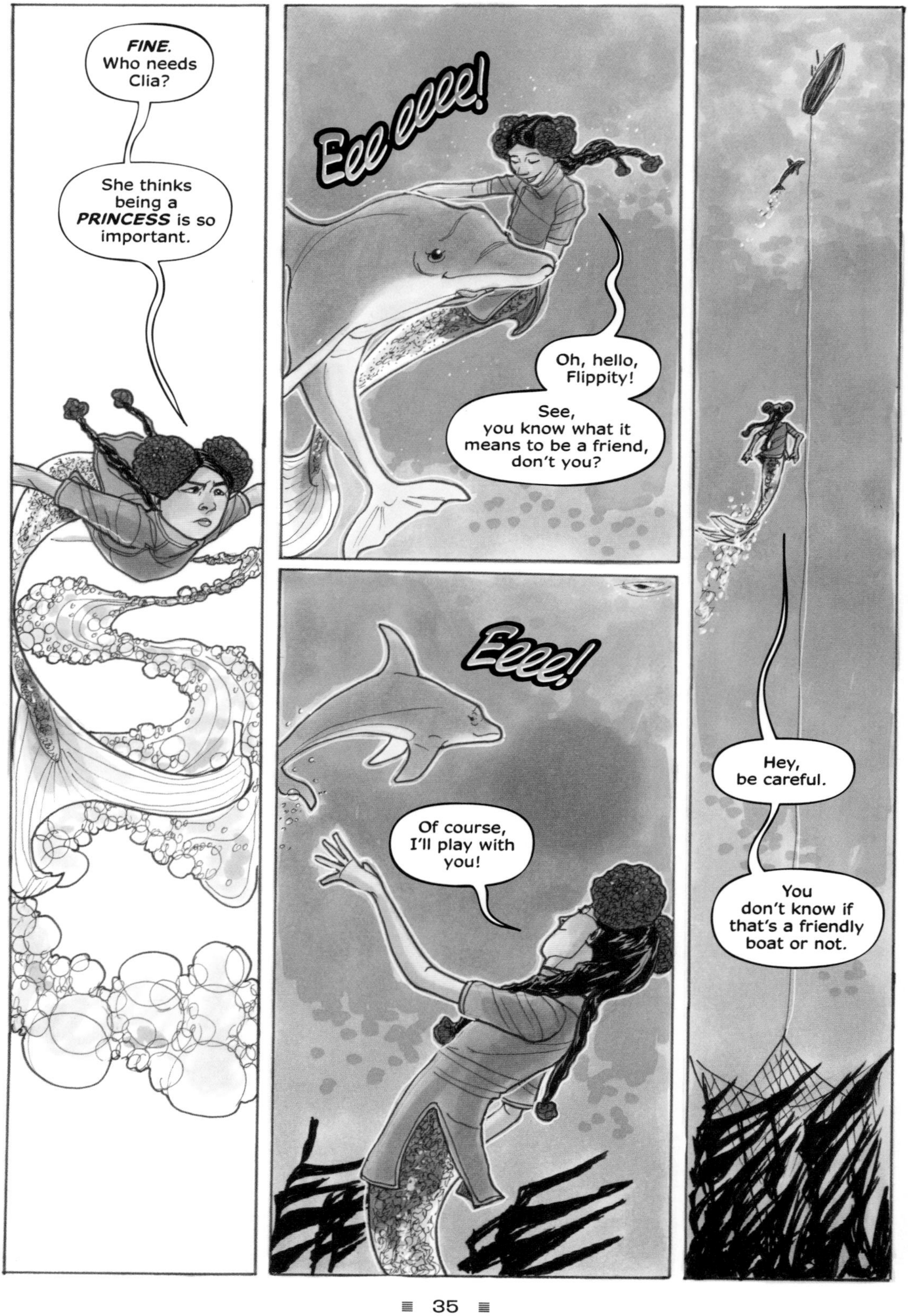
FINE. Who needs Clia?
She thinks being a PRINCESS is so important.
Eee eeee!
Oh, hello, Flippity!
See, you know what it means to be a friend, don't you?
Eeee!
Of course, I'll play with you!
Hey, be careful.
You don't know if that's a friendly boat or not.

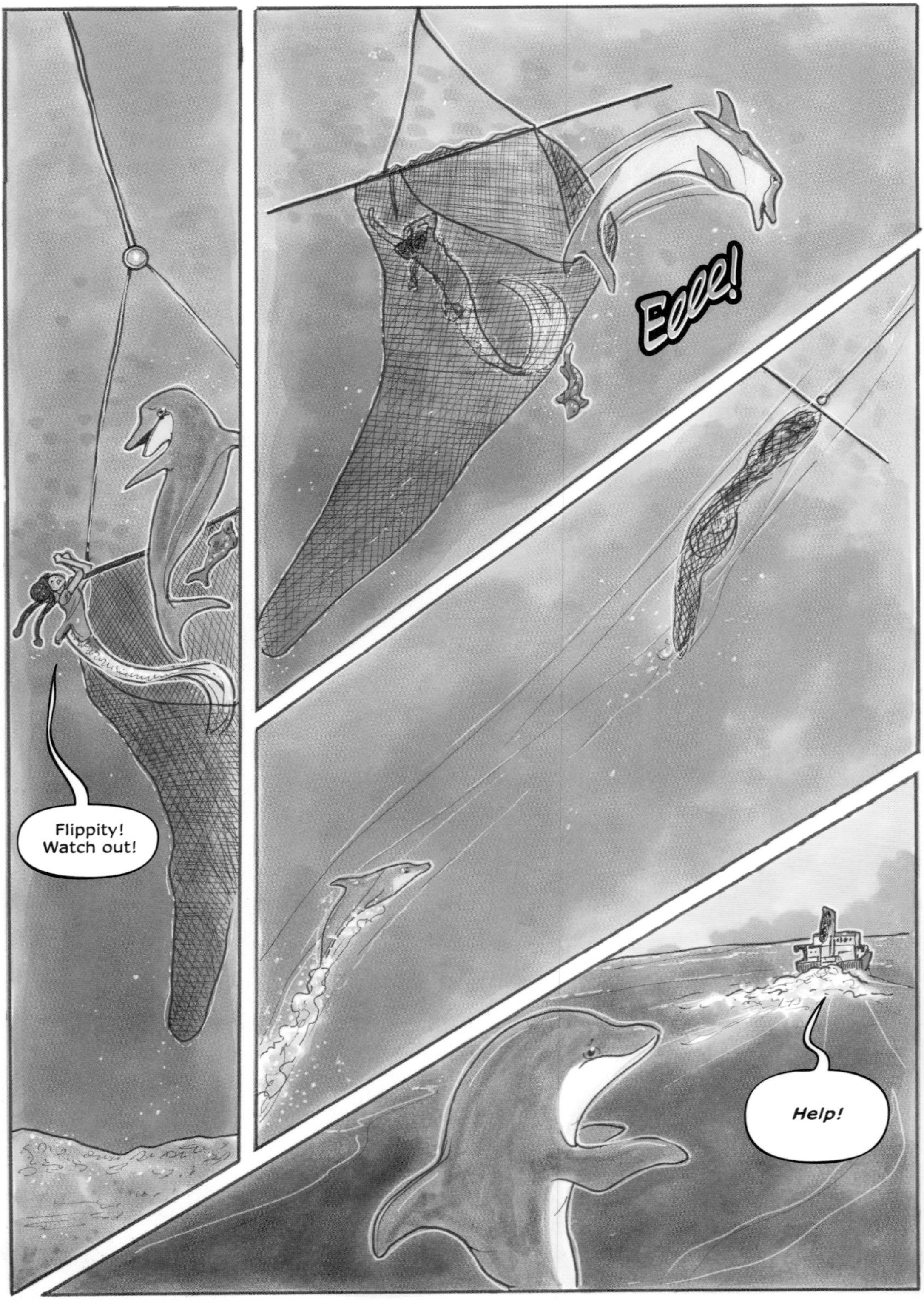
Flippity! Watch out!
Eeee!
Help!

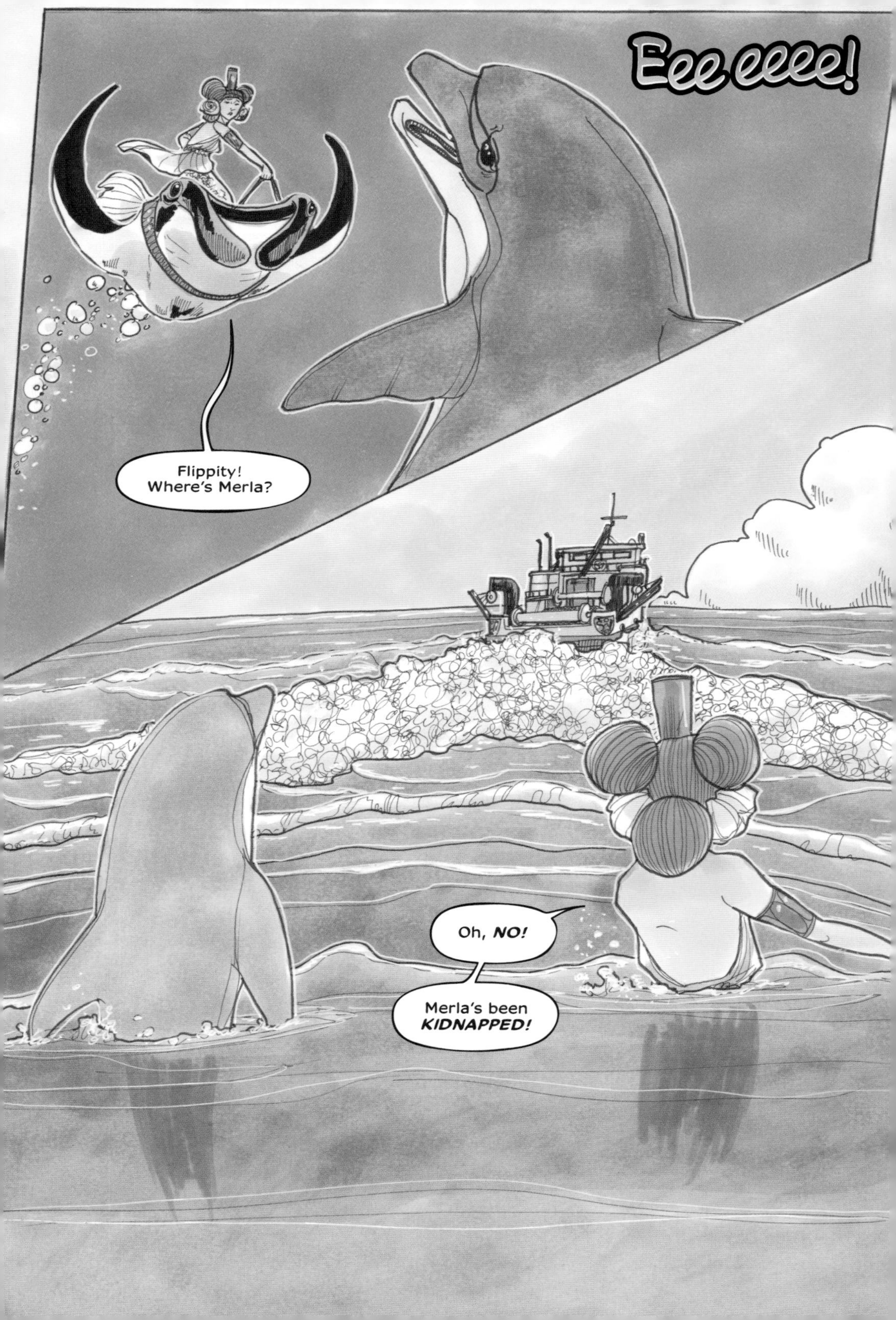

Eee eeee!
Flippity! Where's Merla?
Oh, NO!
Merla's been KIDNAPPED!

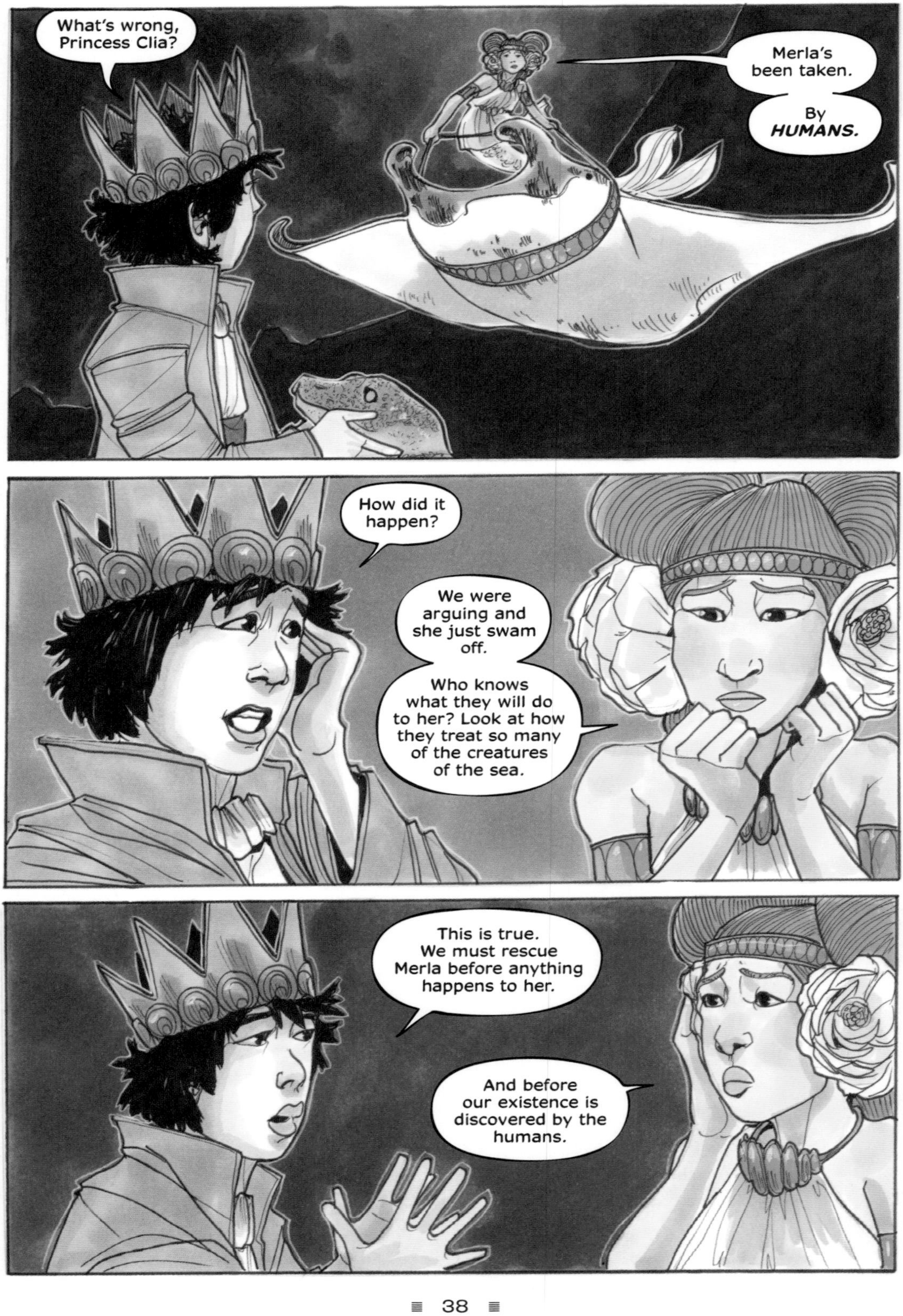
What's wrong, Princess Clia?
Merla's been taken.
By ***HUMANS.***
How did it happen?
We were arguing and she just swam off.
Who knows what they will do to her? Look at how they treat so many of the creatures of the sea.
This is true. We must rescue Merla before anything happens to her.
And before our existence is discovered by the humans.

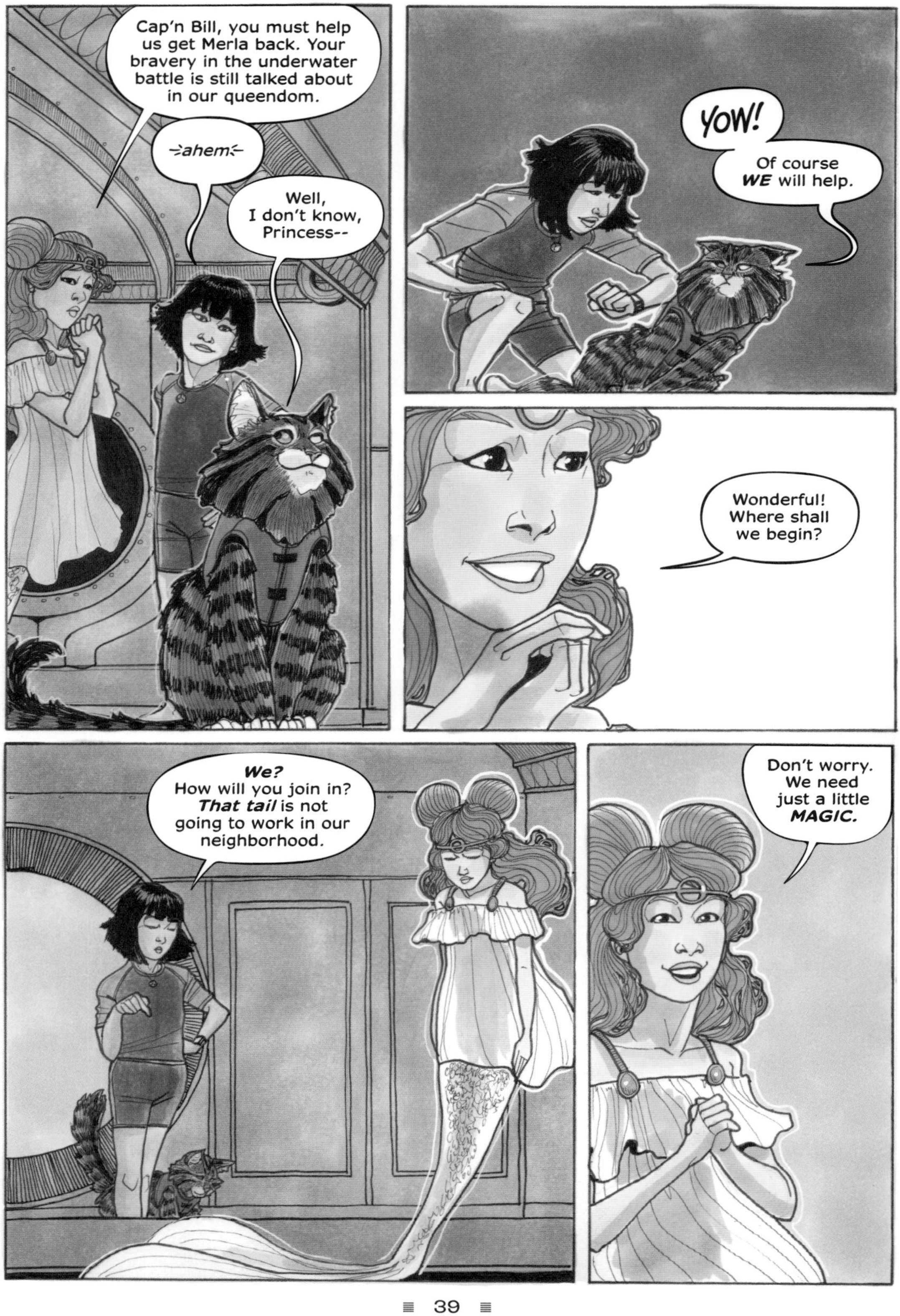
Cap'n Bill, you must help us get Merla back. Your bravery in the underwater battle is still talked about in our queendom.
-ahem-
Well, I don't know, Princess--
YOW!
Of course *WE* will help.
Wonderful! Where shall we begin?
We? How will you join in? *That tail* is not going to work in our neighborhood.
Don't worry. We need just a little *MAGIC.*

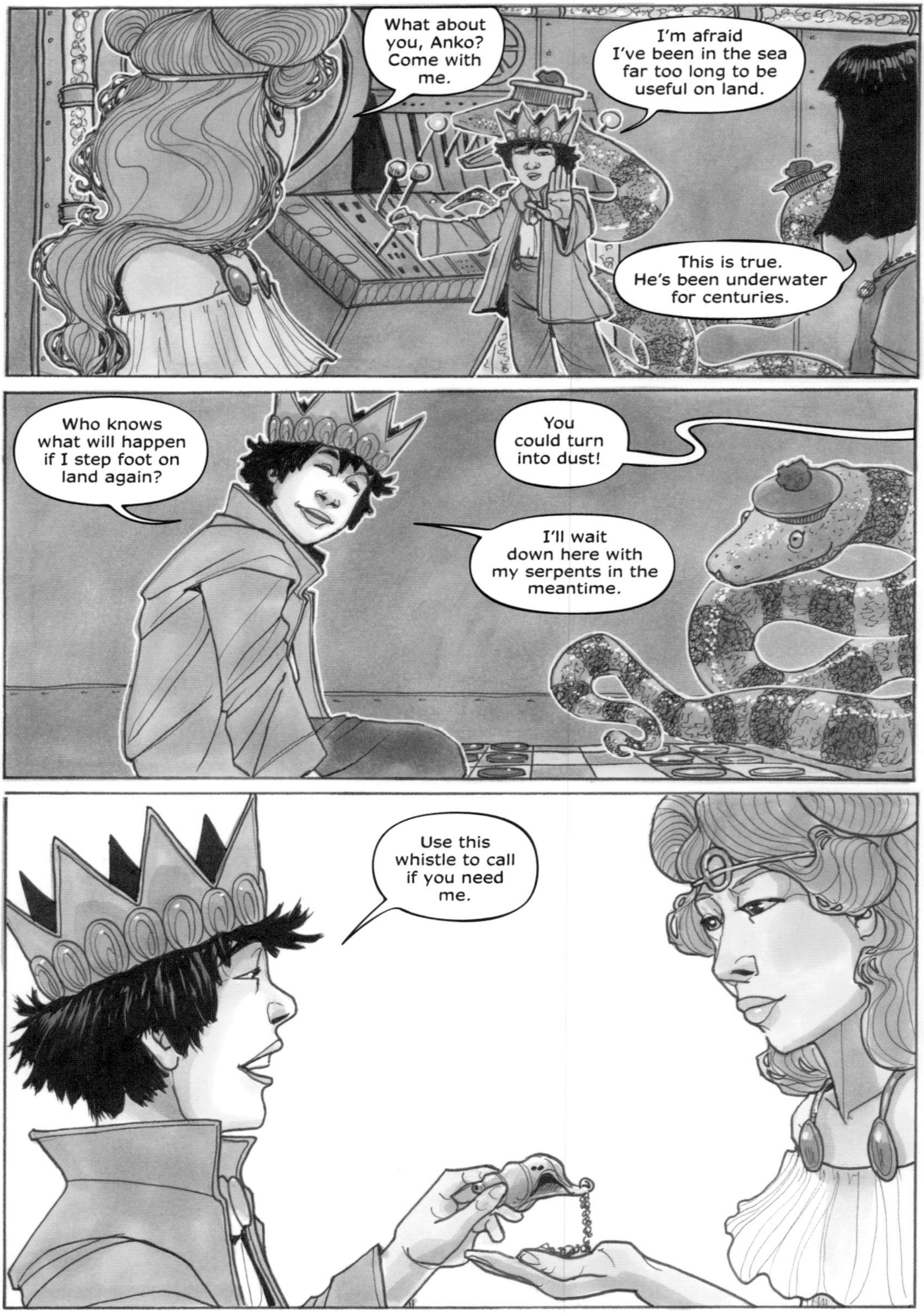
What about you, Anko? Come with me.
I'm afraid I've been in the sea far too long to be useful on land.
This is true. He's been underwater for centuries.
Who knows what will happen if I step foot on land again?
You could turn into dust!
I'll wait down here with my serpents in the meantime.
Use this whistle to call if you need me.

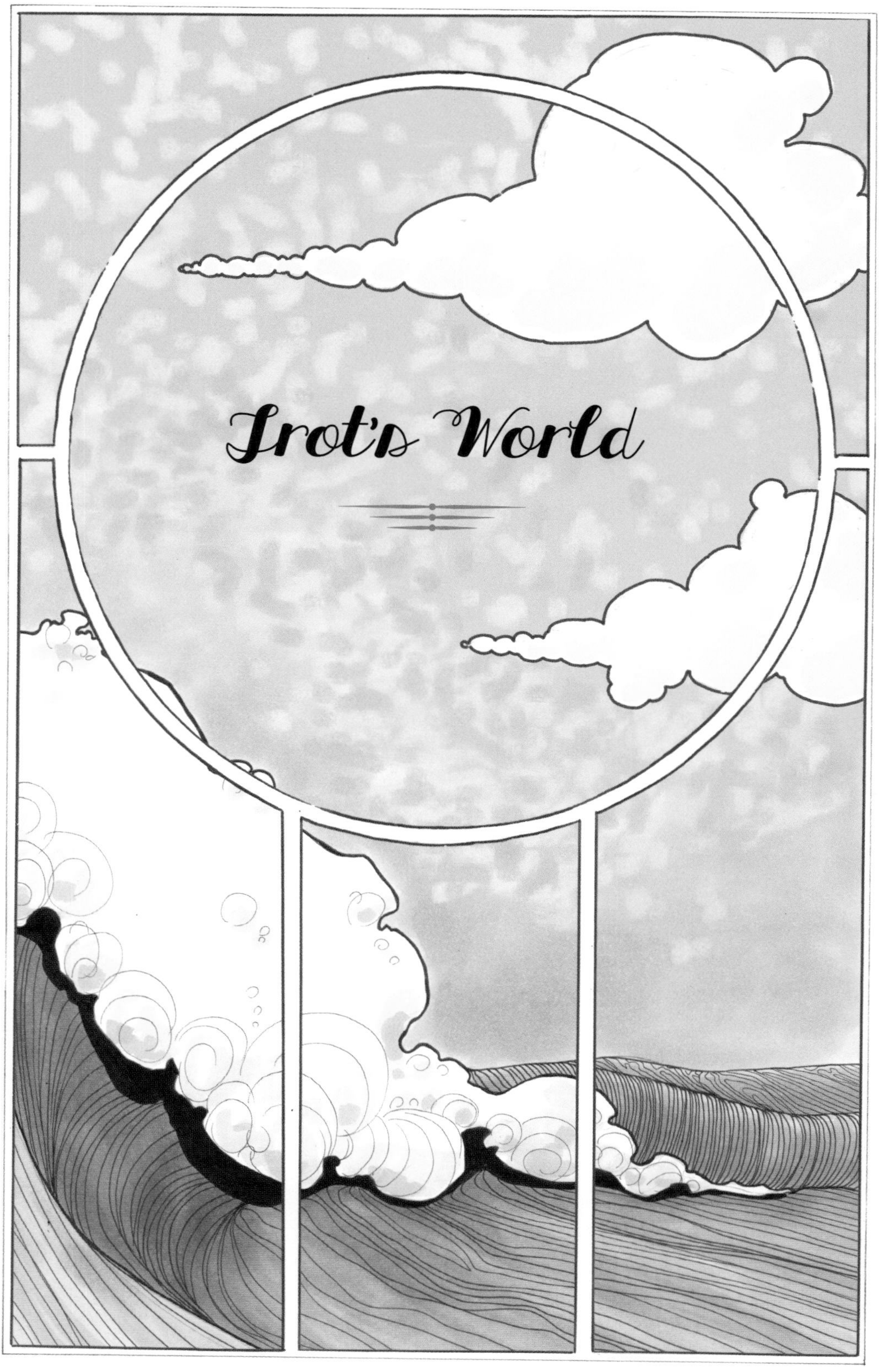
Irot's World

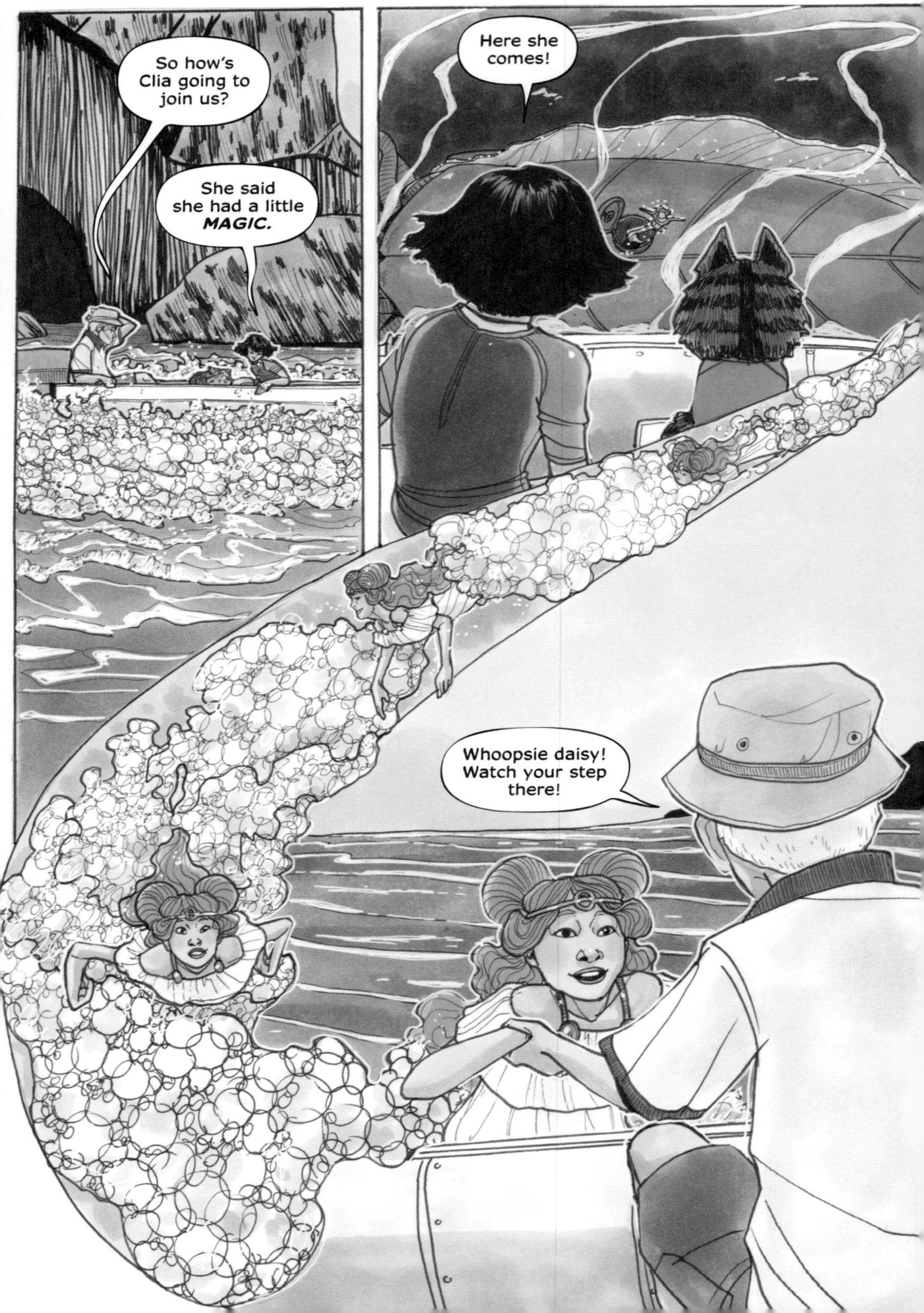
So how's Clia going to join us?
She said she had a little ***MAGIC.***
Here she comes!
Whoopsie daisy! Watch your step there!

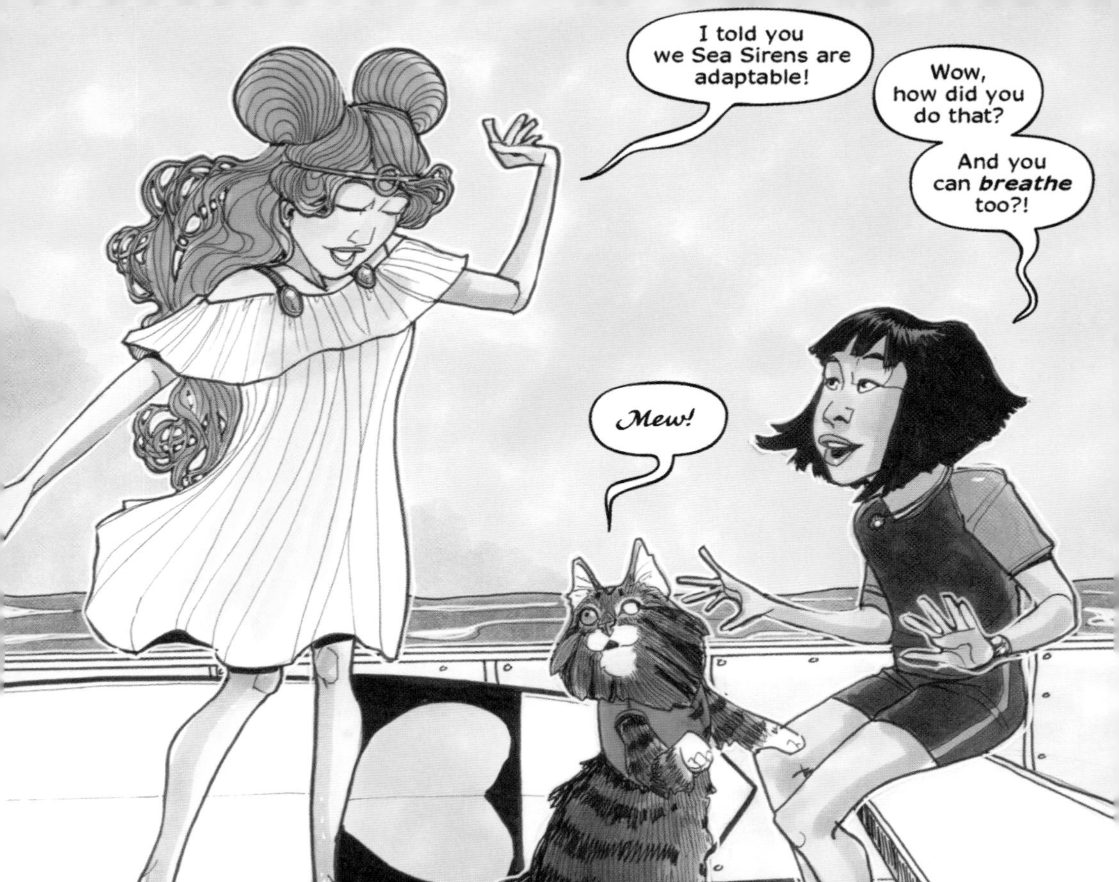
I told you we Sea Sirens are adaptable!
Wow, how did you do that?
And you can ***breathe*** too?!
Mew!

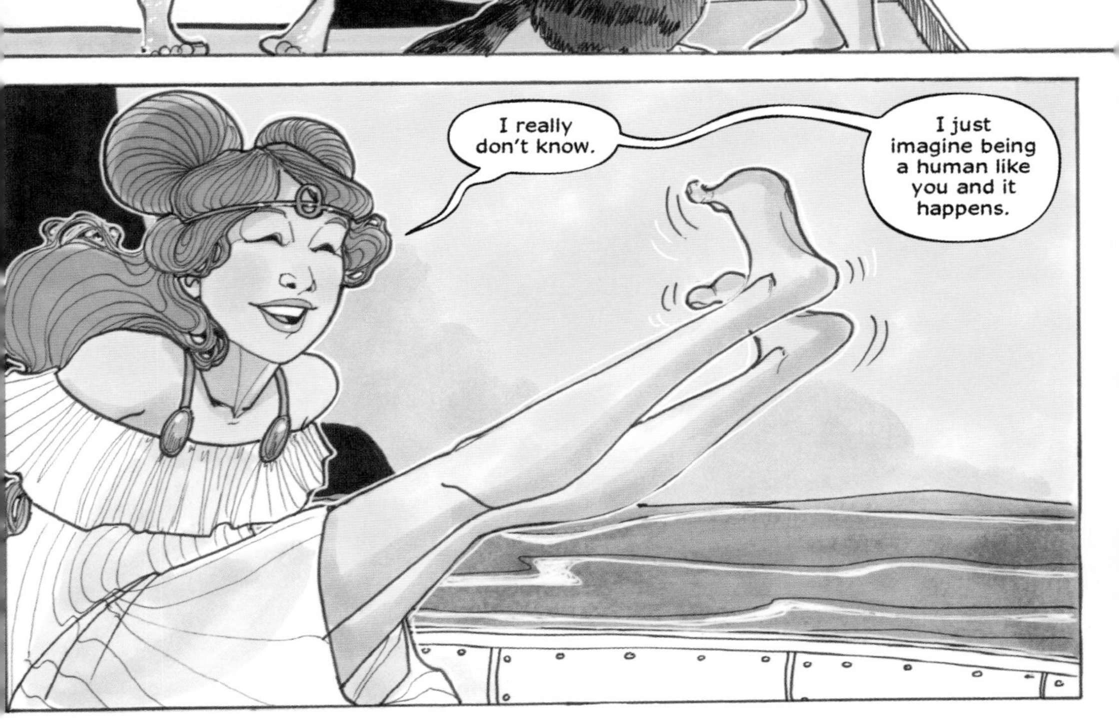
I really don't know.
I just imagine being a human like you and it happens.

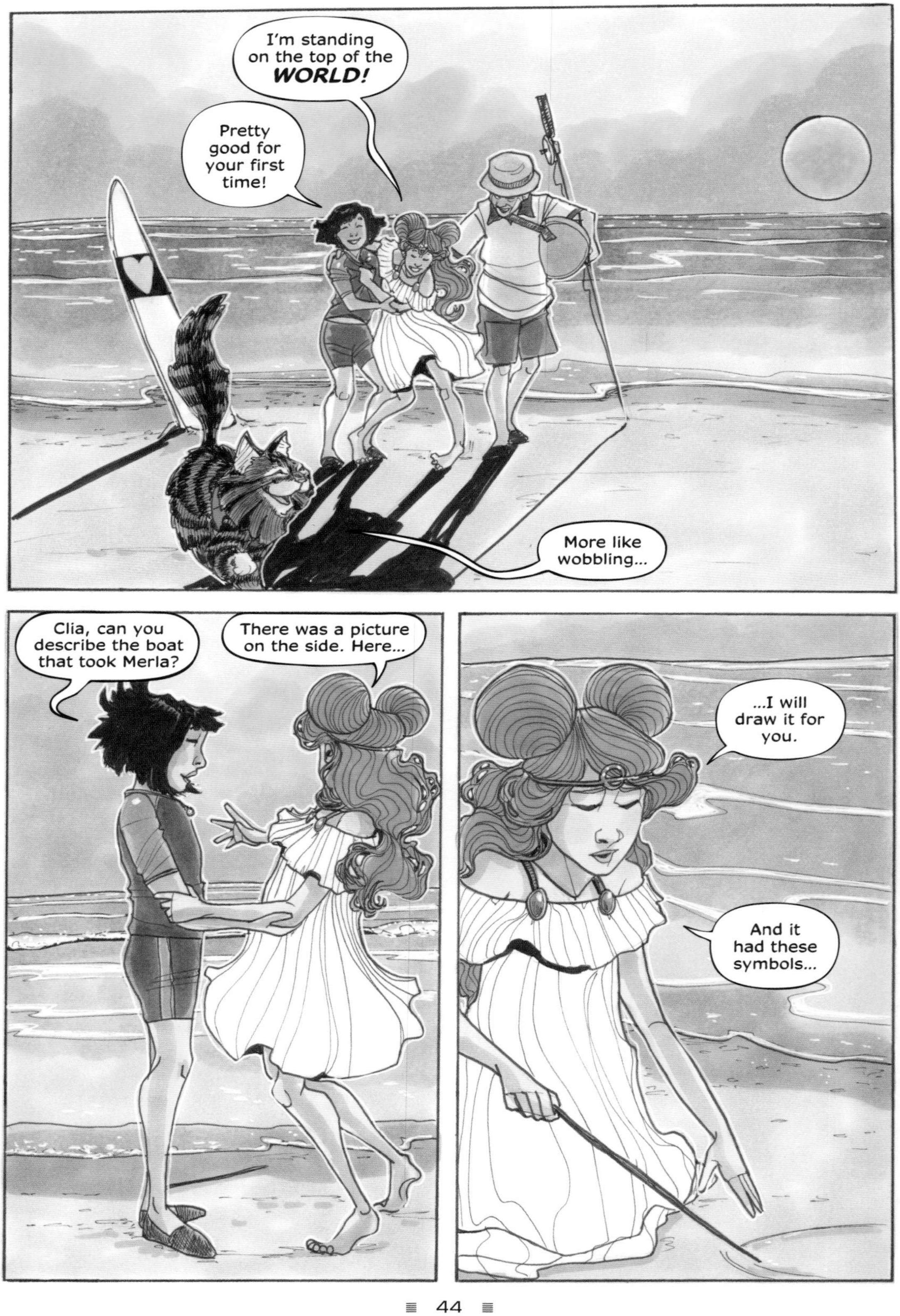
I'm standing on the top of the *WORLD!*
Pretty good for your first time!
More like wobbling...
Clia, can you describe the boat that took Merla?
There was a picture on the side. Here...
...I will draw it for you.
And it had these symbols...

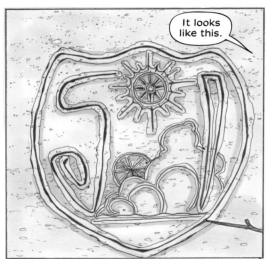

It looks like this.

Why, I haven't seen that in years!

It looks like the sign for Sky Island...

I used to take your mom there when she was about your age.

If it's so great, why haven't you taken me?

...an old amusement park. Great place.

Sky Island closed years ago, long before you were born.

I know someone who knows about this. She hangs out on the pier with us sometimes. She lives up there, not a far walk.

Let's go!

Oh!

Walking may take some practice.

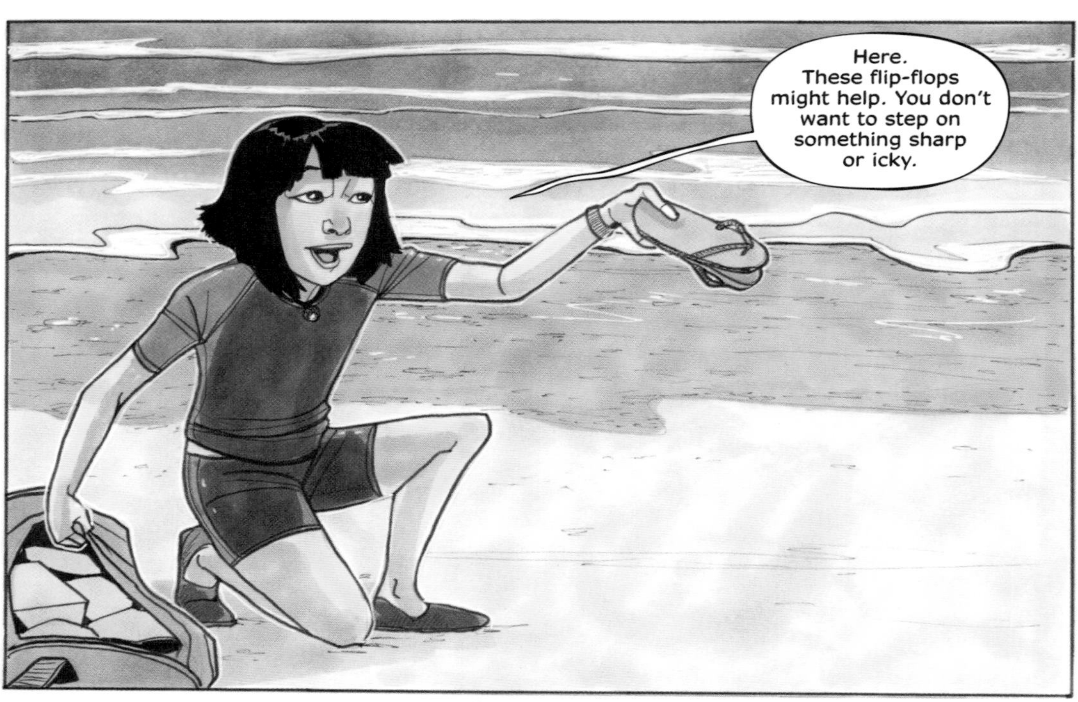
Here.
These flip-flops might help. You don't want to step on something sharp or icky.

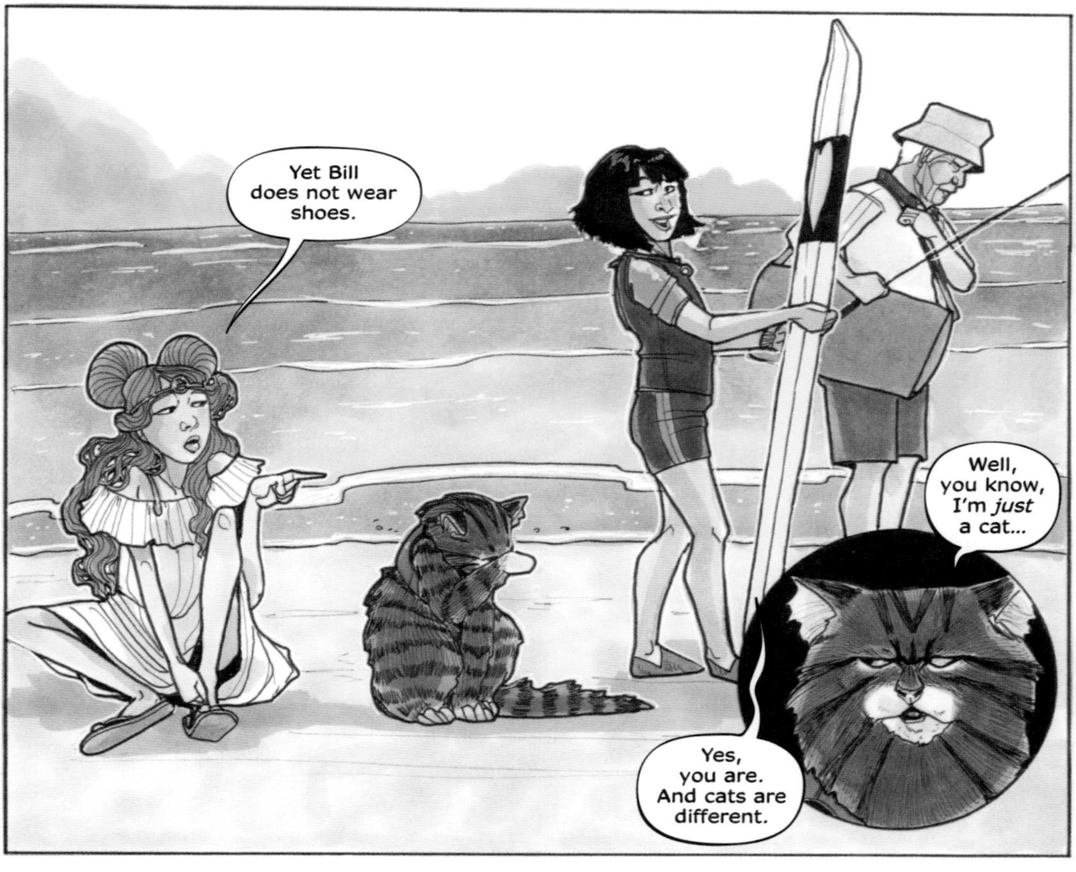
Yet Bill does not wear shoes.
Well, you know, I'm *just* a cat...
Yes, you are. And cats are different.

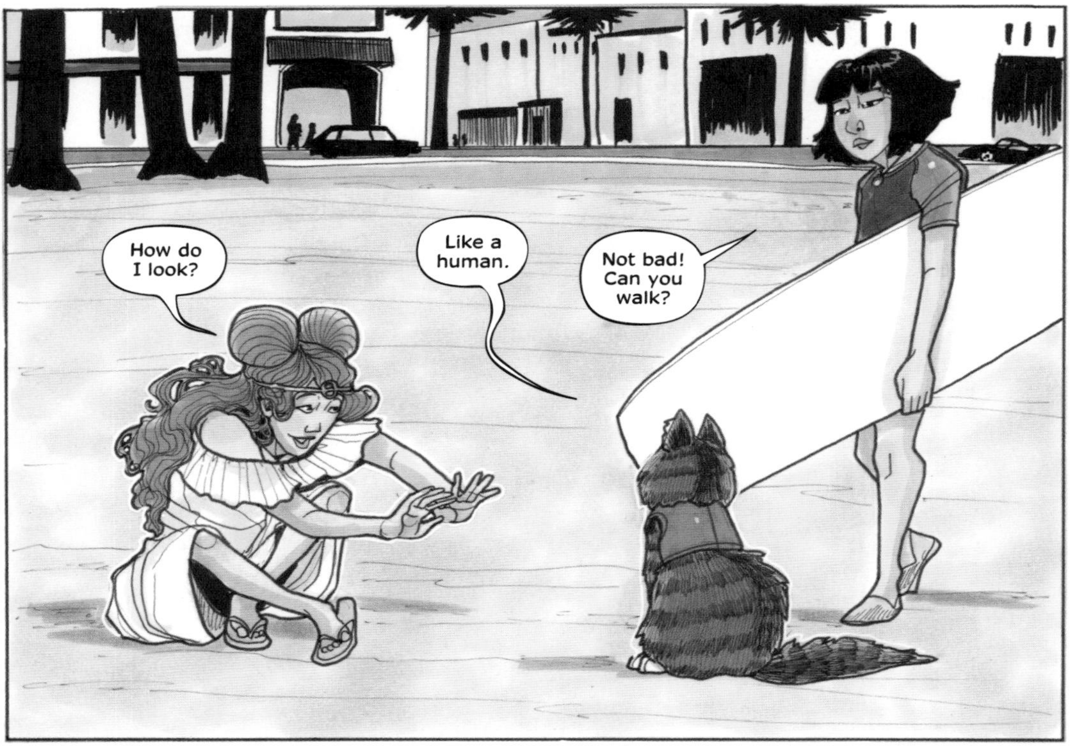
How do I look?
Like a human.
Not bad! Can you walk?

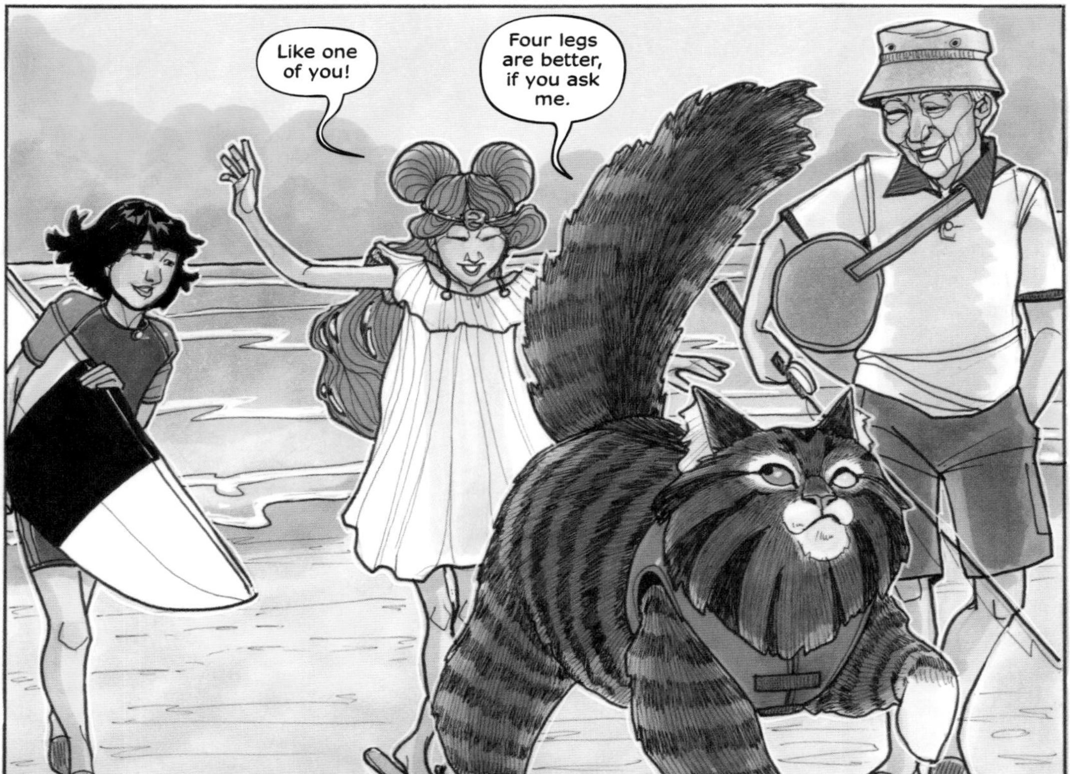
Like one of you!
Four legs are better, if you ask me.

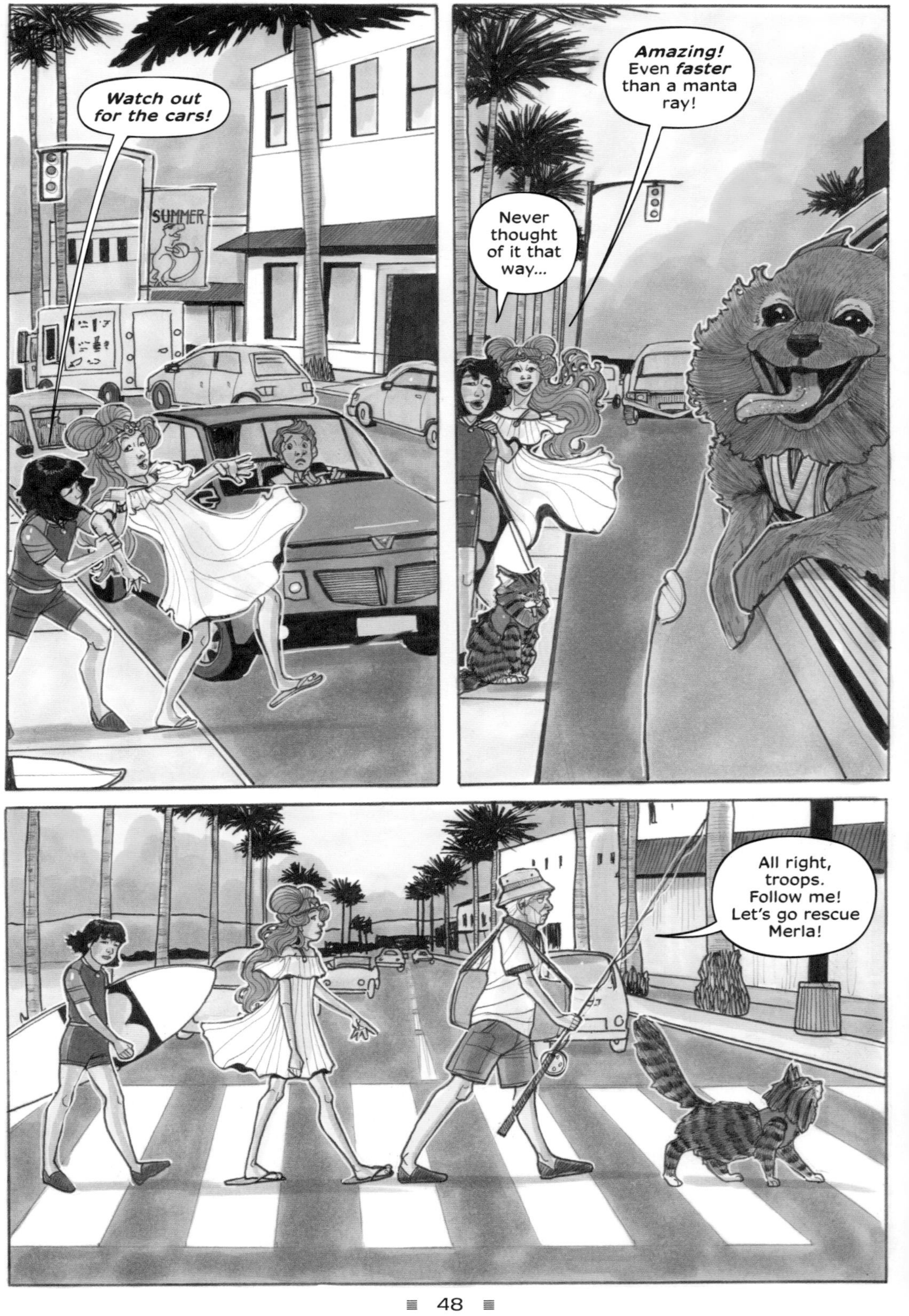
SUMMER
Watch out for the cars!
Amazing! Even *faster* than a manta ray!
Never thought of it that way...
All right, troops. Follow me! Let's go rescue Merla!

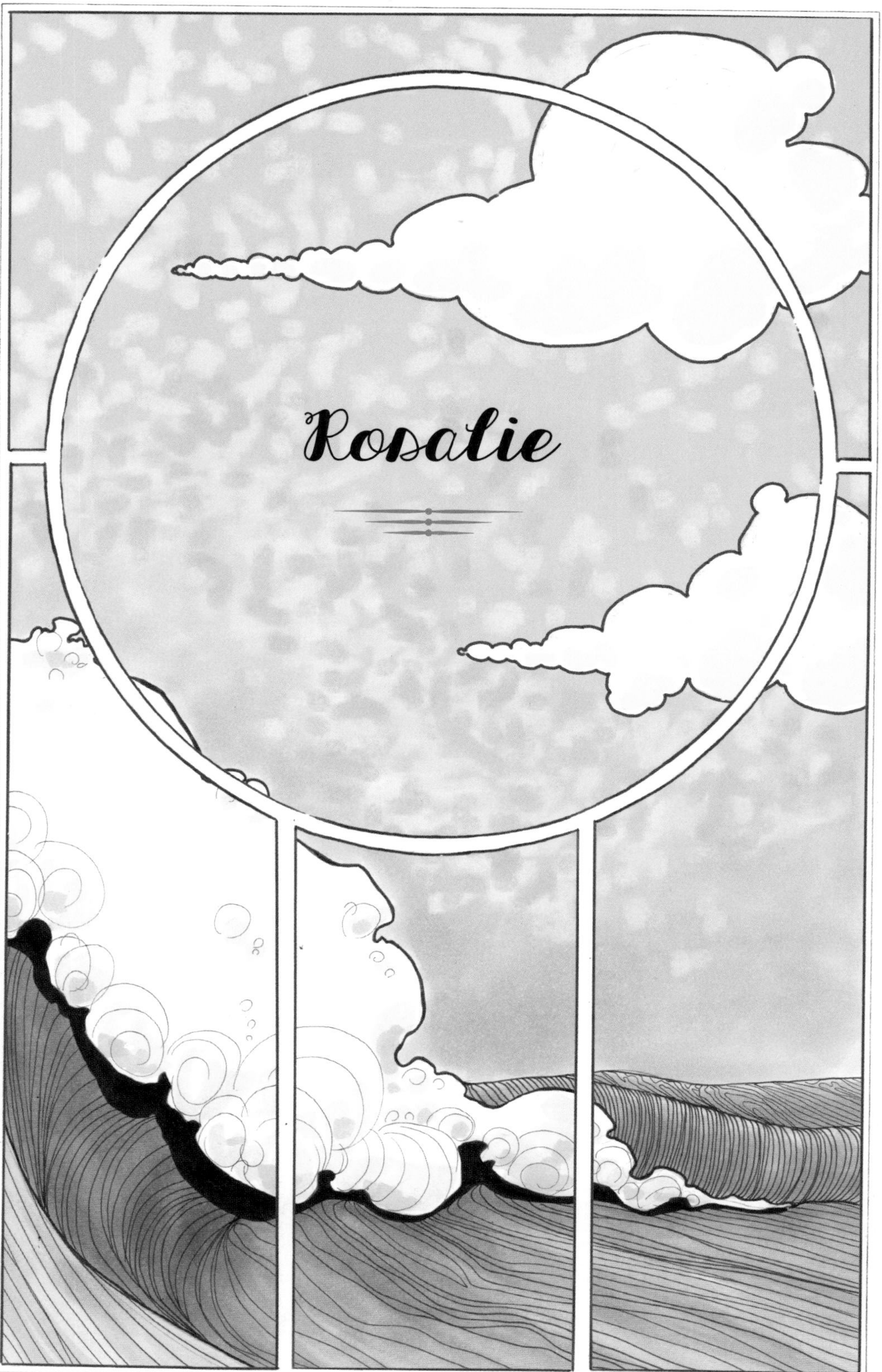
Rosalie

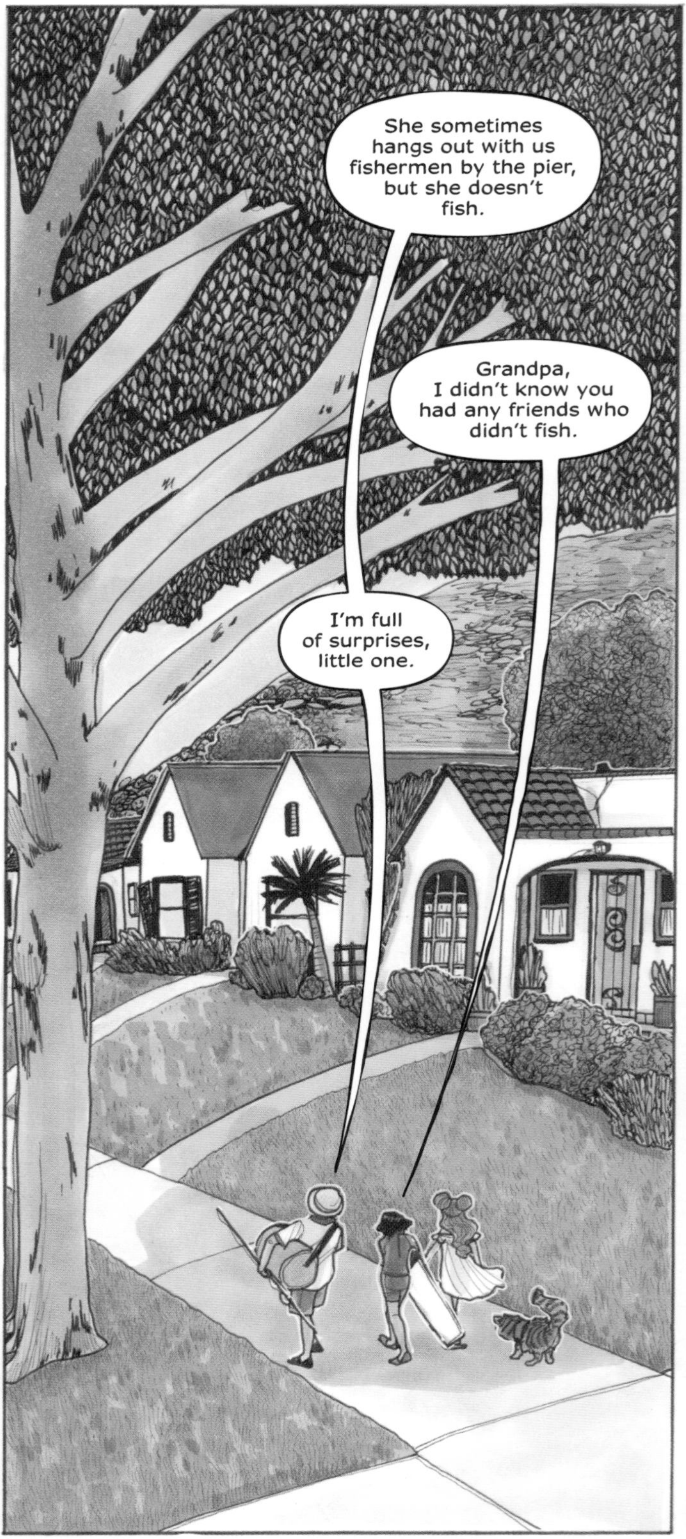
She sometimes hangs out with us fishermen by the pier, but she doesn't fish.
Grandpa, I didn't know you had any friends who didn't fish.
I'm full of surprises, little one.

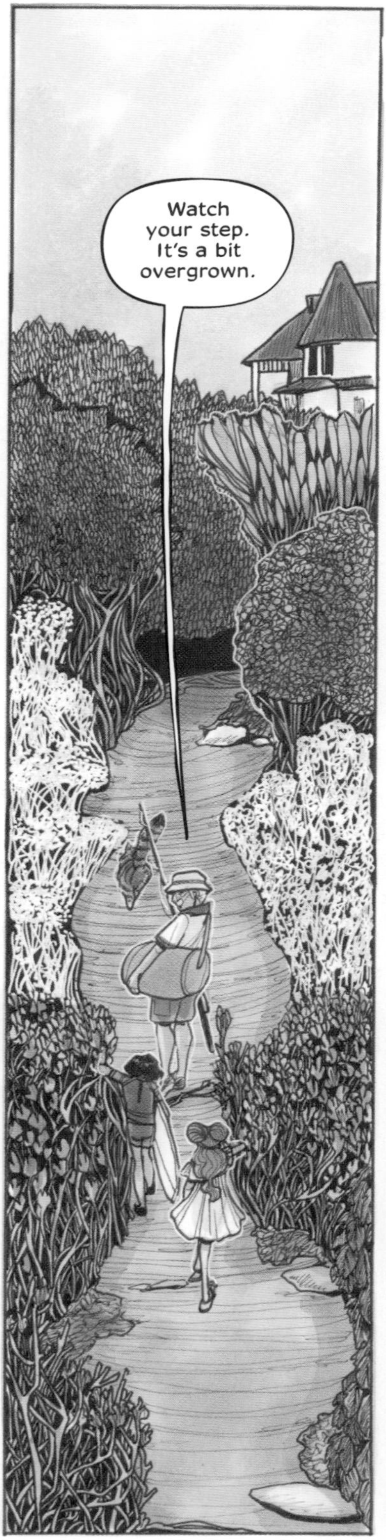
Watch your step. It's a bit overgrown.

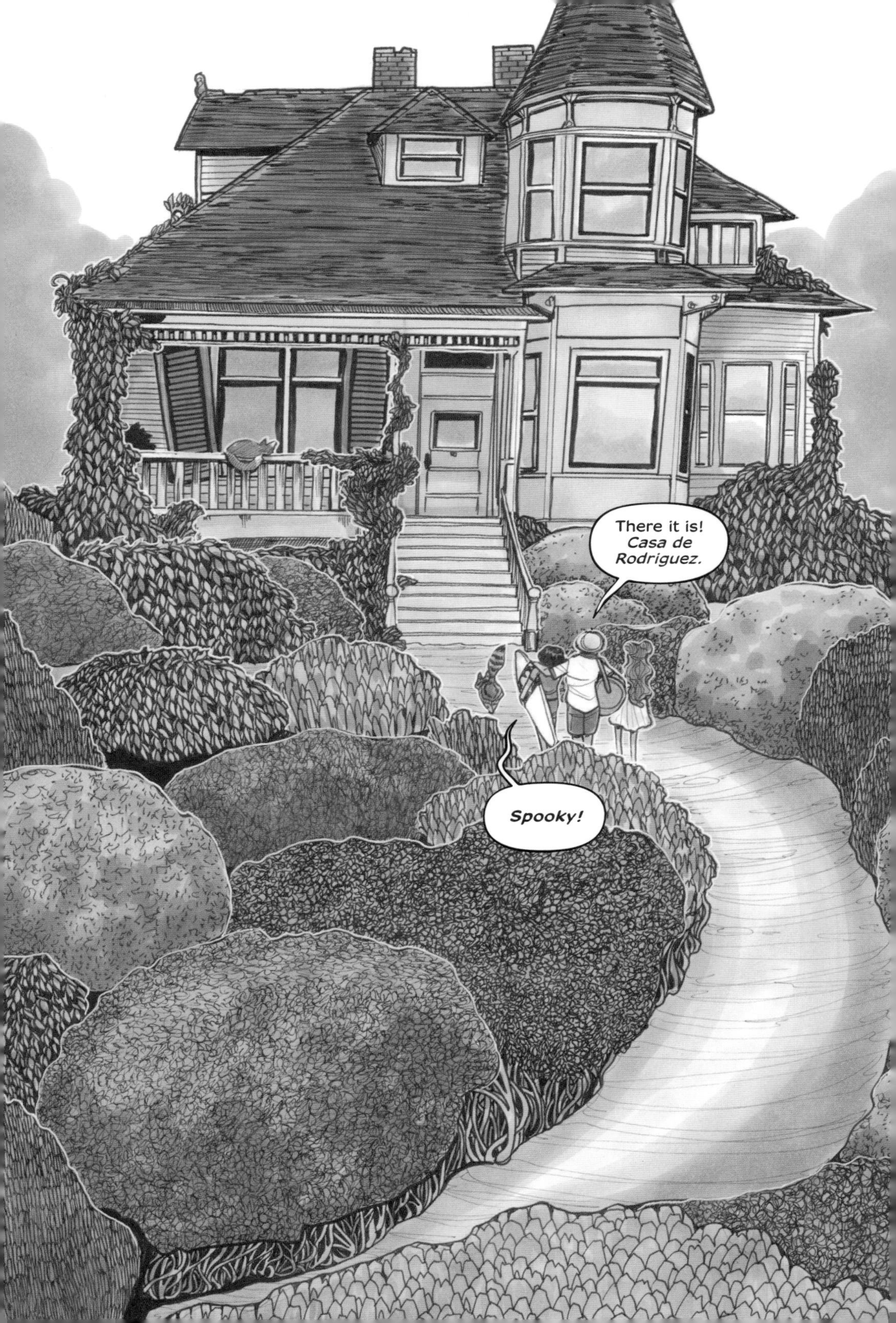
There it is! *Casa de Rodriguez.*
Spooky!

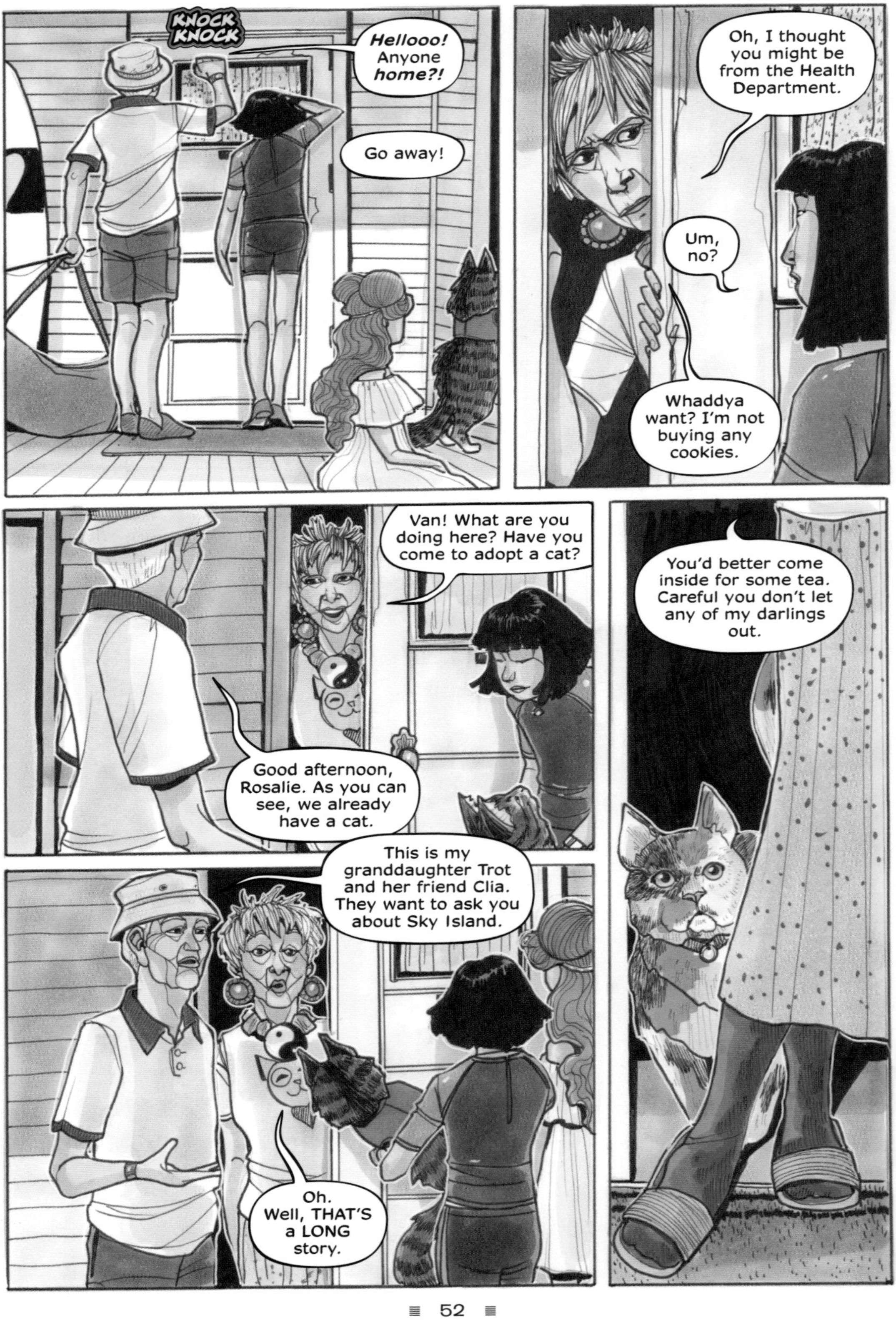
KNOCK KNOCK
Hellooo! Anyone *home?!*
Go away!
Oh, I thought you might be from the Health Department.
Um, no?
Whaddya want? I'm not buying any cookies.
Van! What are you doing here? Have you come to adopt a cat?
Good afternoon, Rosalie. As you can see, we already have a cat.
You'd better come inside for some tea. Careful you don't let any of my darlings out.
This is my granddaughter Trot and her friend Clia. They want to ask you about Sky Island.
Oh. Well, THAT'S a LONG story.

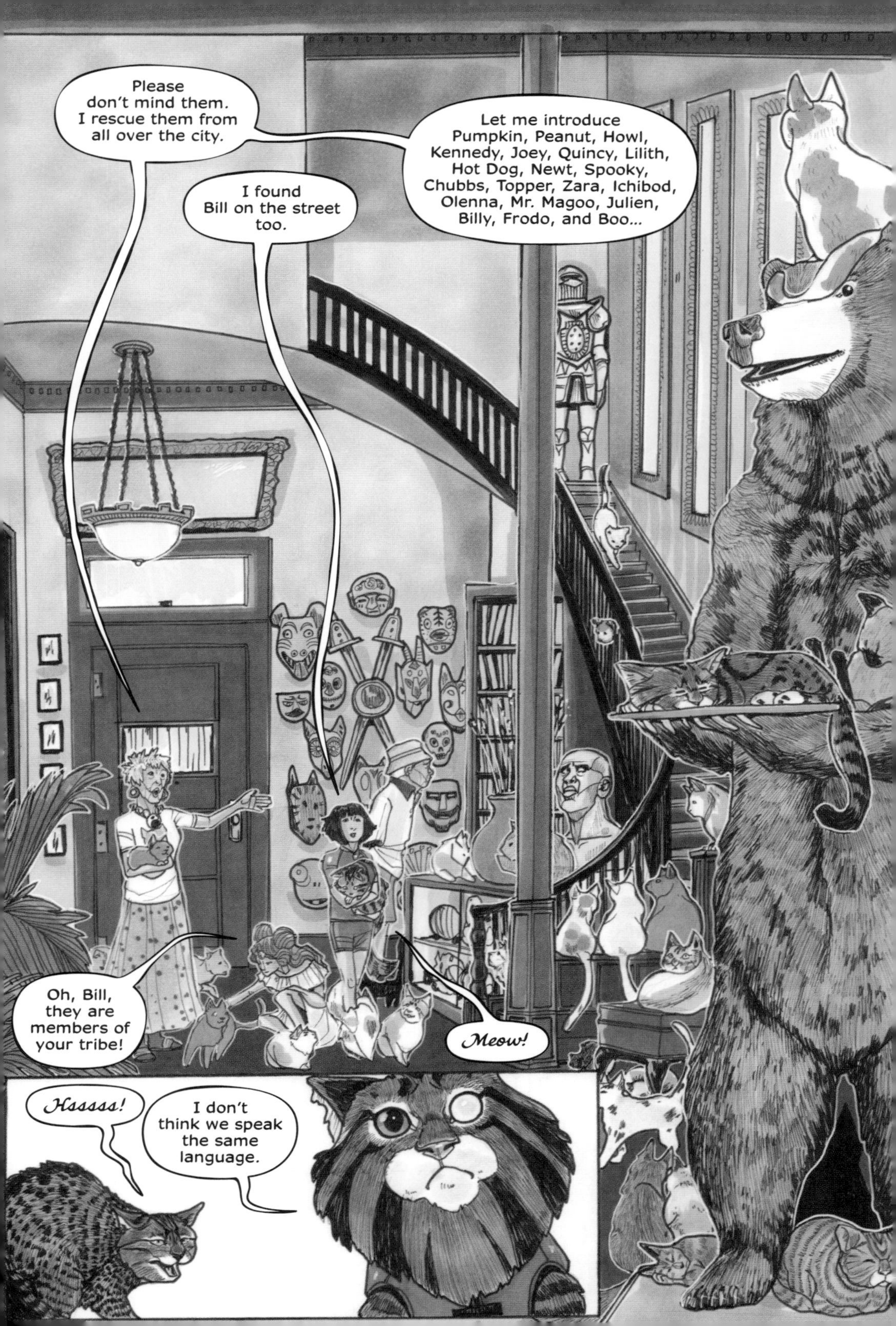
Please don't mind them. I rescue them from all over the city.
Let me introduce Pumpkin, Peanut, Howl, Kennedy, Joey, Quincy, Lilith, Hot Dog, Newt, Spooky, Chubbs, Topper, Zara, Ichibod, Olenna, Mr. Magoo, Julien, Billy, Frodo, and Boo...
I found Bill on the street too.
Oh, Bill, they are members of your tribe!
Meow!
Hssssss!
I don't think we speak the same language.

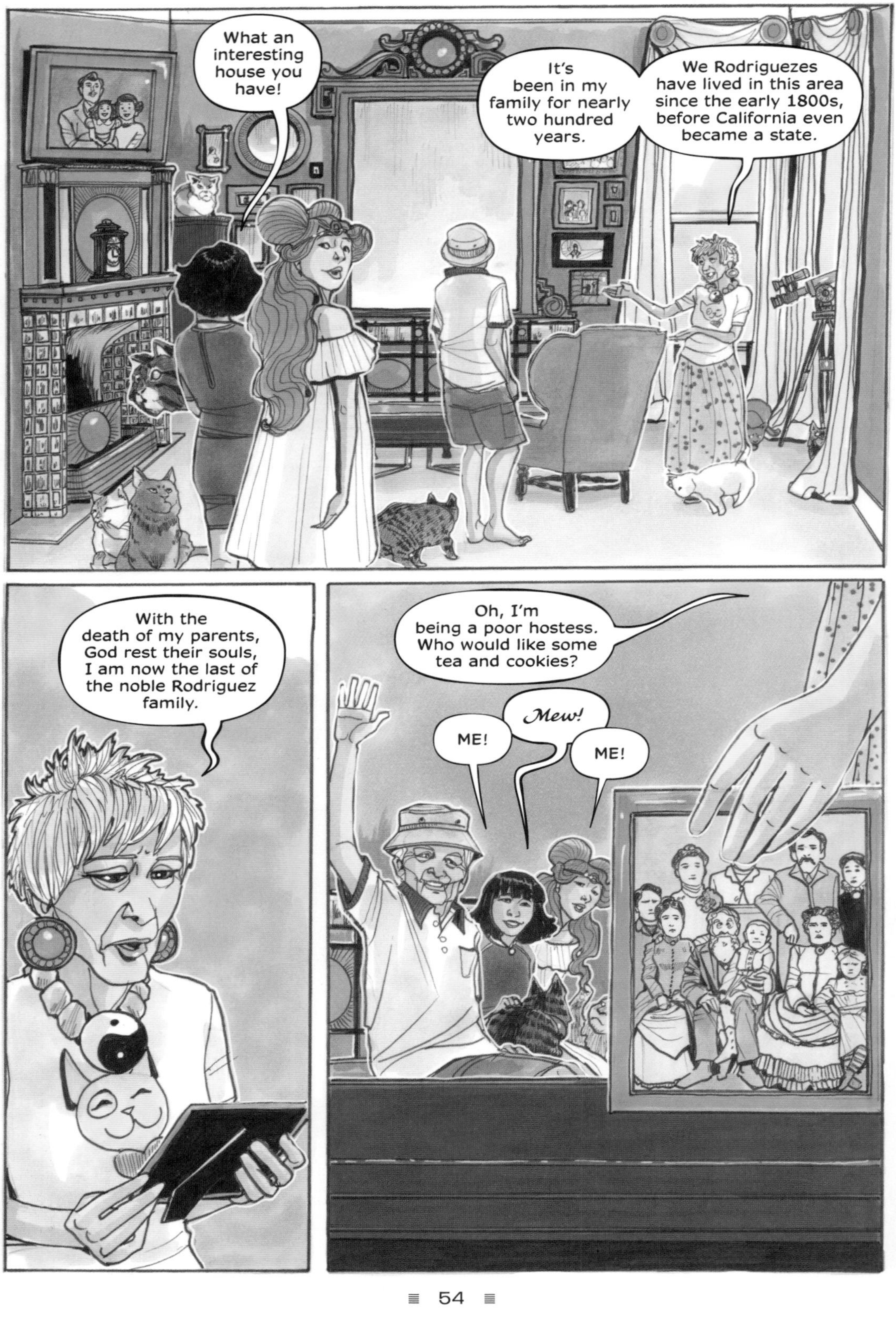
What an interesting house you have!
It's been in my family for nearly two hundred years.
We Rodriguezes have lived in this area since the early 1800s, before California even became a state.
With the death of my parents, God rest their souls, I am now the last of the noble Rodriguez family.
Oh, I'm being a poor hostess. Who would like some tea and cookies?
ME!
Mew!
ME!

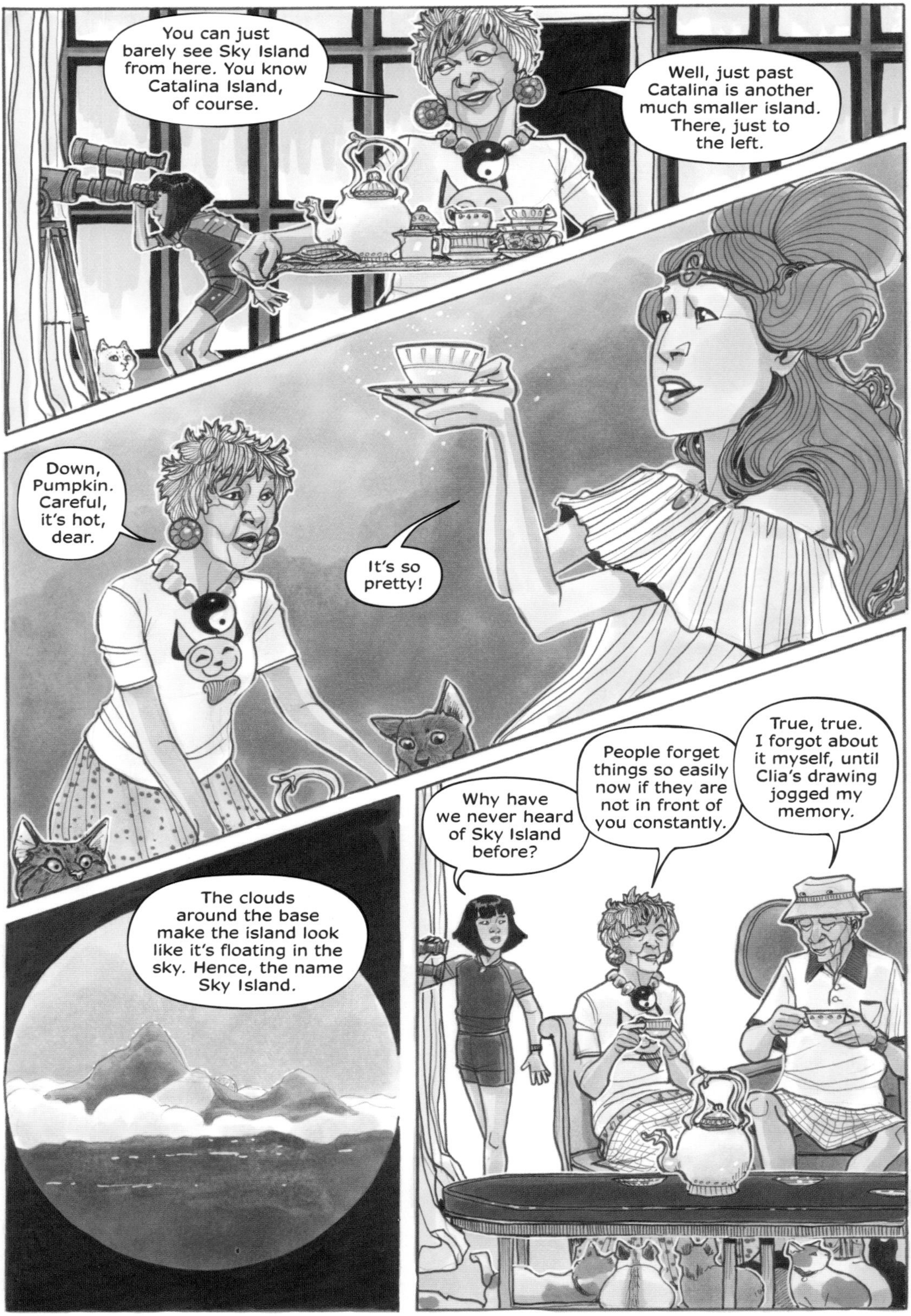
You can just barely see Sky Island from here. You know Catalina Island, of course.
Well, just past Catalina is another much smaller island. There, just to the left.
Down, Pumpkin. Careful, it's hot, dear.
It's so pretty!
The clouds around the base make the island look like it's floating in the sky. Hence, the name Sky Island.
Why have we never heard of Sky Island before?
People forget things so easily now if they are not in front of you constantly.
True, true. I forgot about it myself, until Clia's drawing jogged my memory.

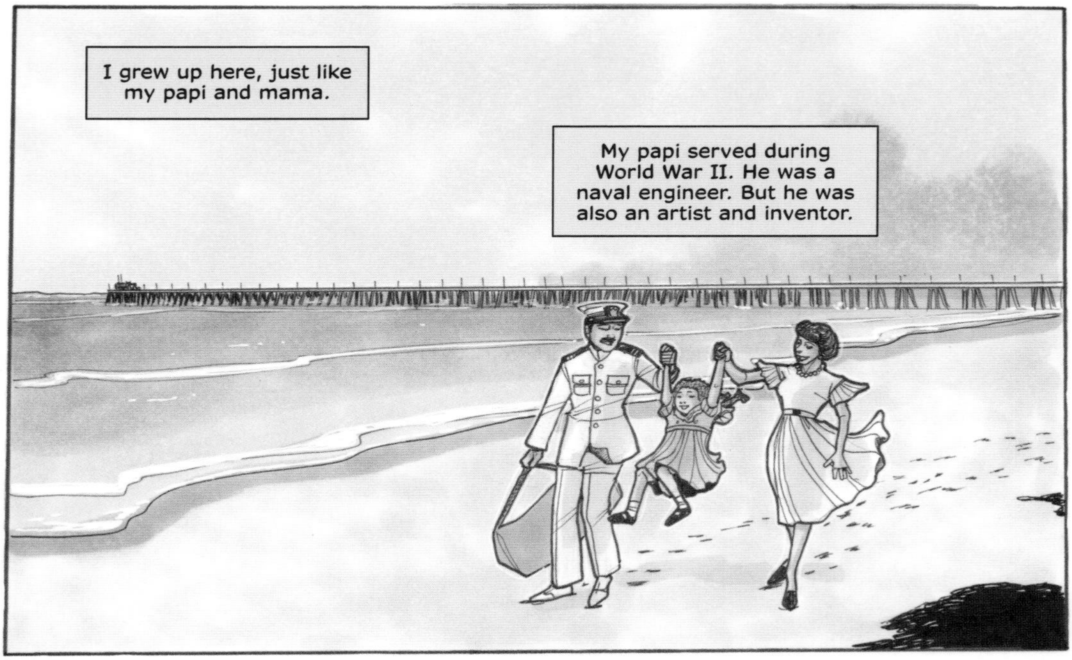
I grew up here, just like my papi and mama.
My papi served during World War II. He was a naval engineer. But he was also an artist and inventor.

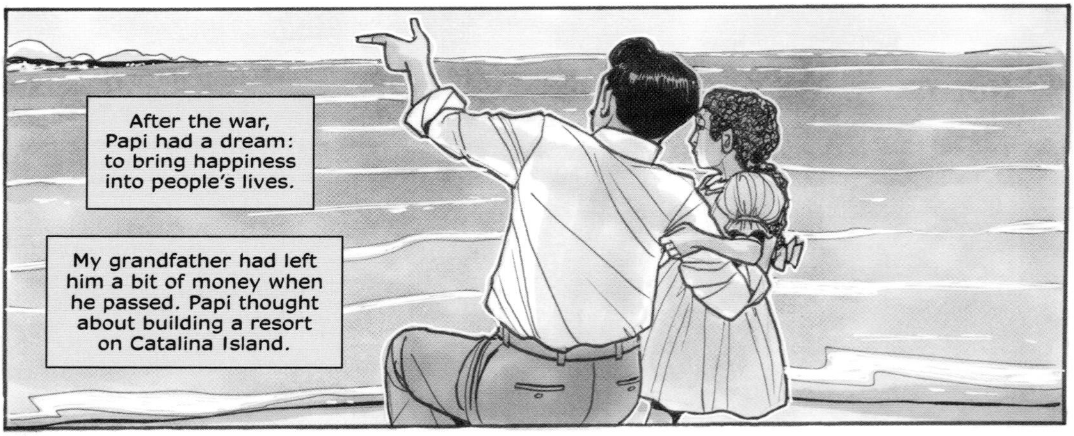
After the war, Papi had a dream: to bring happiness into people's lives.
My grandfather had left him a bit of money when he passed. Papi thought about building a resort on Catalina Island.

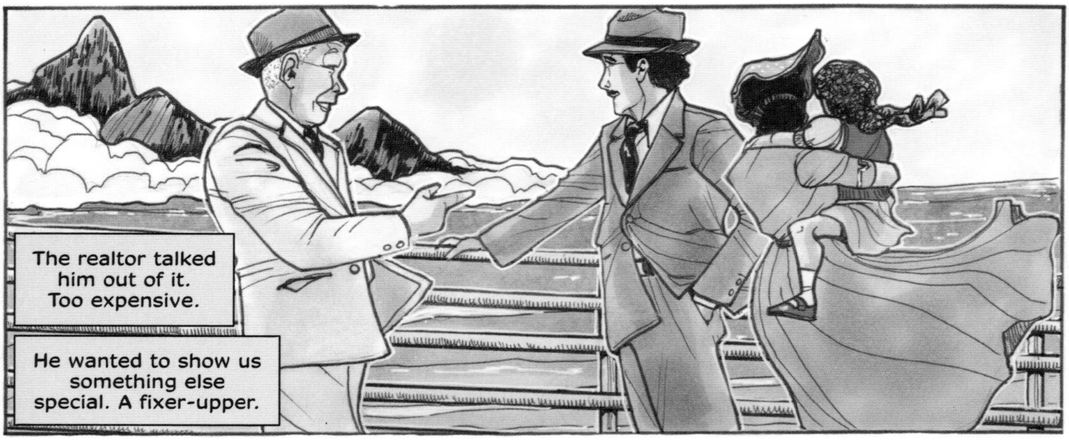
The realtor talked him out of it. Too expensive.
He wanted to show us something else special. A fixer-upper.

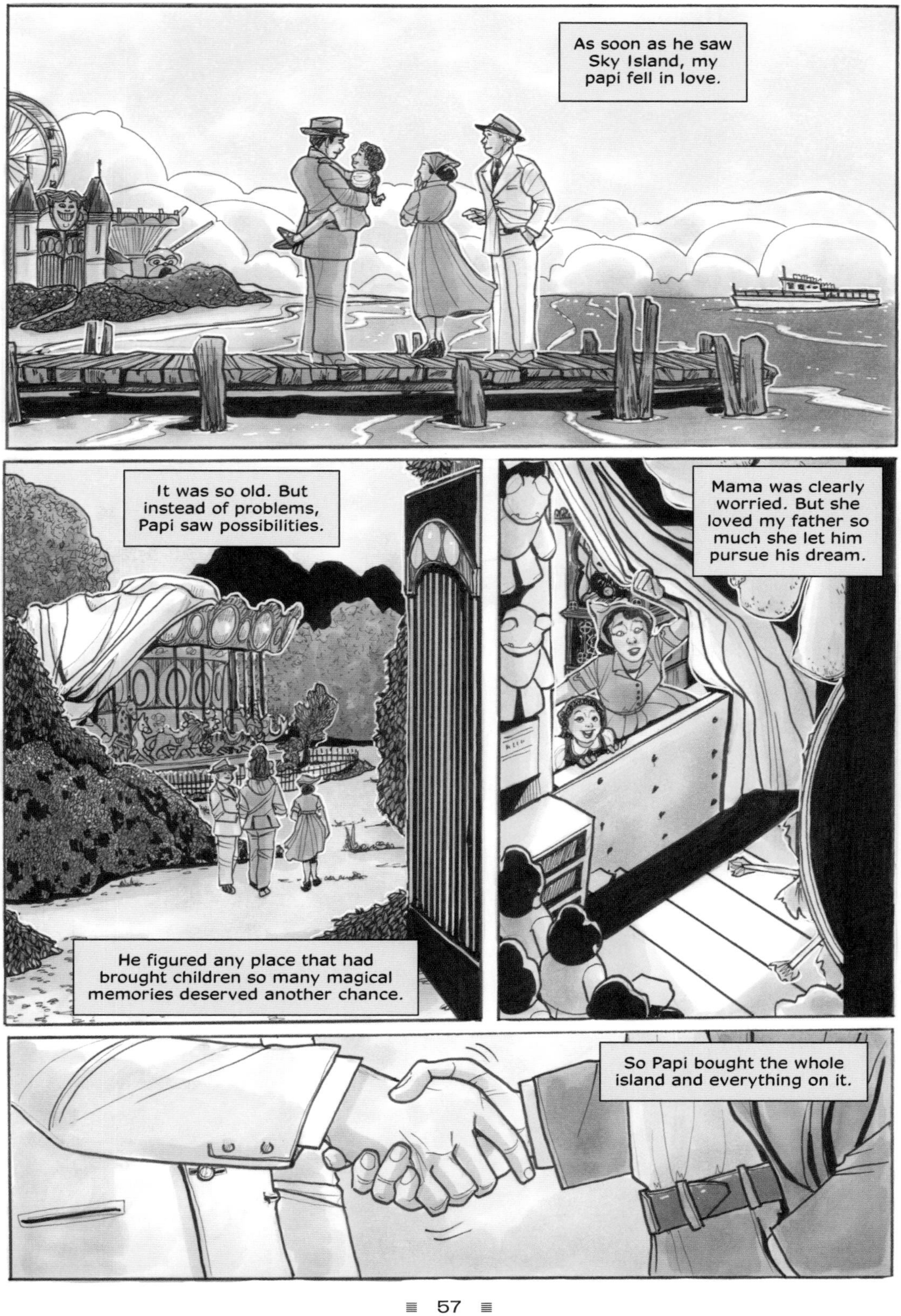
As soon as he saw Sky Island, my papi fell in love.
It was so old. But instead of problems, Papi saw possibilities.
He figured any place that had brought children so many magical memories deserved another chance.
Mama was clearly worried. But she loved my father so much she let him pursue his dream.
So Papi bought the whole island and everything on it.

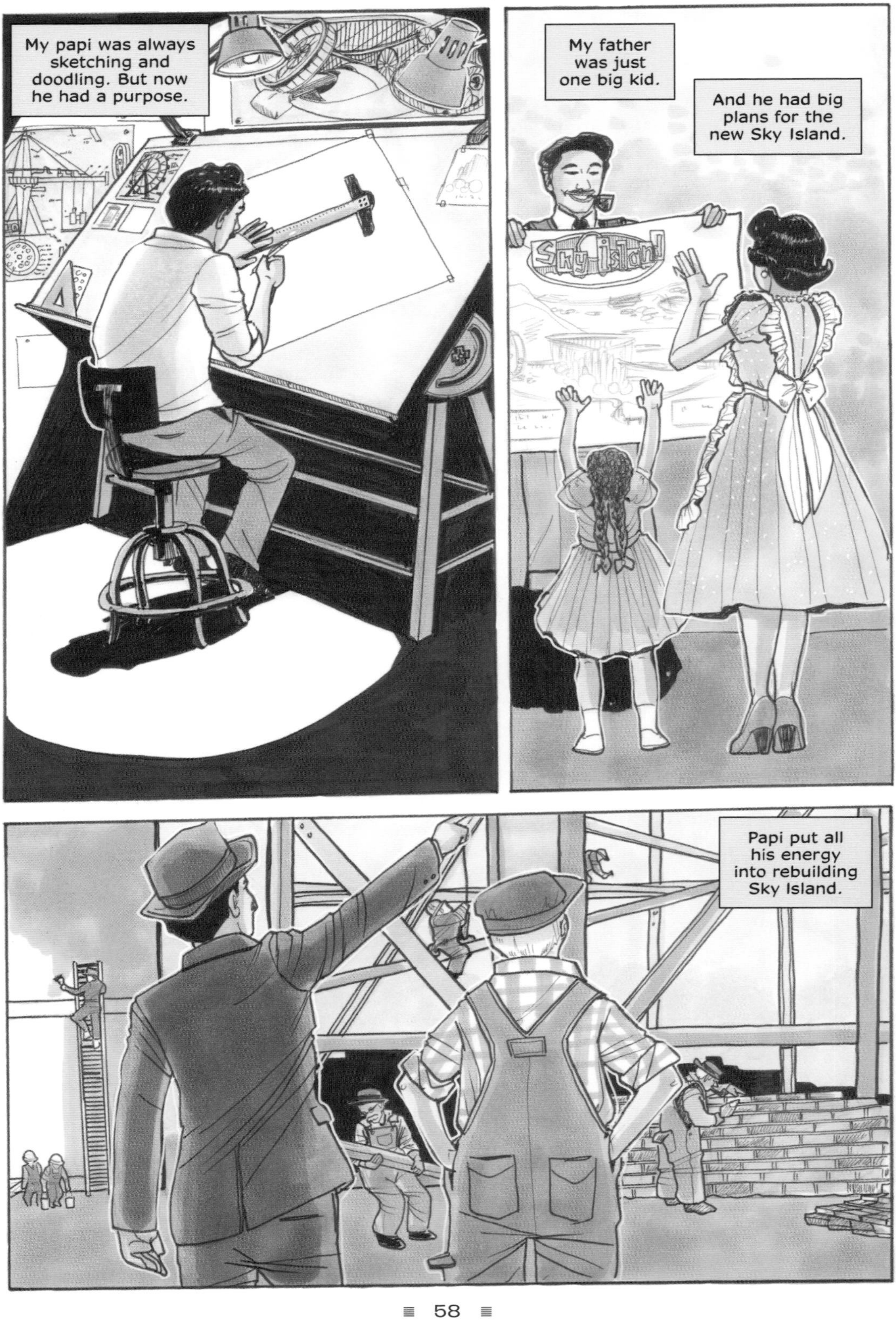
My papi was always sketching and doodling. But now he had a purpose.
My father was just one big kid.
And he had big plans for the new Sky Island.
Sky Island
Papi put all his energy into rebuilding Sky Island.

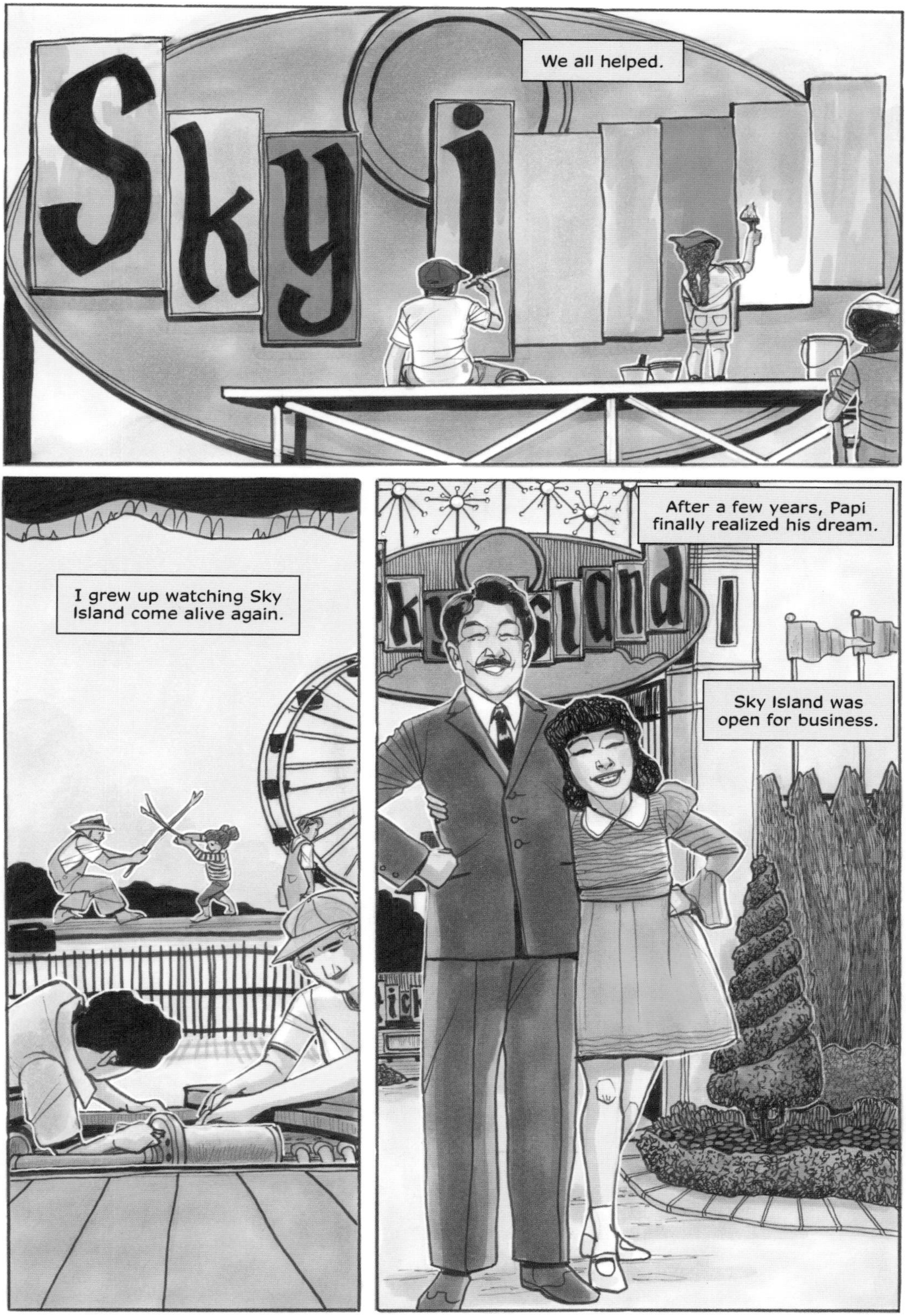
We all helped.
I grew up watching Sky Island come alive again.
After a few years, Papi finally realized his dream.
Sky Island was open for business.

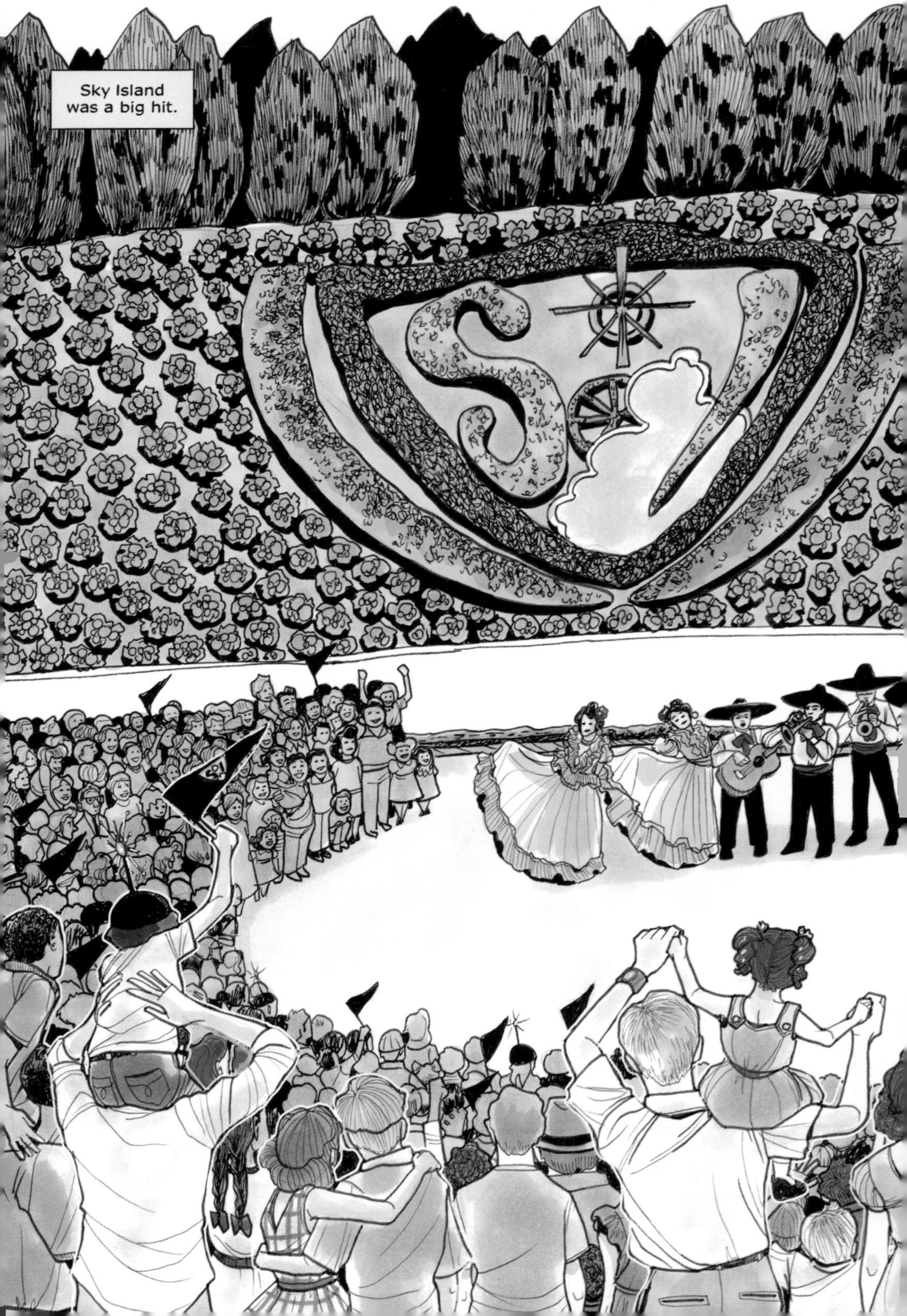
Sky Island
was a big hit.

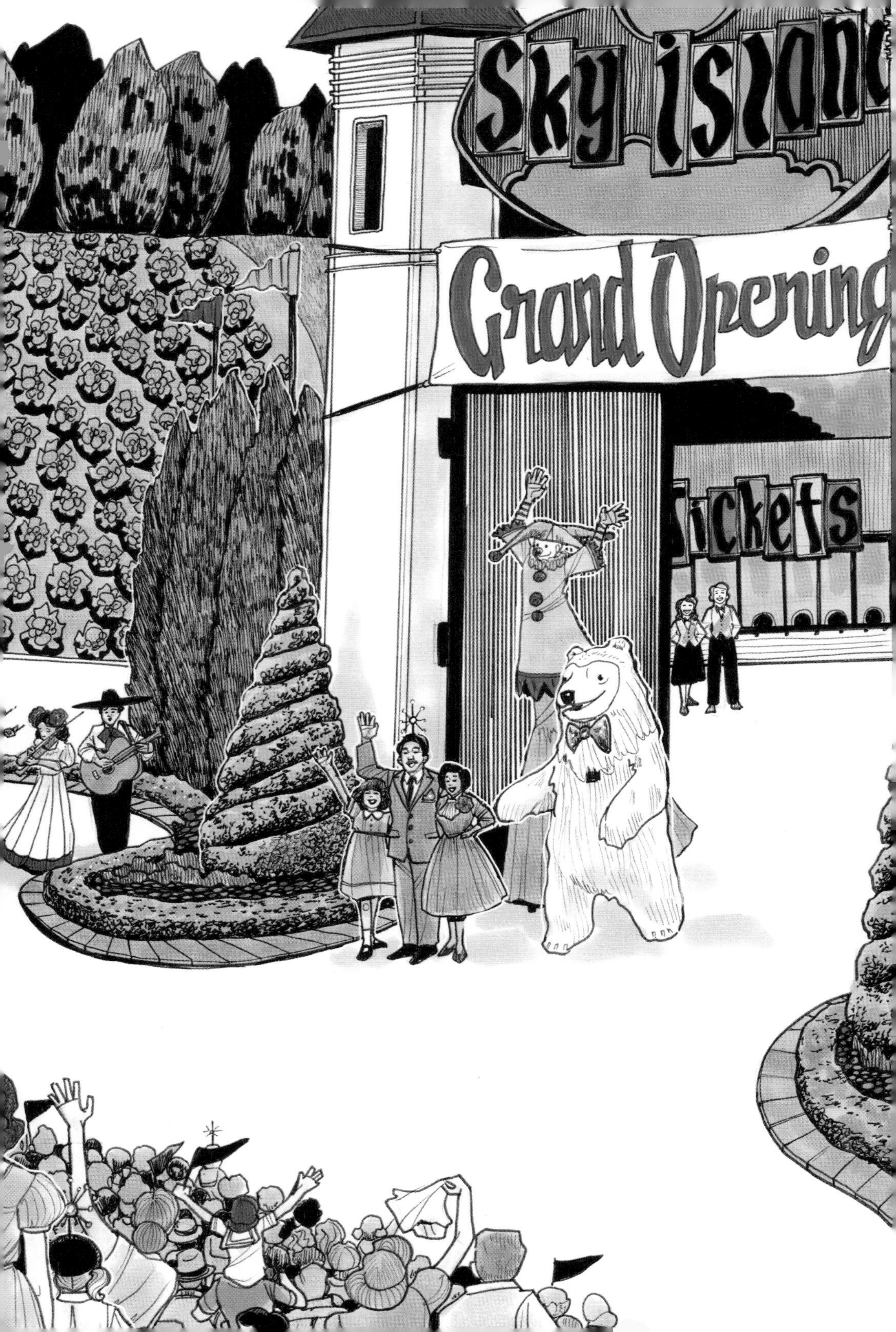
Sky Islan
Grand Opening
ickets

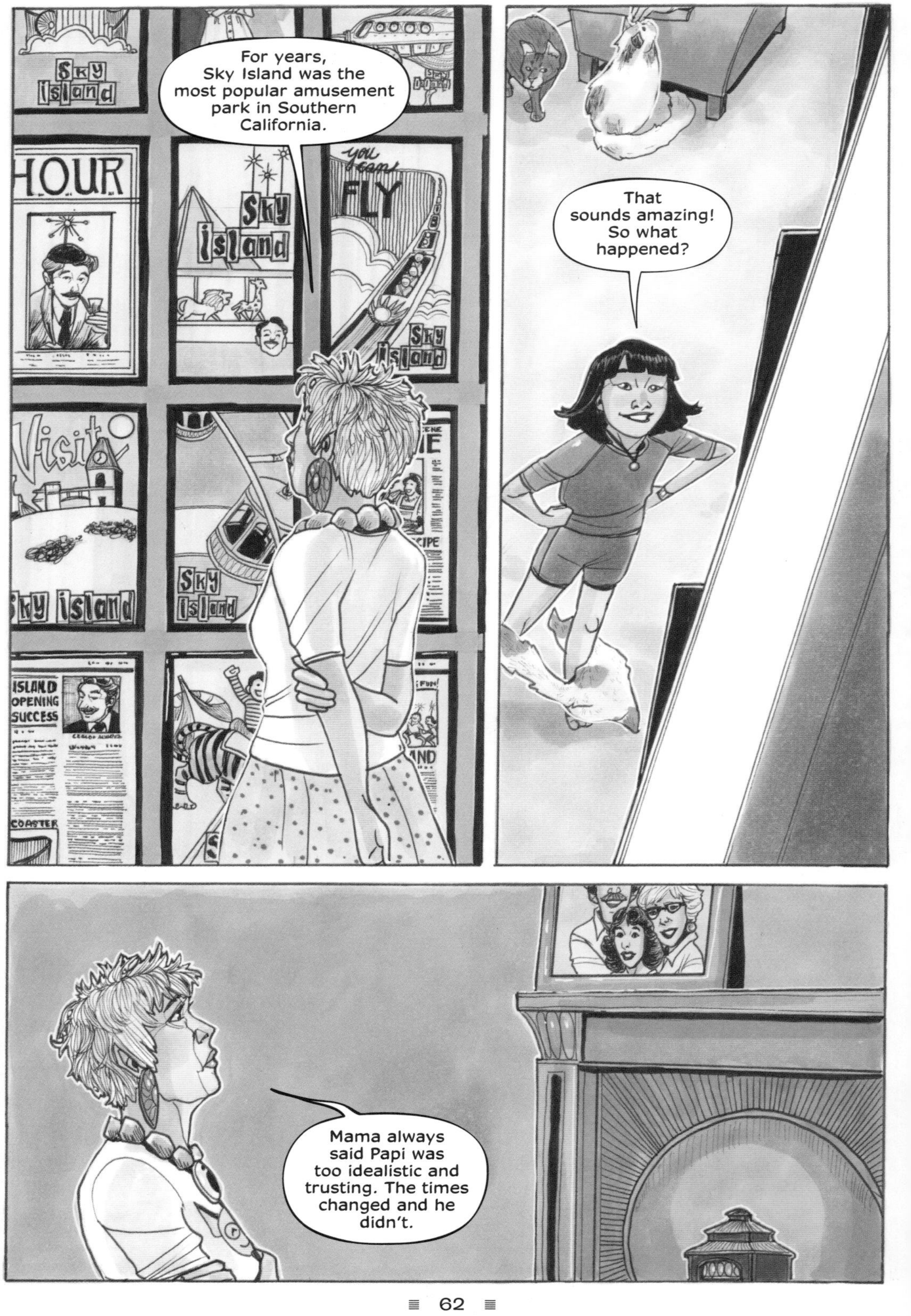
For years, Sky Island was the most popular amusement park in Southern California.
Sky Island
HOUR
you can't FLY
Sky Island
Sky Island
Visit
Sky Island
Sky Island
ISLAND OPENING SUCCESS
COASTER
FUN!
That sounds amazing! So what happened?
Mama always said Papi was too idealistic and trusting. The times changed and he didn't.

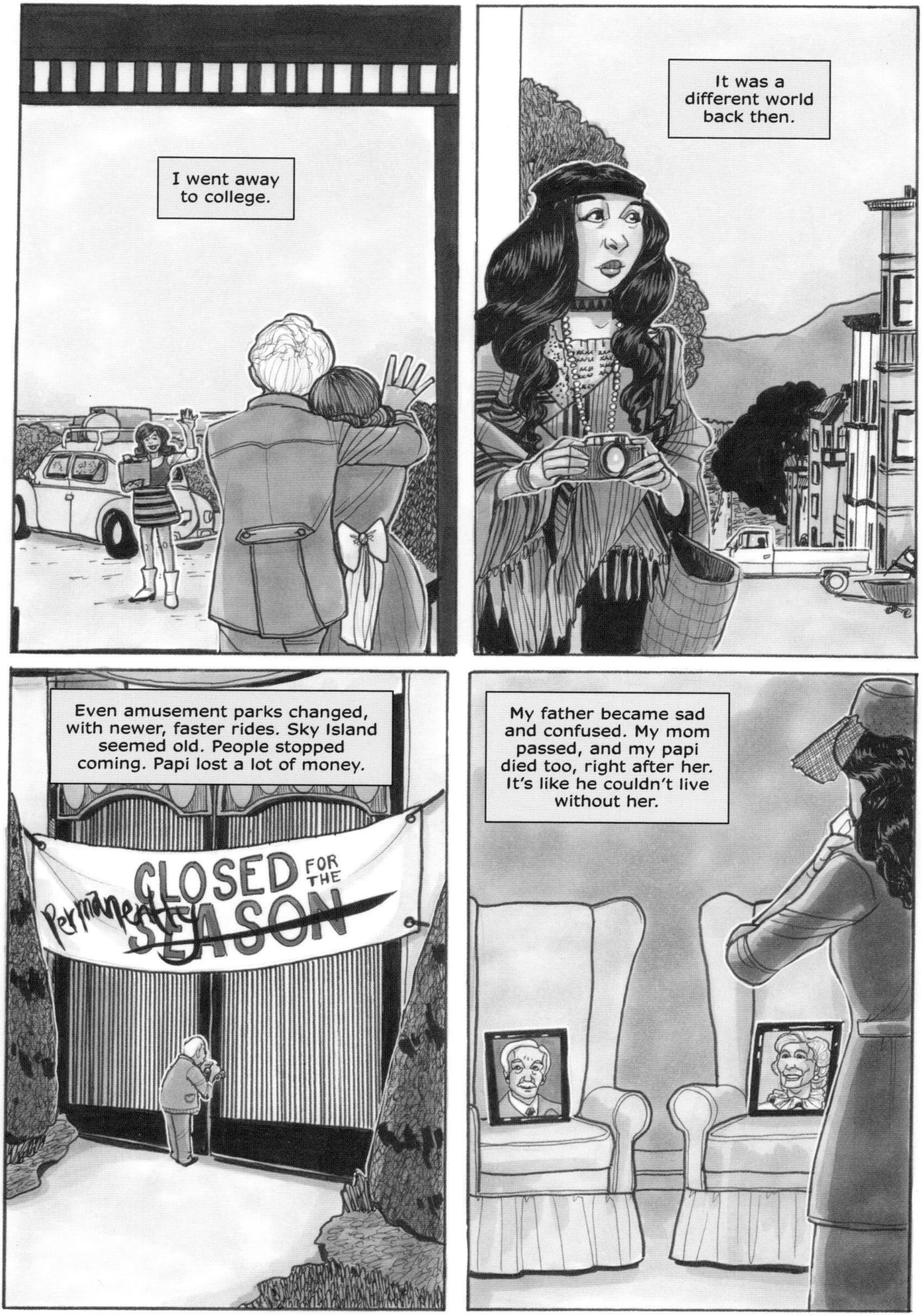
I went away to college.
It was a different world back then.
Even amusement parks changed, with newer, faster rides. Sky Island seemed old. People stopped coming. Papi lost a lot of money.
CLOSED FOR THE
Permanently
SEASON
My father became sad and confused. My mom passed, and my papi died too, right after her. It's like he couldn't live without her.

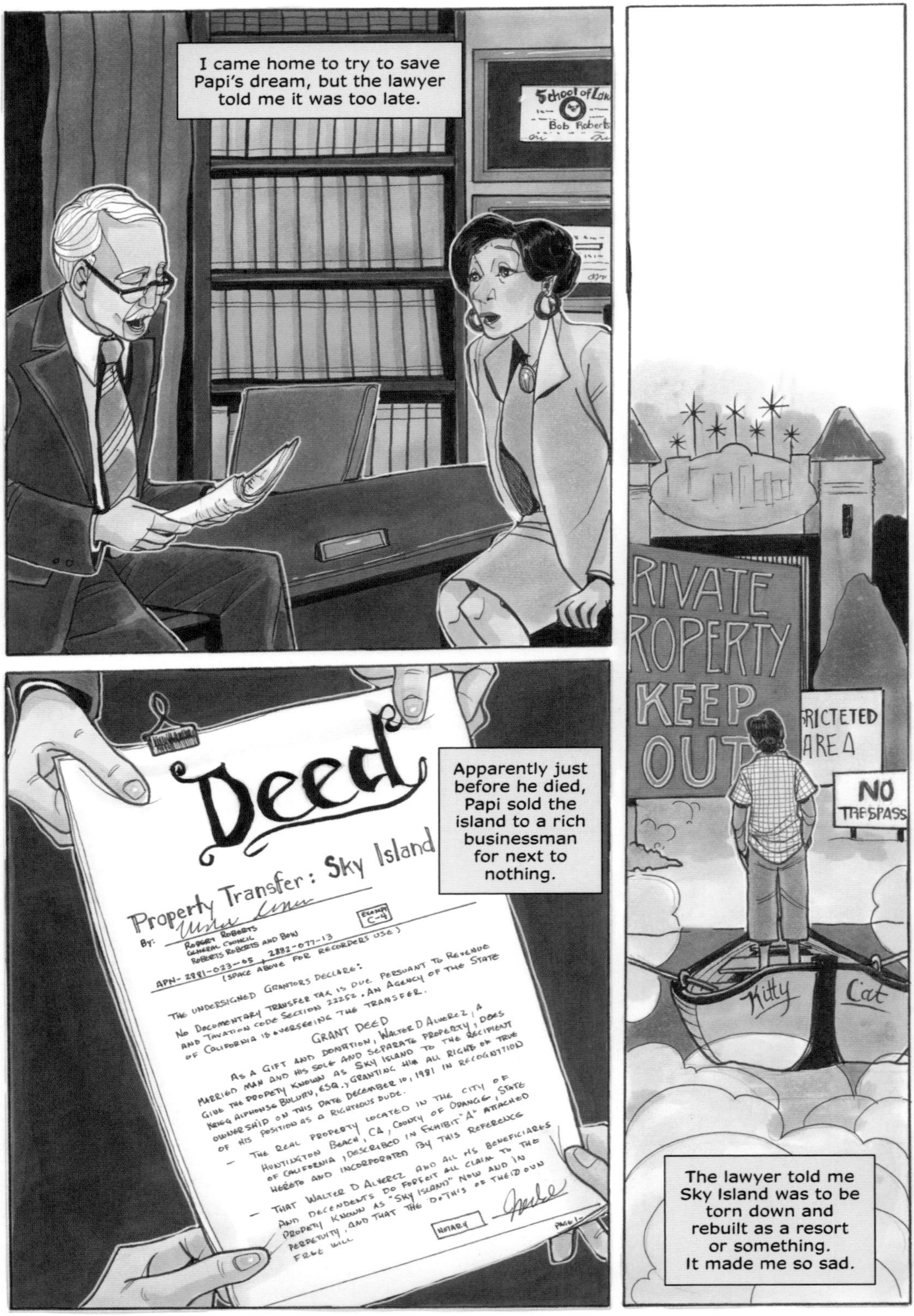
I came home to try to save Papi's dream, but the lawyer told me it was too late.
School of Law
Bob Roberts
Deed
Property Transfer: Sky Island
By:
APN- 2881-023-65 + 2882-077-13
(SPACE ABOVE FOR RECORDERS USE)
THE UNDERSIGNED GRANTORS DECLARE:
GRANT DEED
NOTARY
Apparently just before he died, Papi sold the island to a rich businessman for next to nothing.
RIVATE ROPERTY KEEP OUT
RICTETED AREA
NO TRESPASS
Kitty Cat
The lawyer told me Sky Island was to be torn down and rebuilt as a resort or something. It made me so sad.

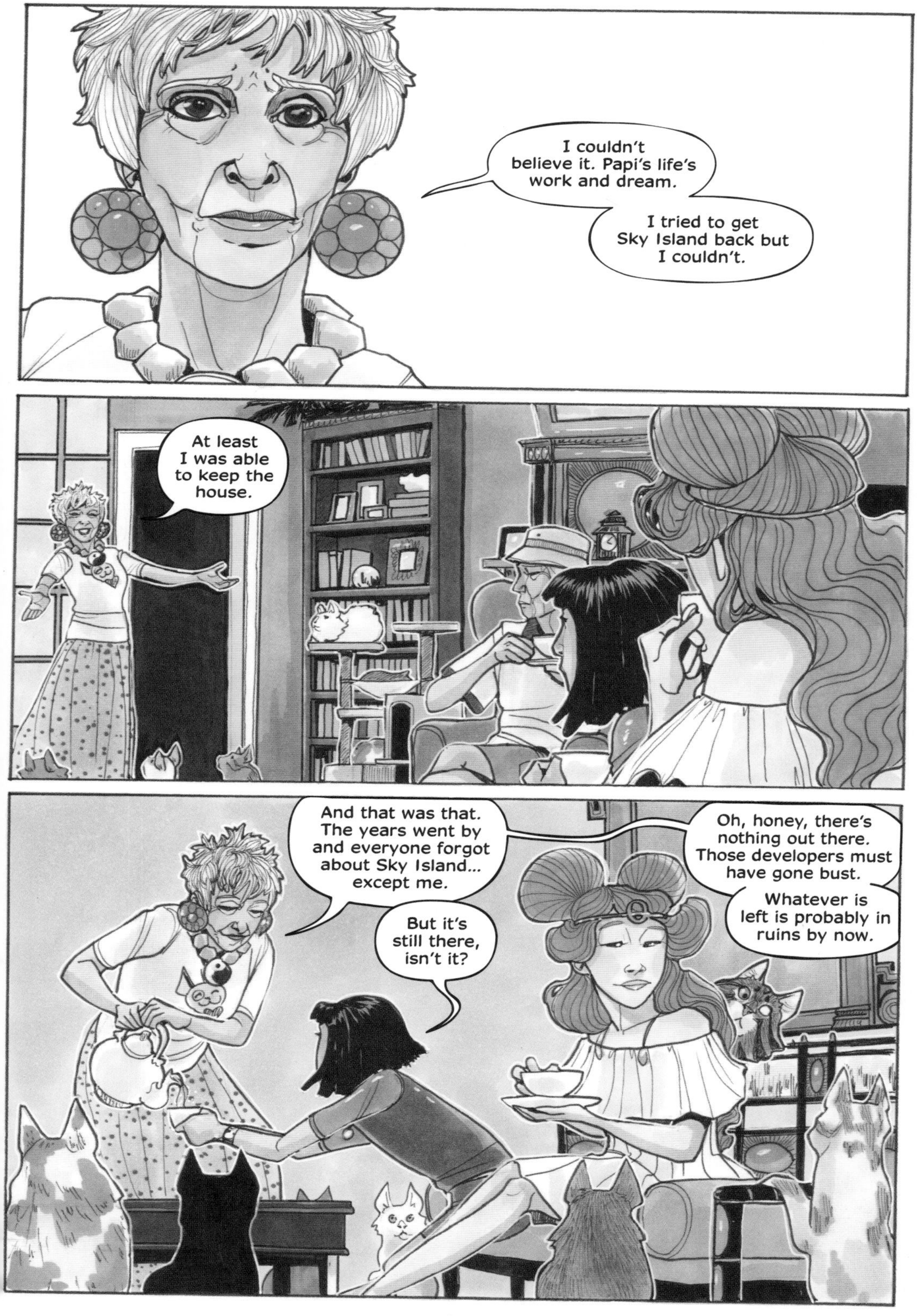
I couldn't believe it. Papi's life's work and dream.
I tried to get Sky Island back but I couldn't.
At least I was able to keep the house.
And that was that. The years went by and everyone forgot about Sky Island... except me.
But it's still there, isn't it?
Oh, honey, there's nothing out there. Those developers must have gone bust.
Whatever is left is probably in ruins by now.

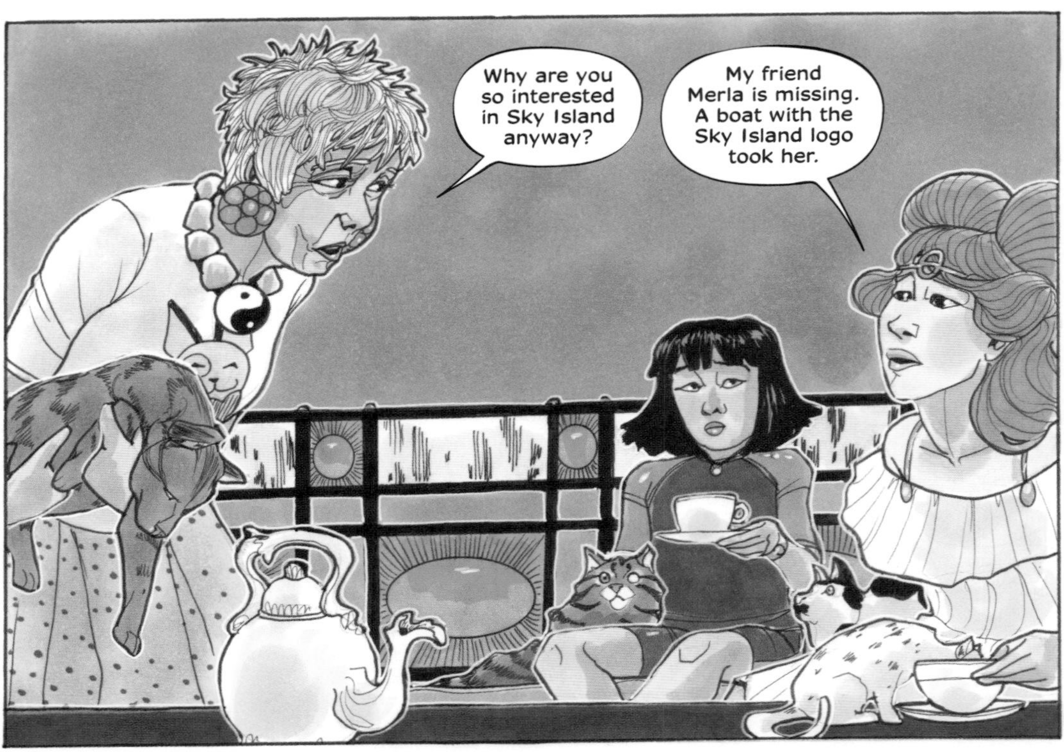
Why are you so interested in Sky Island anyway?
My friend Merla is missing. A boat with the Sky Island logo took her.

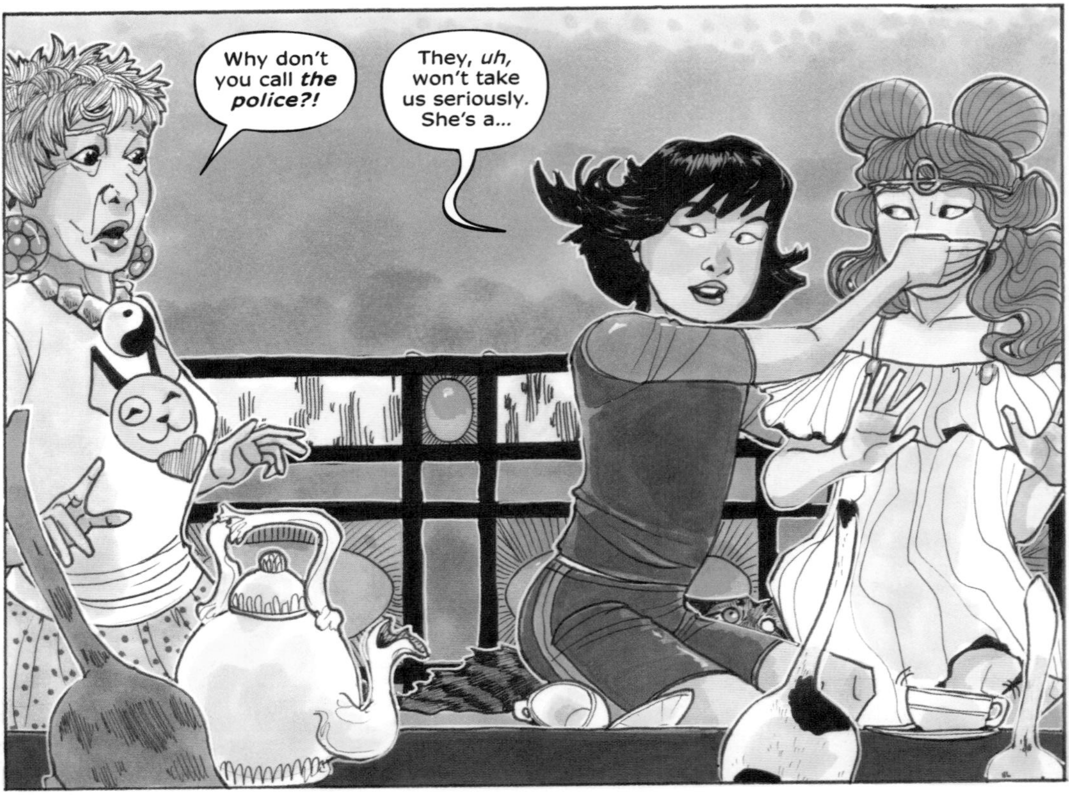
Why don't you call *the police?!*
They, *uh,* won't take us seriously. She's a...

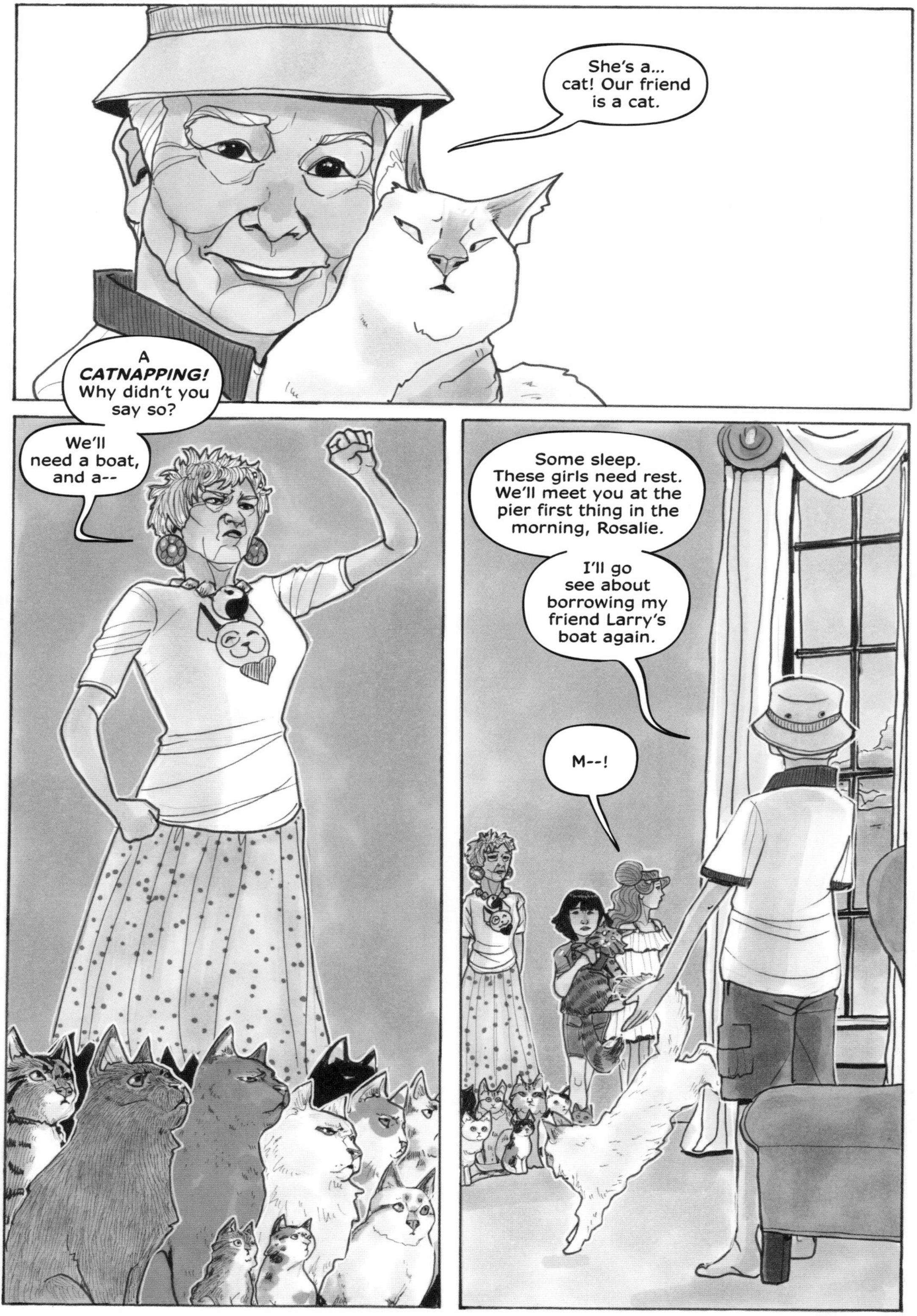
She's a... cat! Our friend is a cat.
A *CATNAPPING!* Why didn't you say so?
We'll need a boat, and a--
Some sleep. These girls need rest. We'll meet you at the pier first thing in the morning, Rosalie.
I'll go see about borrowing my friend Larry's boat again.
M--!

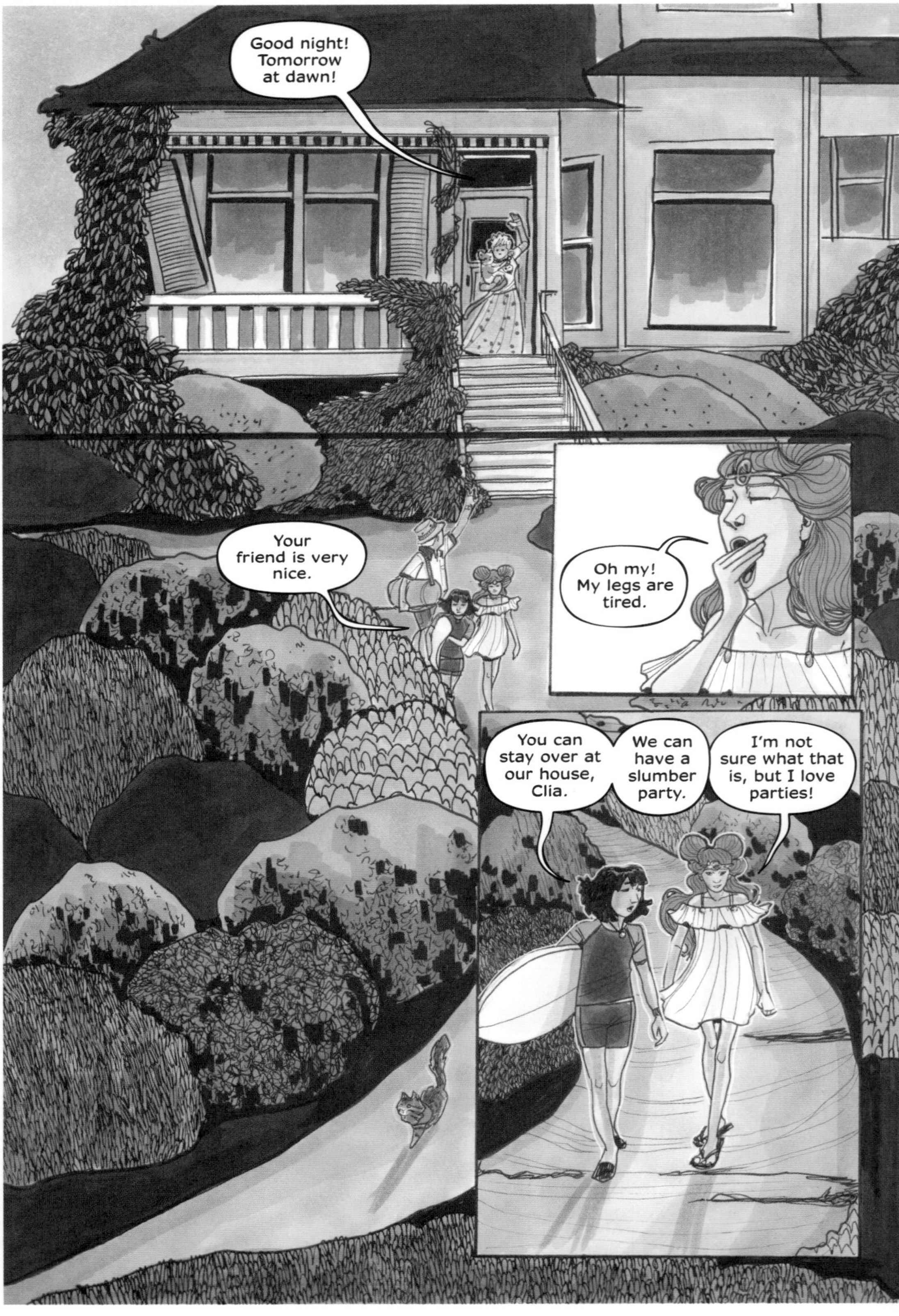
Good night! Tomorrow at dawn!
Your friend is very nice.
Oh my! My legs are tired.
You can stay over at our house, Clia.
We can have a slumber party.
I'm not sure what that is, but I love parties!

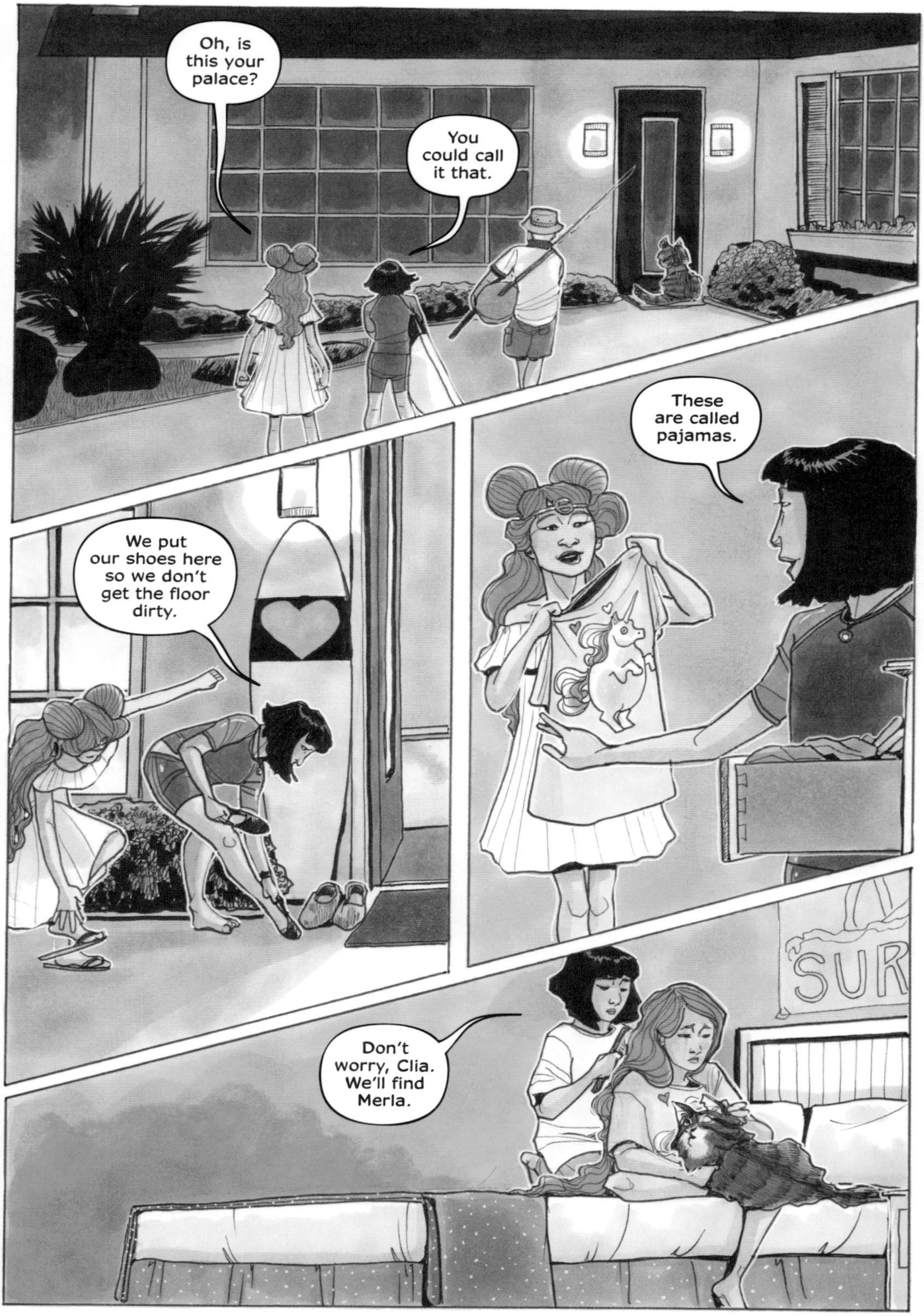
Oh, is this your palace?
You could call it that.
We put our shoes here so we don't get the floor dirty.
These are called pajamas.
SUR
Don't worry, Clia. We'll find Merla.

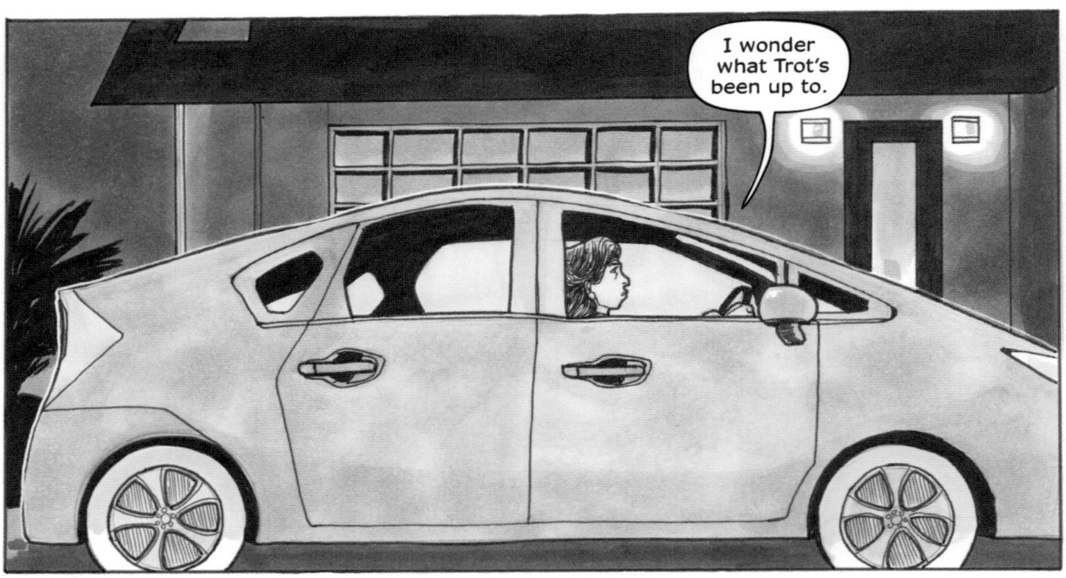
I wonder what Trot's been up to.

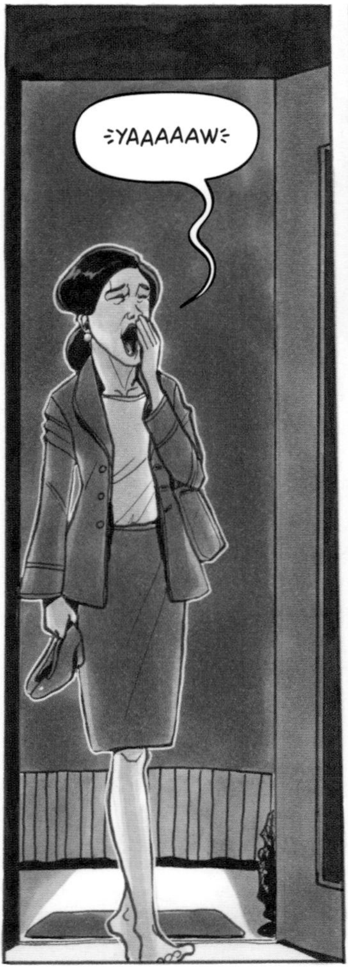
YAAAAAW

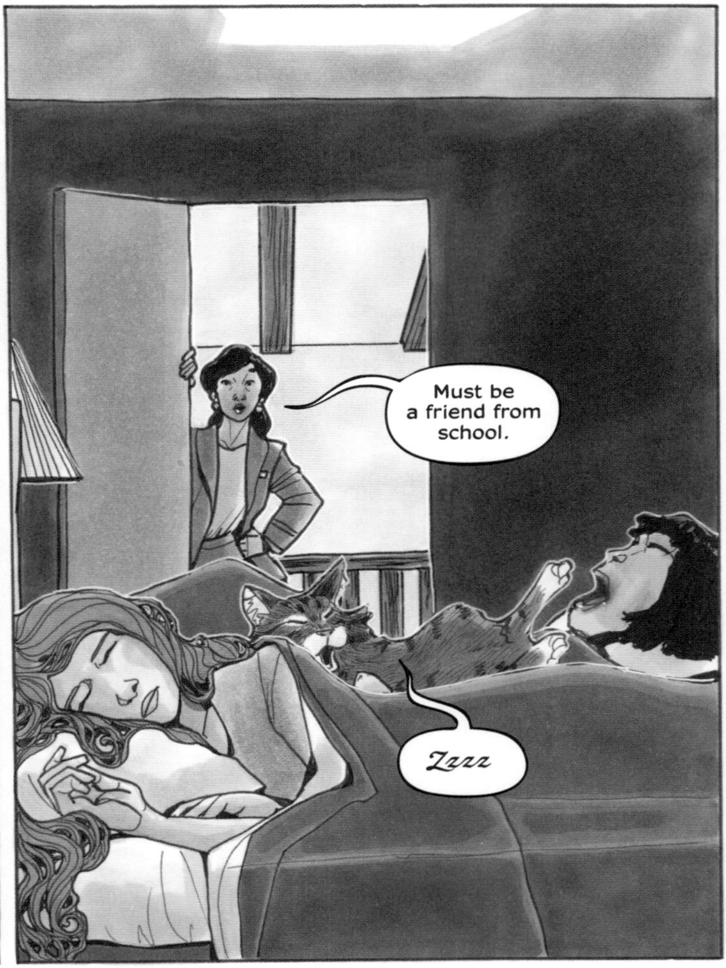
Must be a friend from school.
Zzzz

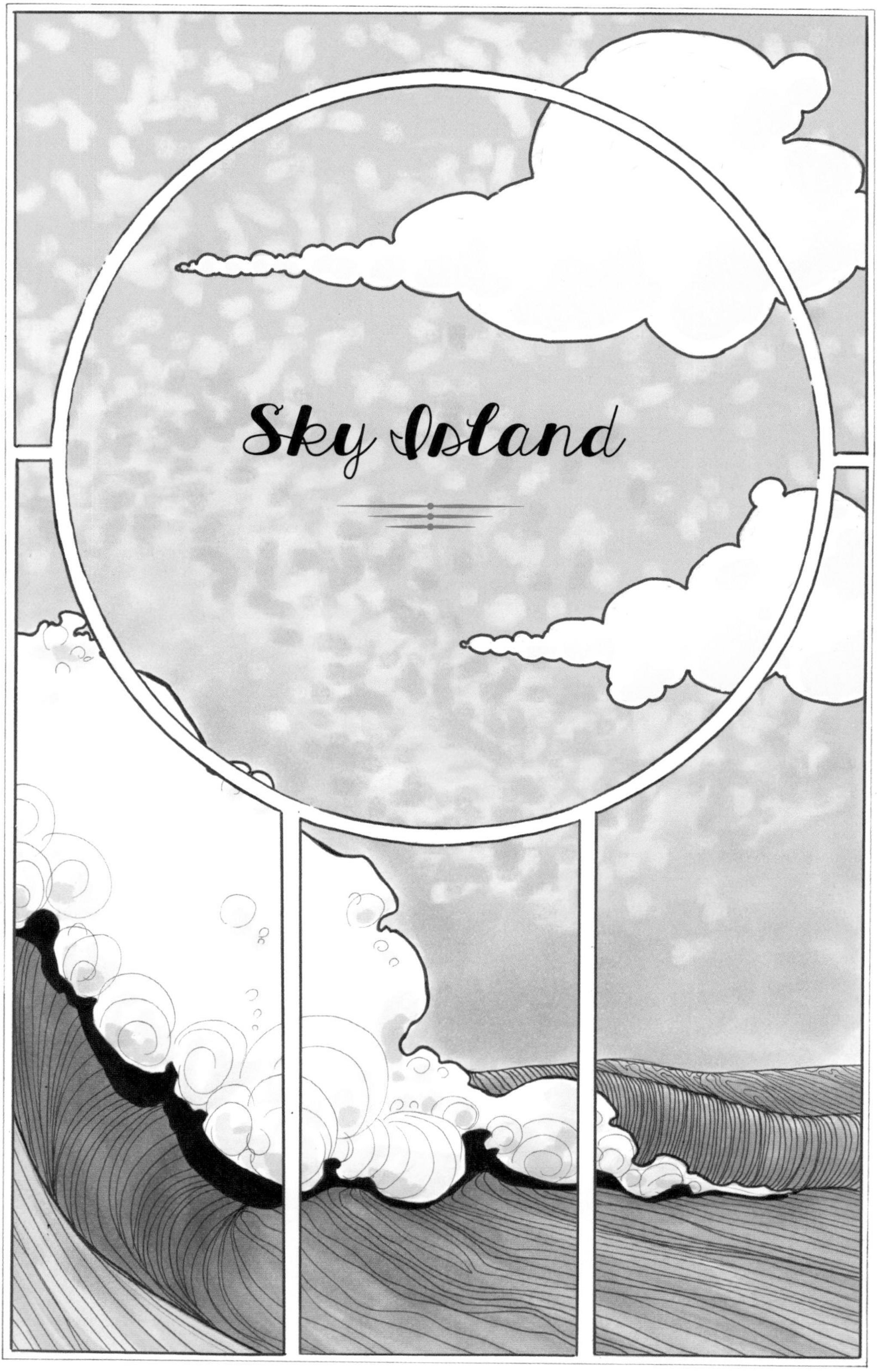
Sky Island

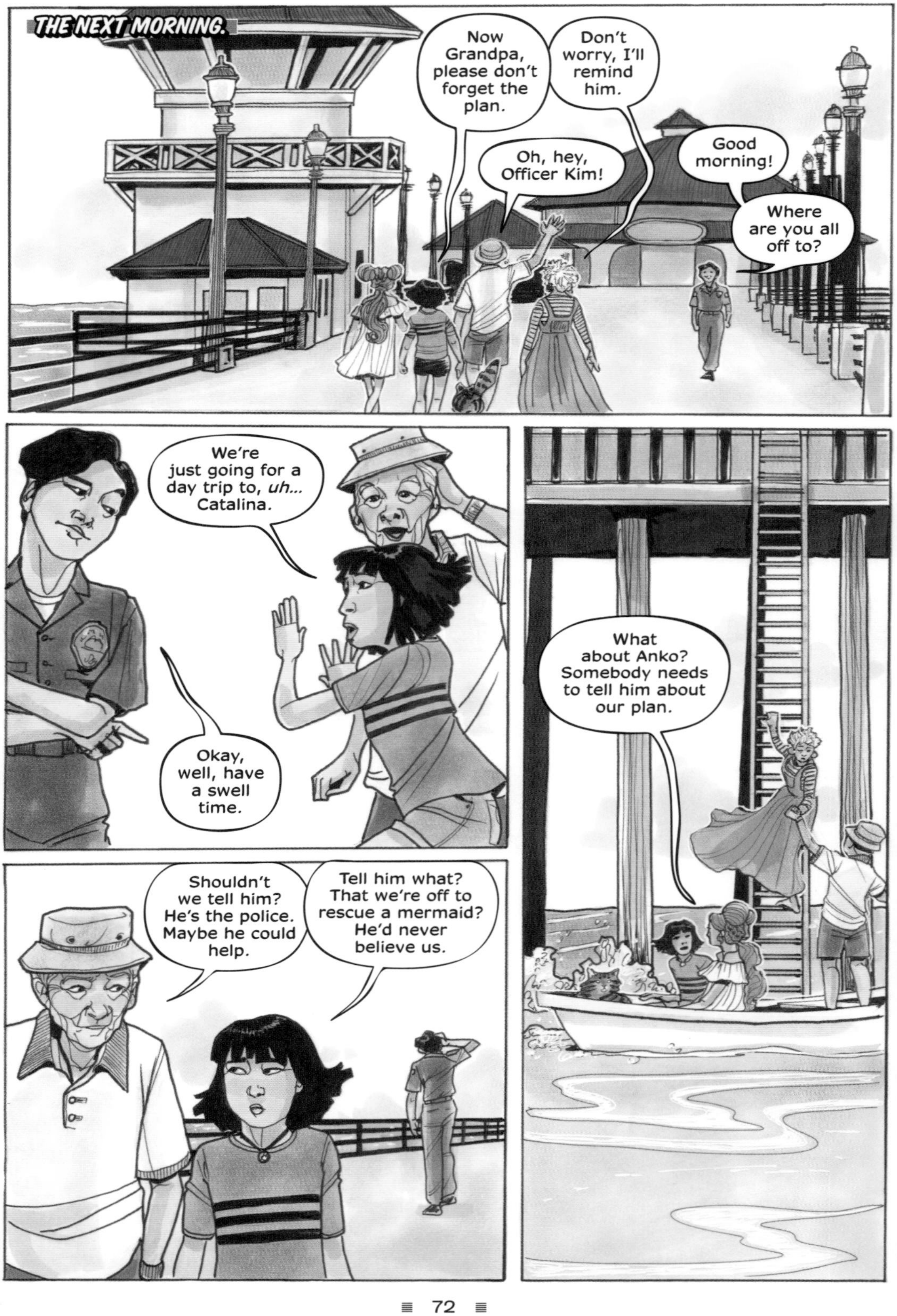
THE NEXT MORNING.
Now Grandpa, please don't forget the plan.
Don't worry, I'll remind him.
Oh, hey, Officer Kim!
Good morning!
Where are you all off to?
We're just going for a day trip to, *uh...* Catalina.
Okay, well, have a swell time.
What about Anko? Somebody needs to tell him about our plan.
Shouldn't we tell him? He's the police. Maybe he could help.
Tell him what? That we're off to rescue a mermaid? He'd never believe us.

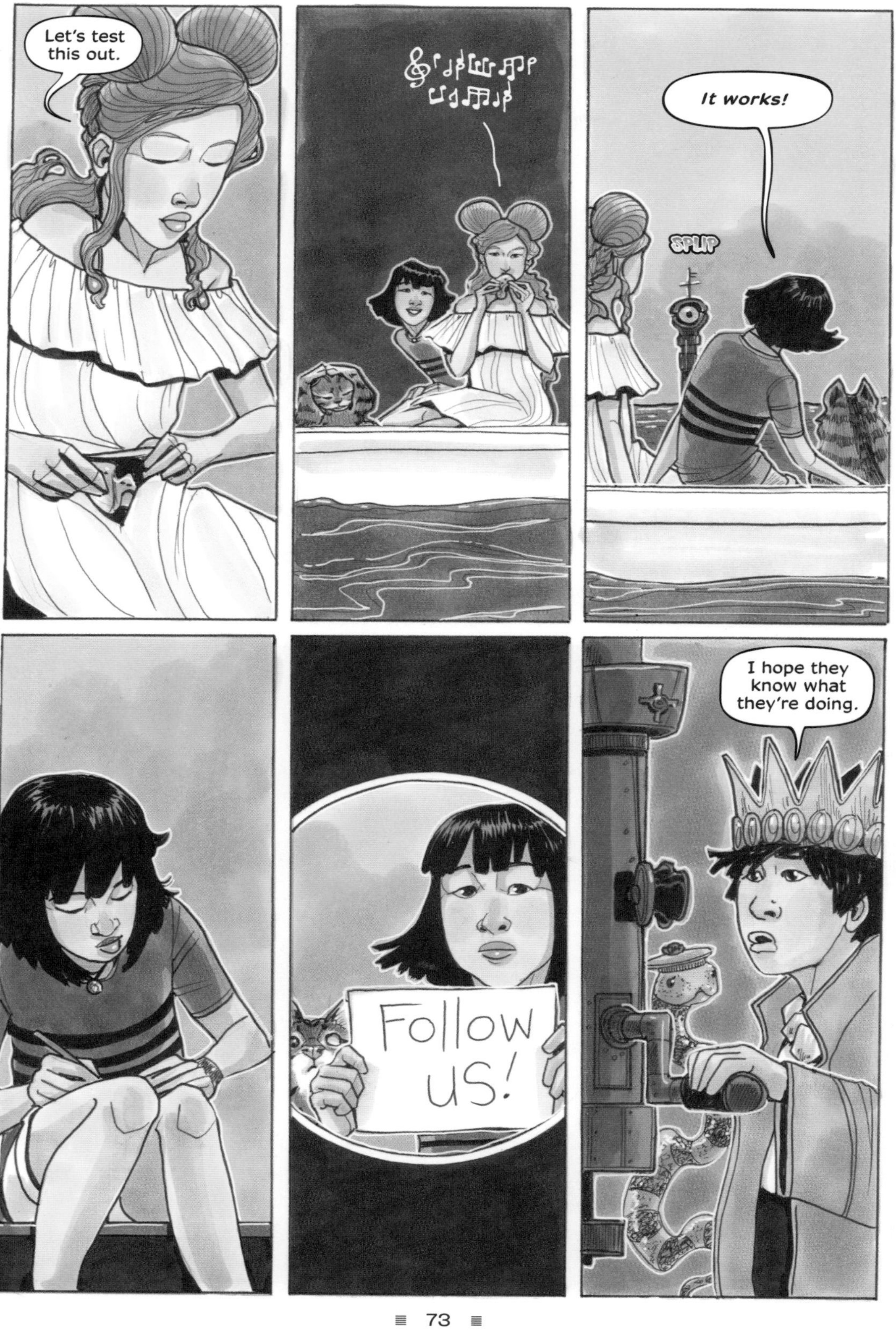
Let's test this out.
It works!
SPLIP
I hope they know what they're doing.
Follow us!

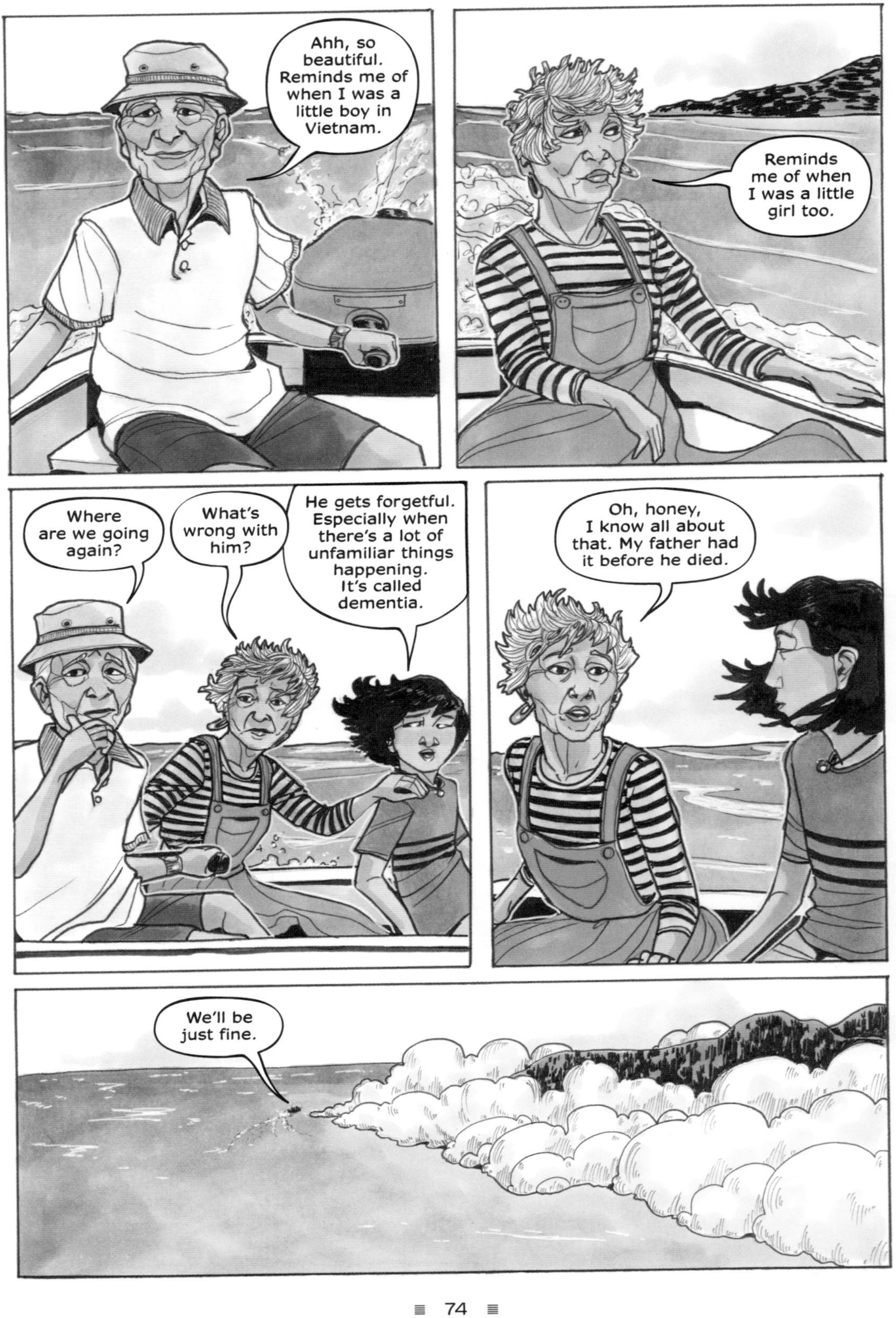
Ahh, so beautiful. Reminds me of when I was a little boy in Vietnam.
Reminds me of when I was a little girl too.
Where are we going again?
What's wrong with him?
He gets forgetful. Especially when there's a lot of unfamiliar things happening. It's called dementia.
Oh, honey, I know all about that. My father had it before he died.
We'll be just fine.

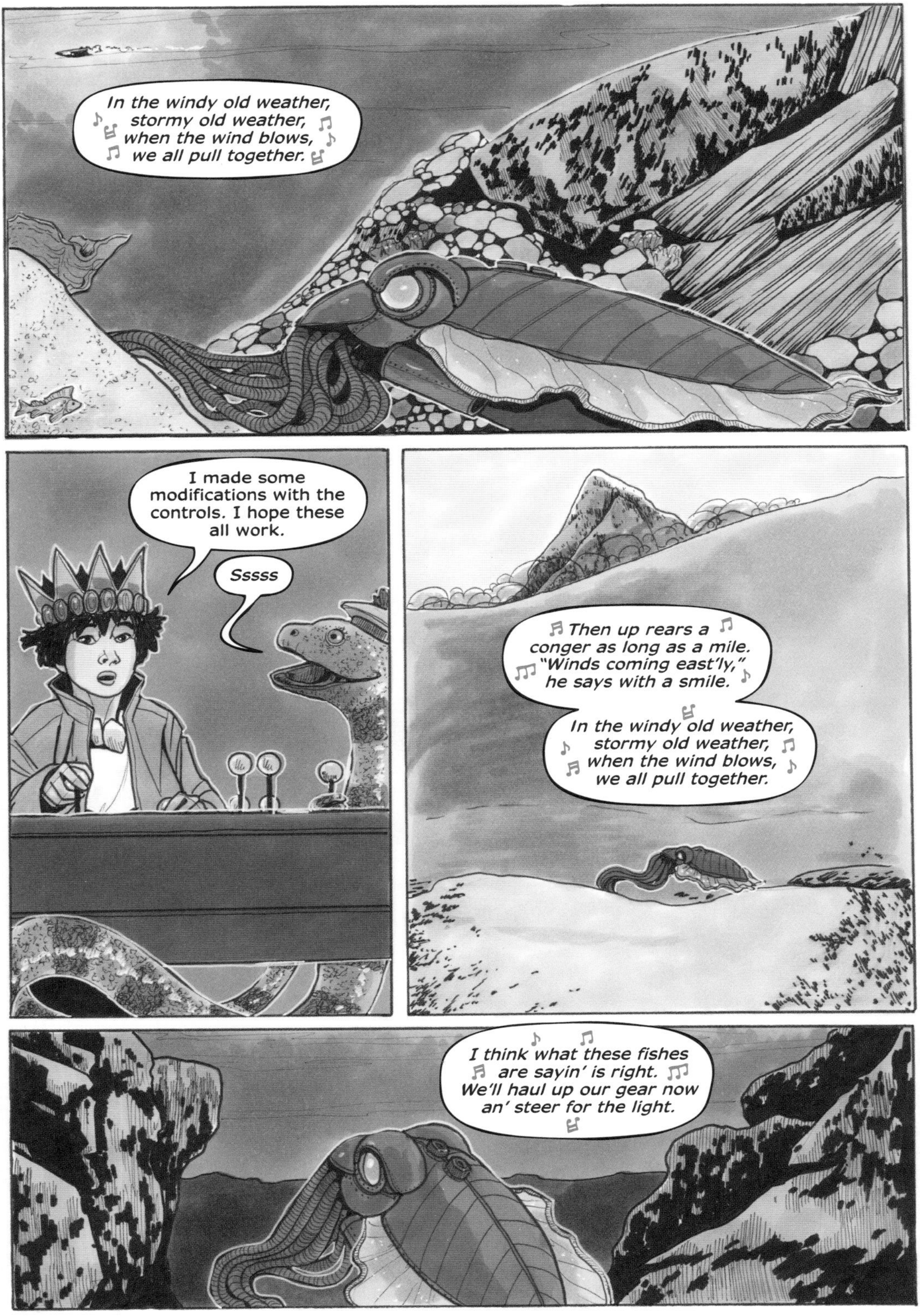
In the windy old weather, stormy old weather, when the wind blows, we all pull together.
I made some modifications with the controls. I hope these all work.
Sssss
Then up rears a conger as long as a mile. "Winds coming east'ly," he says with a smile.
In the windy old weather, stormy old weather, when the wind blows, we all pull together.
I think what these fishes are sayin' is right. We'll haul up our gear now an' steer for the light.

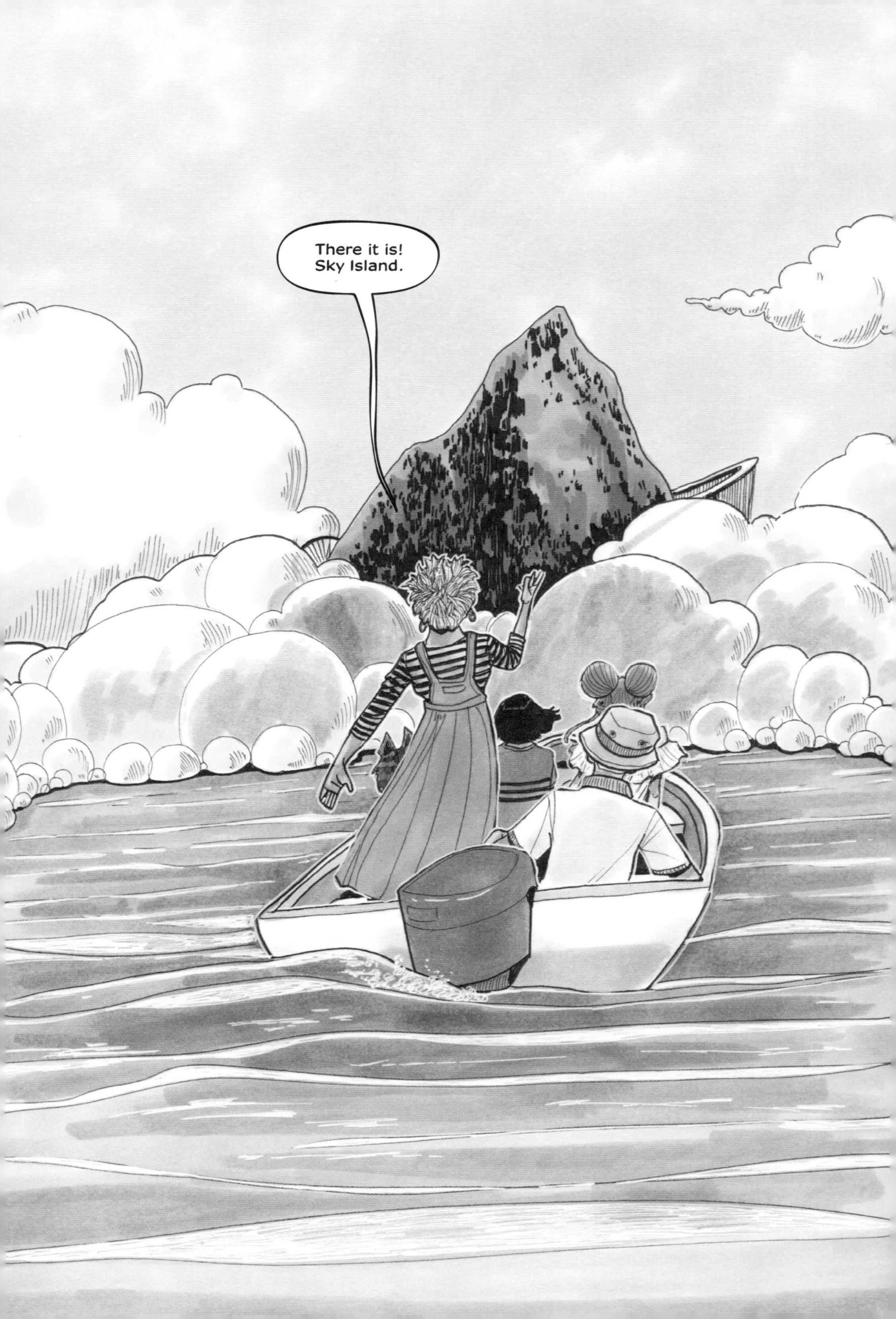
There it is! Sky Island.

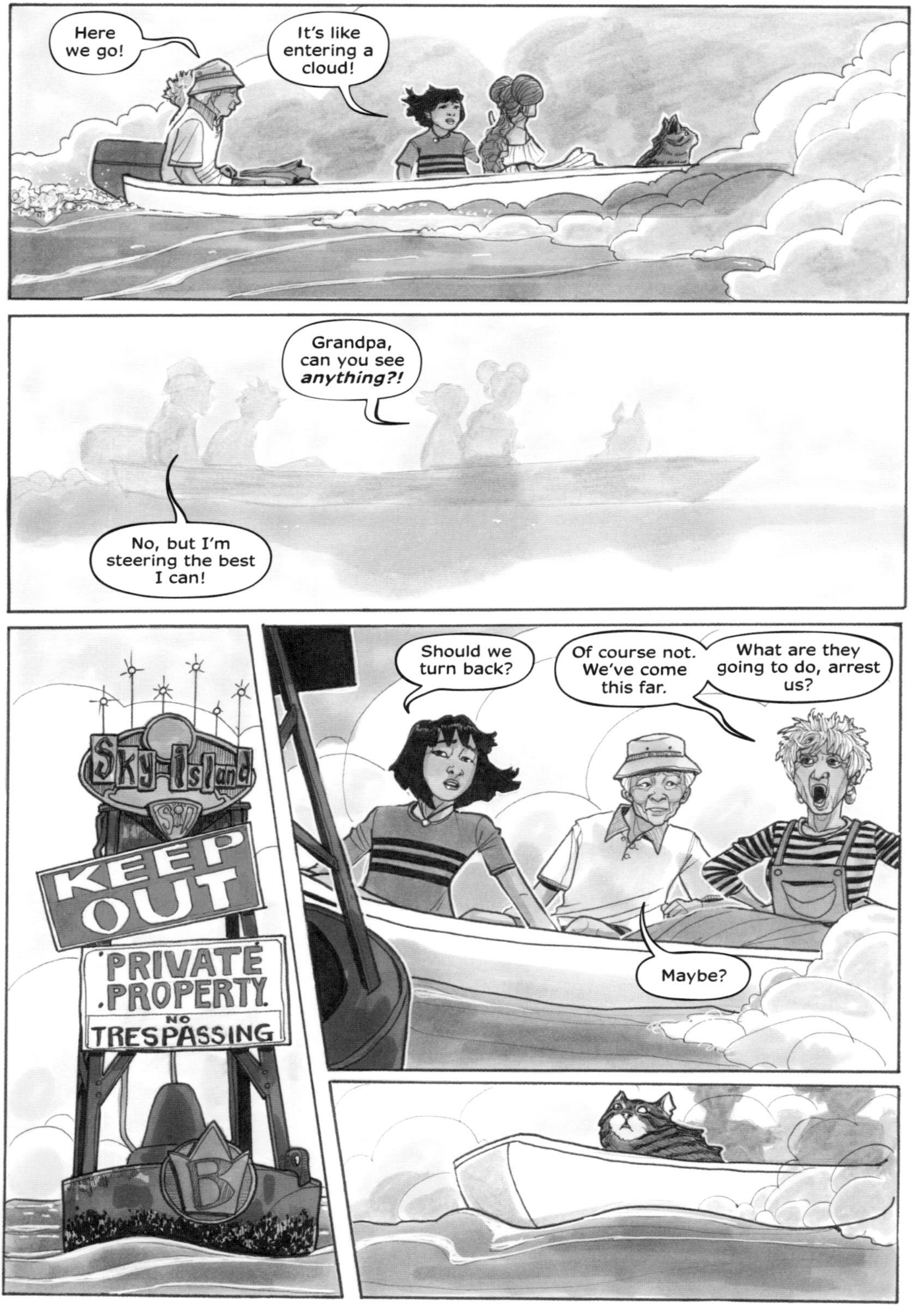

Here we go!
It's like entering a cloud!
Grandpa, can you see *anything?!*
No, but I'm steering the best I can!
Sky Island
KEEP OUT
PRIVATE PROPERTY
NO TRESPASSING
B
Should we turn back?
Of course not. We've come this far.
What are they going to do, arrest us?
Maybe?

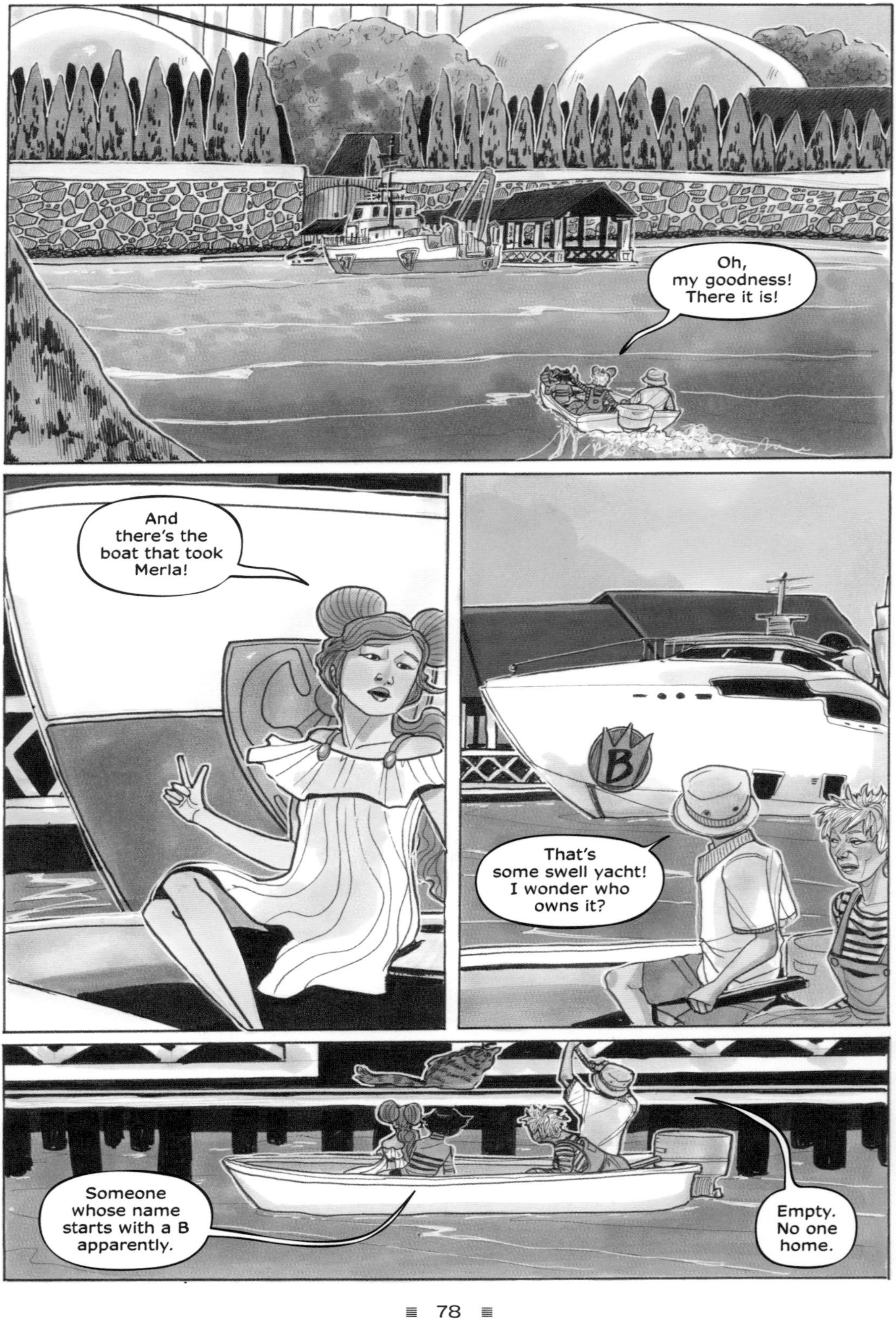
Oh, my goodness! There it is!
And there's the boat that took Merla!
That's some swell yacht! I wonder who owns it?
Someone whose name starts with a B apparently.
Empty. No one home.

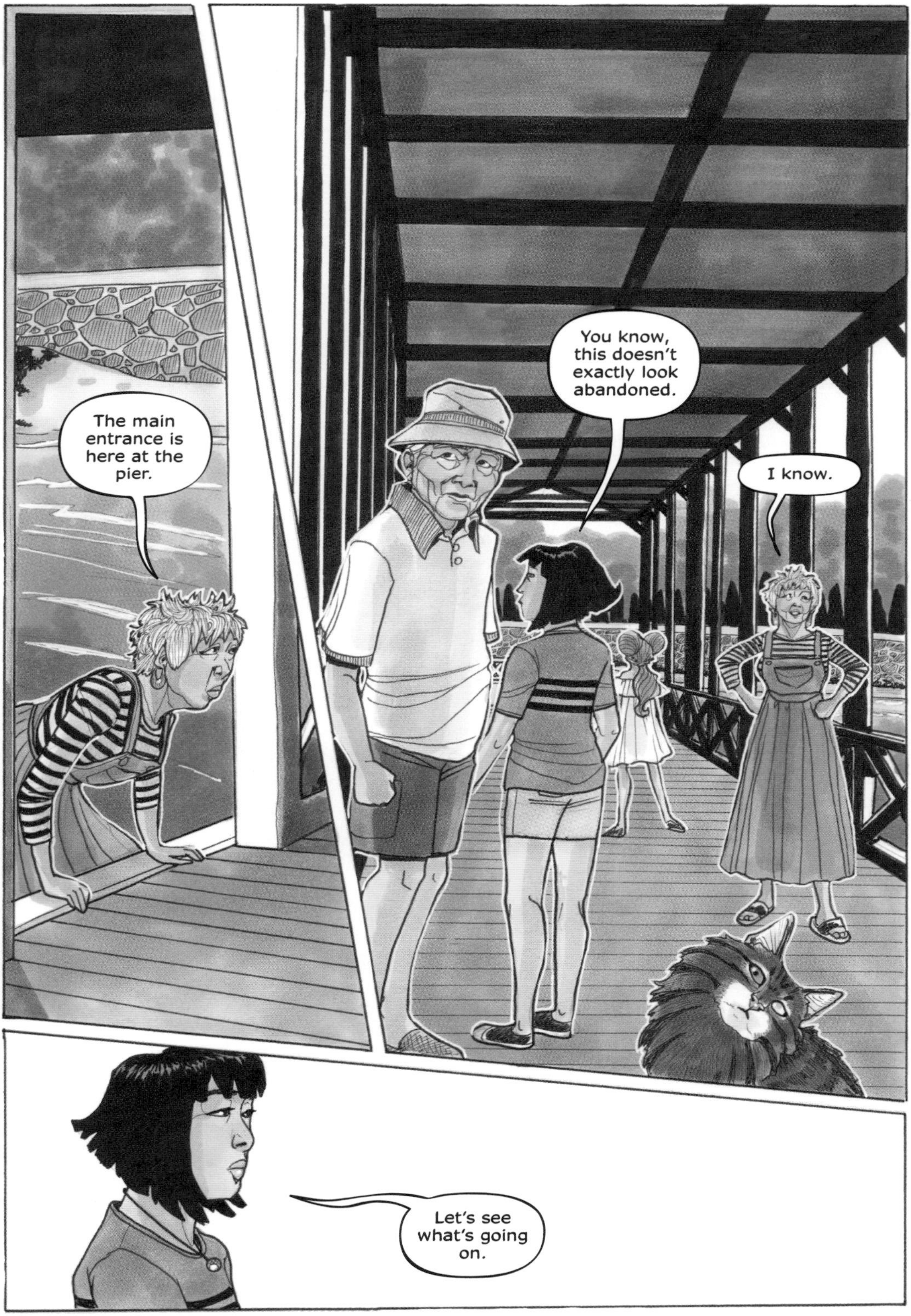
The main entrance is here at the pier.
You know, this doesn't exactly look abandoned.
I know.
Let's see what's going on.

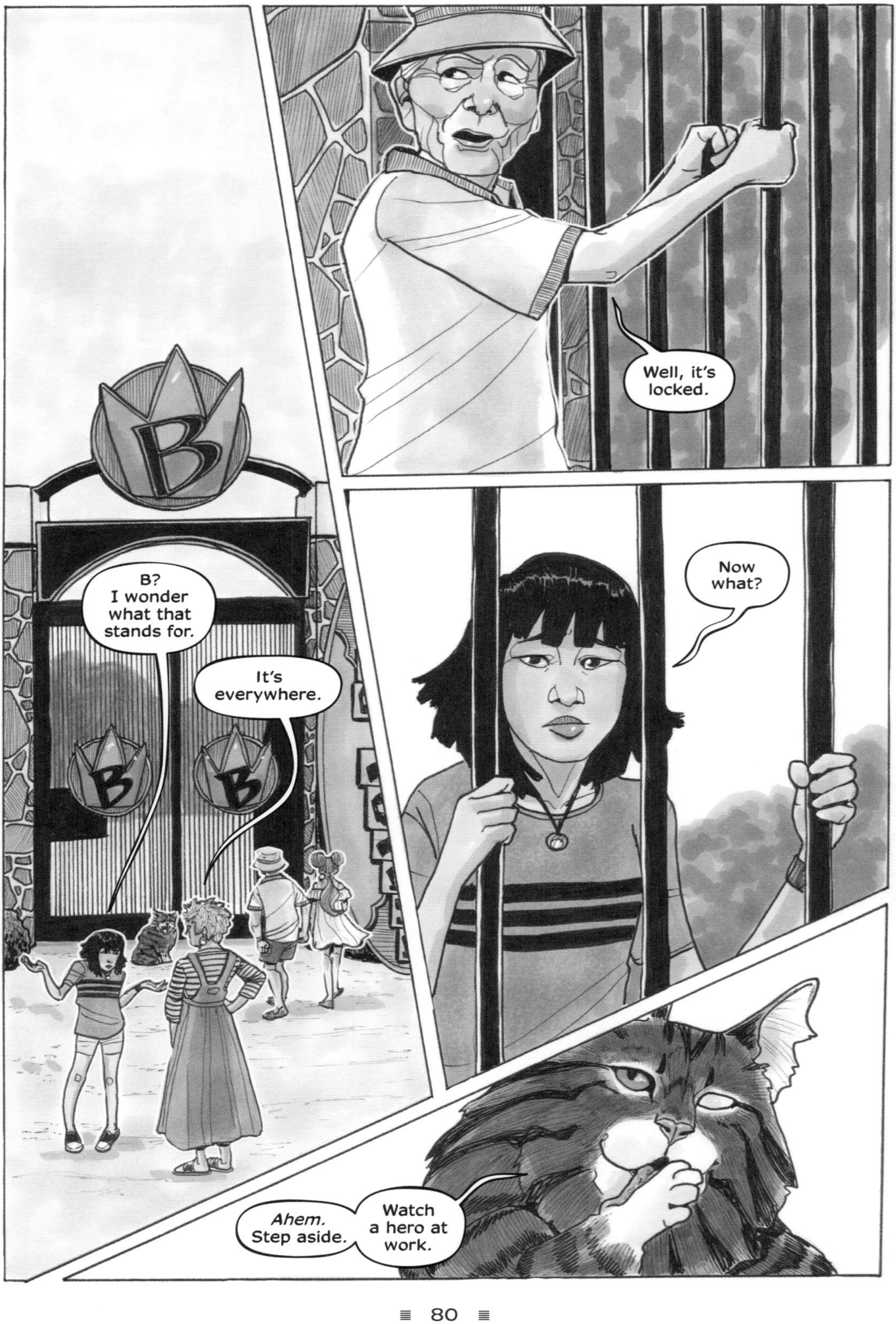
B?
I wonder what that stands for.
It's everywhere.
Well, it's locked.
Now what?
Ahem. Step aside.
Watch a hero at work.

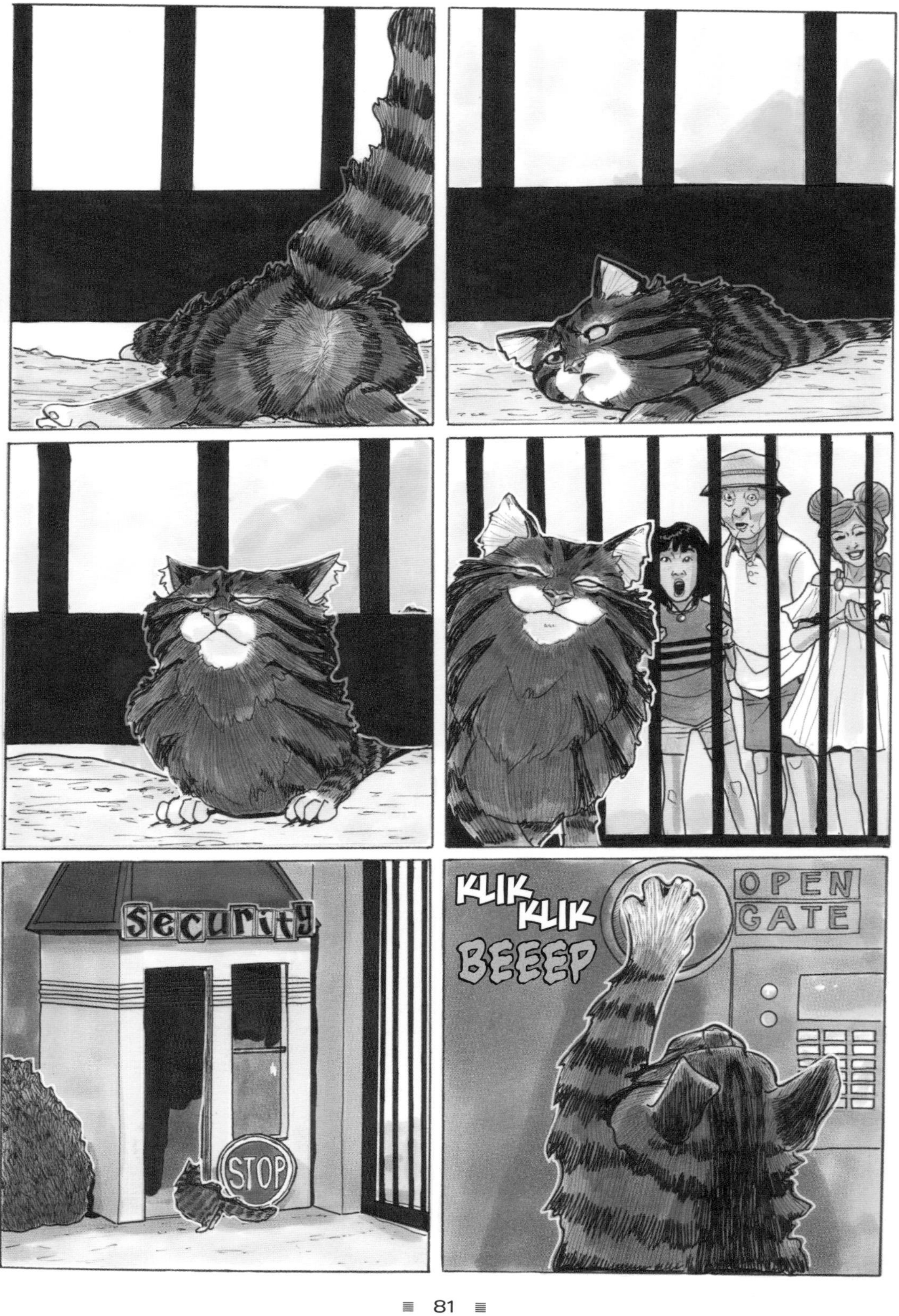
Security
STOP
KLIK
KLIK
BEEEP
OPEN GATE

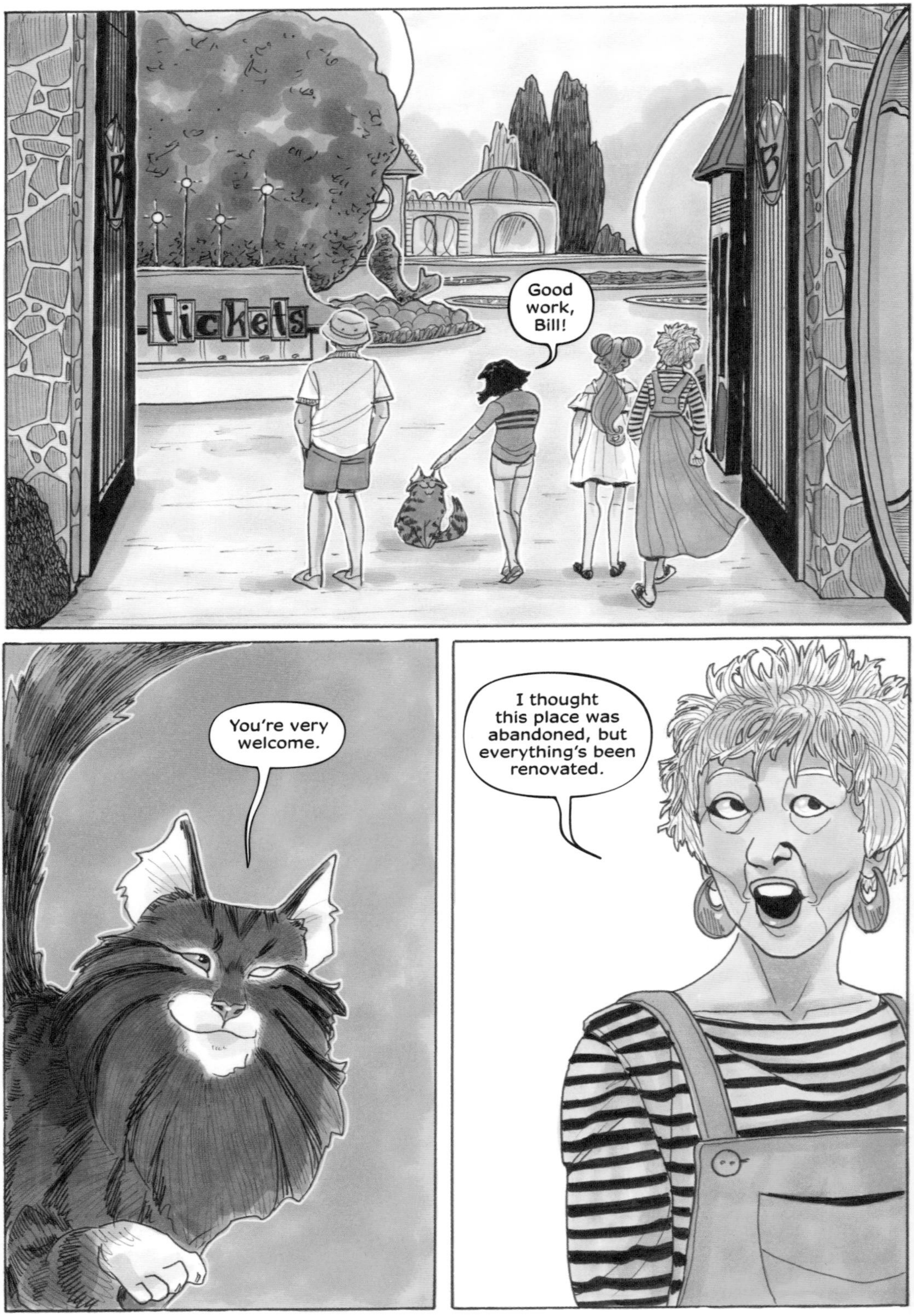
tickets
Good work, Bill!
You're very welcome.
I thought this place was abandoned, but everything's been renovated.

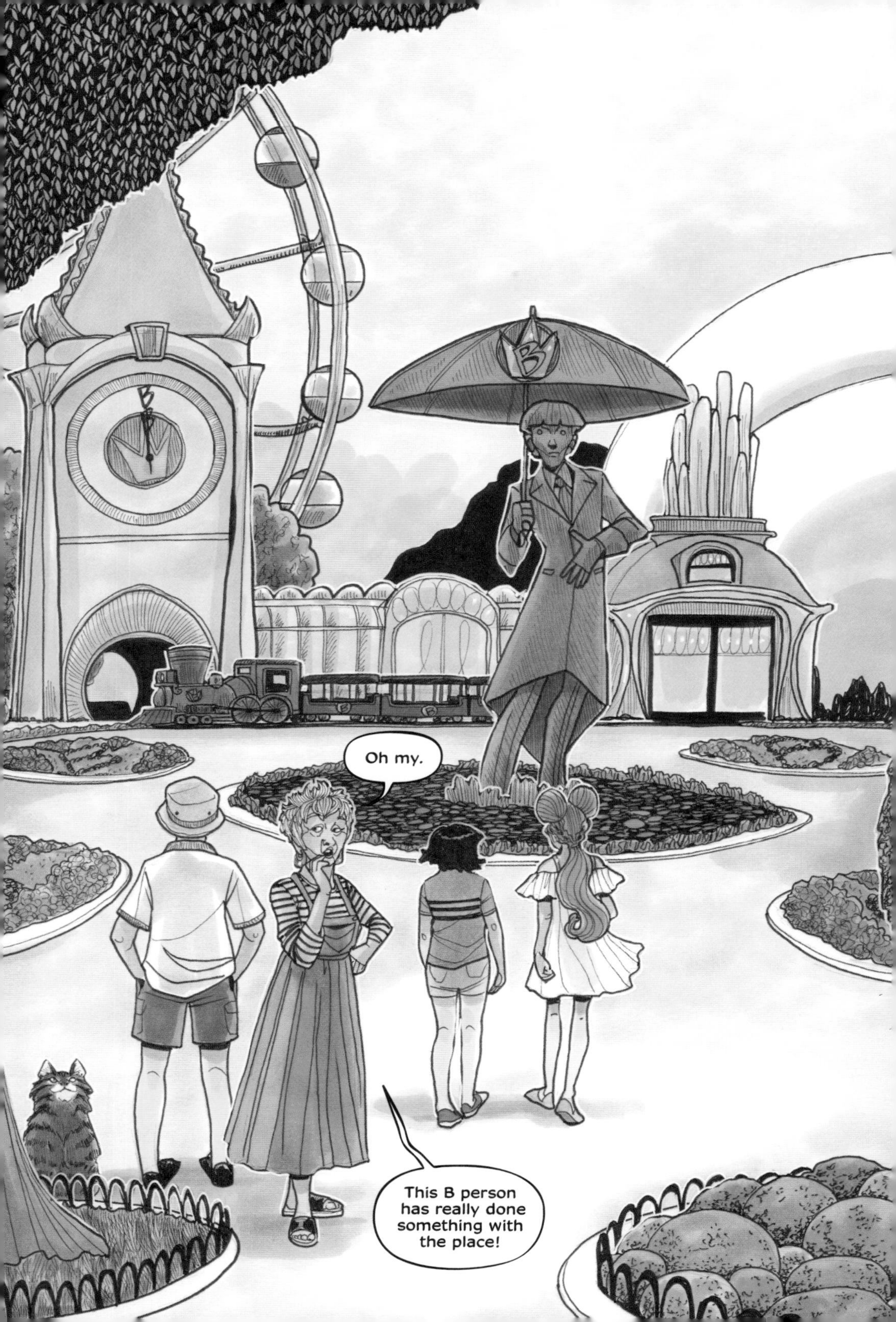
Oh my.
This B person has really done something with the place!

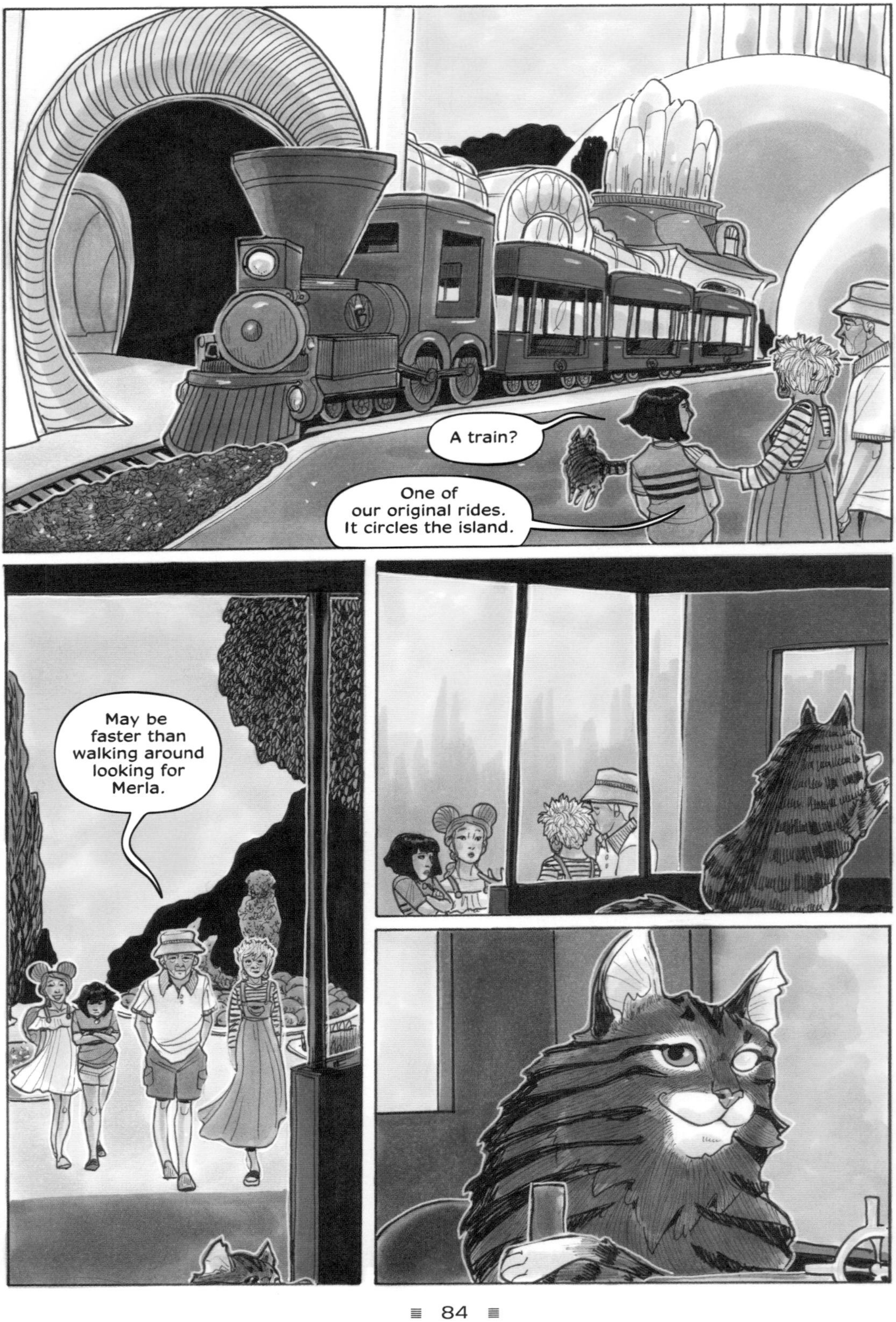
A train?
One of our original rides. It circles the island.
May be faster than walking around looking for Merla.

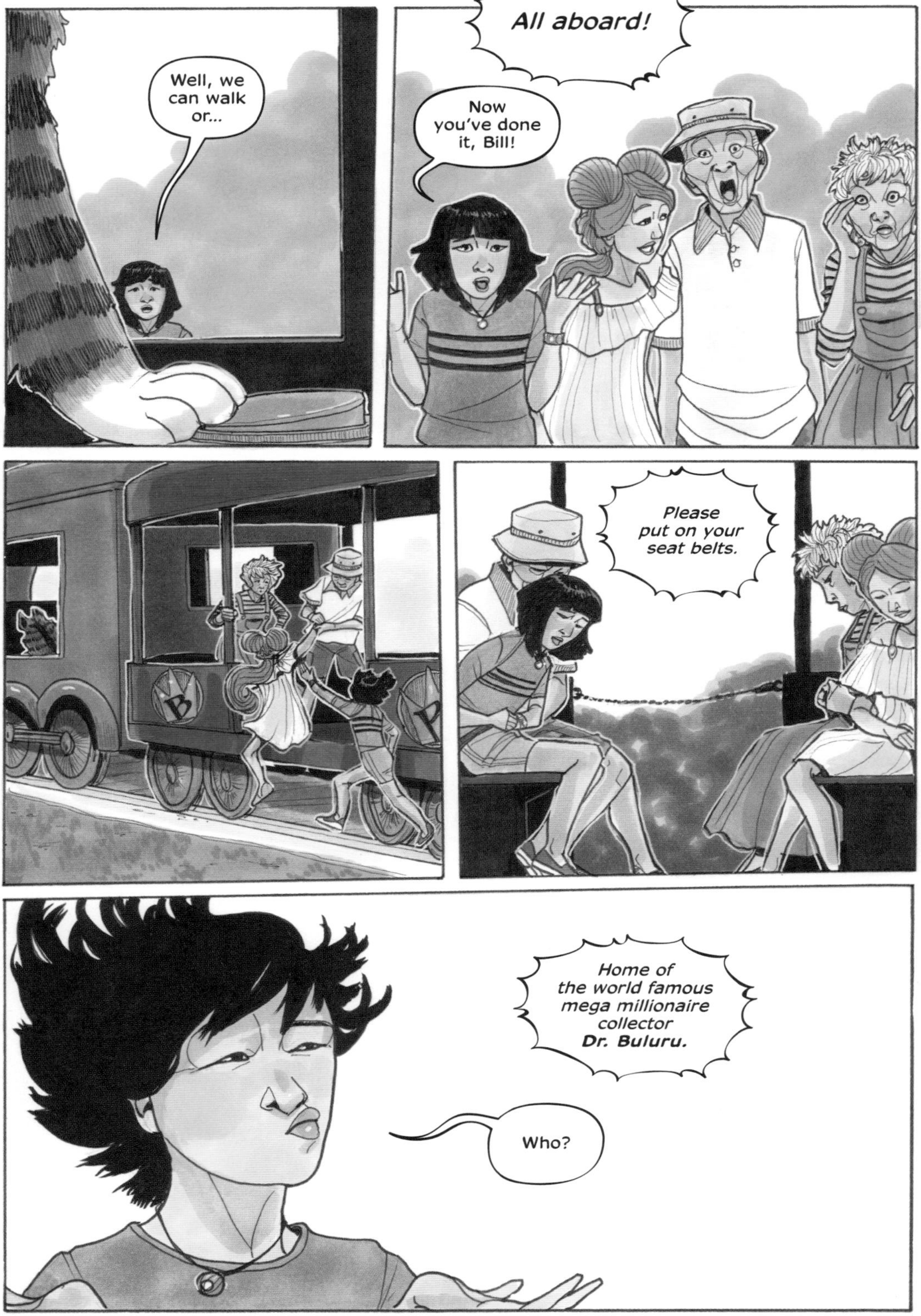
Well, we can walk or...
All aboard!
Now you've done it, Bill!
Please put on your seat belts.
Home of the world famous mega millionaire collector **Dr. Buluru.**
Who?

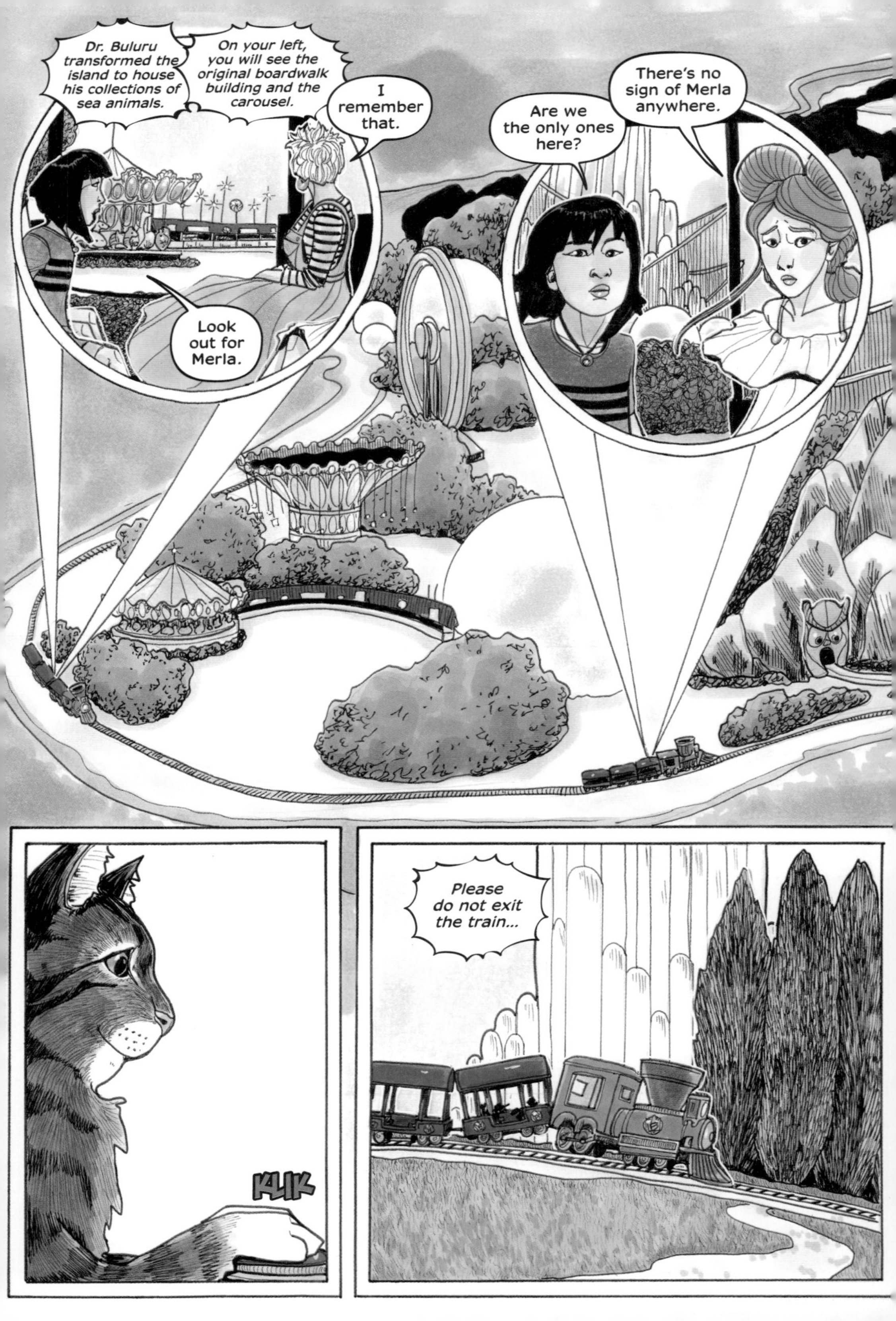

Dr. Buluru transformed the island to house his collections of sea animals.
On your left, you will see the original boardwalk building and the carousel.
I remember that.
Look out for Merla.
Are we the only ones here?
There's no sign of Merla anywhere.
KLIK
Please do not exit the train...

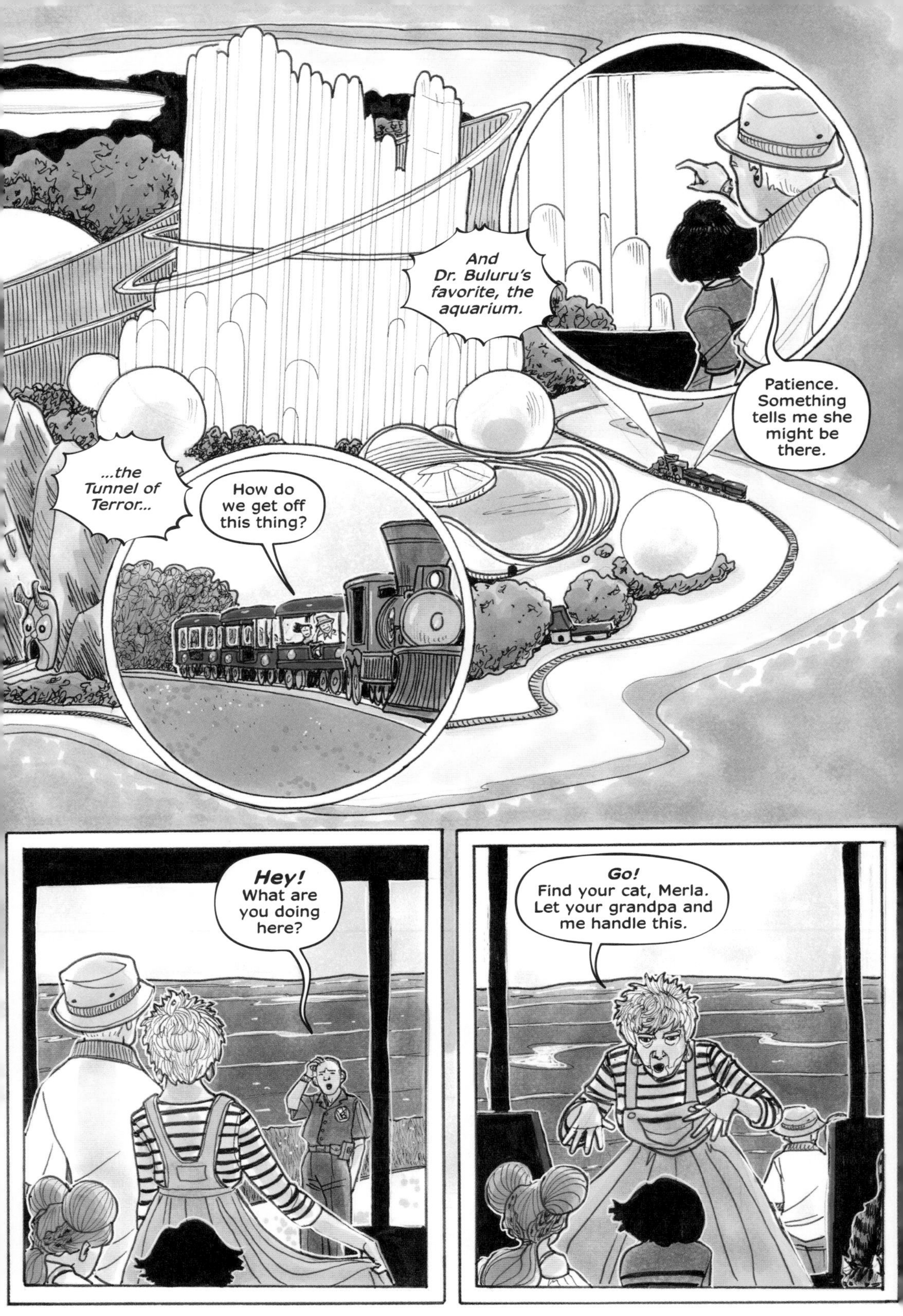
...the Tunnel of Terror...
How do we get off this thing?
And Dr. Buluru's favorite, the aquarium.
Patience. Something tells me she might be there.
Hey! What are you doing here?
Go! Find your cat, Merla. Let your grandpa and me handle this.

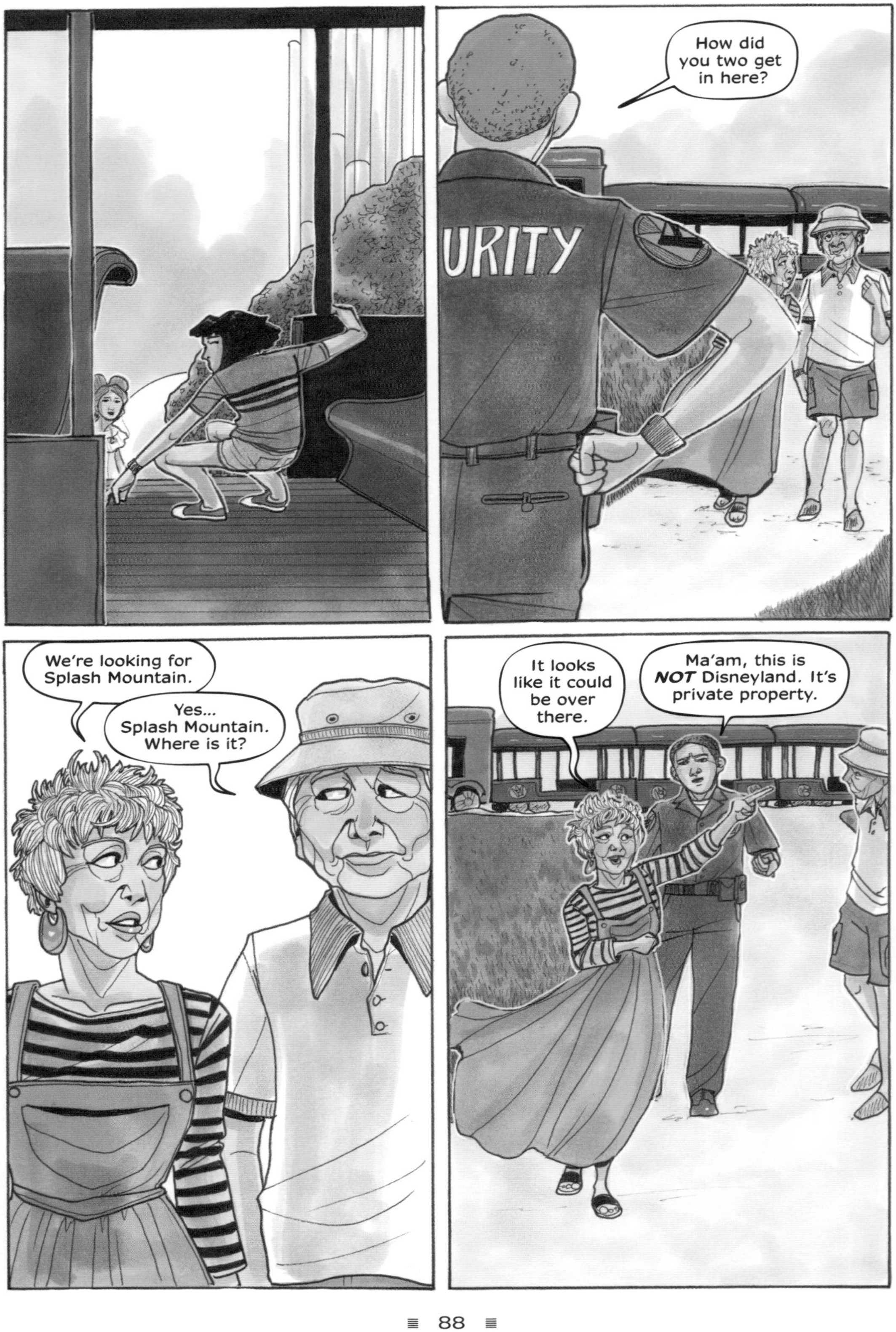
How did you two get in here?
URITY
We're looking for Splash Mountain.
Yes... Splash Mountain. Where is it?
It looks like it could be over there.
Ma'am, this is ***NOT*** Disneyland. It's private property.

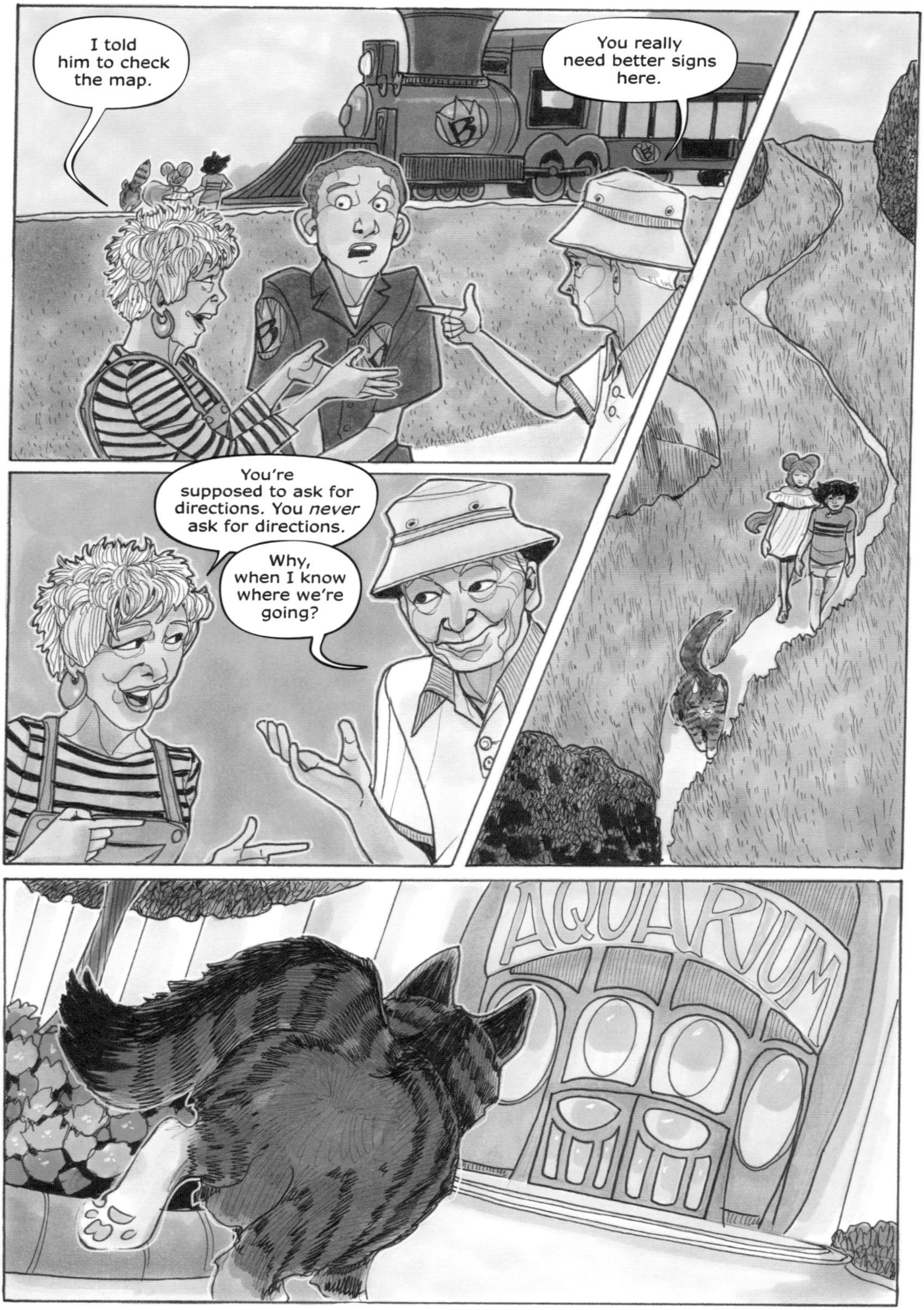
I told him to check the map.
You really need better signs here.
You're supposed to ask for directions. You *never* ask for directions.
Why, when I know where we're going?
AQUARIUM

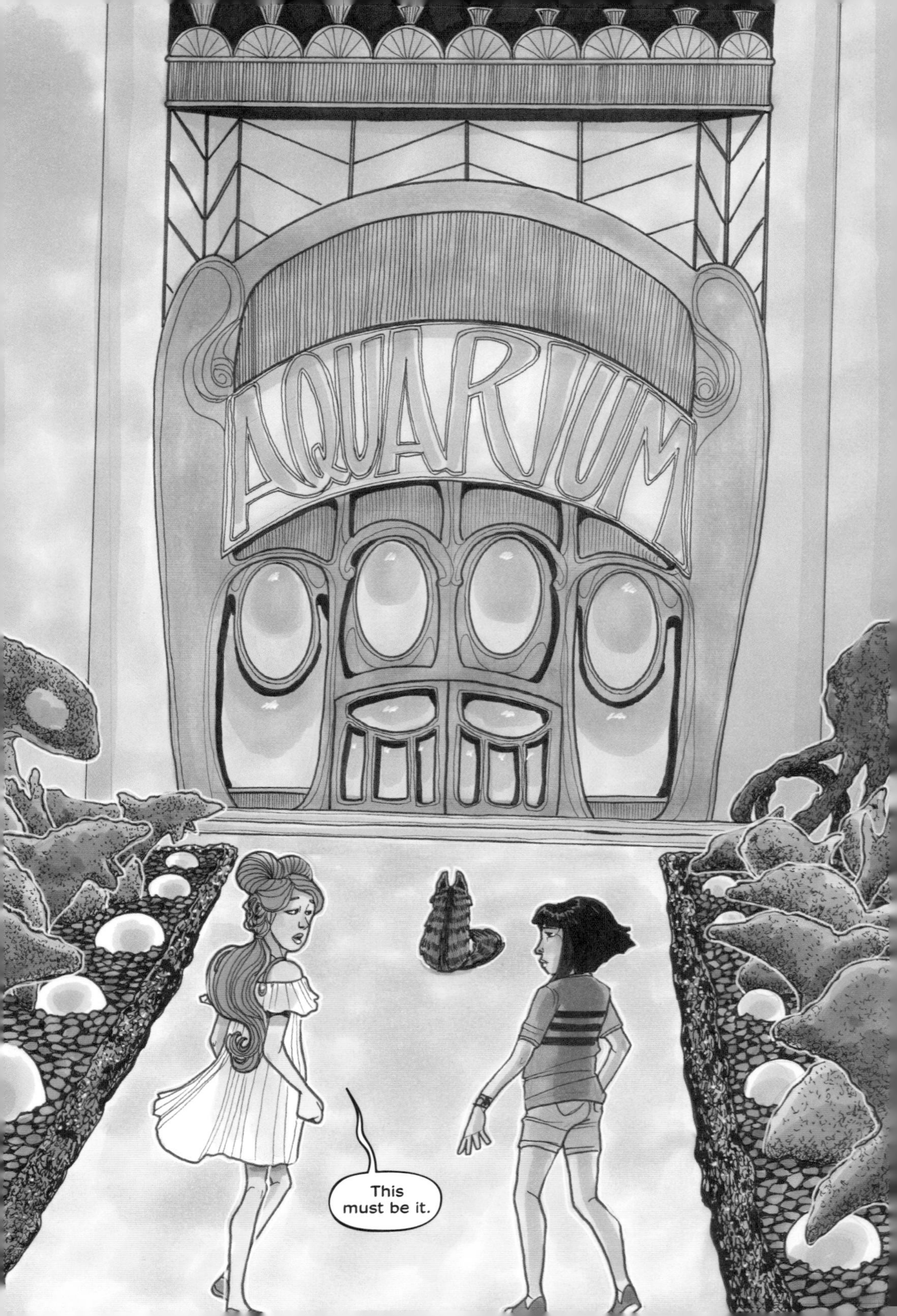
AQUARIUM
This must be it.

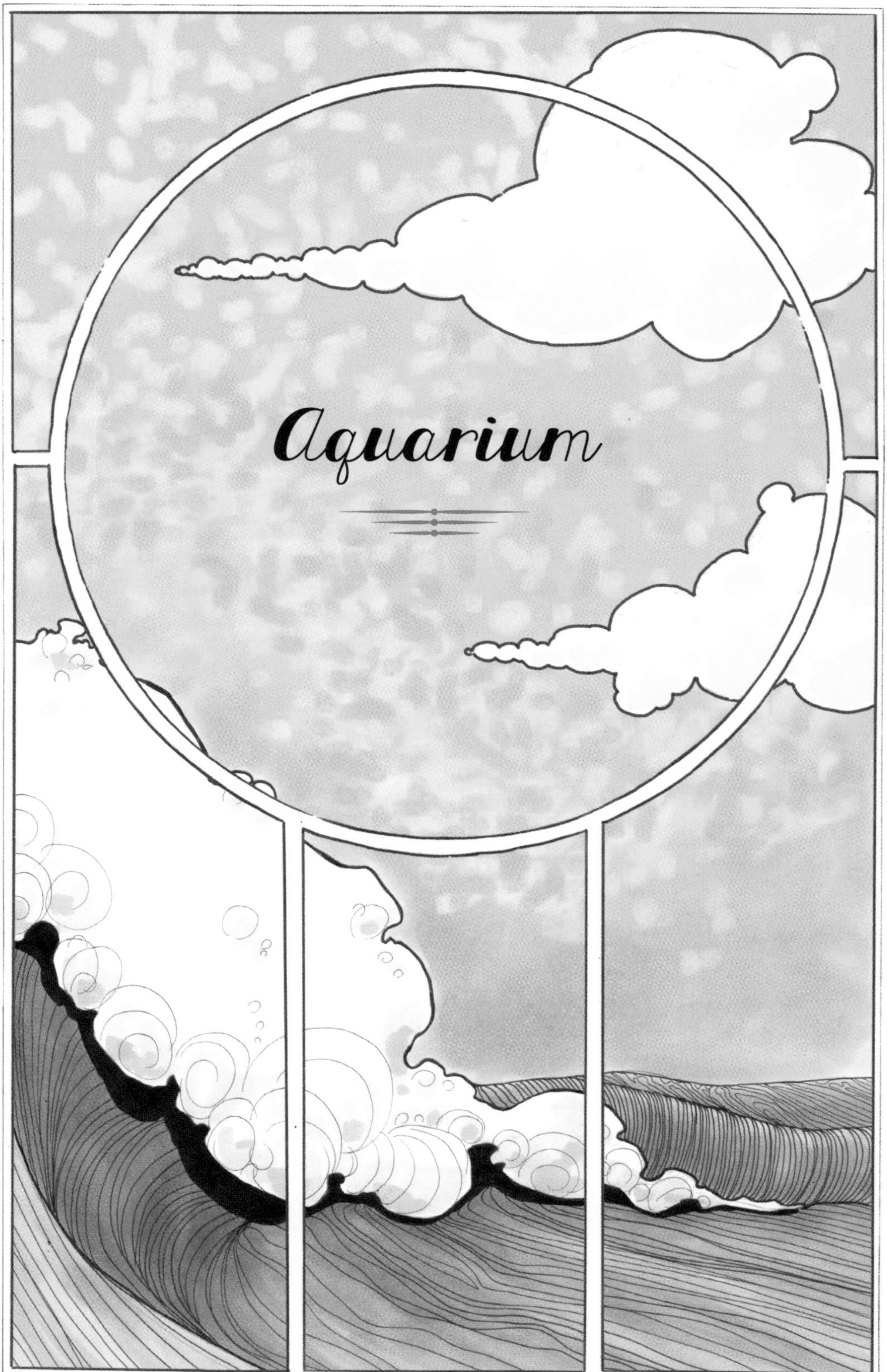
Aquarium

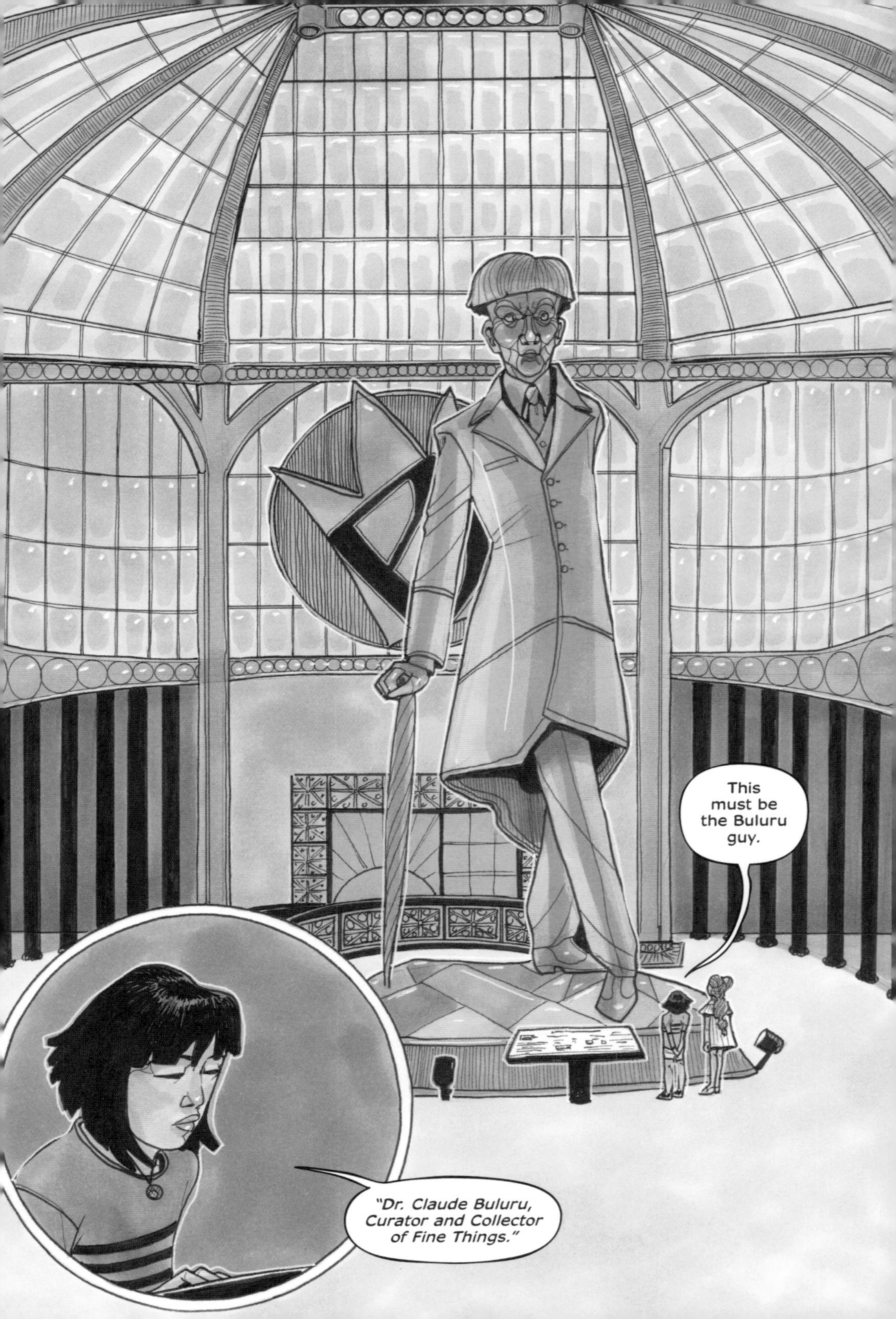
This must be the Buluru guy.
"Dr. Claude Buluru, Curator and Collector of Fine Things."

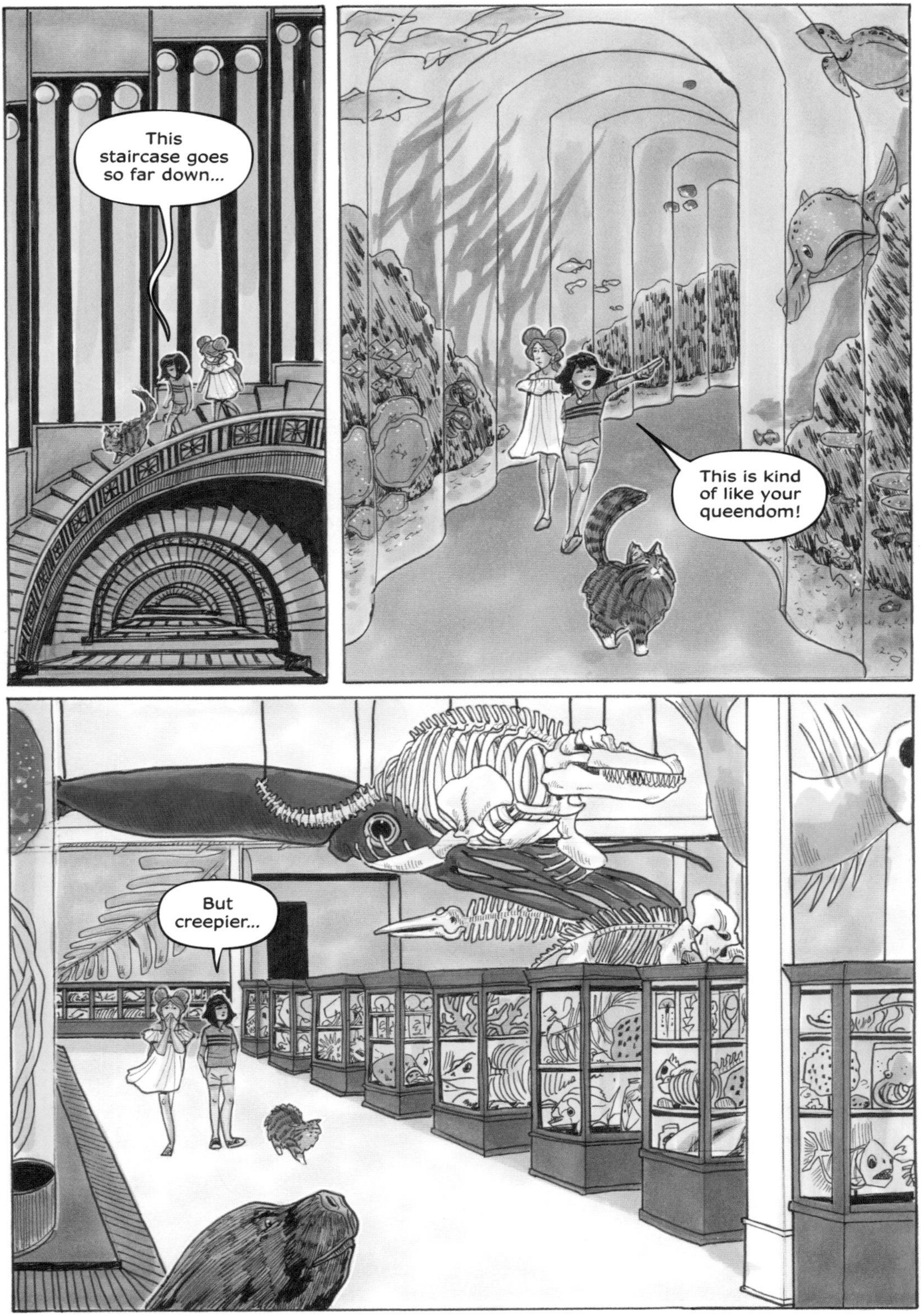
This staircase goes so far down...
This is kind of like your queendom!
But creepier...

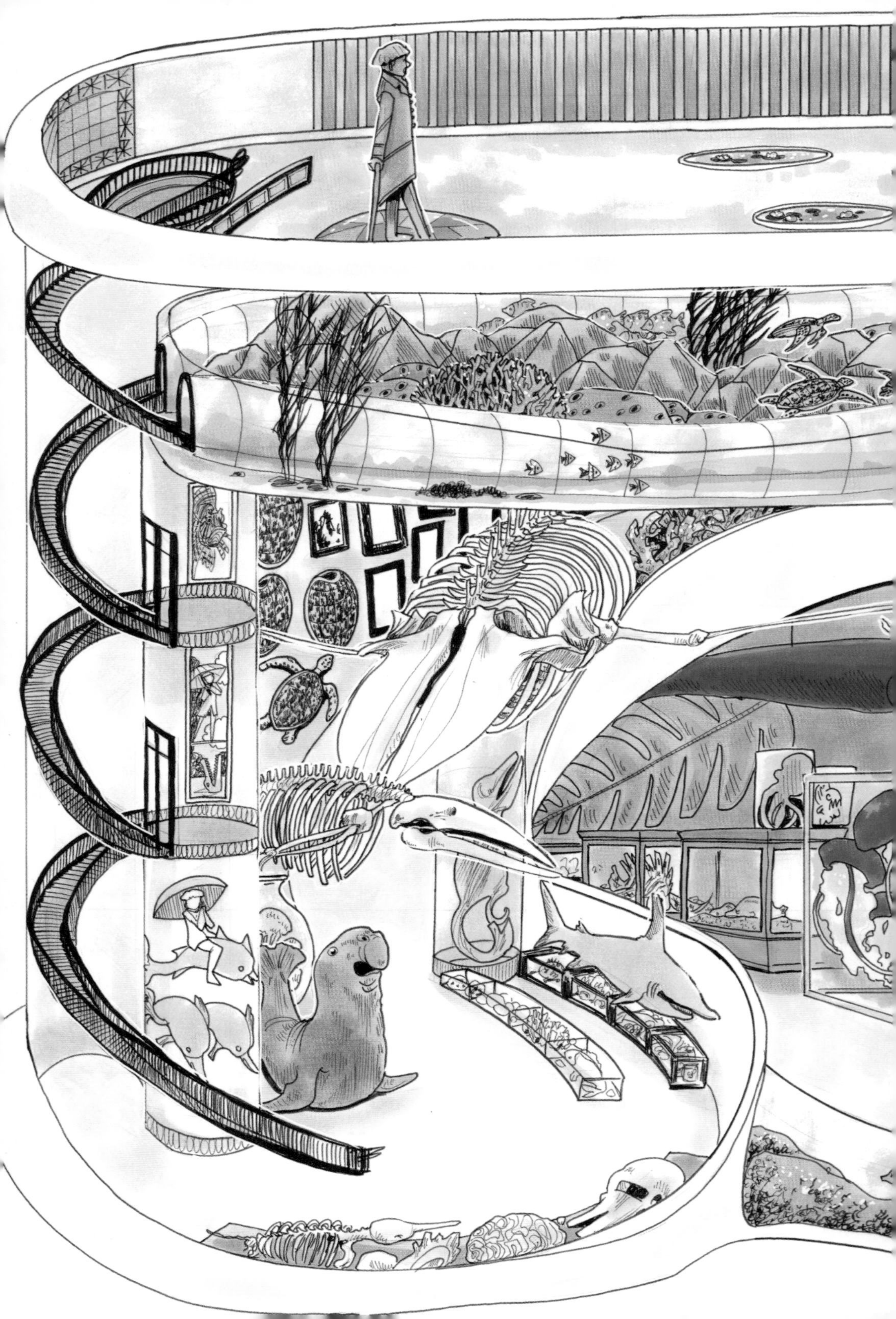

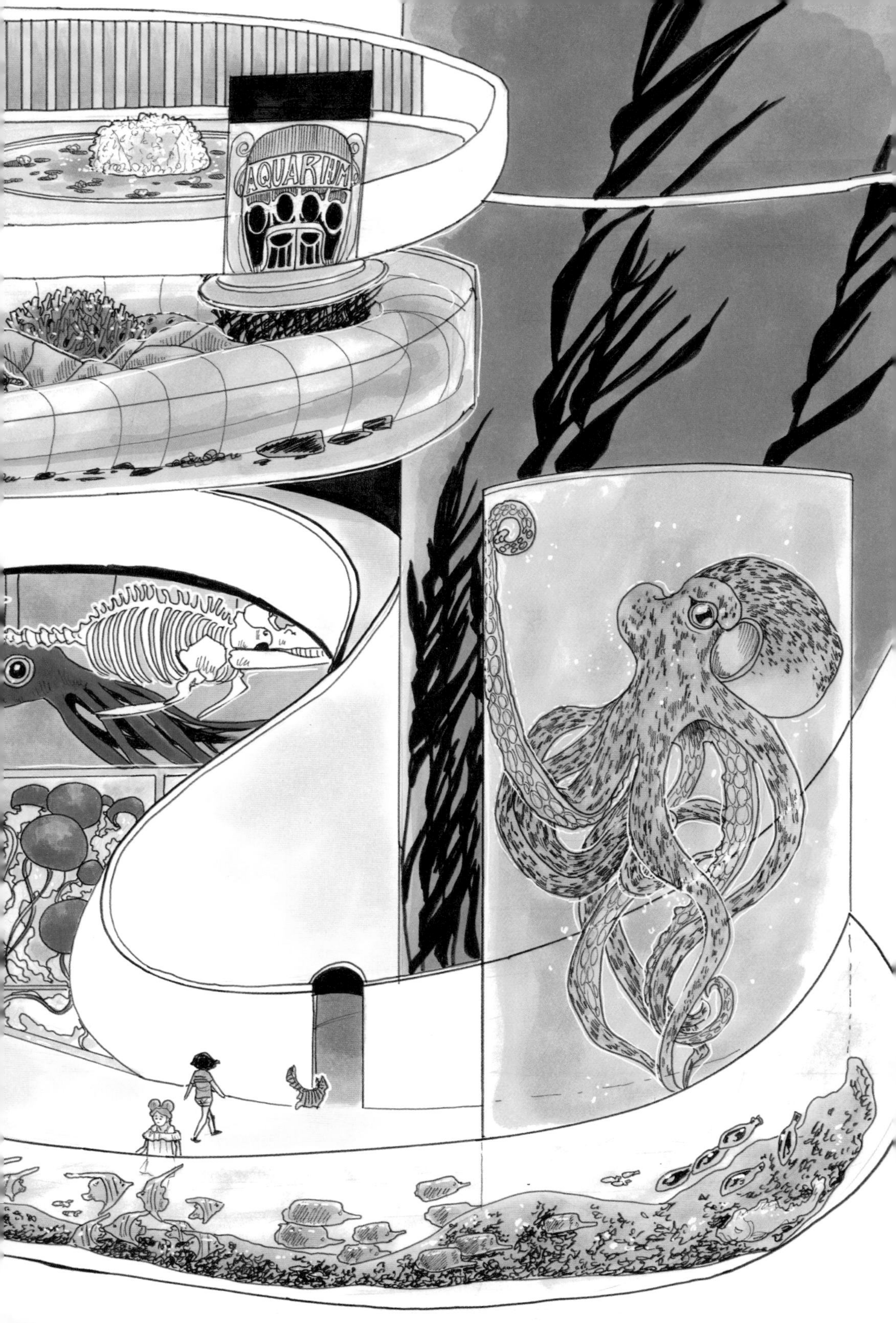
AQUARIUM

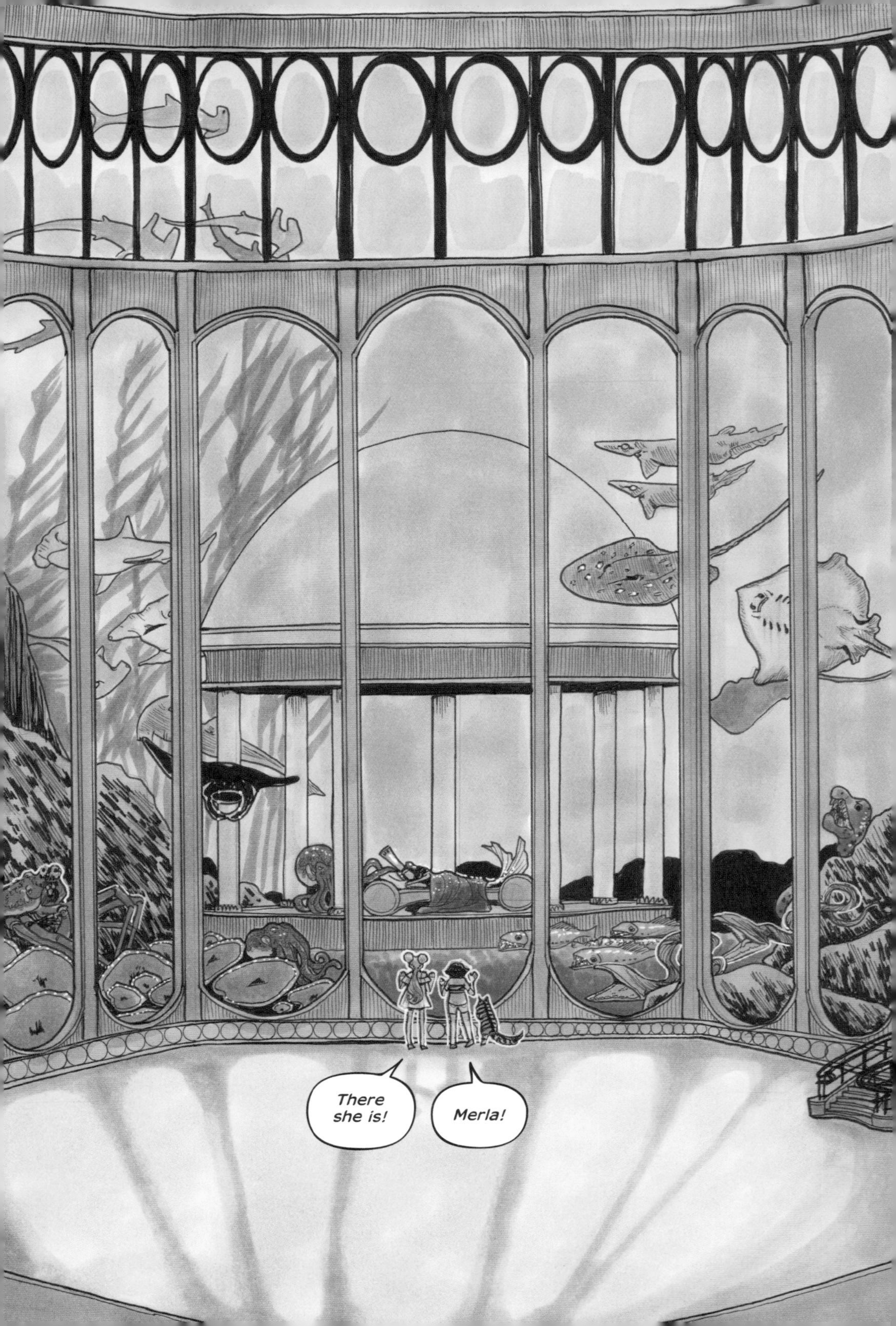
There she is!
Merla!

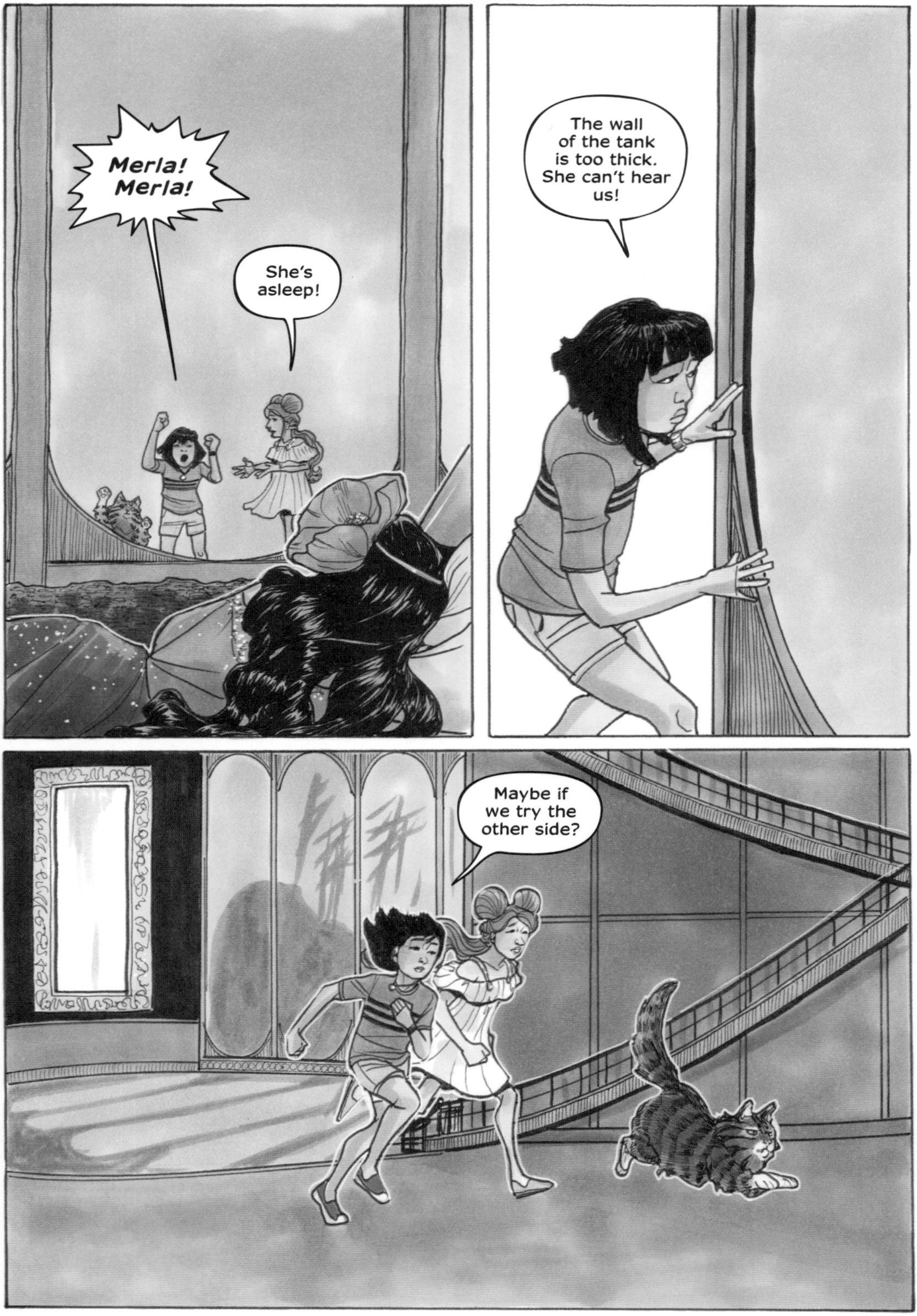
Merla! Merla!
She's asleep!
The wall of the tank is too thick. She can't hear us!
Maybe if we try the other side?

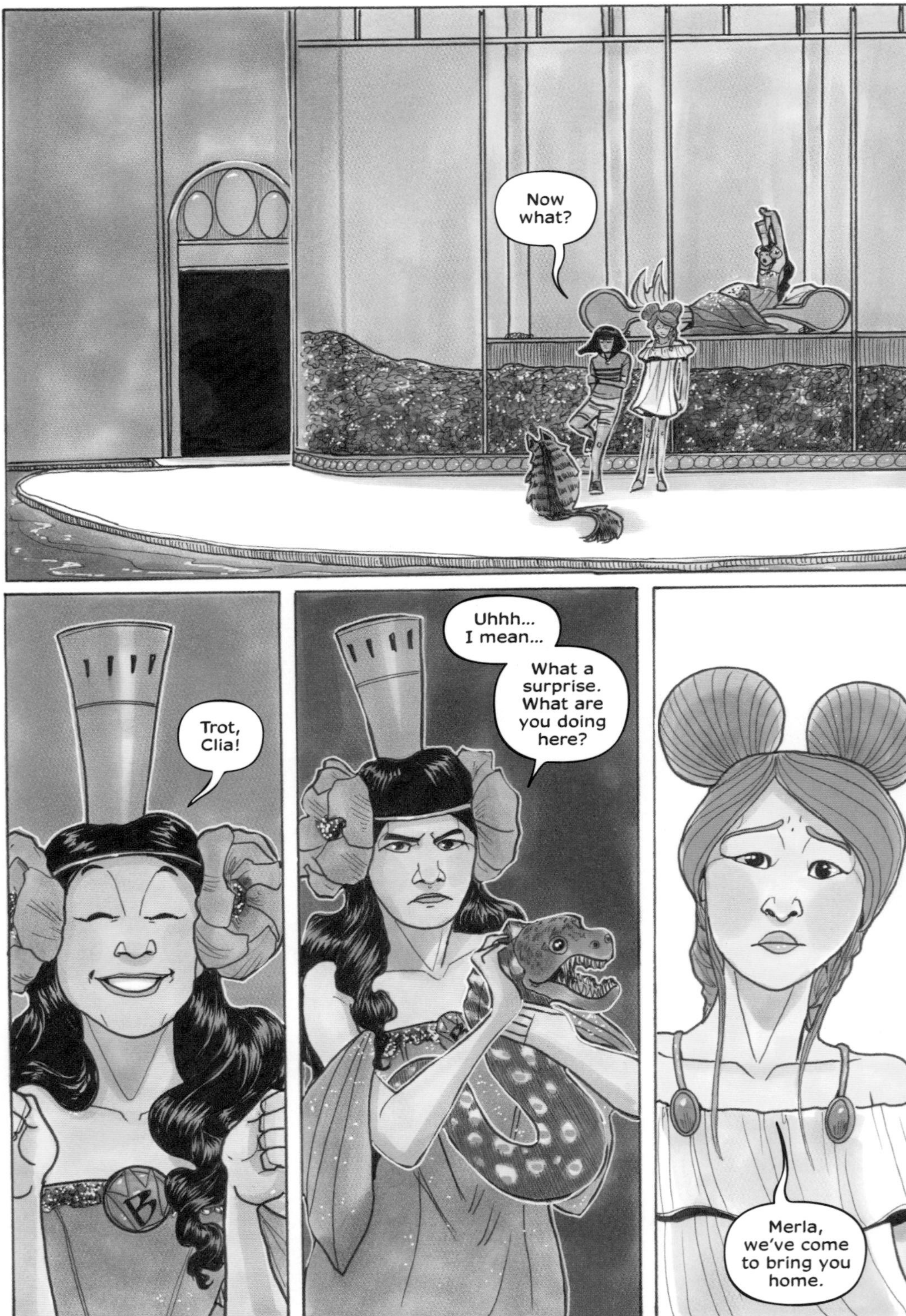
Now what?
Trot, Clia!
Uhhh... I mean...
What a surprise. What are you doing here?
Merla, we've come to bring you home.

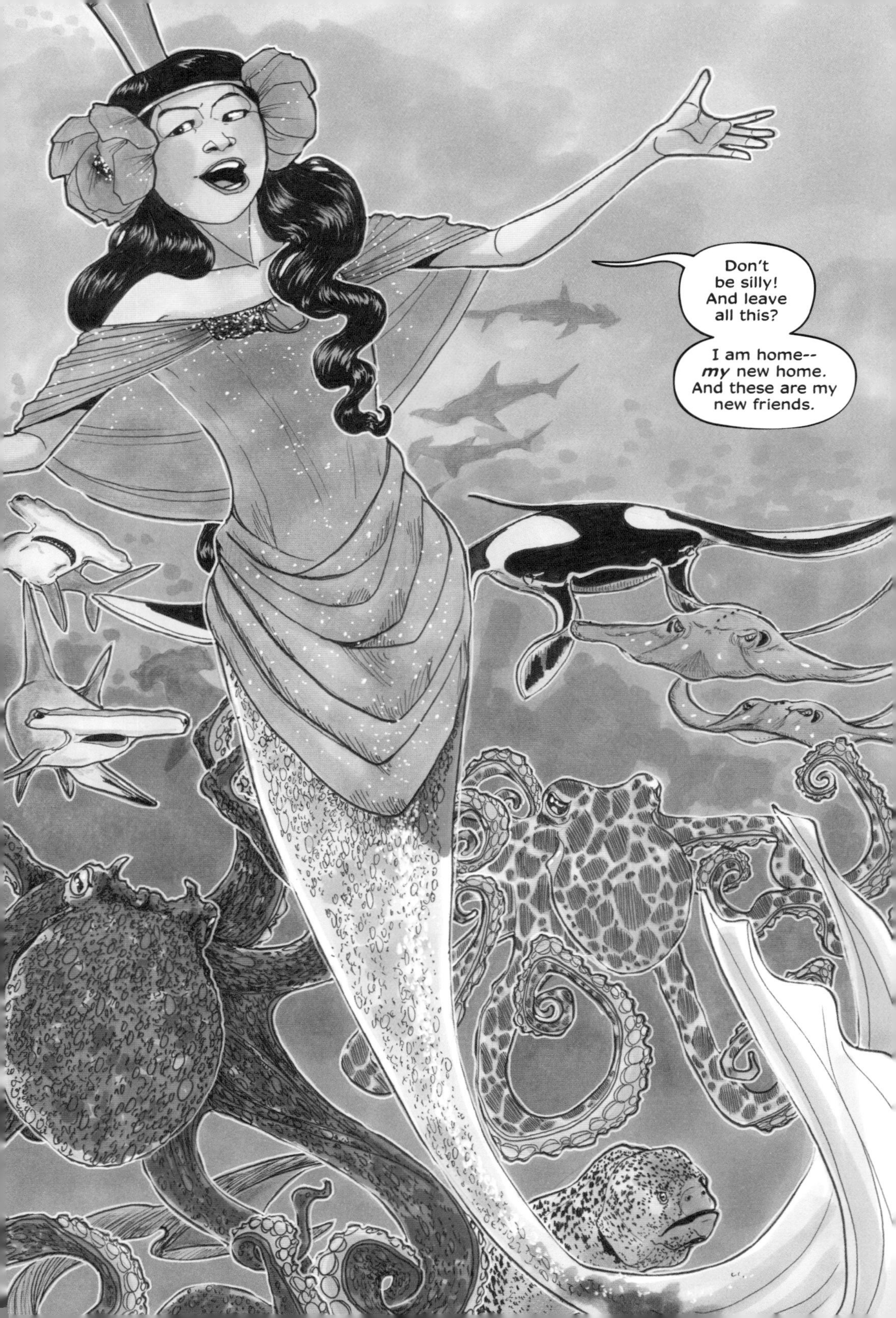
Don't be silly! And leave all this?
I am home-- *my* new home. And these are my new friends.

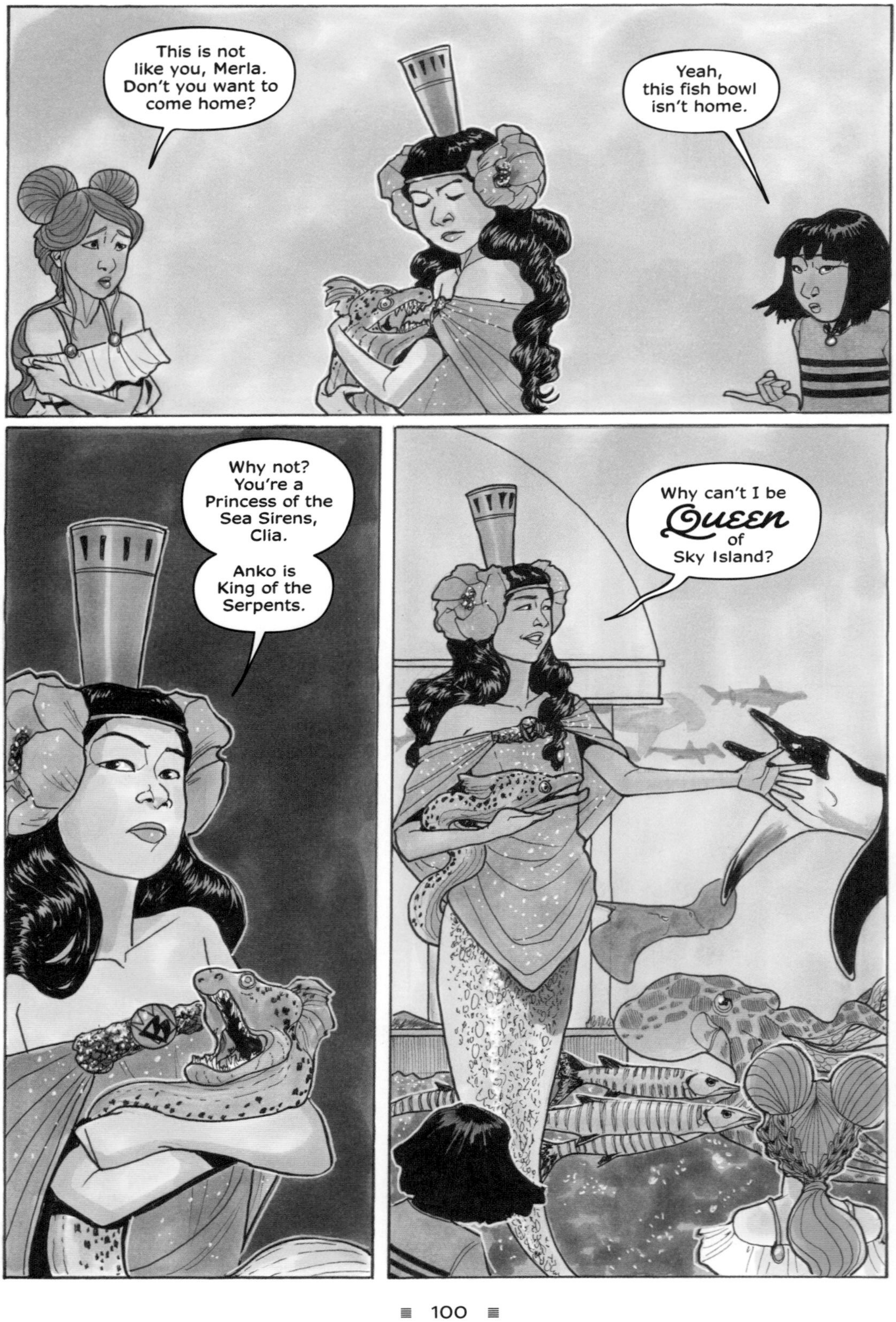
This is not like you, Merla. Don't you want to come home?
Yeah, this fish bowl isn't home.
Why not? You're a Princess of the Sea Sirens, Clia.
Anko is King of the Serpents.
Why can't I be QUEEN of Sky Island?

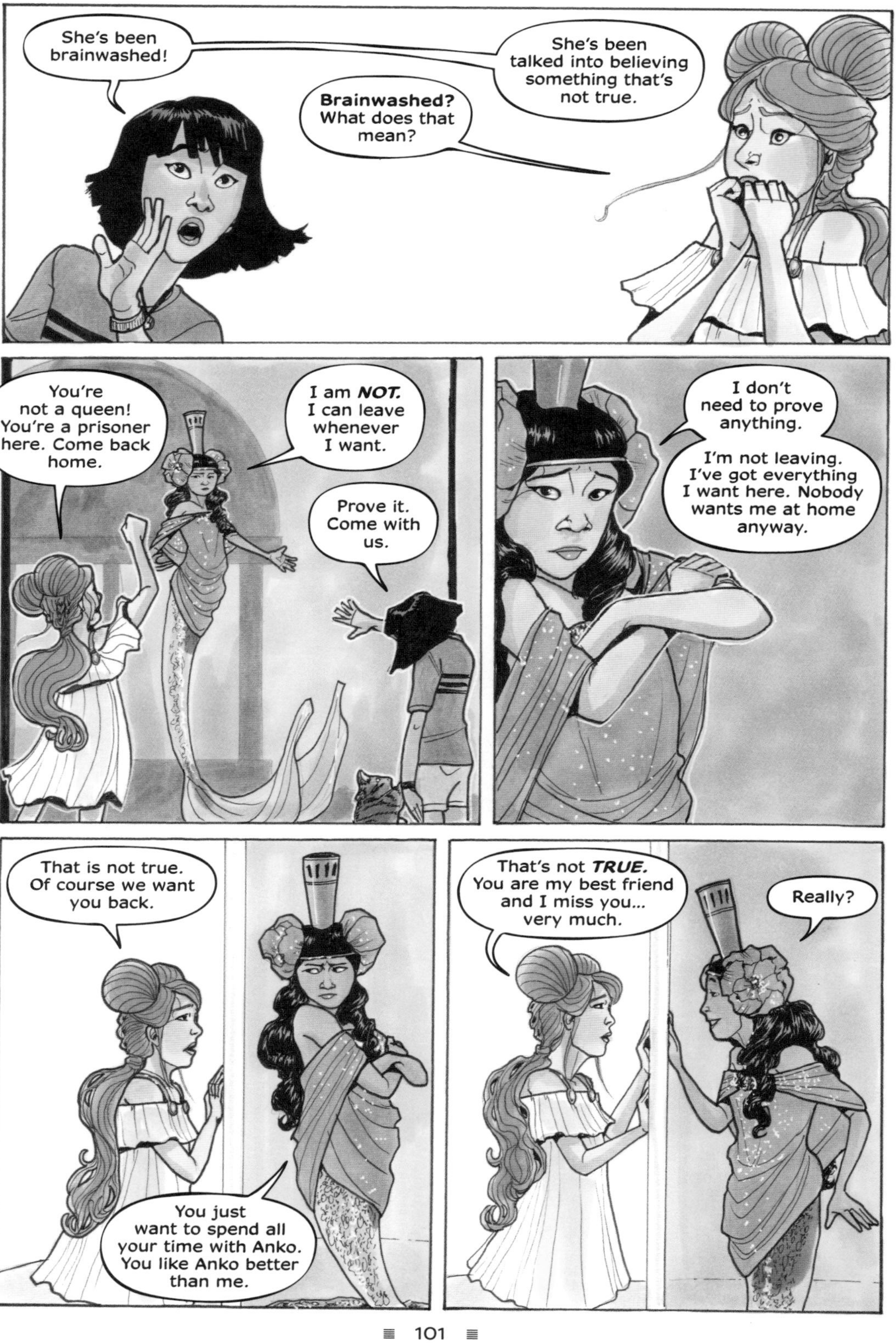
She's been brainwashed!
Brainwashed? What does that mean?
She's been talked into believing something that's not true.
You're not a queen! You're a prisoner here. Come back home.
I am ***NOT.*** I can leave whenever I want.
Prove it. Come with us.
I don't need to prove anything.
I'm not leaving. I've got everything I want here. Nobody wants me at home anyway.
That is not true. Of course we want you back.
You just want to spend all your time with Anko. You like Anko better than me.
That's not ***TRUE.*** You are my best friend and I miss you... very much.
Really?

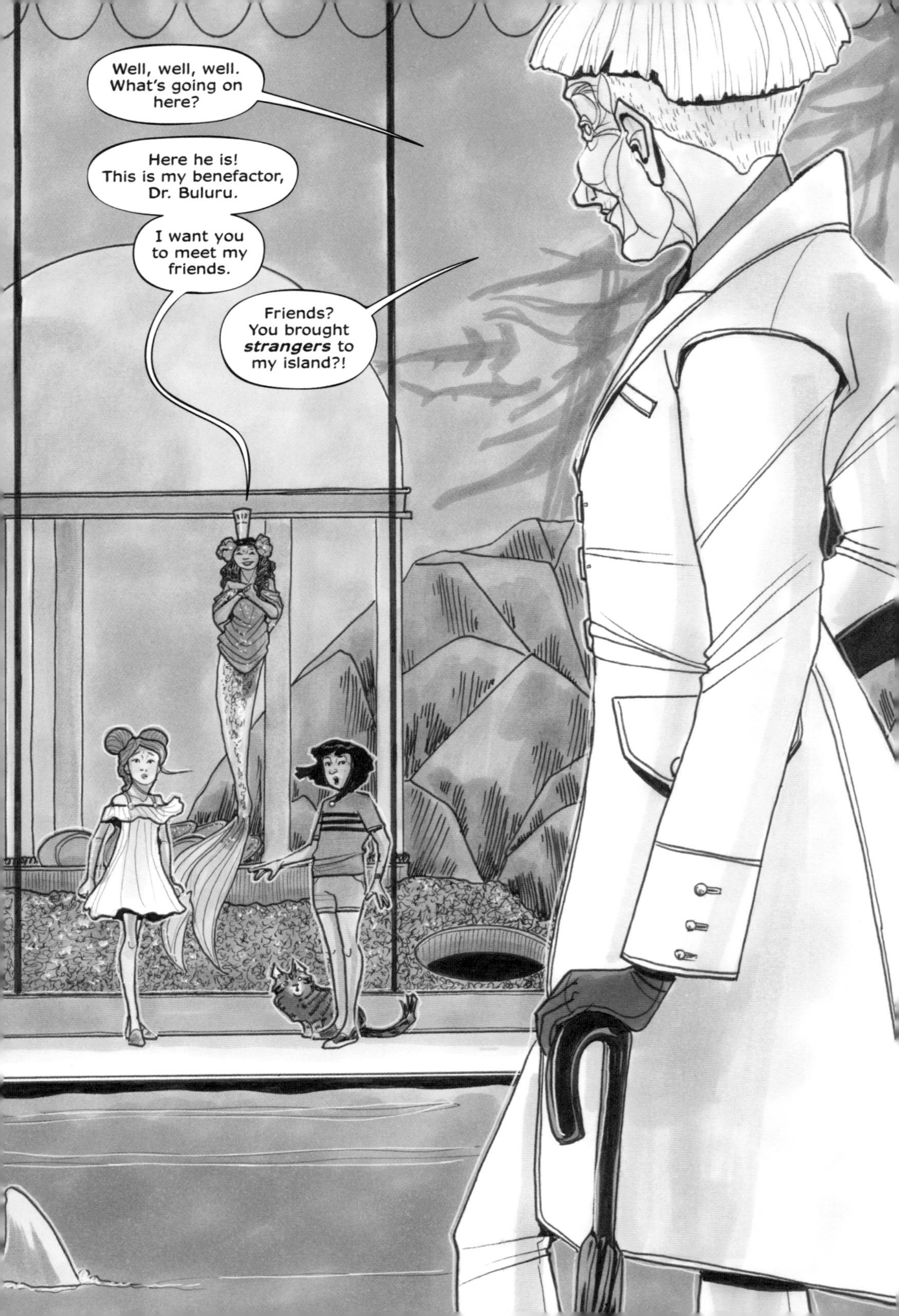
Well, well, well. What's going on here?
Here he is! This is my benefactor, Dr. Buluru.
I want you to meet my friends.
Friends? You brought *strangers* to my island?!

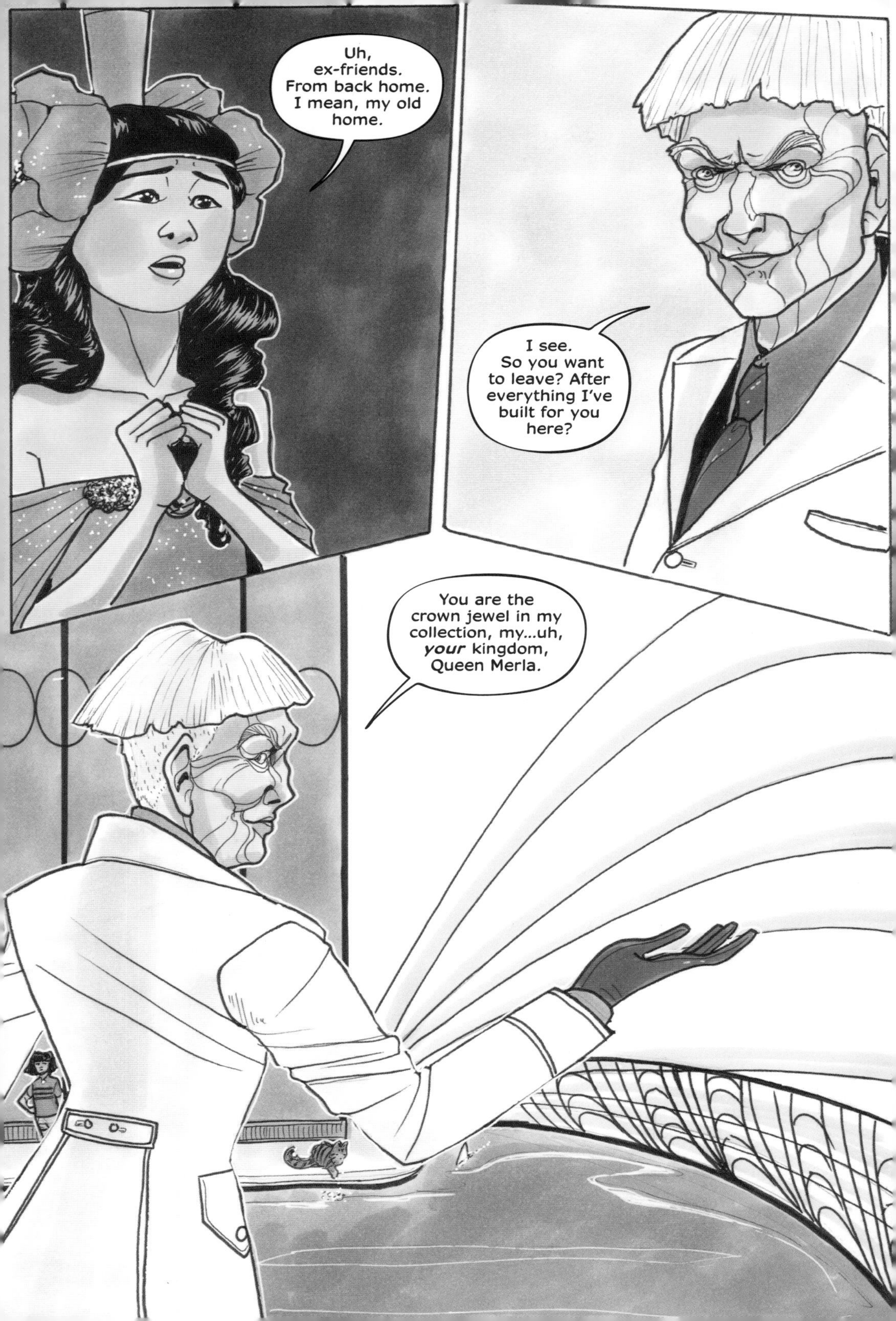
Uh, ex-friends. From back home. I mean, my old home.
I see. So you want to leave? After everything I've built for you here?
You are the crown jewel in my collection, my...uh, *your* kingdom, Queen Merla.

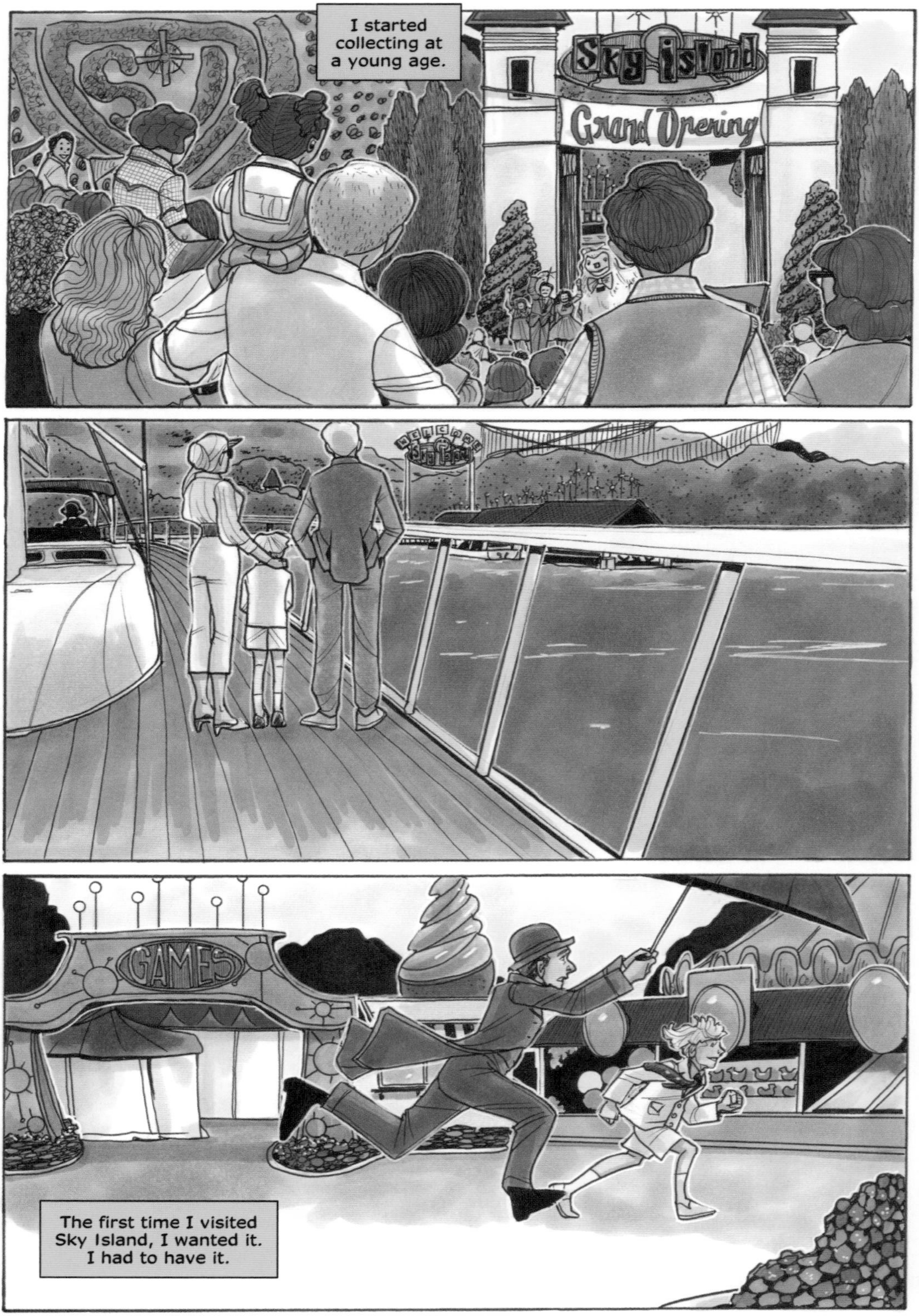
I started collecting at a young age.
Sky Island
Grand Opening
GAMES
The first time I visited Sky Island, I wanted it. I had to have it.

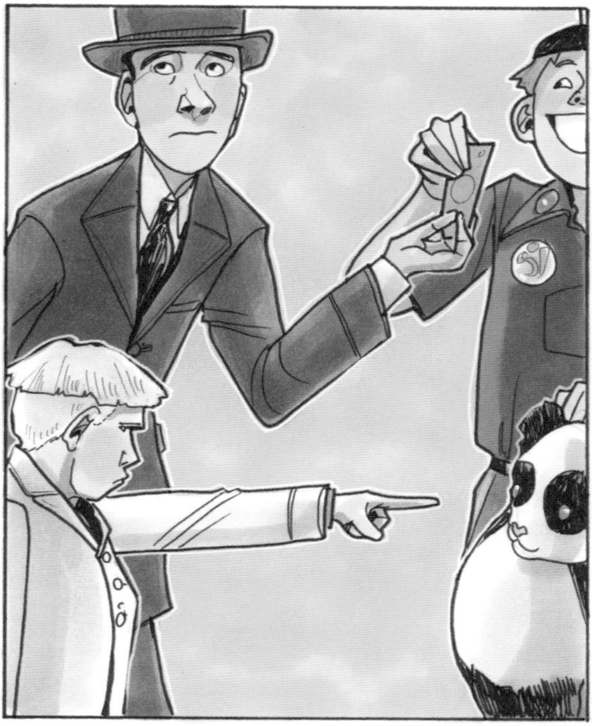

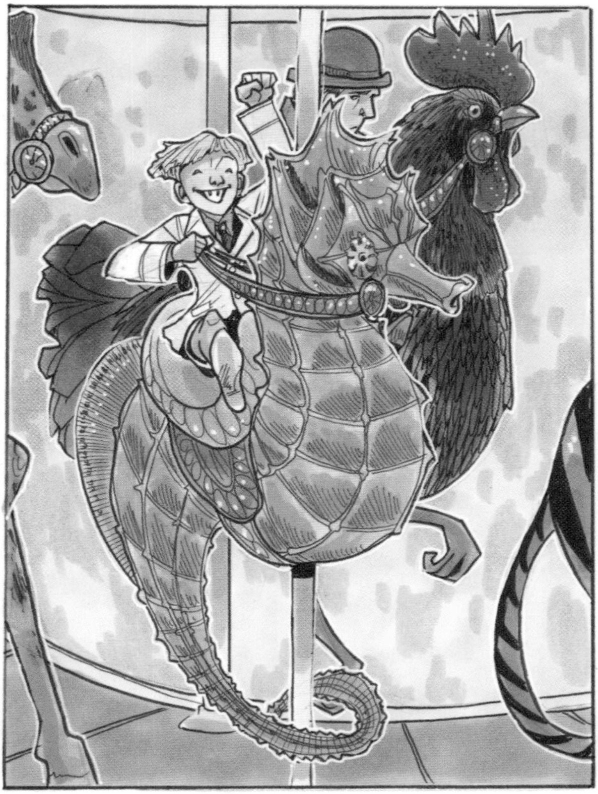

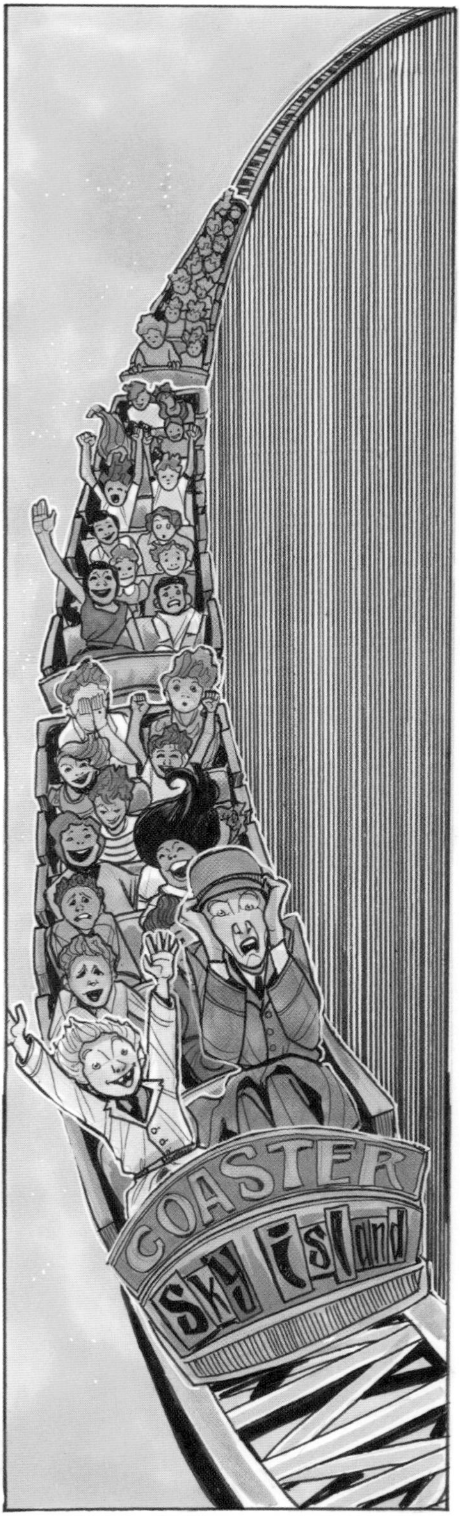
COASTER
Sky island

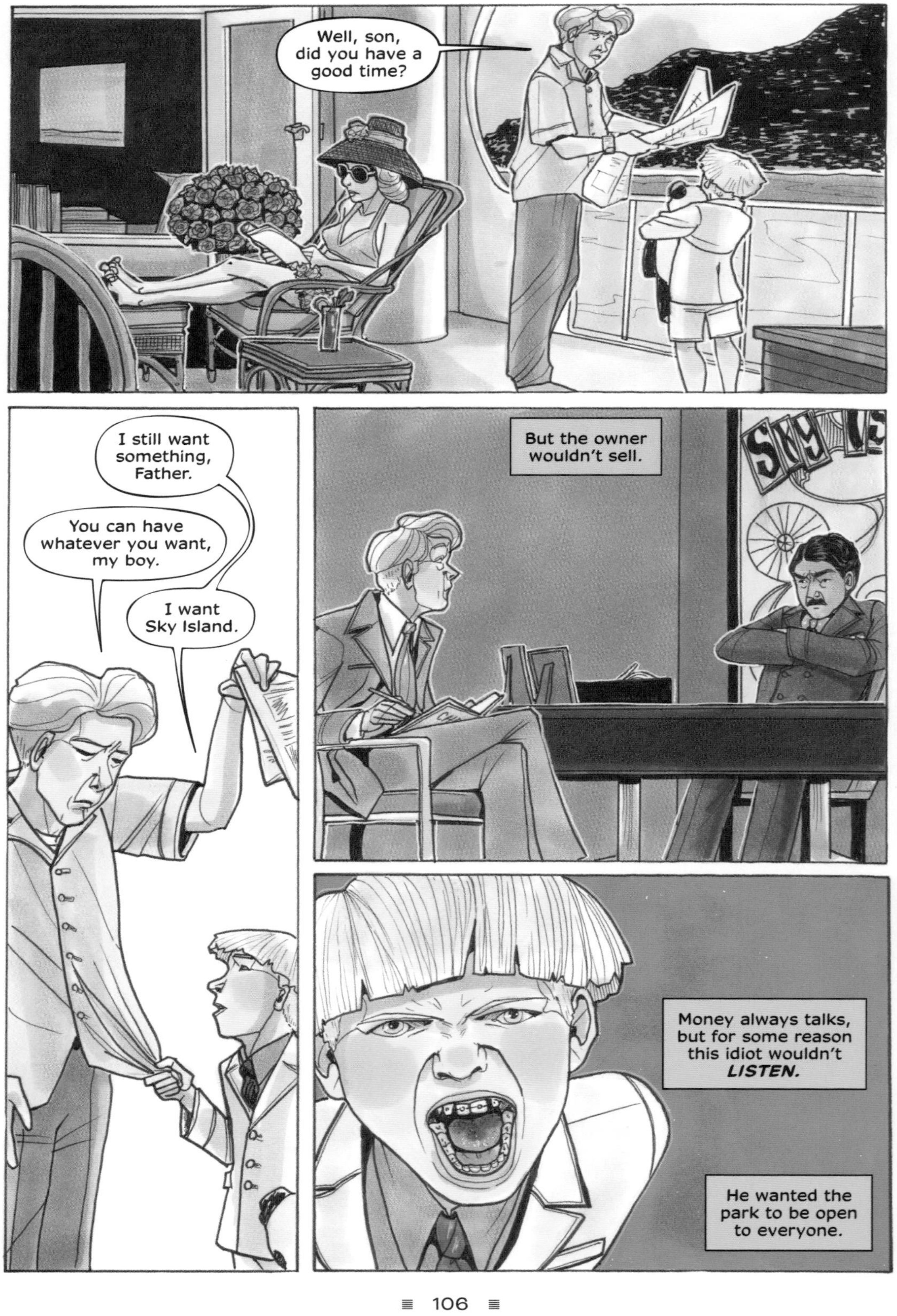
Well, son, did you have a good time?
I still want something, Father.
You can have whatever you want, my boy.
I want Sky Island.
But the owner wouldn't sell.
Money always talks, but for some reason this idiot wouldn't ***LISTEN.***
He wanted the park to be open to everyone.

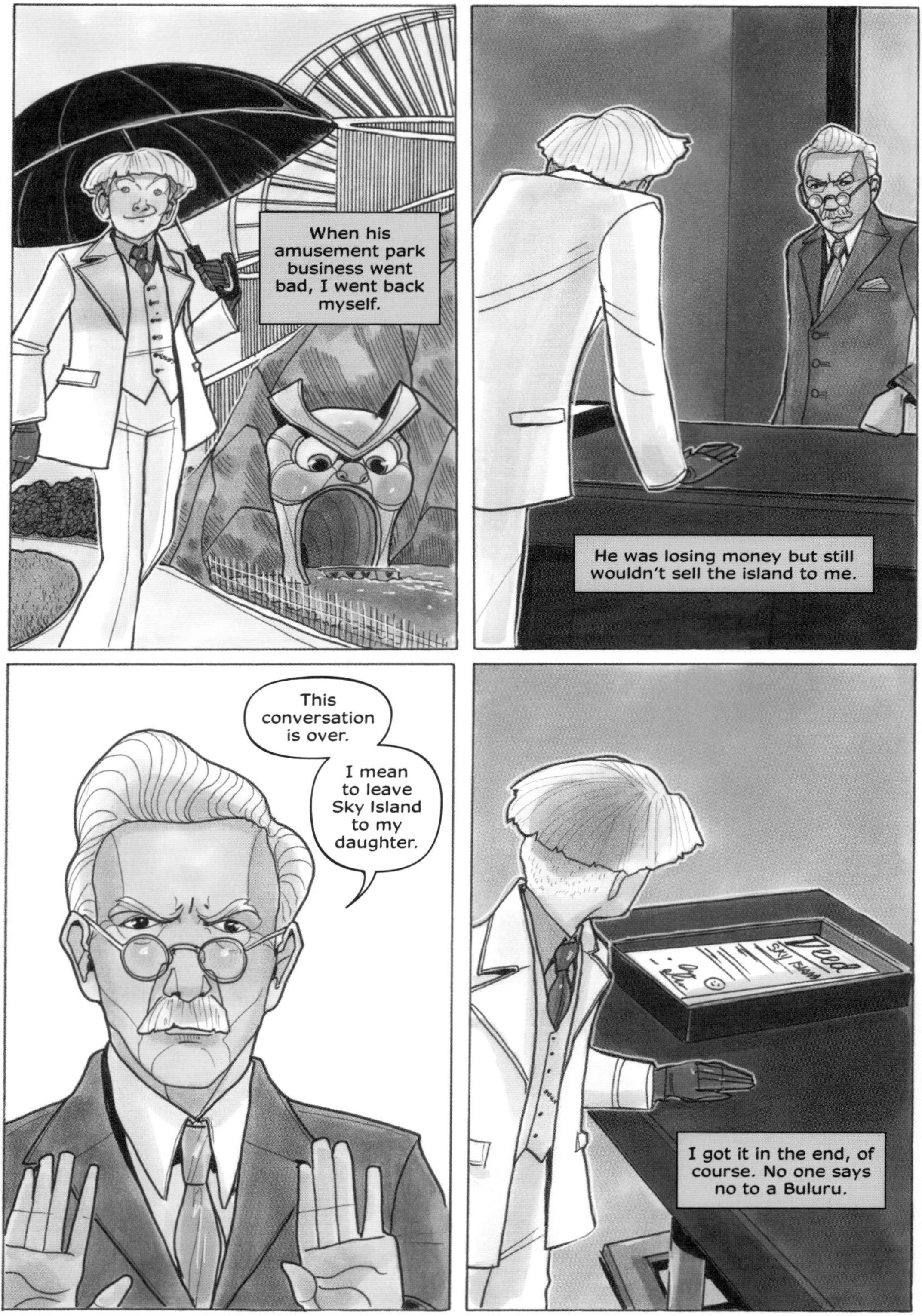
When his amusement park business went bad, I went back myself.
He was losing money but still wouldn't sell the island to me.
This conversation is over.
I mean to leave Sky Island to my daughter.
I got it in the end, of course. No one says no to a Buluru.

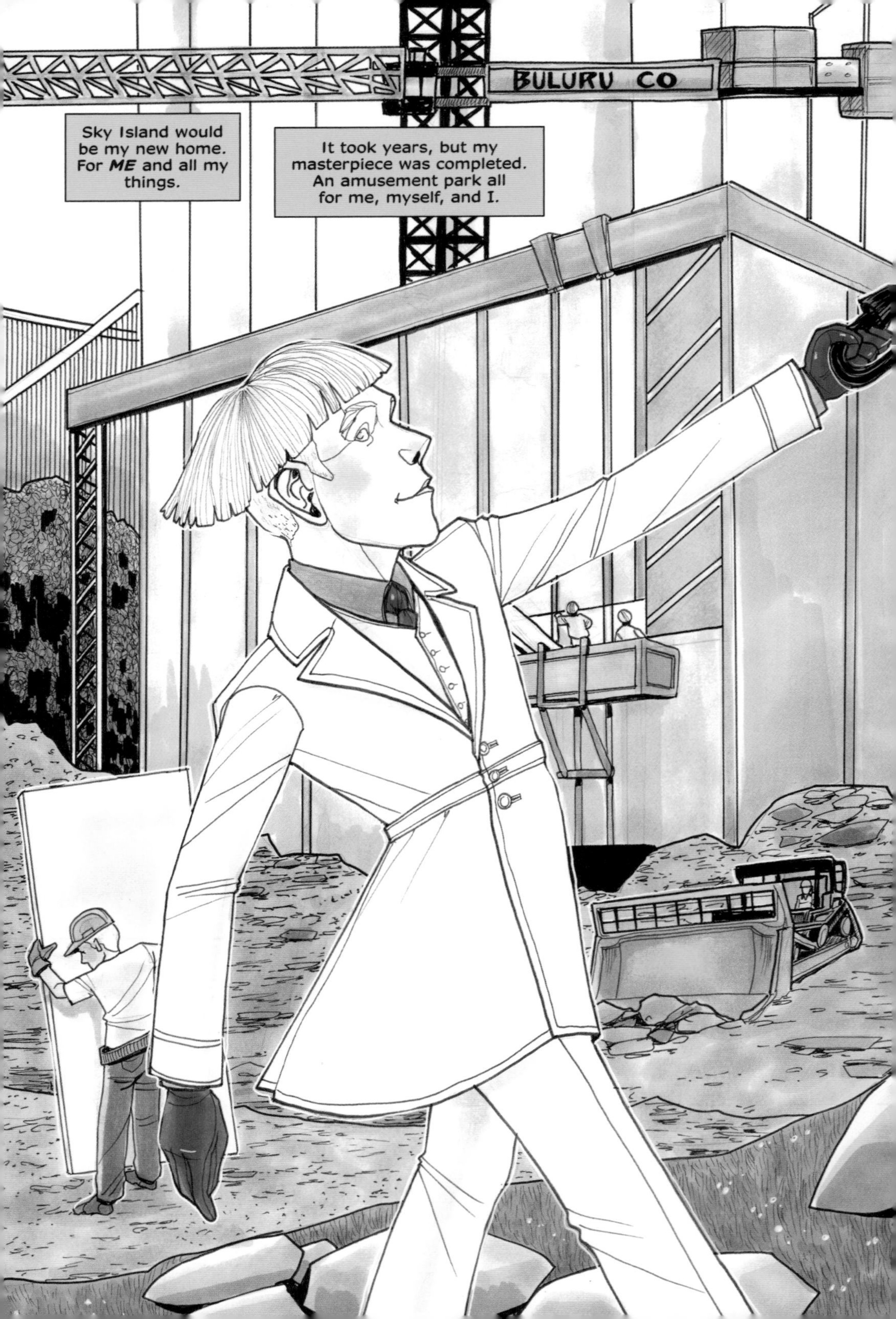
BULURU CO
Sky Island would be my new home. For ***ME*** and all my things.
It took years, but my masterpiece was completed. An amusement park all for me, myself, and I.

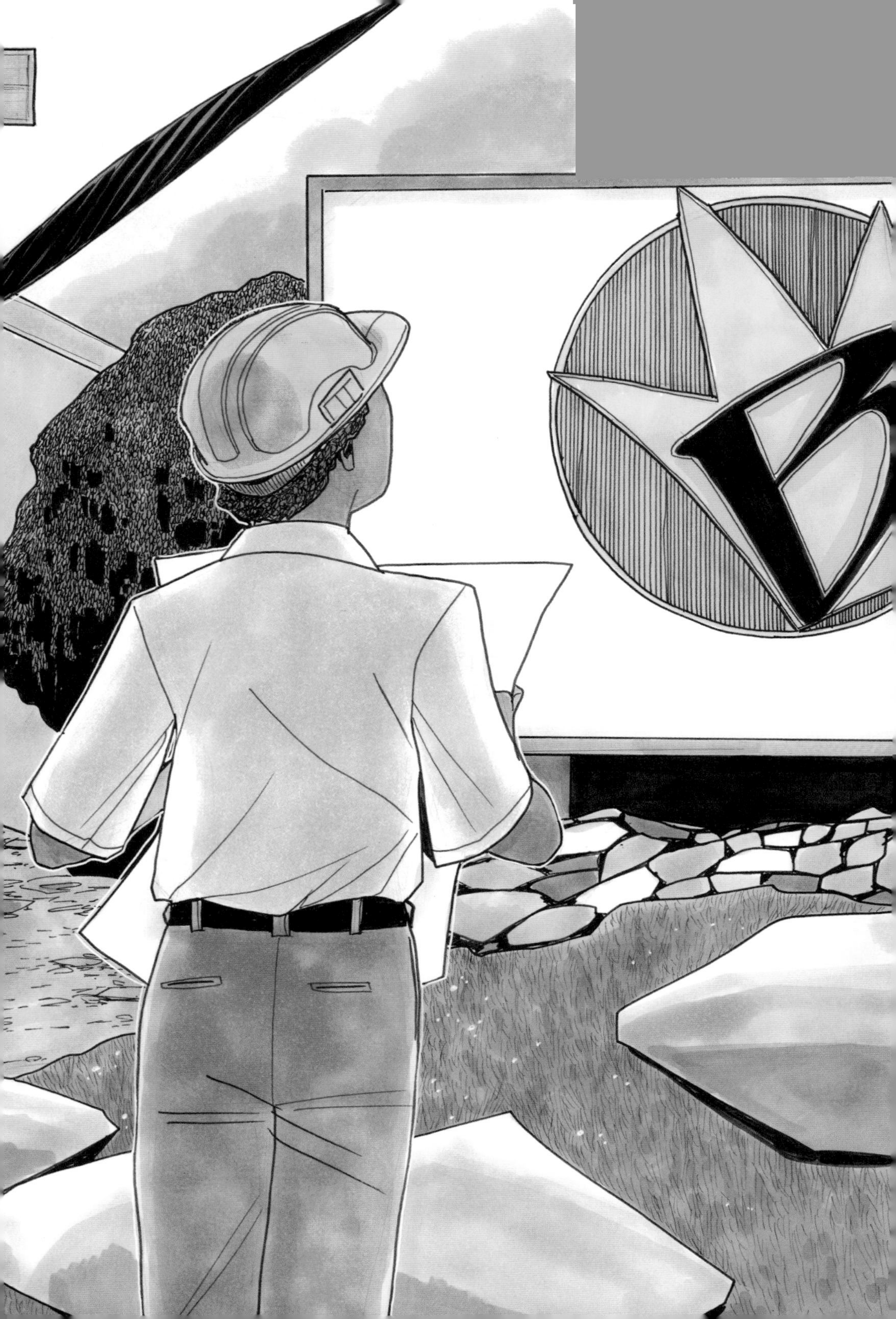

But it wasn't complete. I needed to stock the aquarium. And I was still looking for the rarest sea creature of all. There were rumors of course, but no one had seen one for centuries.

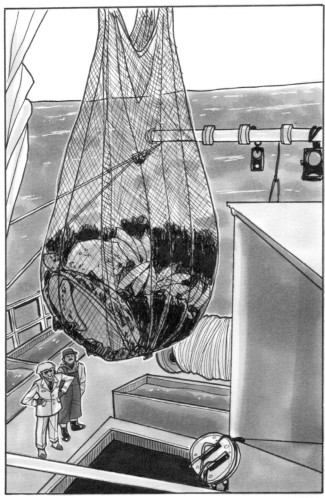

And then, at last I found a legendary Sea Siren.

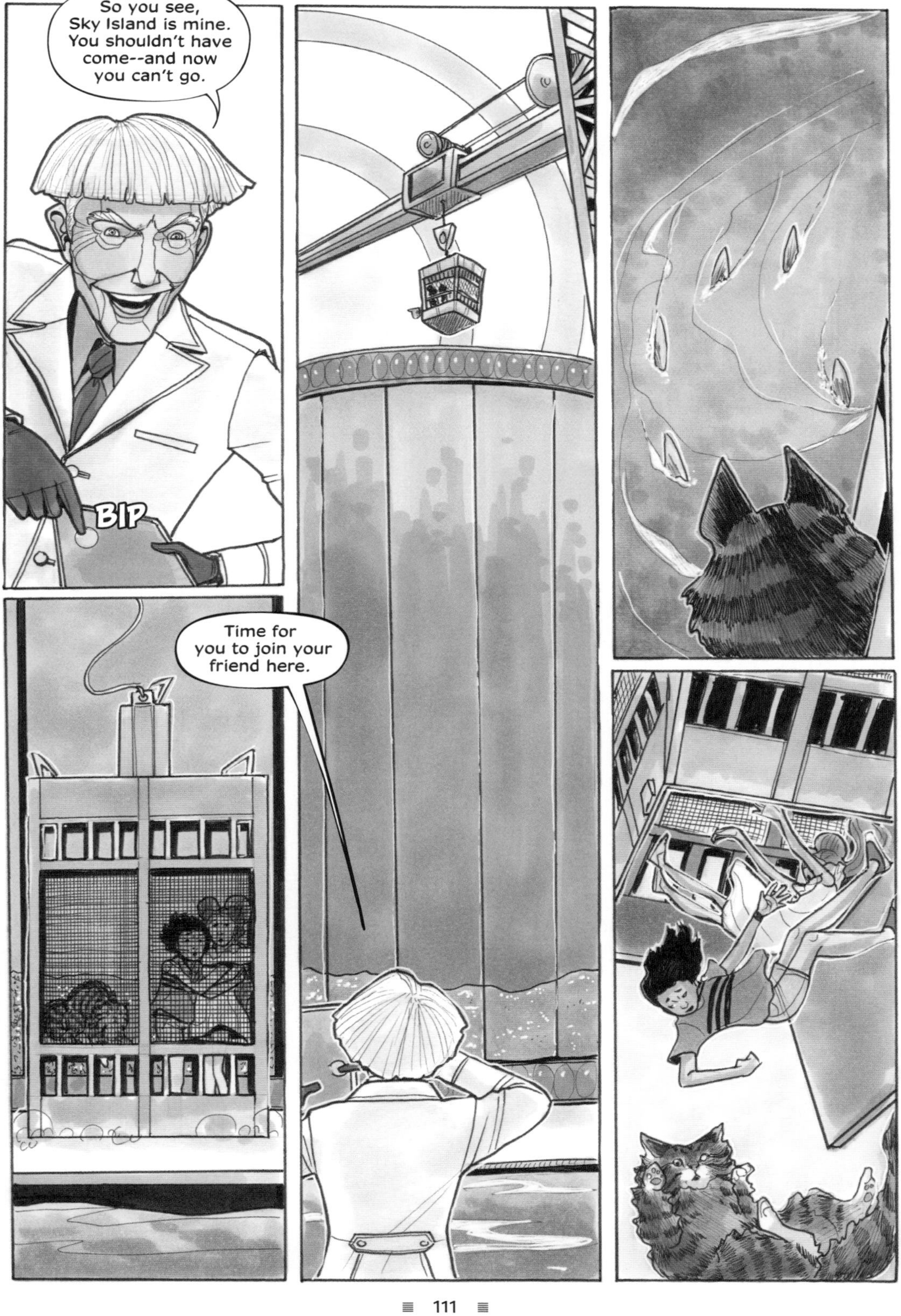
So you see, Sky Island is mine. You shouldn't have come--and now you can't go.
BIP
Time for you to join your friend here.

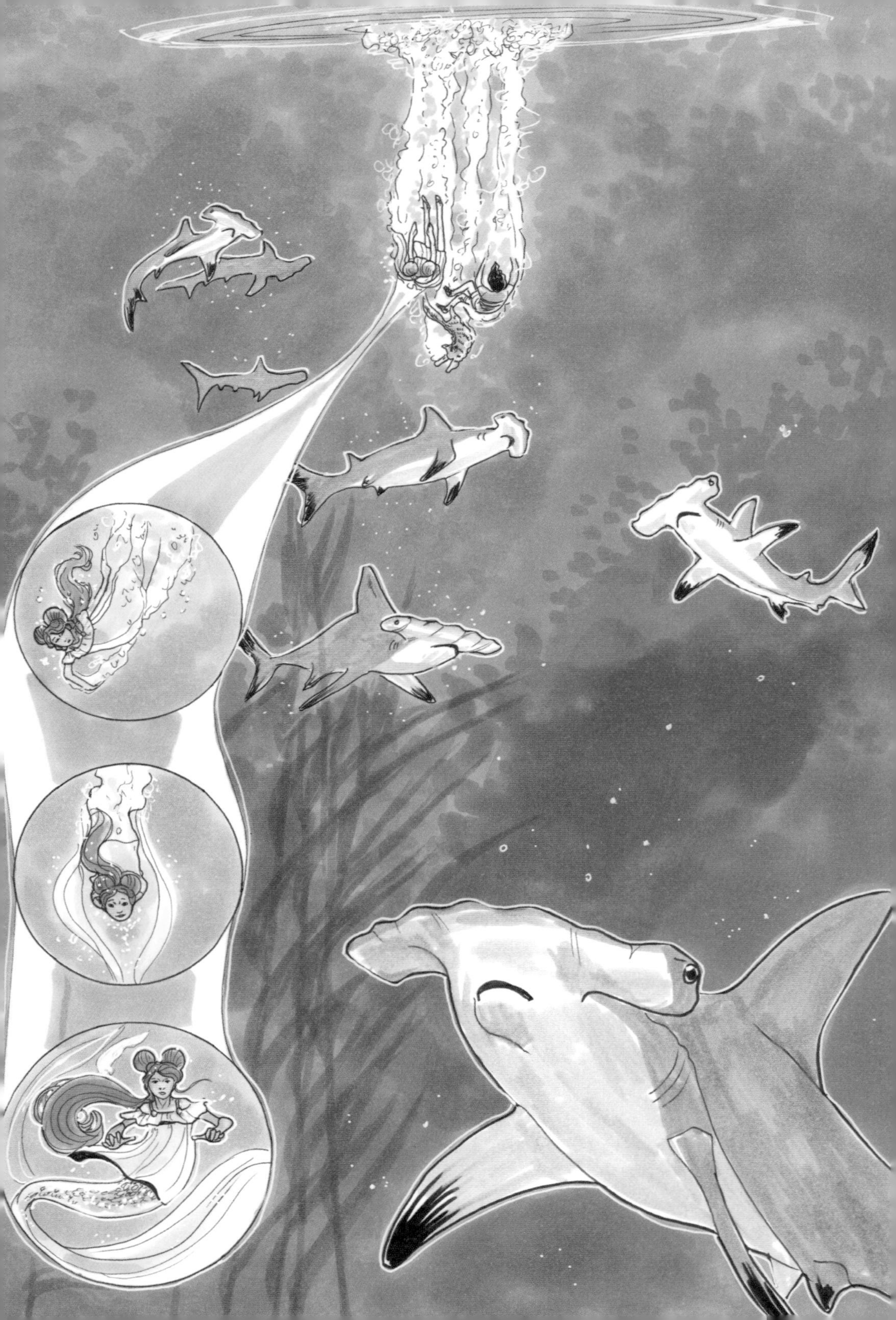

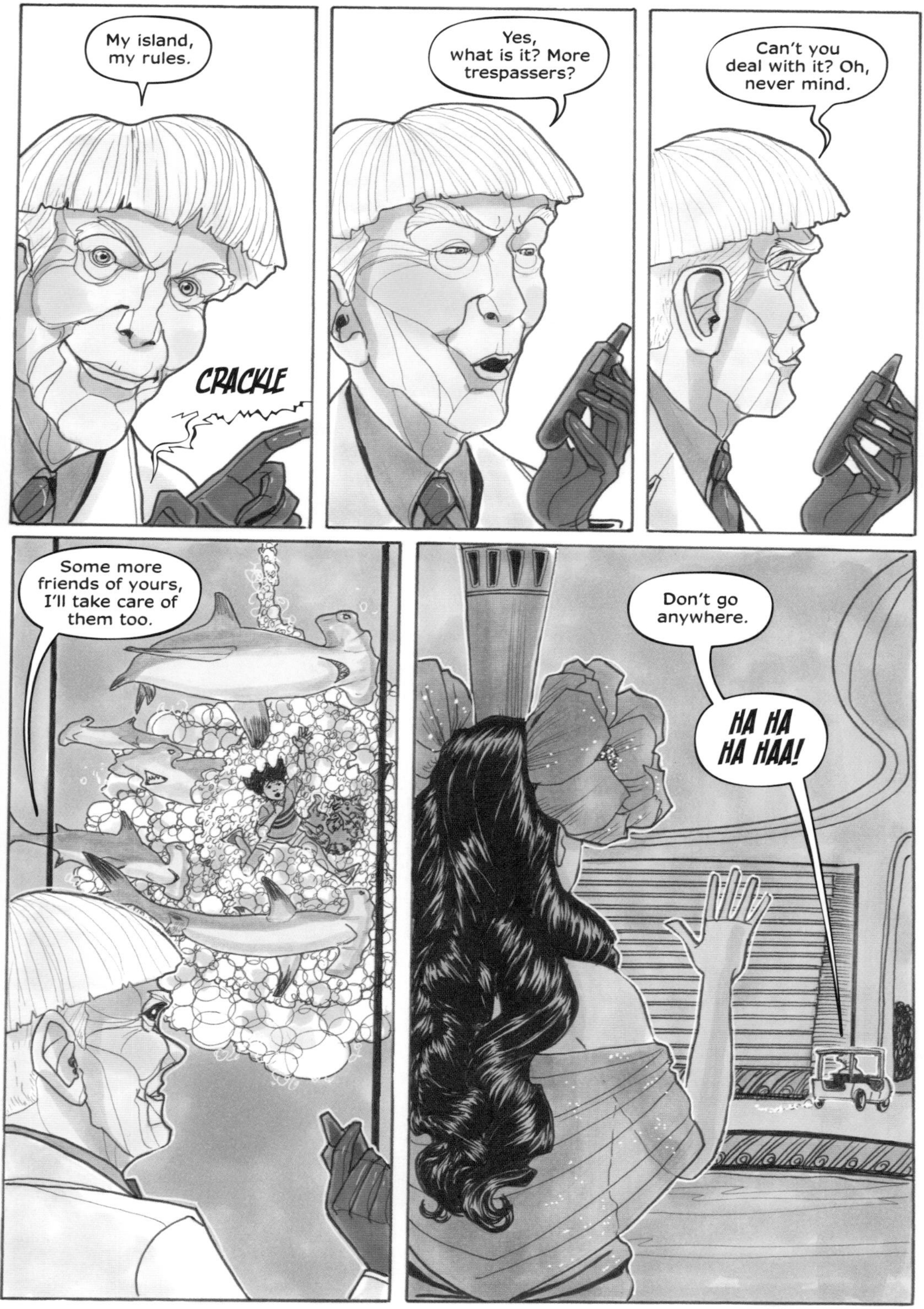
My island, my rules.
CRACKLE
Yes, what is it? More trespassers?
Can't you deal with it? Oh, never mind.
Some more friends of yours, I'll take care of them too.
Don't go anywhere.
HA HA HA HAA!

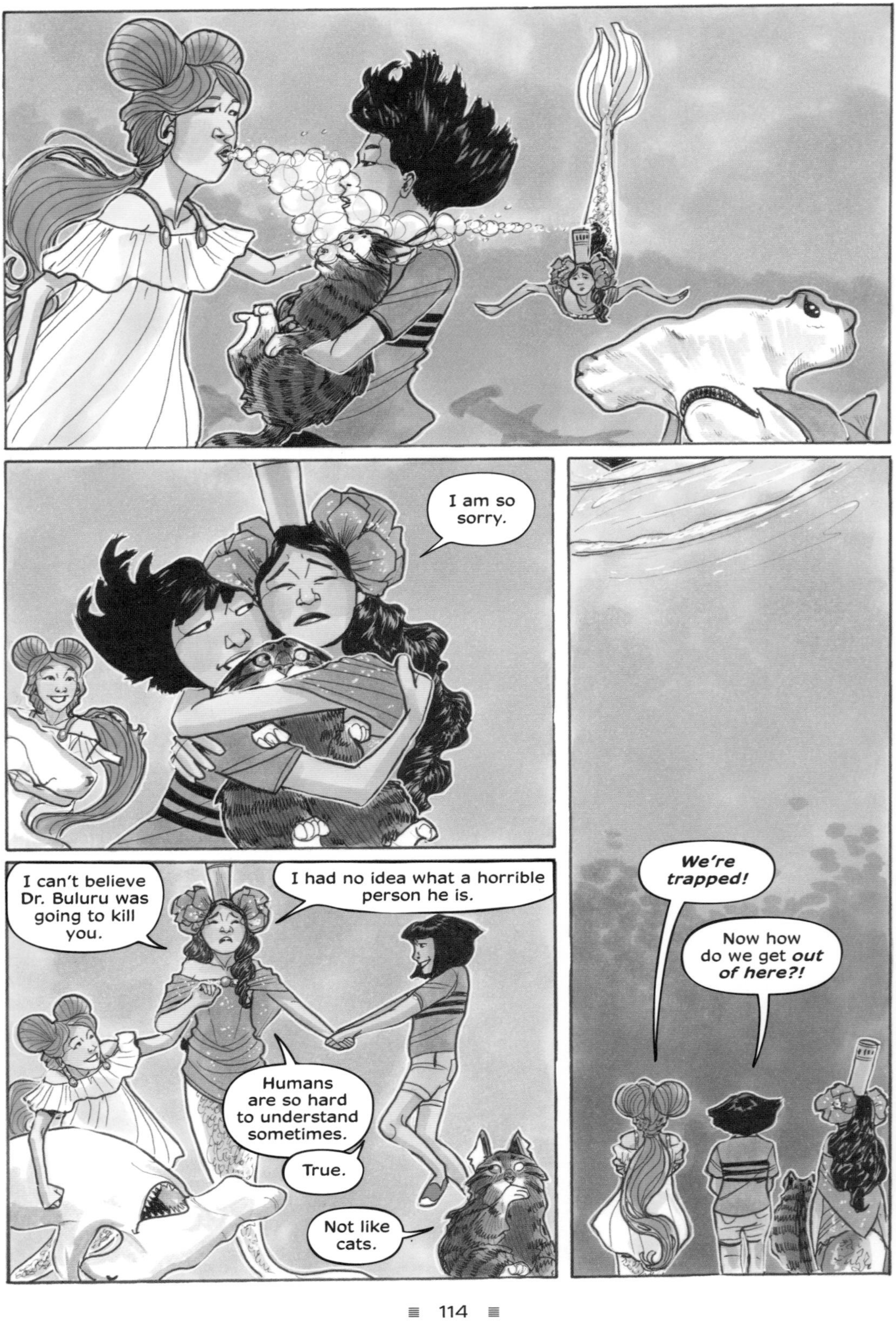

I am so sorry.
I can't believe Dr. Buluru was going to kill you.
I had no idea what a horrible person he is.
Humans are so hard to understand sometimes.
True.
Not like cats.
We're trapped!
Now how do we get *out of here?!*

Cap'n Bill to the Rescue

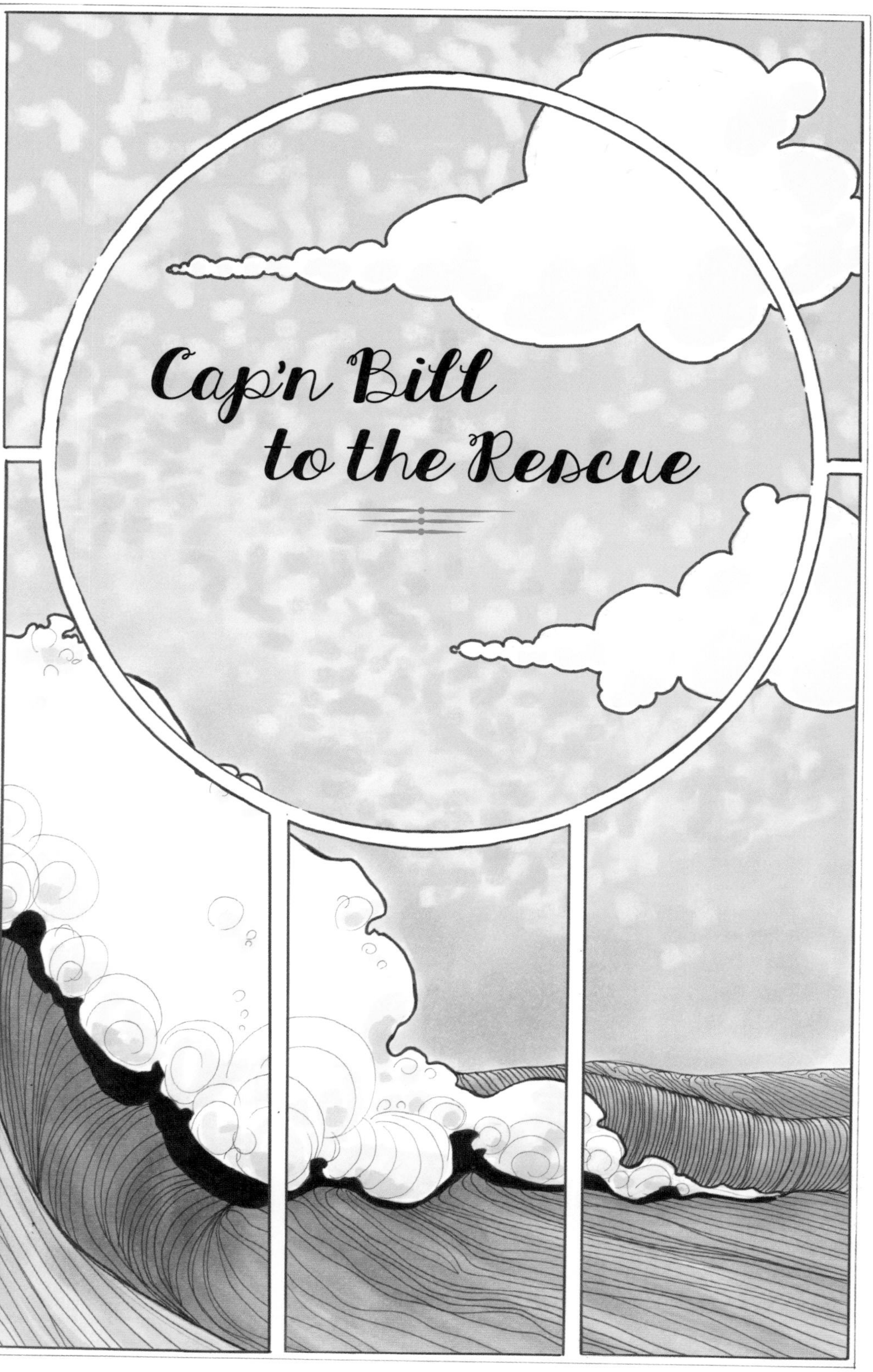

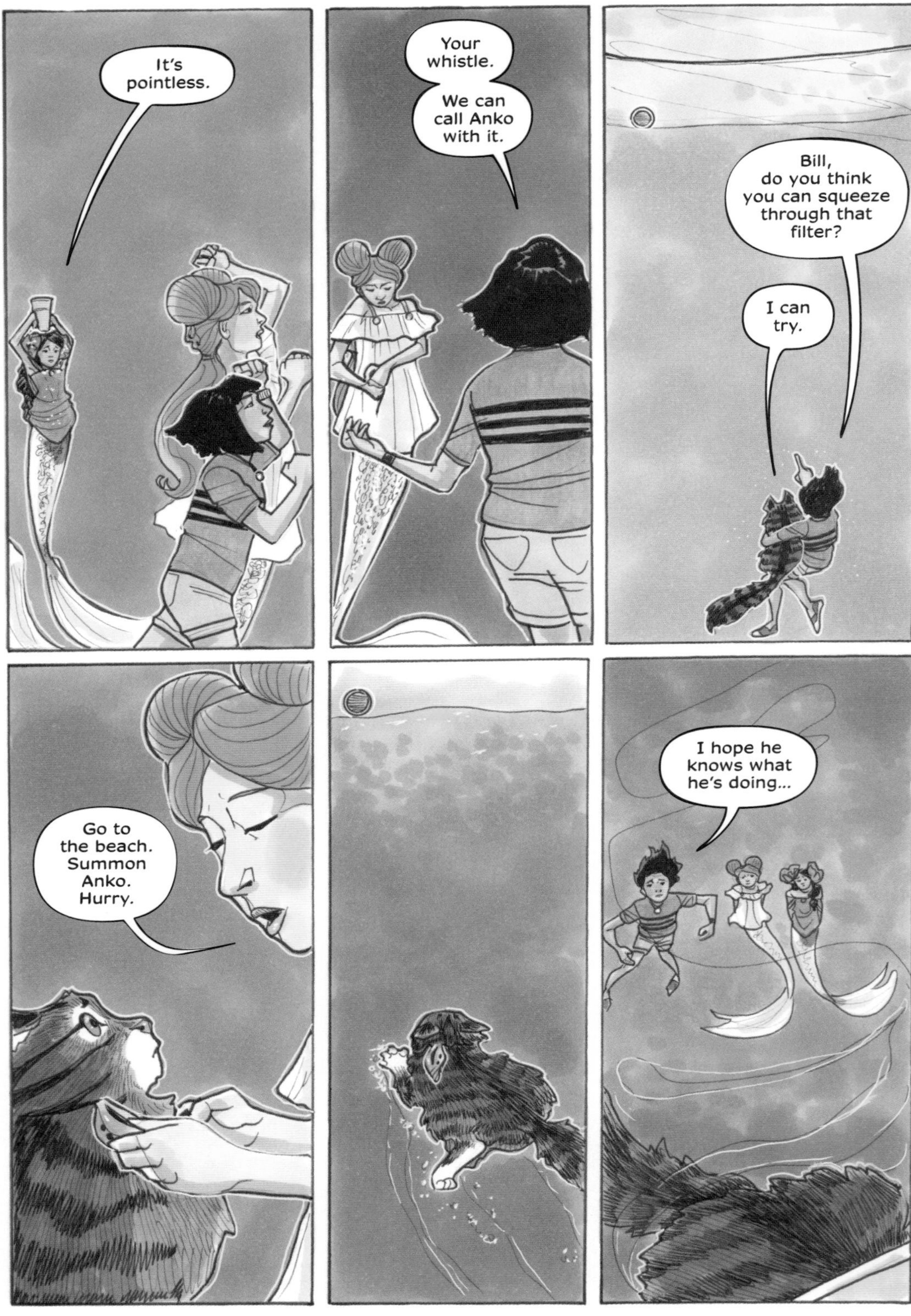
It's pointless.
Your whistle.
We can call Anko with it.
Bill, do you think you can squeeze through that filter?
I can try.
Go to the beach. Summon Anko. Hurry.
I hope he knows what he's doing...

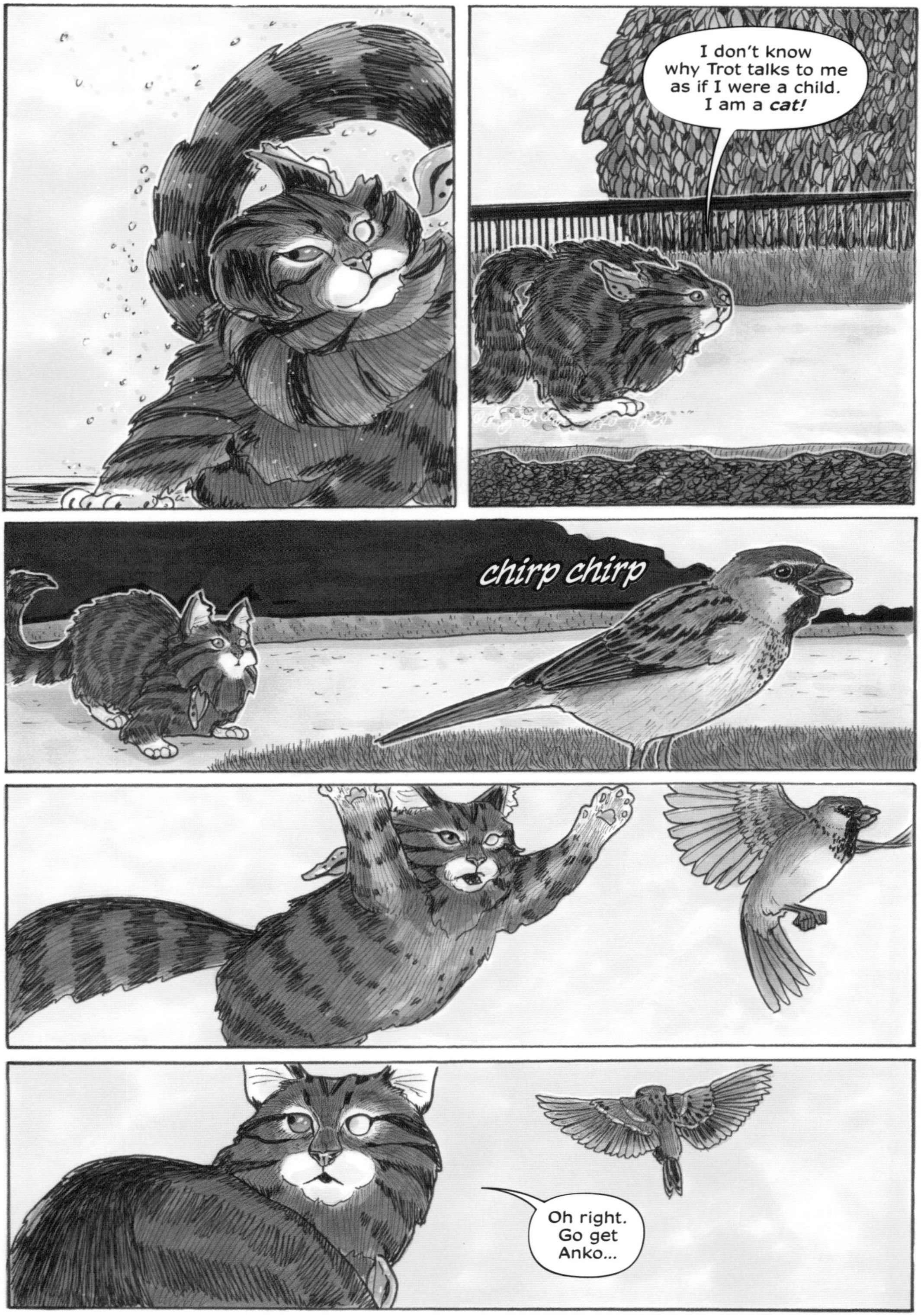
I don't know why Trot talks to me as if I were a child. I am a ***cat!***
chirp chirp
Oh right. Go get Anko...

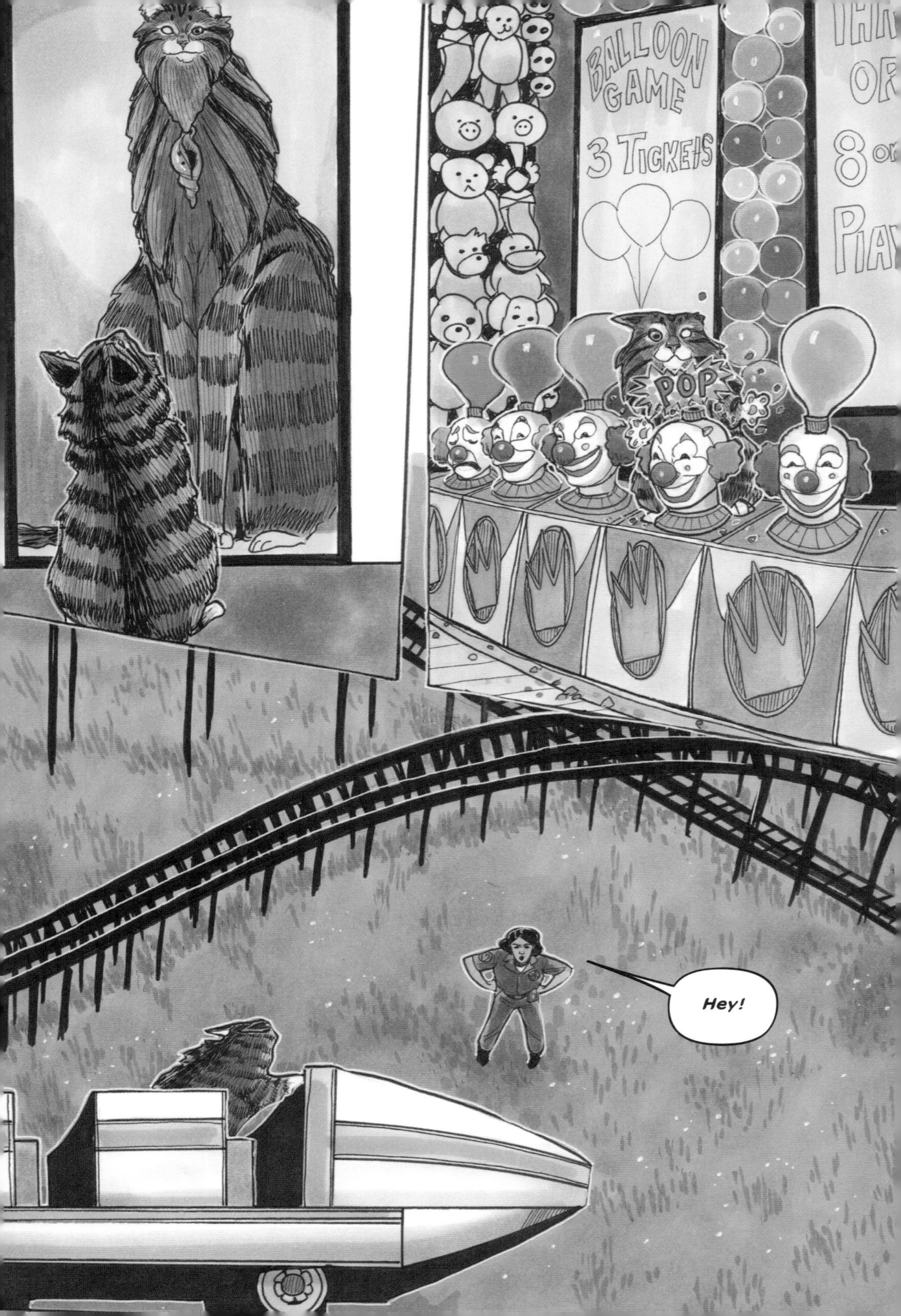
BALLOON GAME
3 Tickets
POP
Hey!

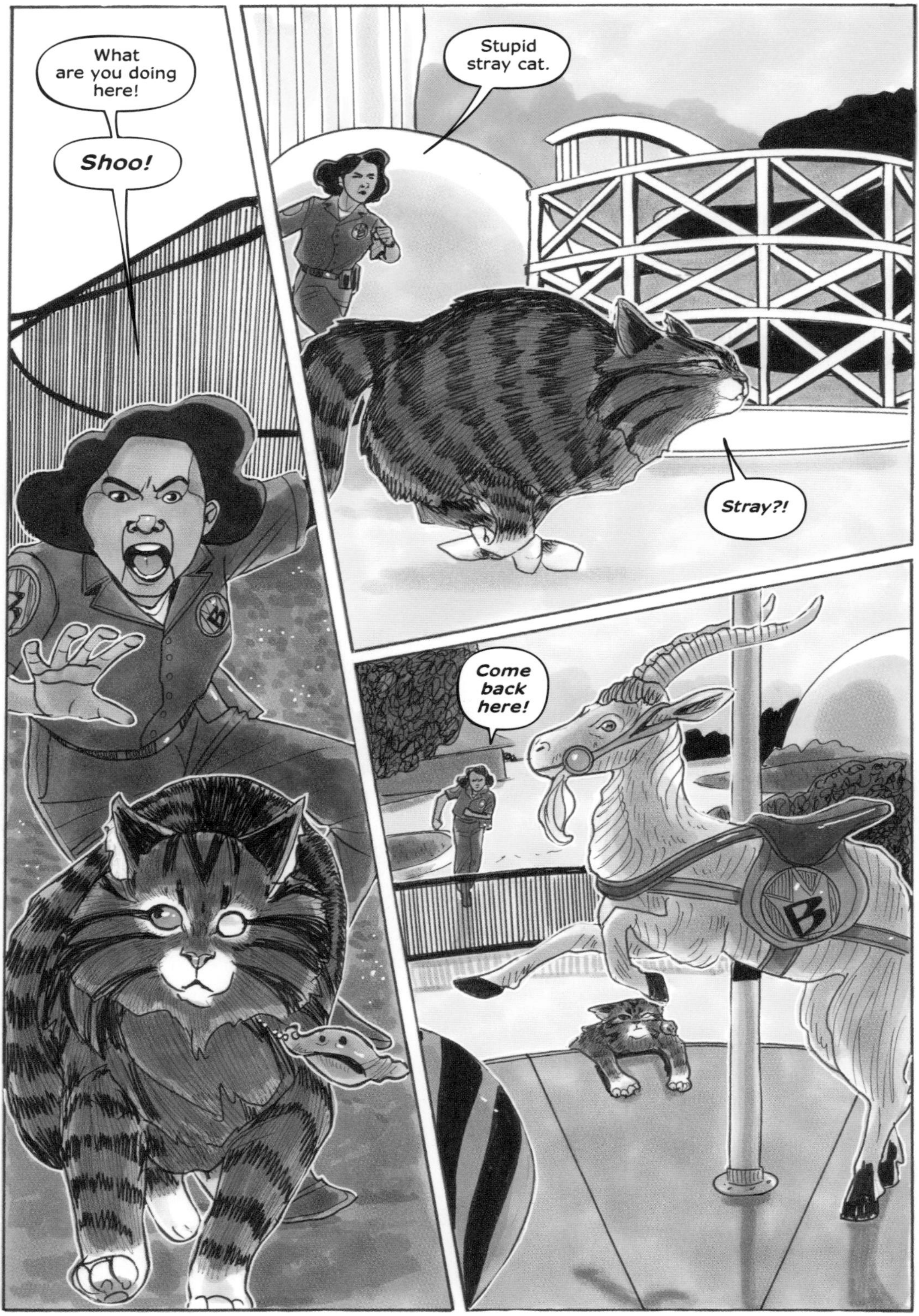
What are you doing here!
Shoo!
Stupid stray cat.
Stray?!
Come back here!

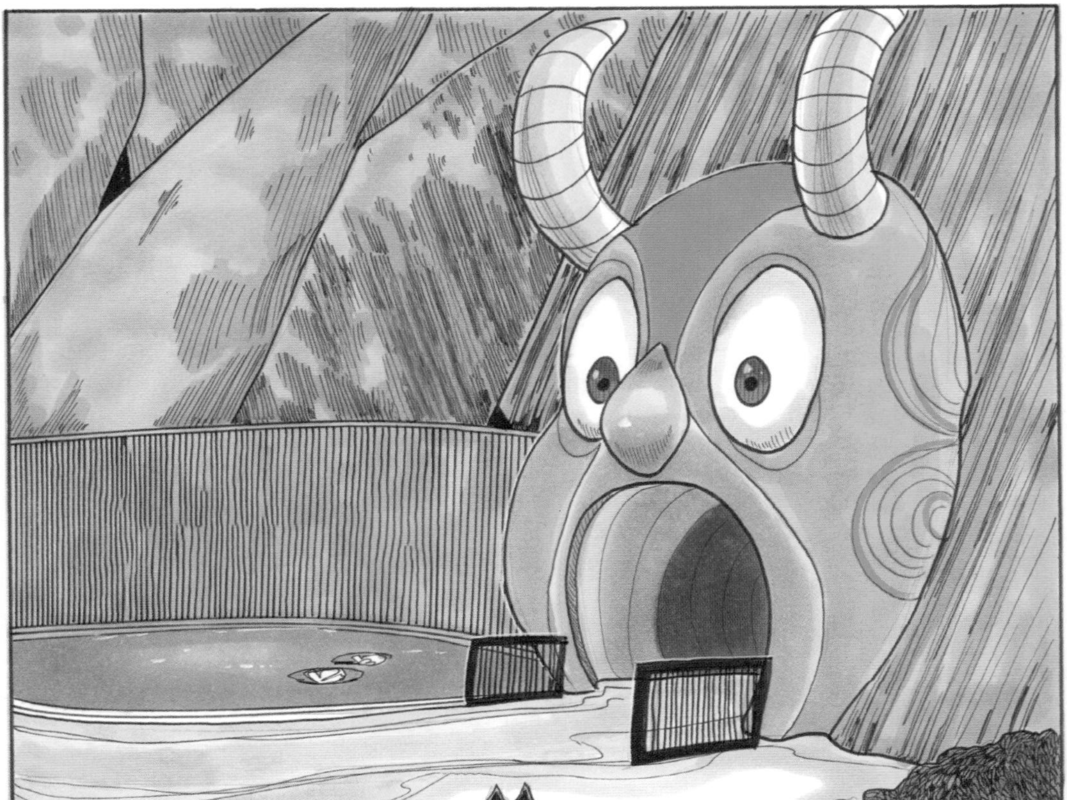

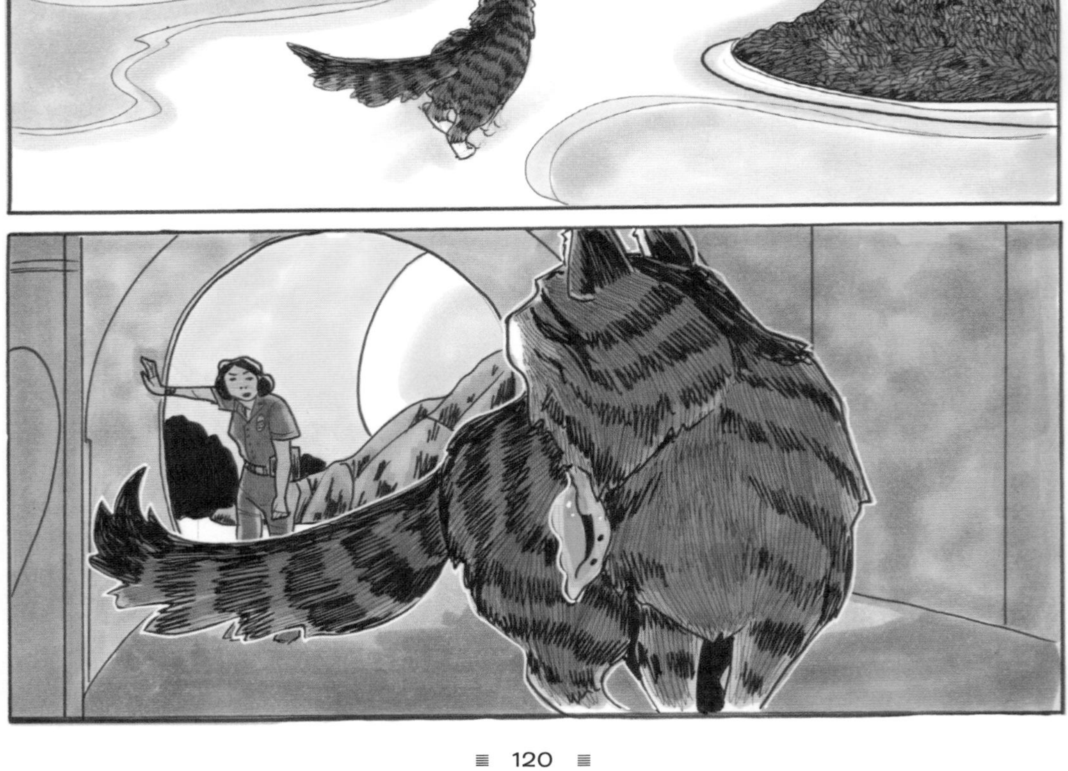

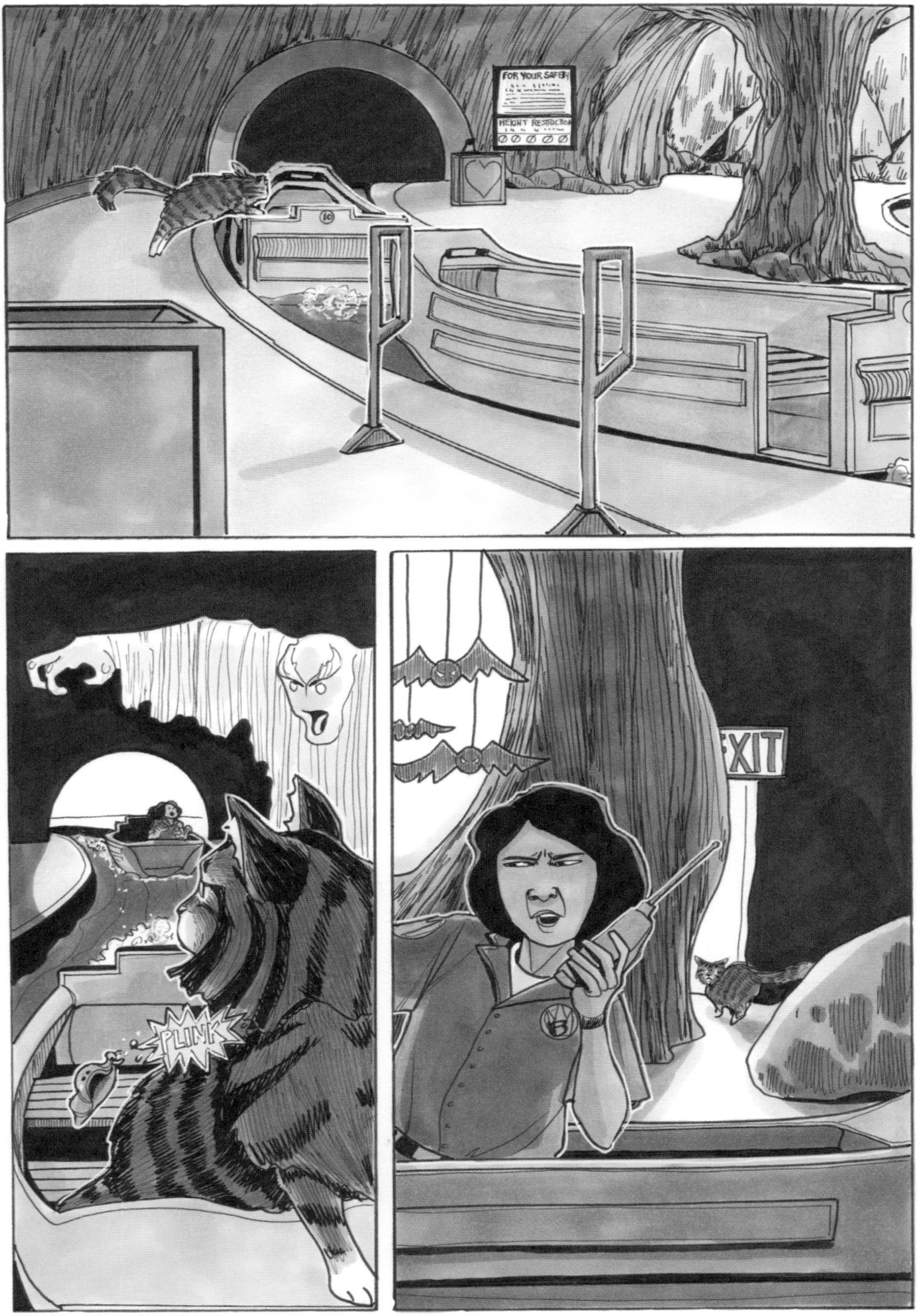
FOR YOUR SAFETY
HEIGHT RESTRICTION
EXIT
PLINK

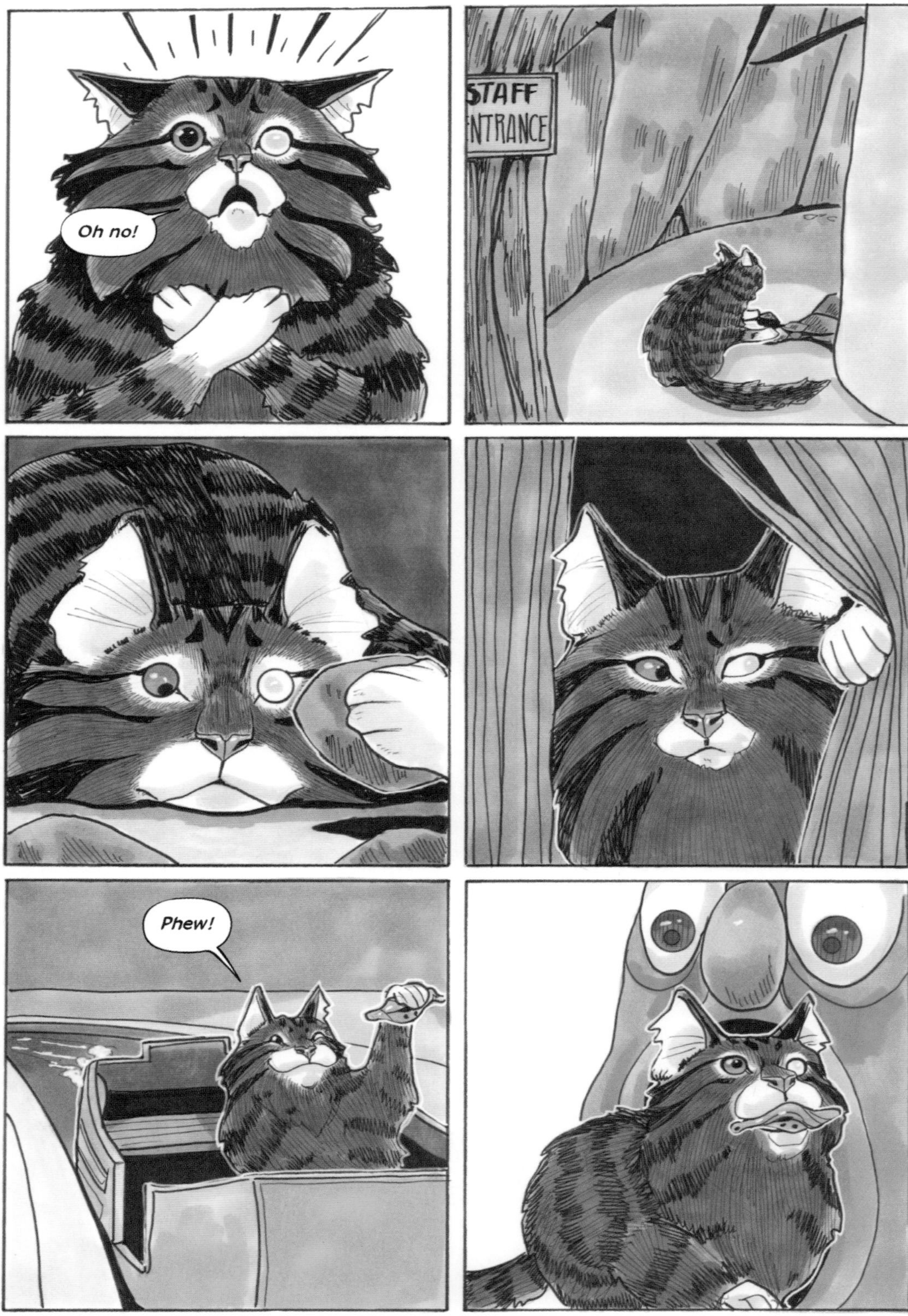

Oh no!
STAFF
ENTRANCE
Phew!

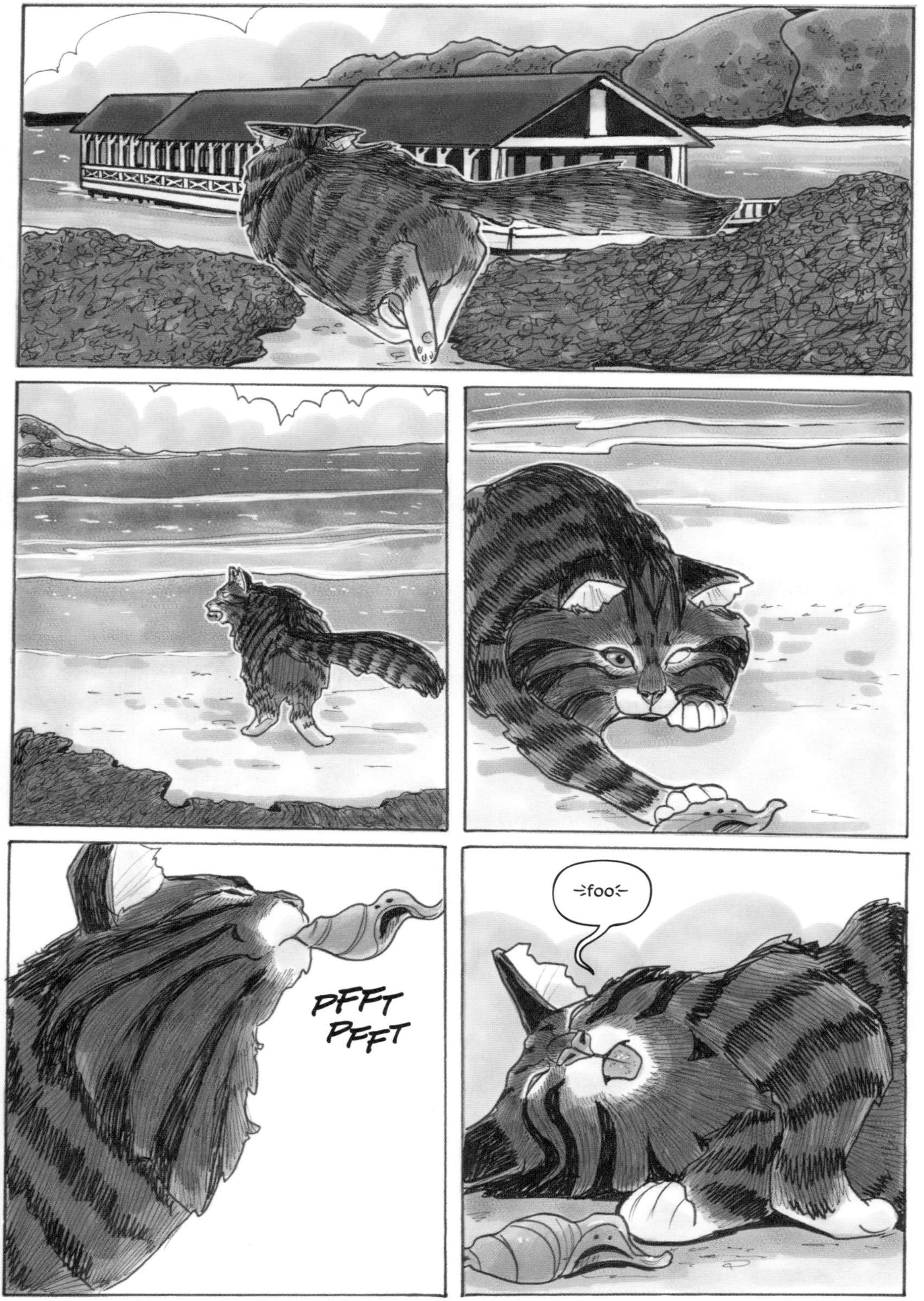
PFFT
PFFT
foo

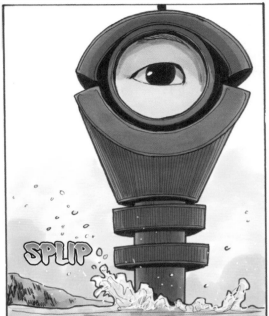

SPLIP

What is that cat doing?

Whew. I hope he got that.

Clearly the cat is trying to tell us something is wrong. Let's go see.

kachunk kachunk

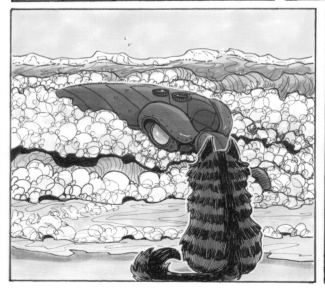

Get in, Bill!

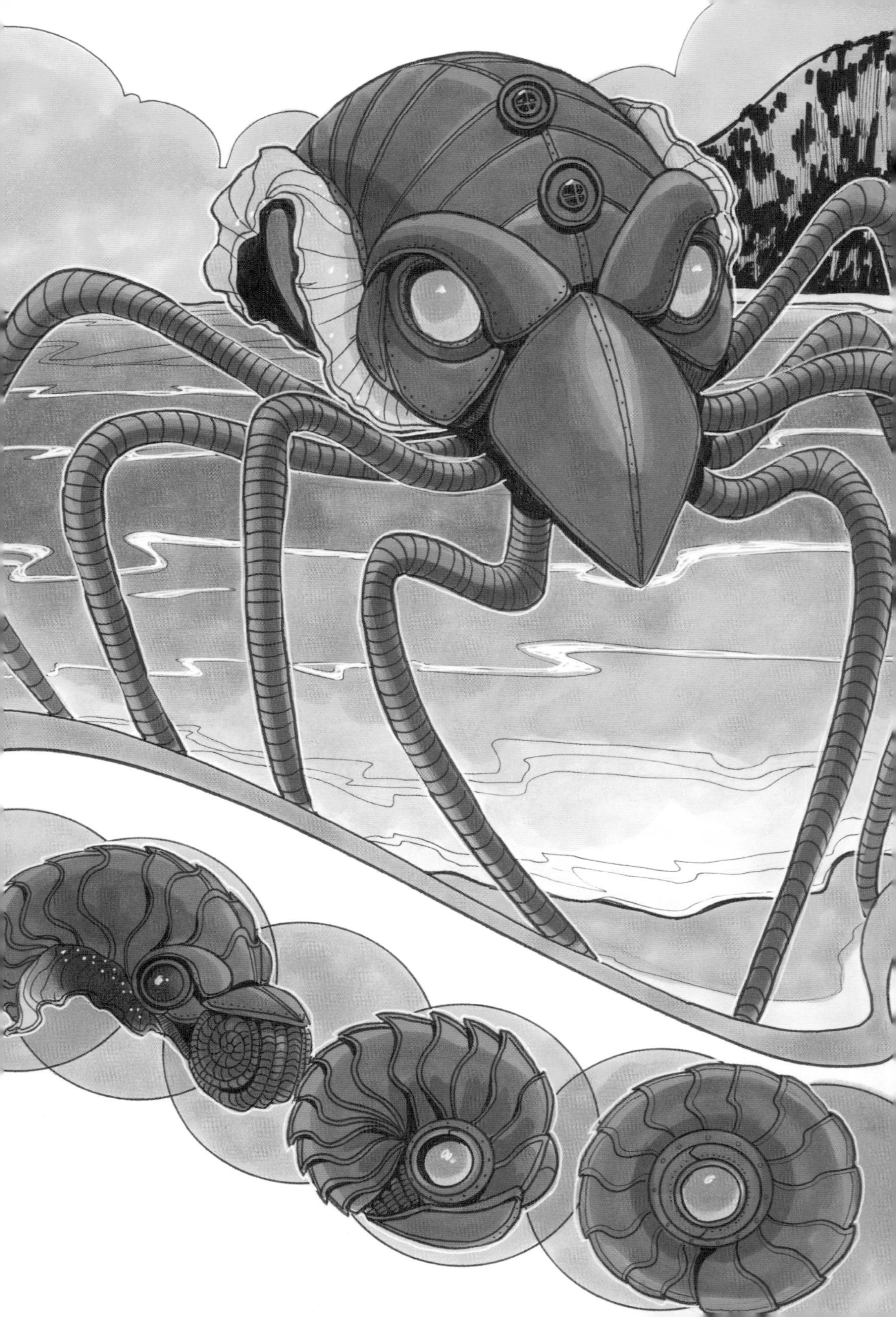

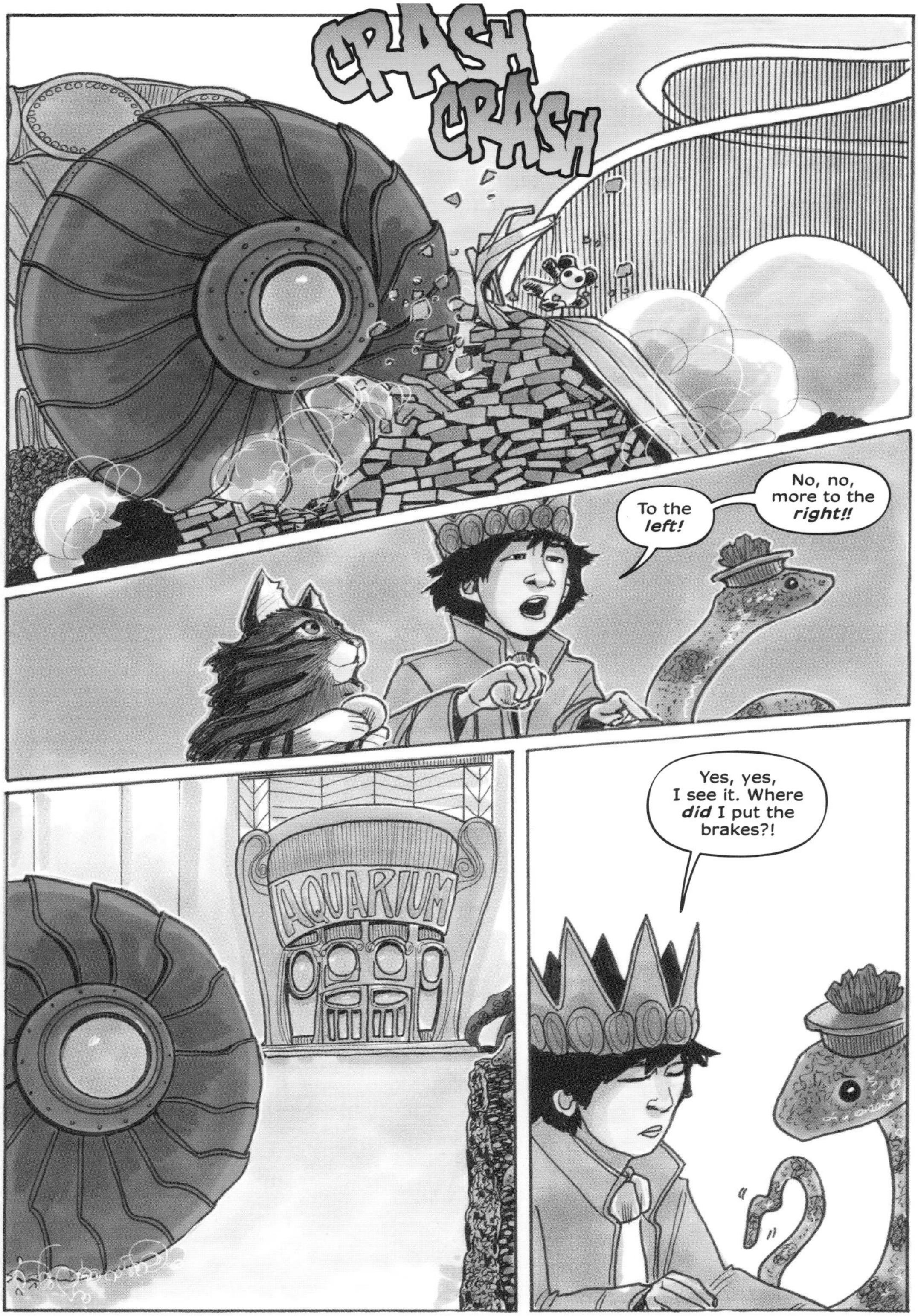
CRASH
CRASH
To the *left!*
No, no, more to the *right!!*
AQUARIUM
Yes, yes, I see it. Where *did* I put the brakes?!

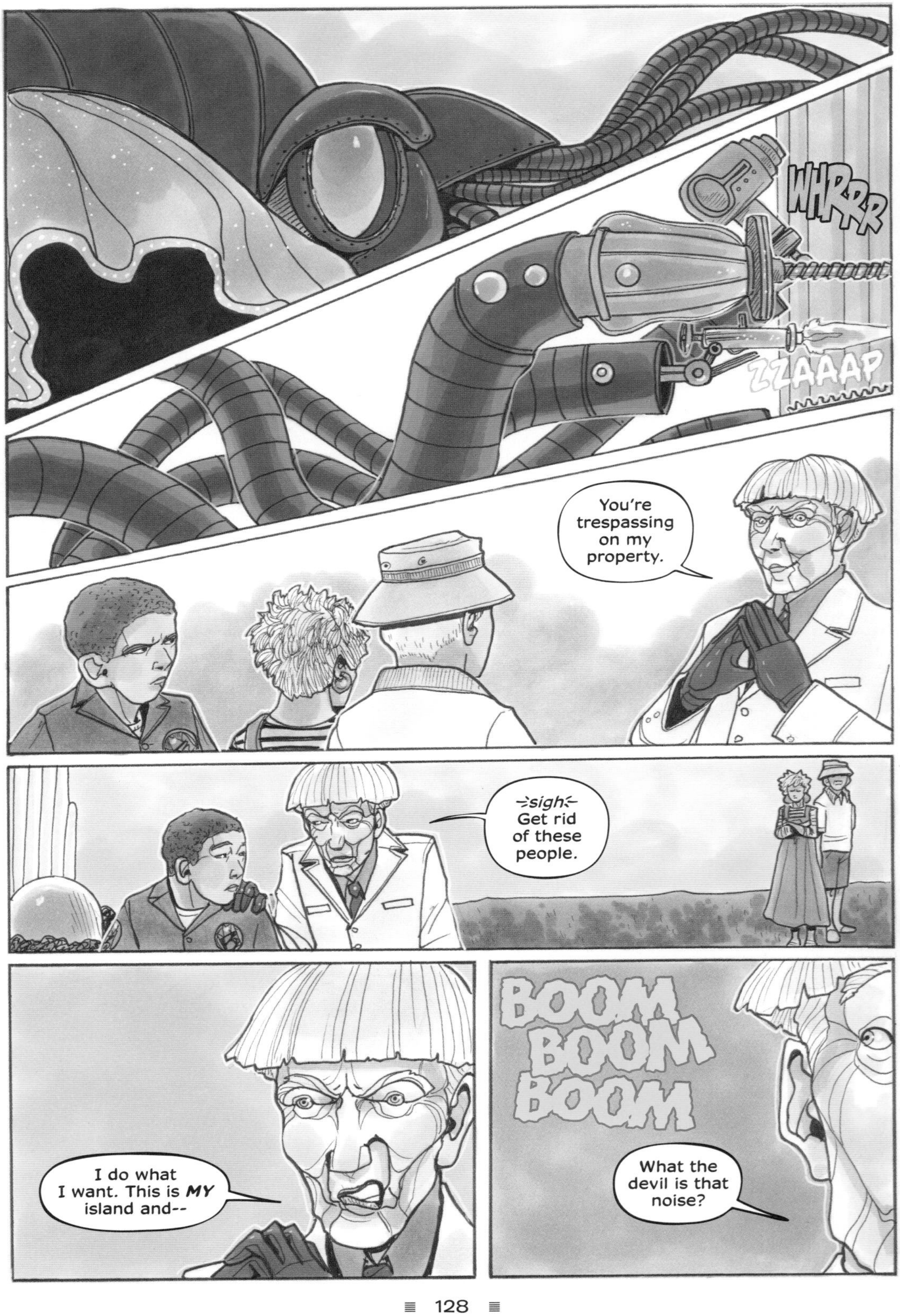
WHRRR
ZZAAAP
You're trespassing on my property.
sigh
Get rid of these people.
I do what I want. This is ***MY*** island and--
BOOM BOOM BOOM
What the devil is that noise?

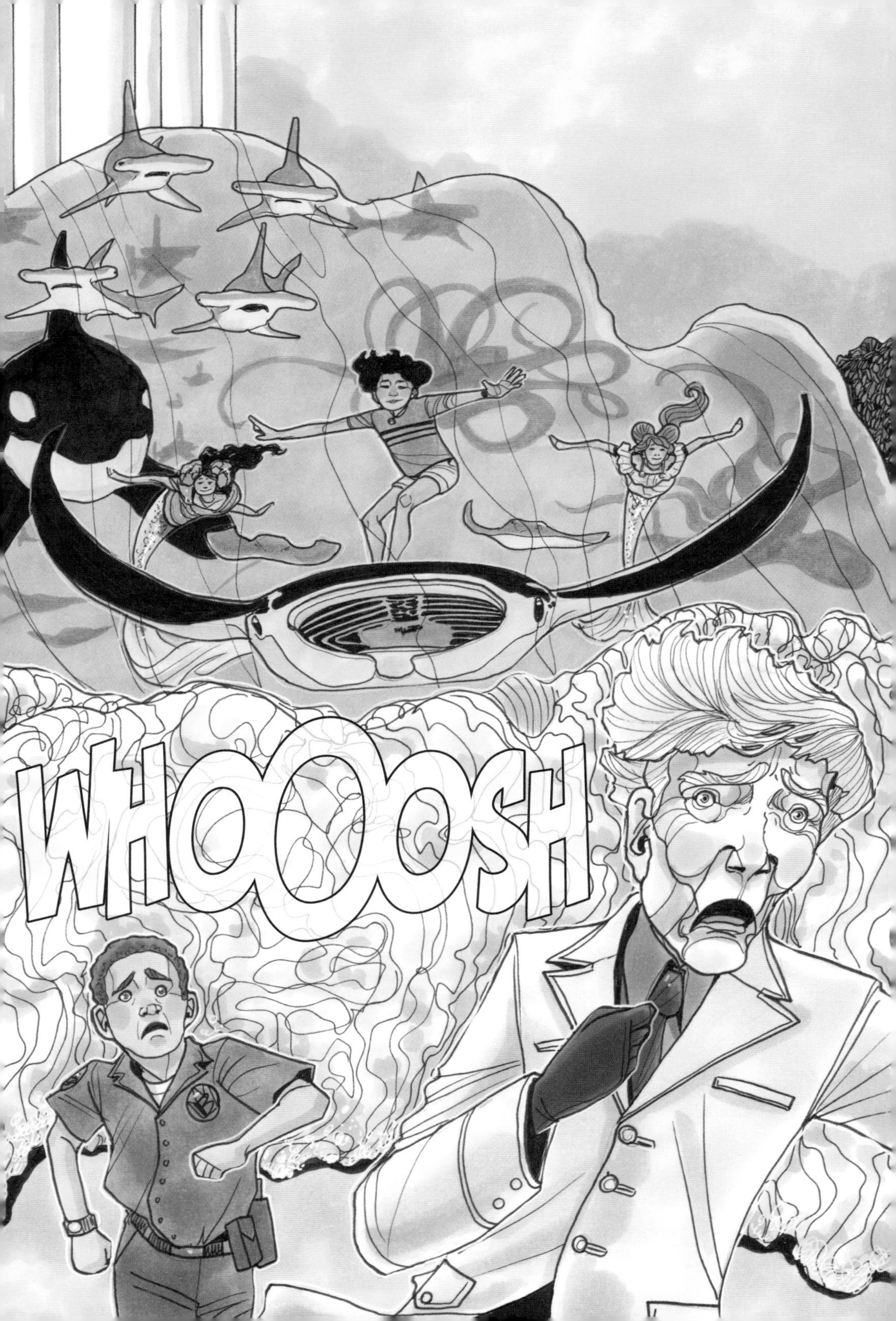
WHOOOSH

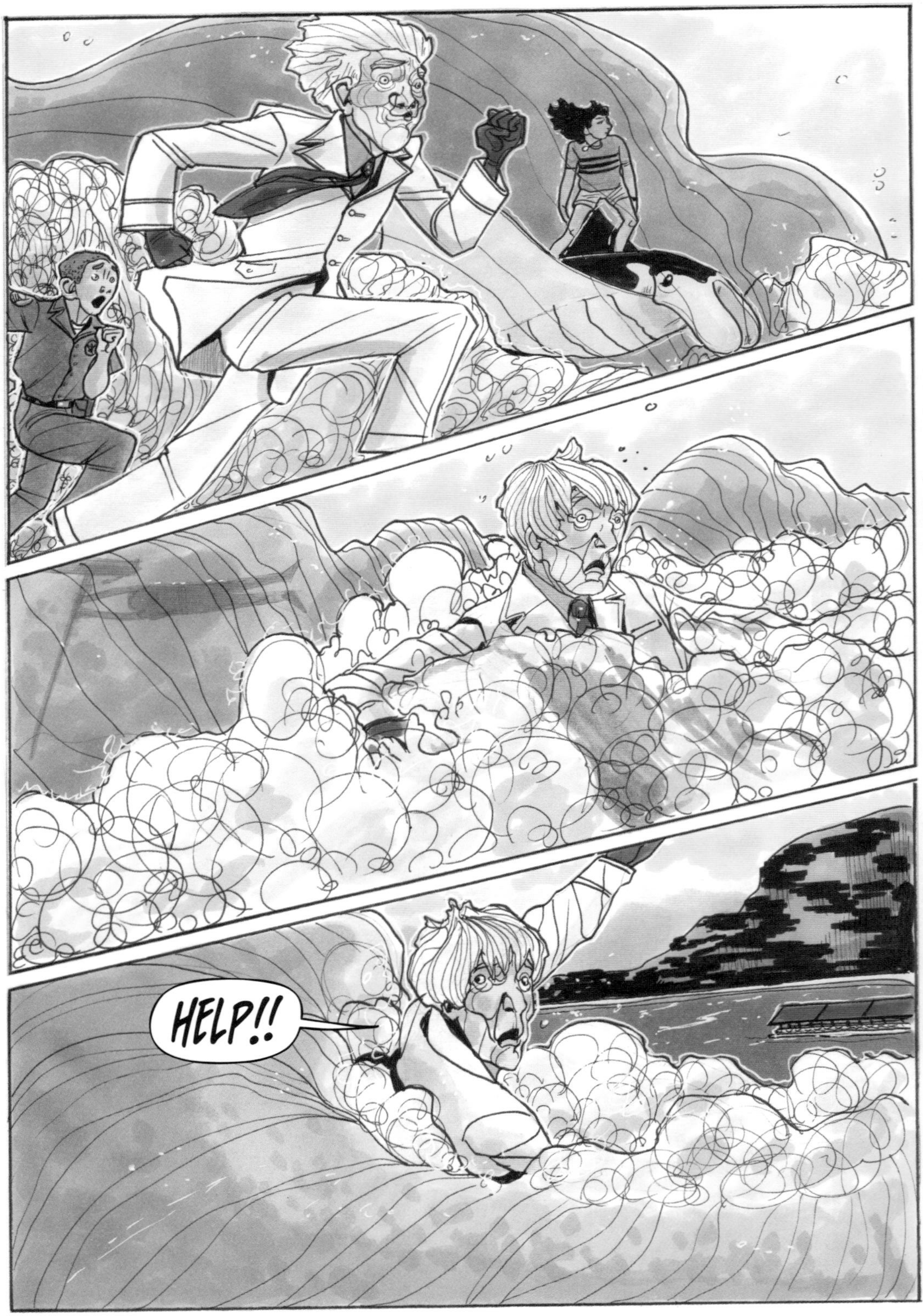
HELP!!

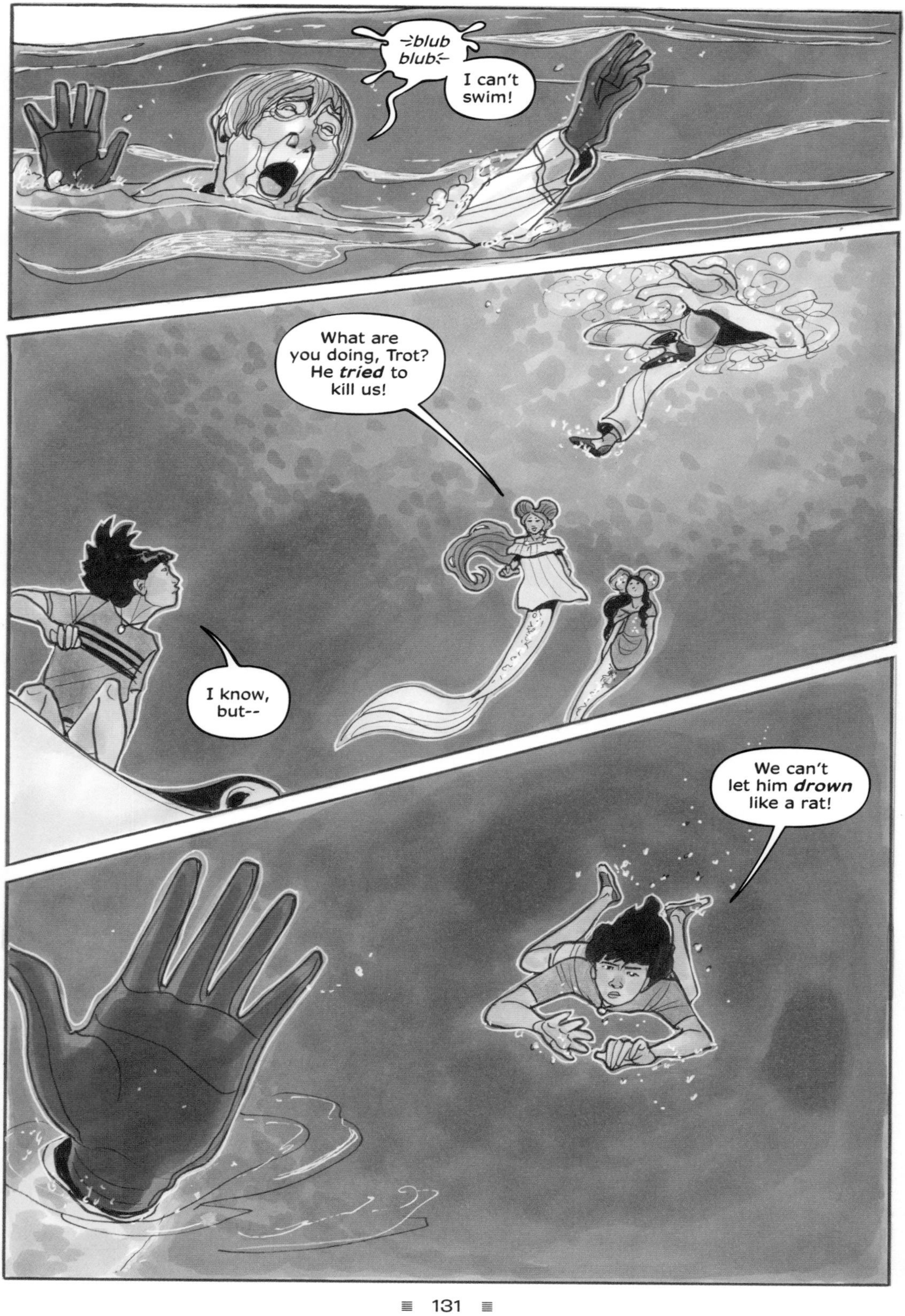

blub blub
I can't swim!
What are you doing, Trot? He *tried* to kill us!
I know, but--
We can't let him *drown* like a rat!

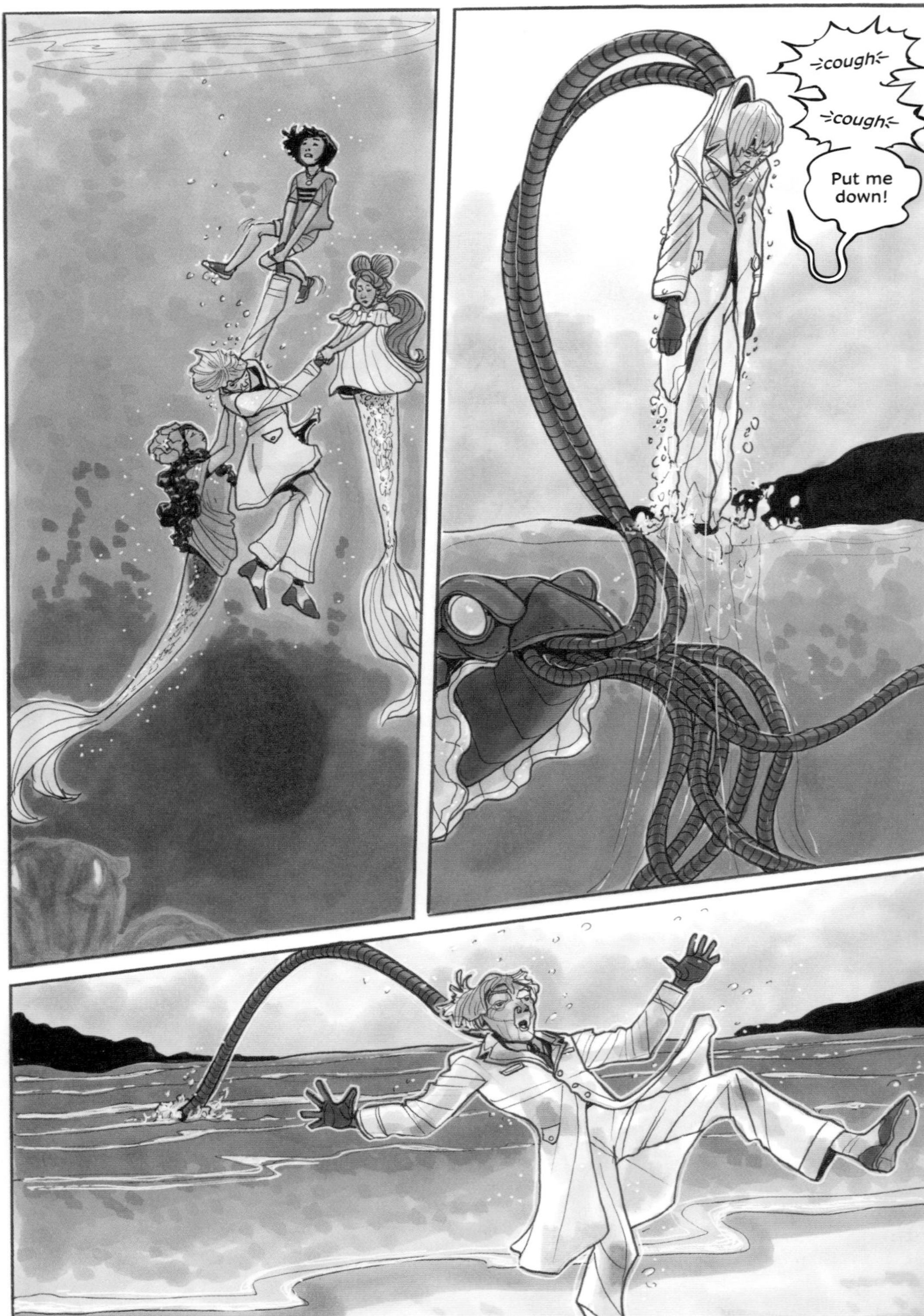

cough
cough
Put me down!

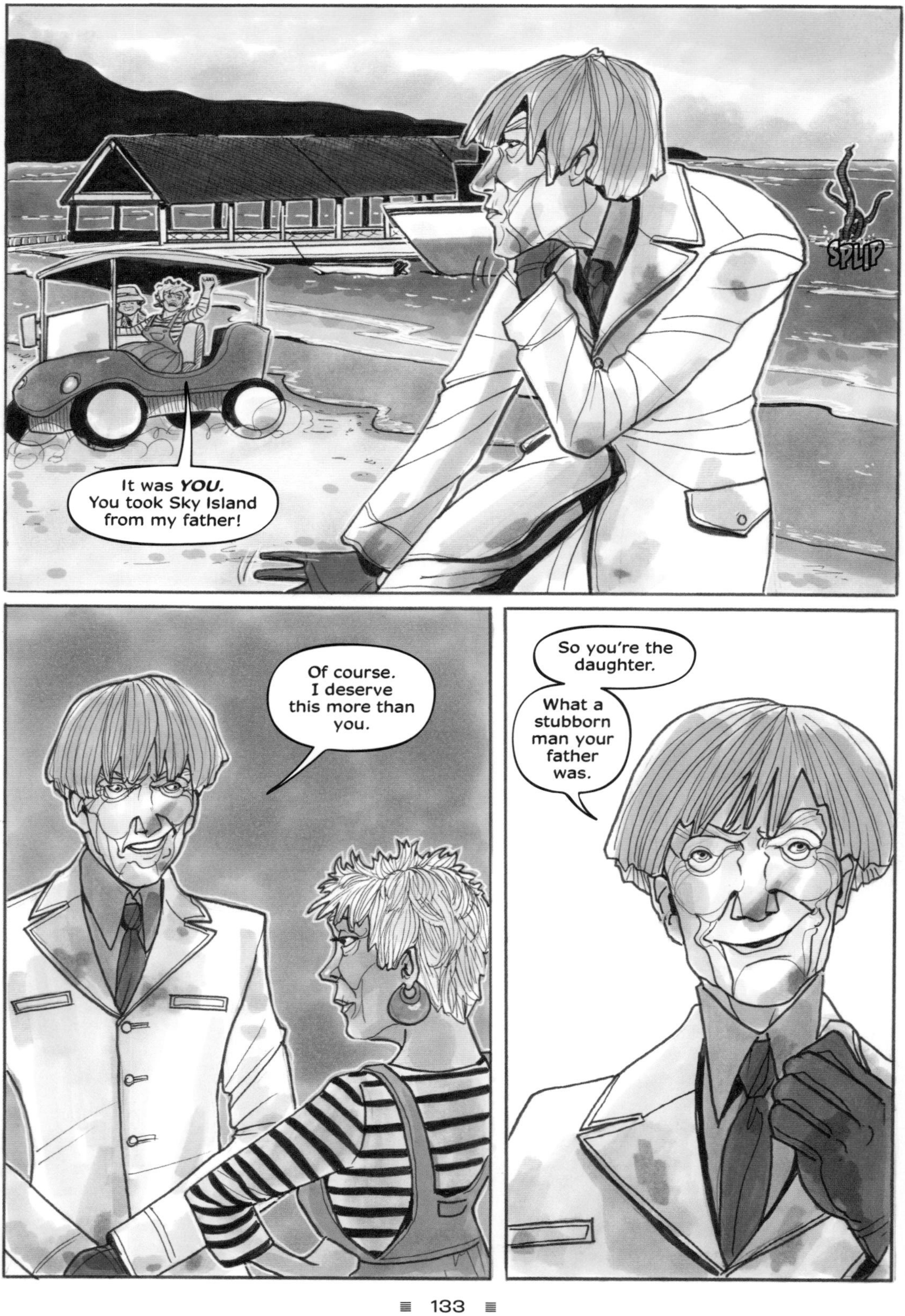
SPLIP
It was **YOU.** You took Sky Island from my father!
Of course. I deserve this more than you.
So you're the daughter.
What a stubborn man your father was.

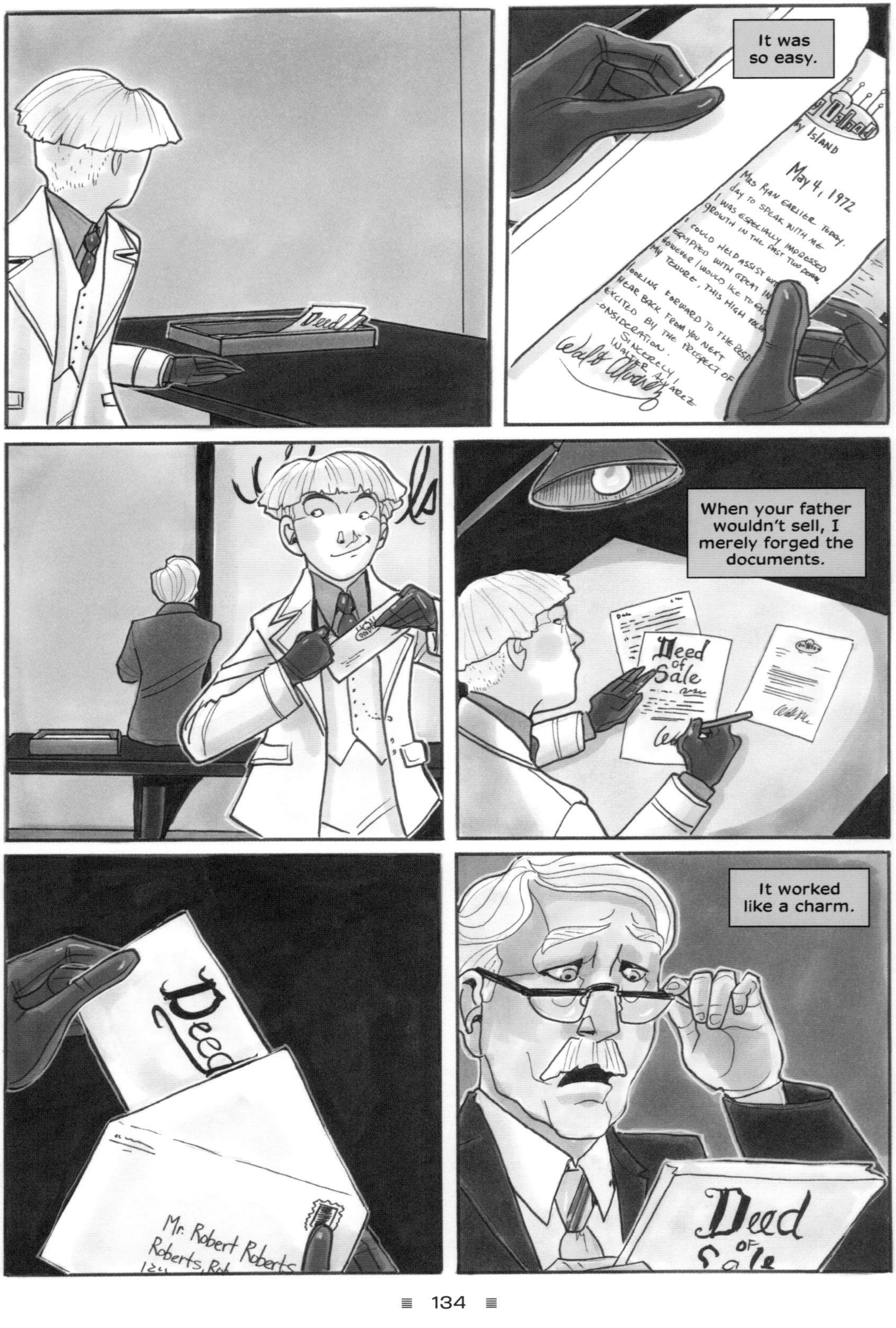
It was so easy.
May 4, 1972
When your father wouldn't sell, I merely forged the documents.
Deed of Sale
Mr. Robert Roberts
It worked like a charm.
Deed of Sale

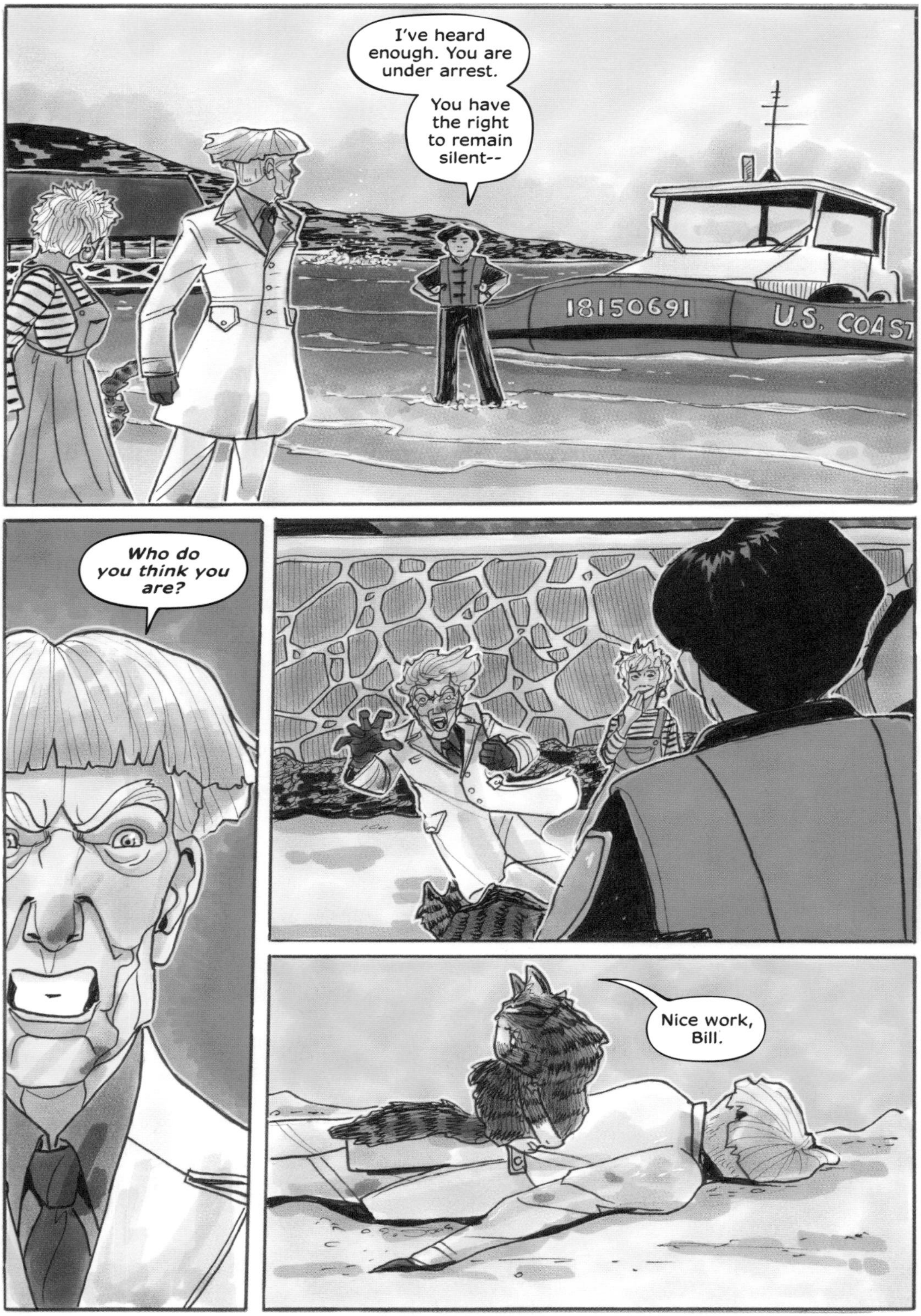
I've heard enough. You are under arrest.
You have the right to remain silent--
18150691
U.S. COAST
Who do you think you are?
Nice work, Bill.

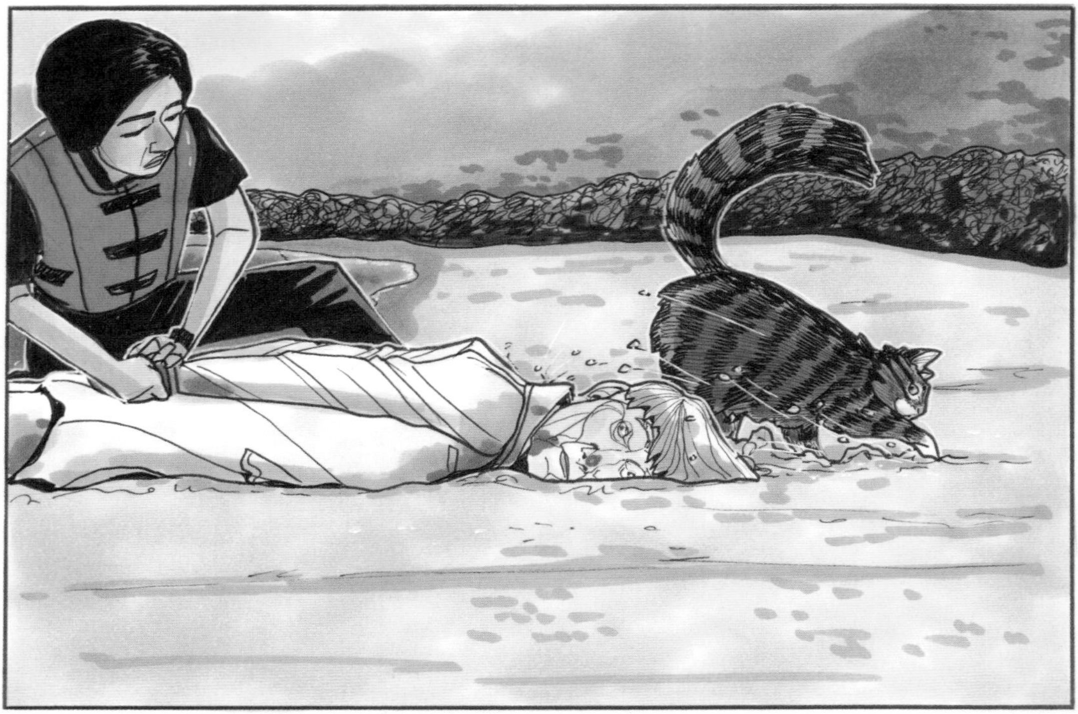

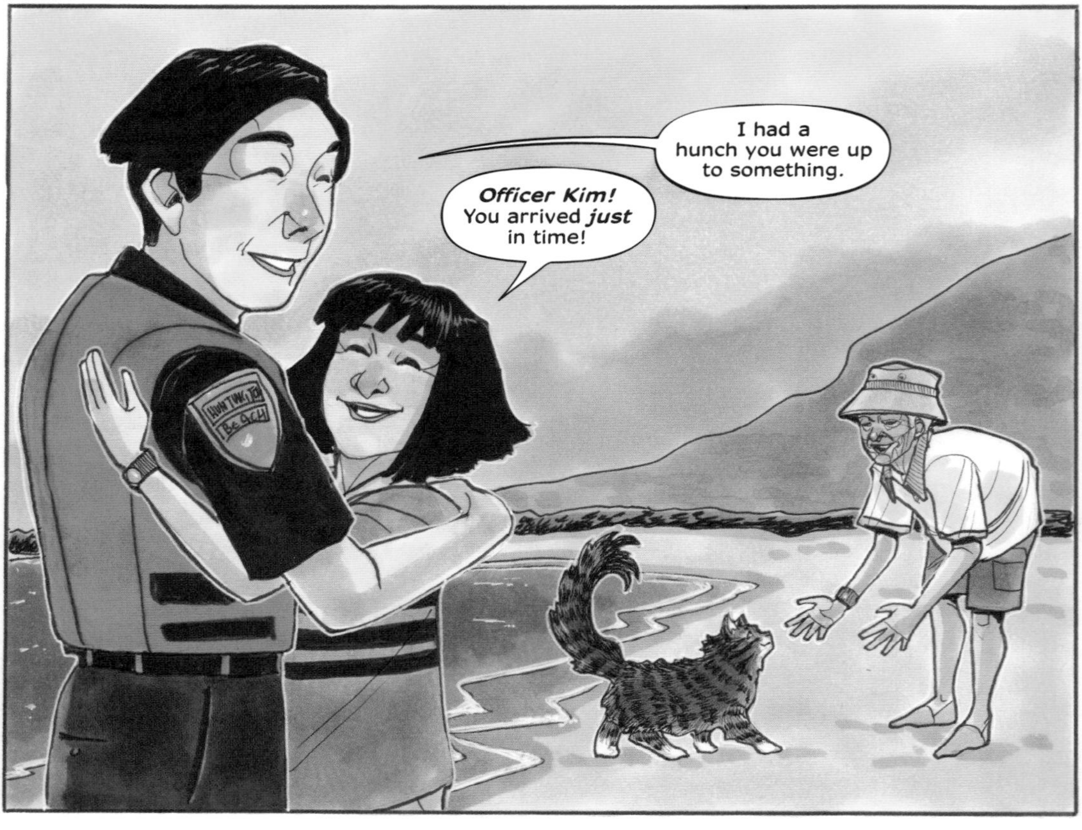
Officer Kim! You arrived *just* in time!
I had a hunch you were up to something.
HUNTINGTON BEACH

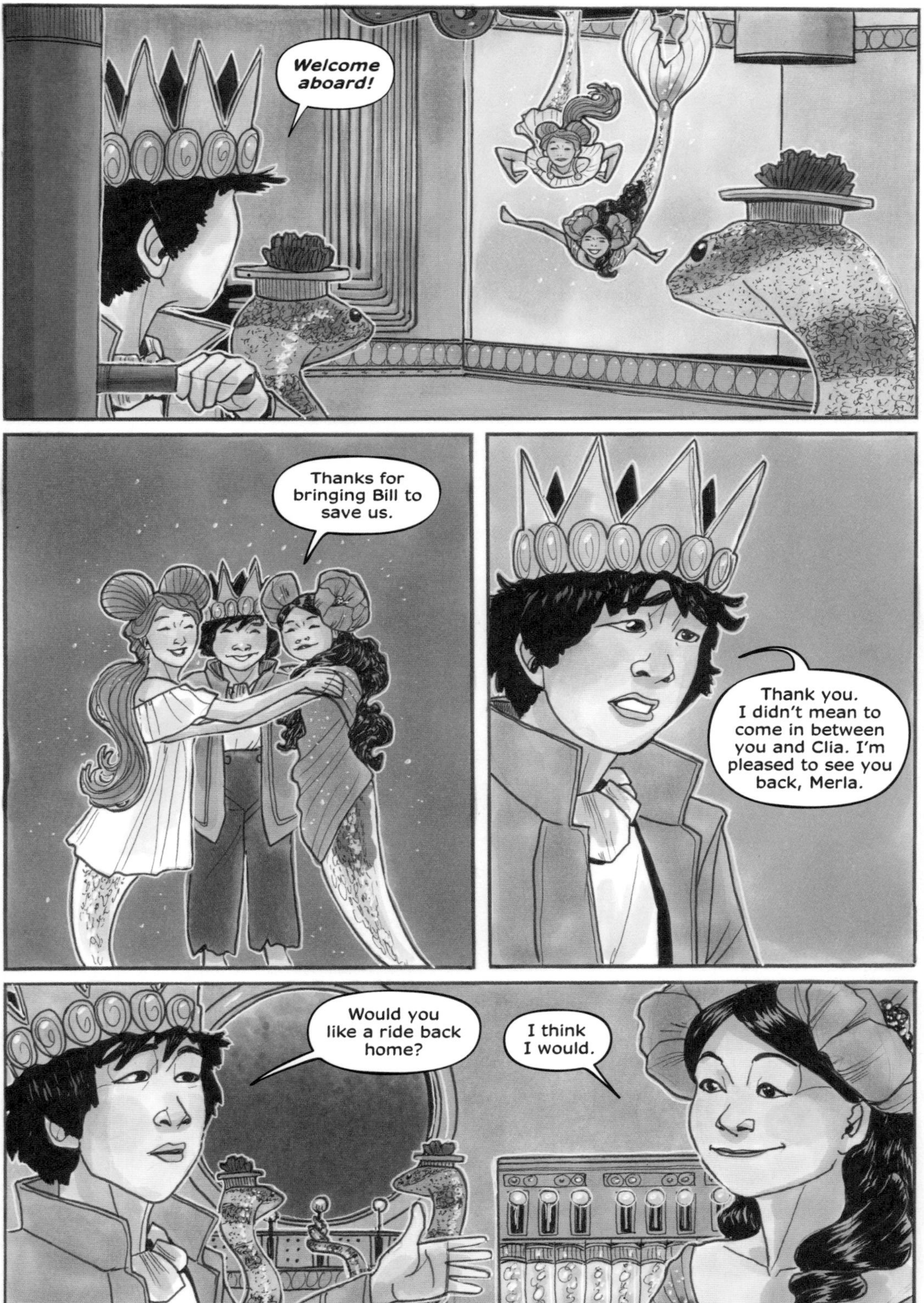
Welcome aboard!
Thanks for bringing Bill to save us.
Thank you. I didn't mean to come in between you and Clia. I'm pleased to see you back, Merla.
Would you like a ride back home?
I think I would.

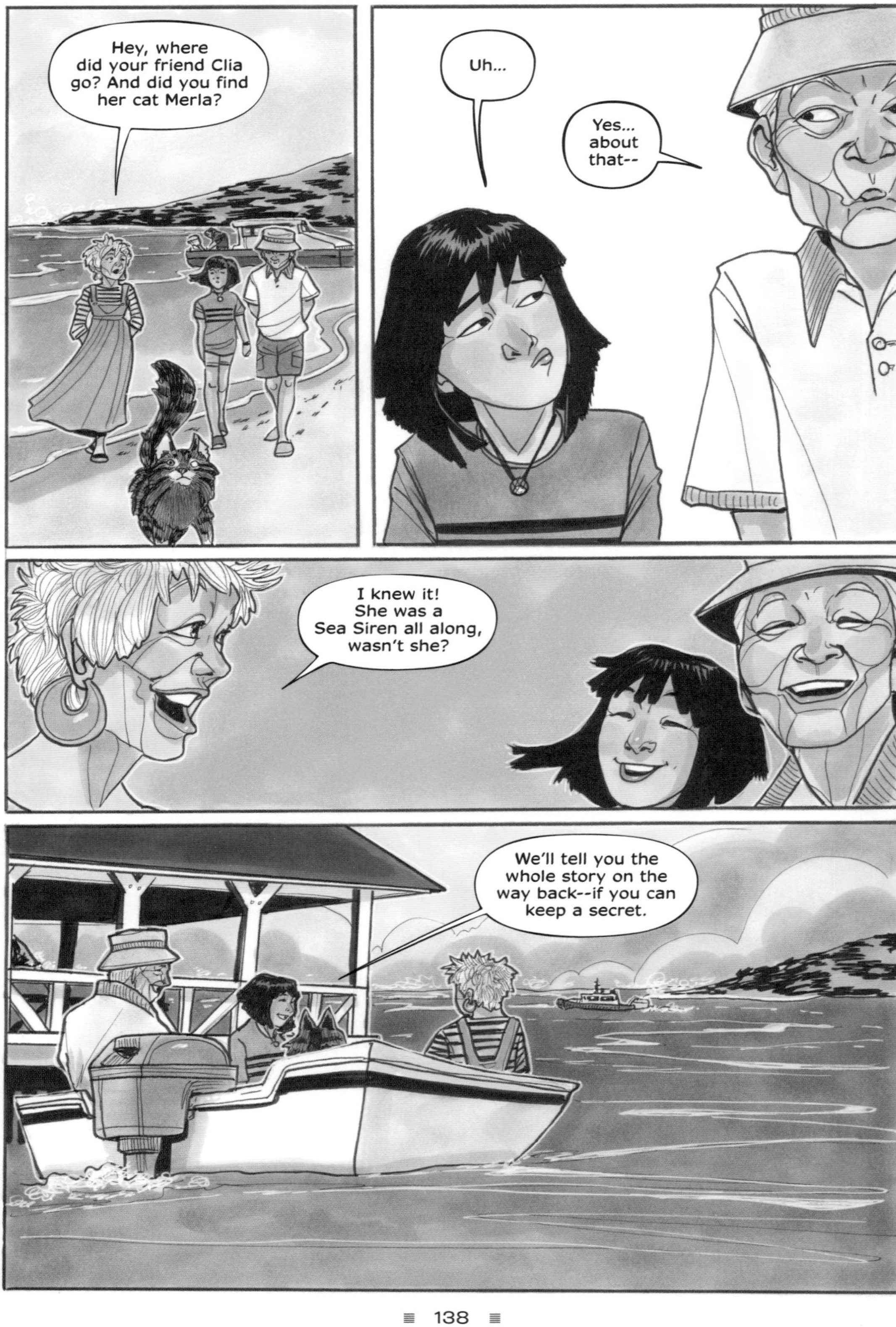
Hey, where did your friend Clia go? And did you find her cat Merla?
Uh...
Yes... about that--
I knew it! She was a Sea Siren all along, wasn't she?
We'll tell you the whole story on the way back--if you can keep a secret.

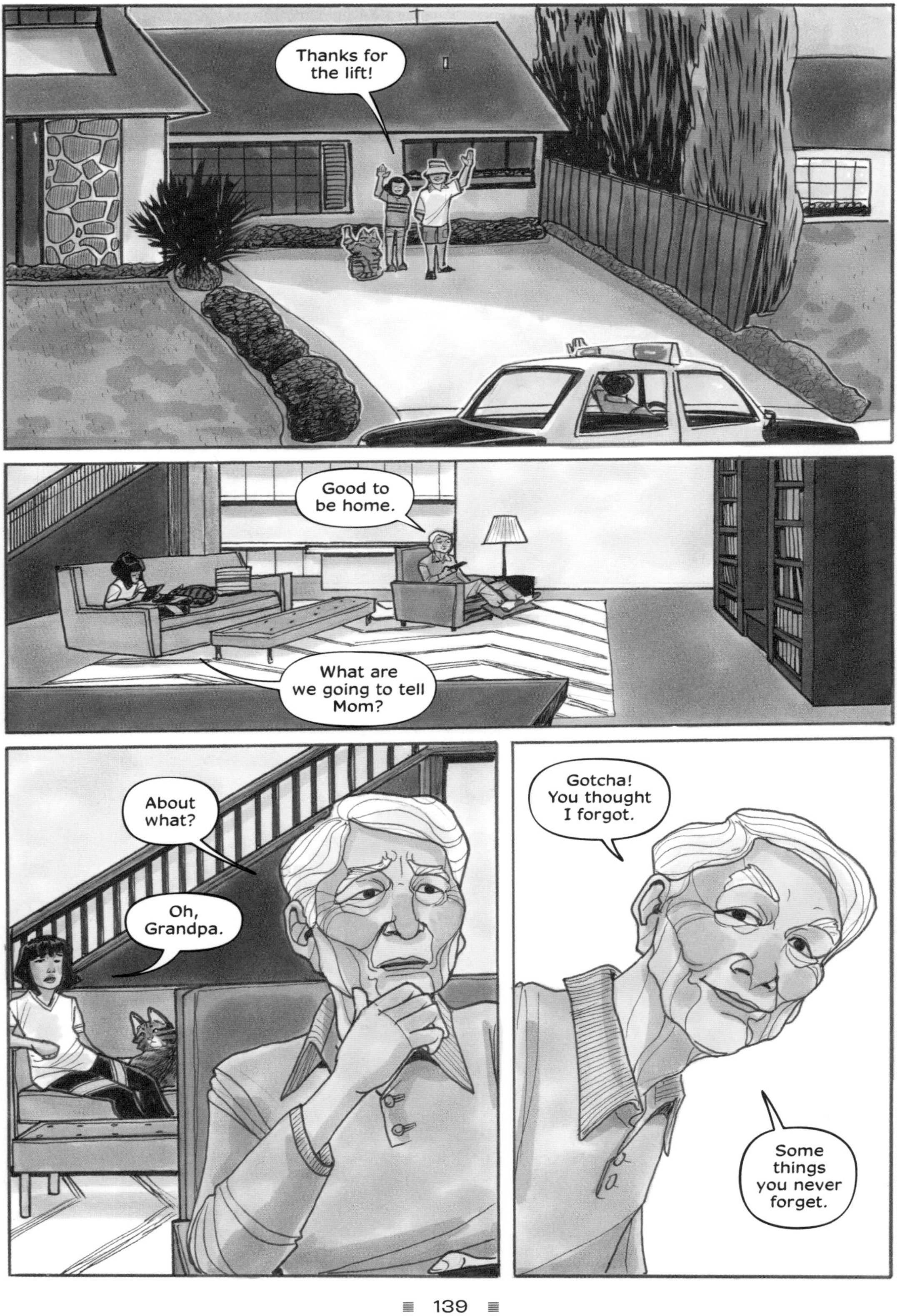
Thanks for the lift!
Good to be home.
What are we going to tell Mom?
About what?
Oh, Grandpa.
Gotcha! You thought I forgot.
Some things you never forget.

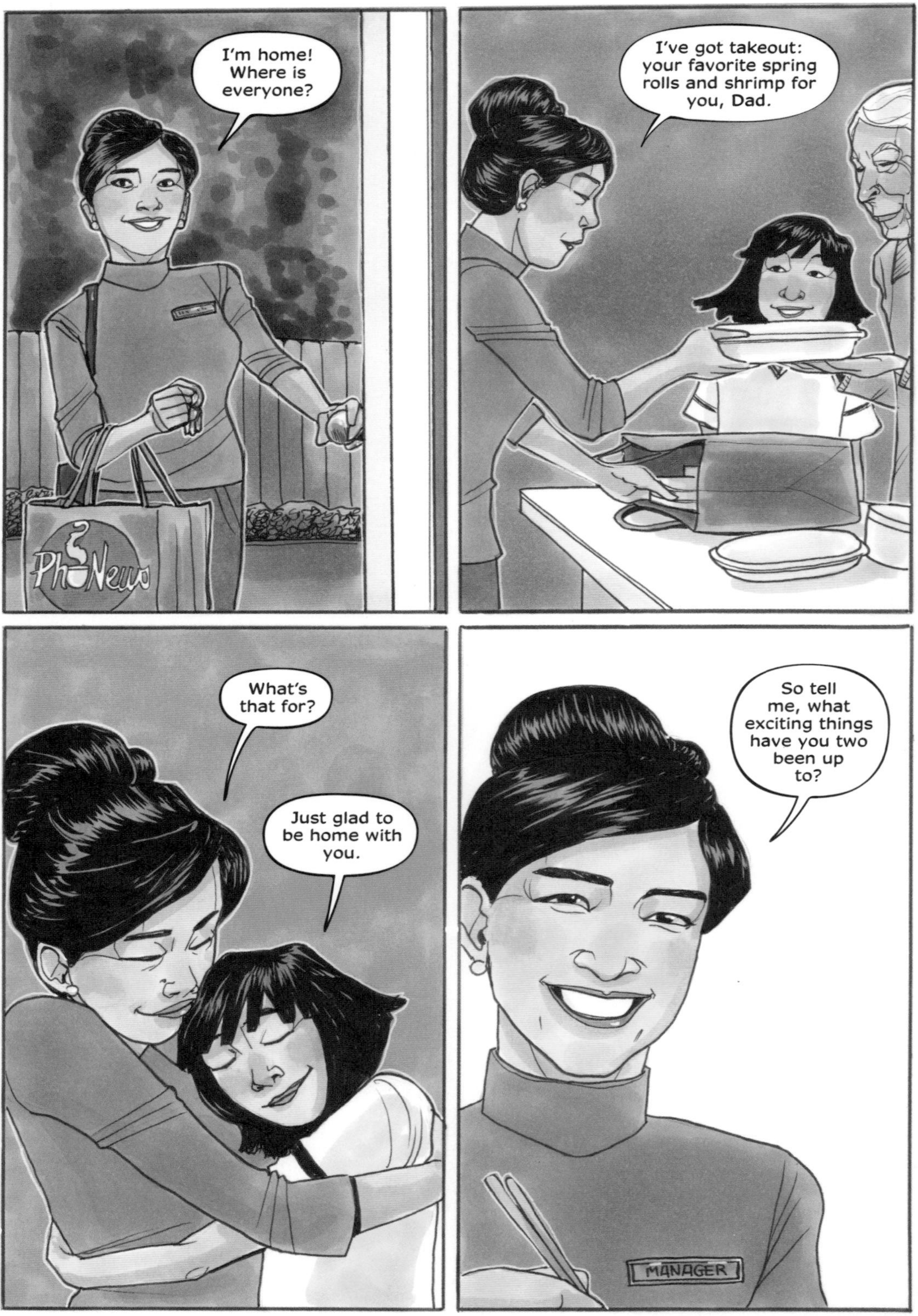
I'm home! Where is everyone?
I've got takeout: your favorite spring rolls and shrimp for you, Dad.
What's that for?
Just glad to be home with you.
So tell me, what exciting things have you two been up to?
MANAGER

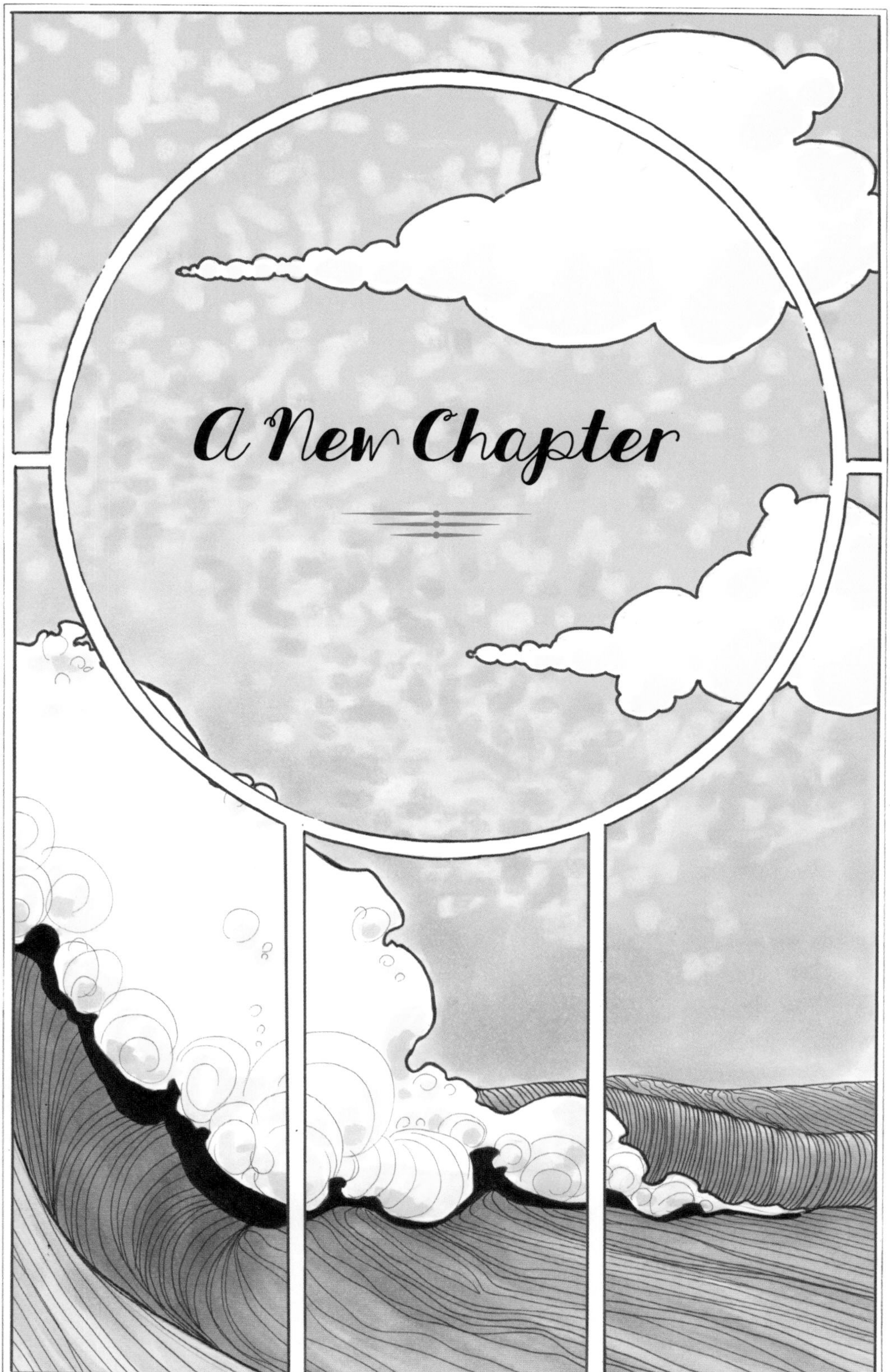
A New Chapter

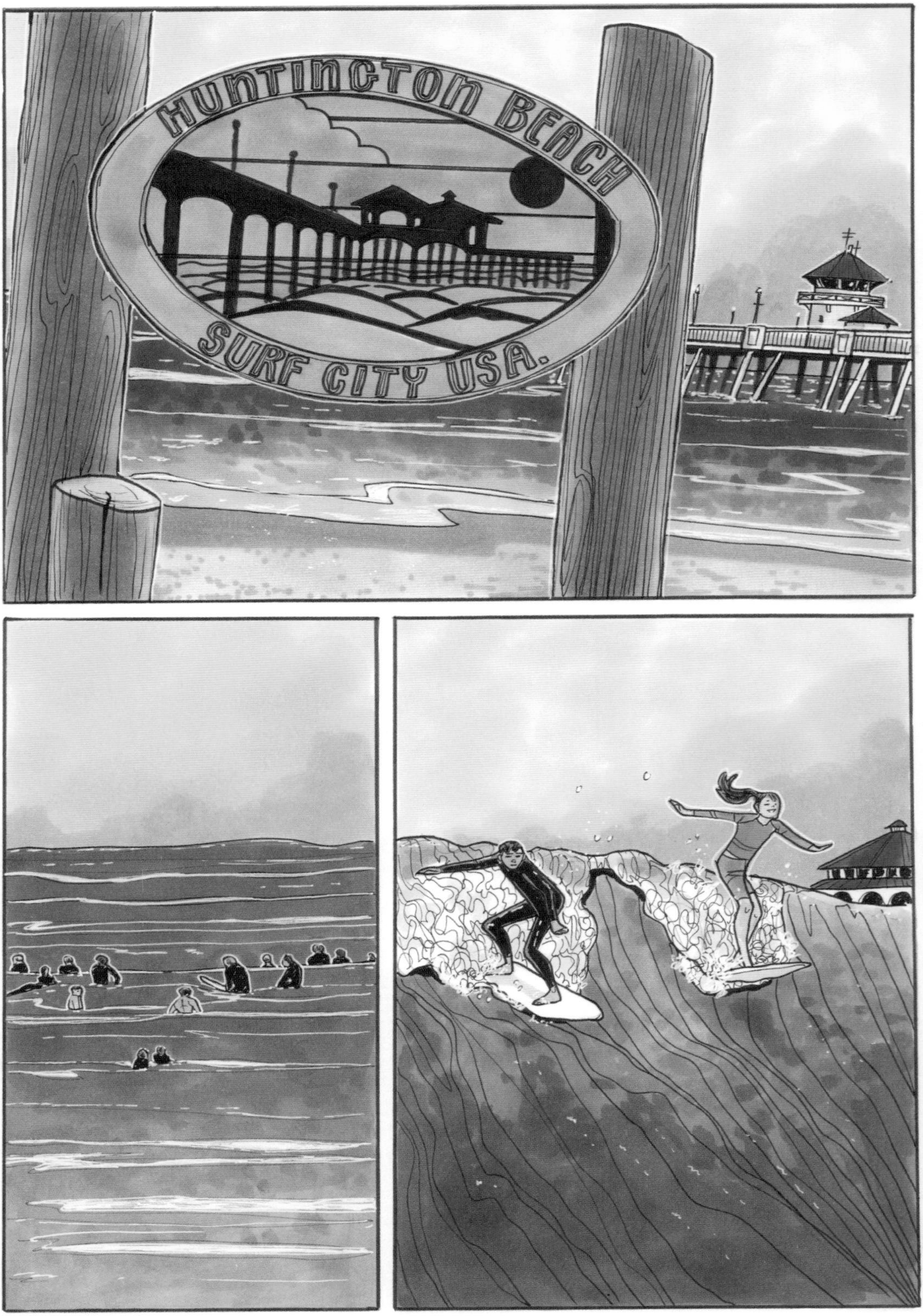
HUNTINGTON BEACH
SURF CITY USA.

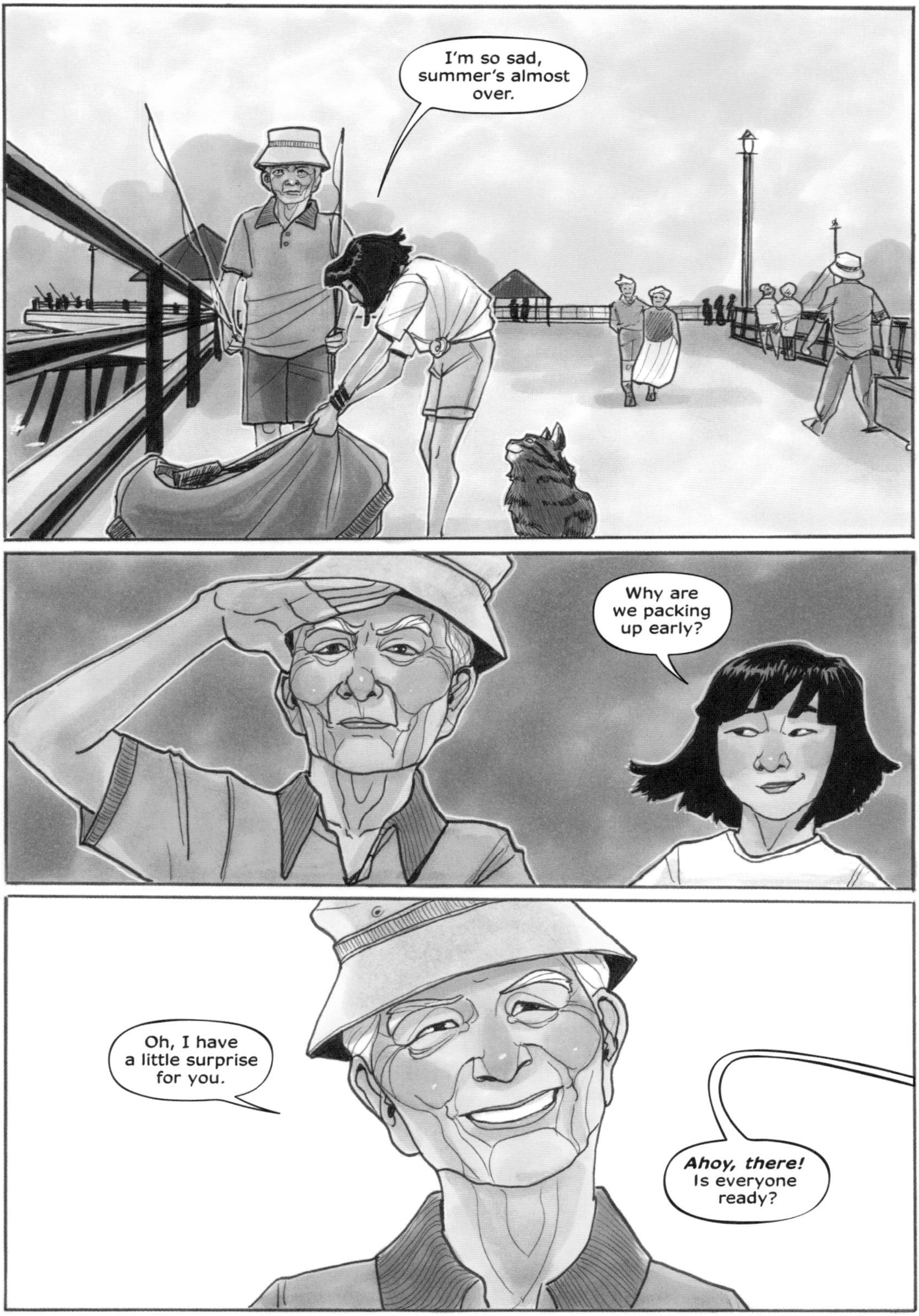
I'm so sad, summer's almost over.
Why are we packing up early?
Oh, I have a little surprise for you.
Ahoy, there! Is everyone ready?

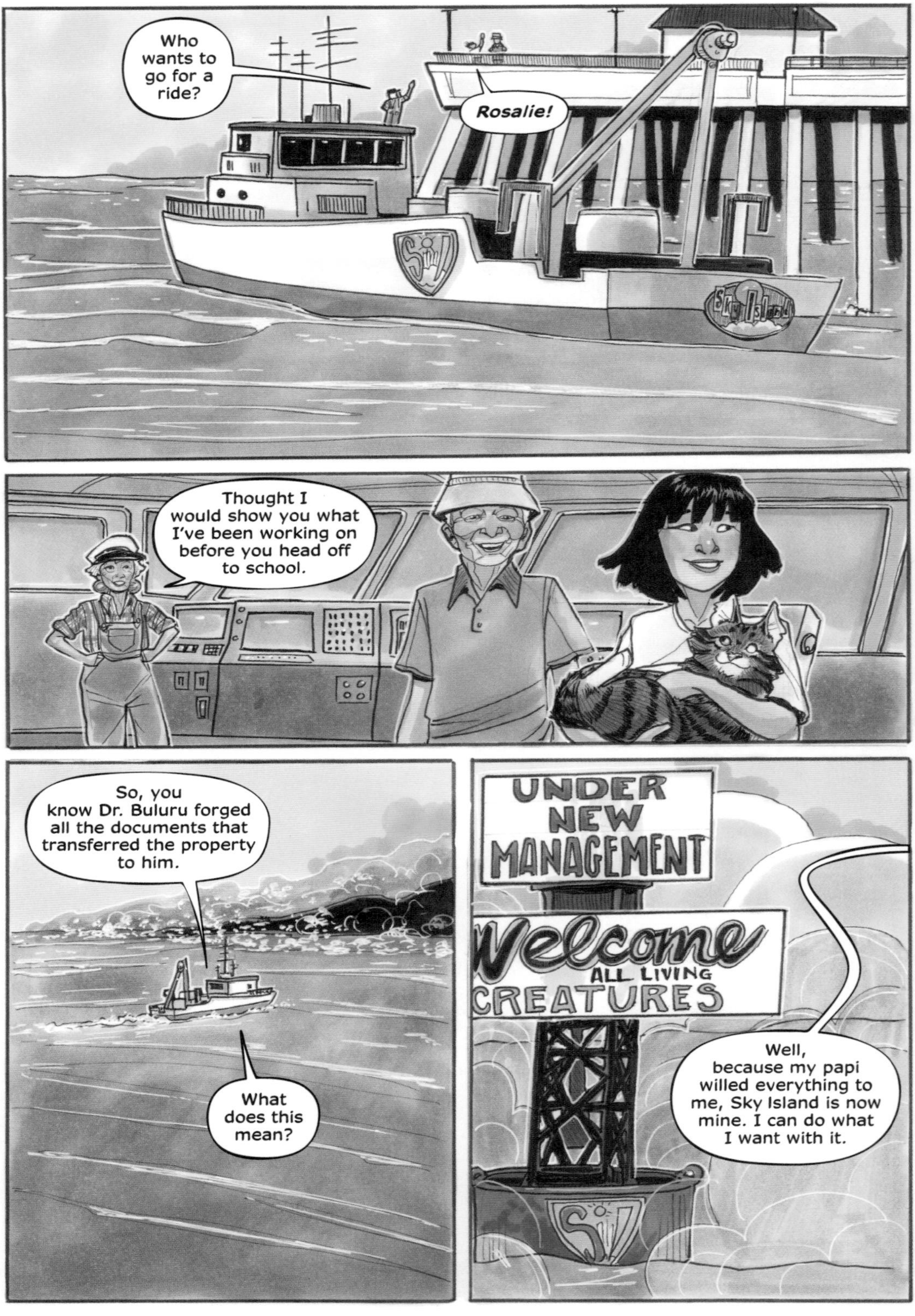

Who wants to go for a ride?
Rosalie!
Thought I would show you what I've been working on before you head off to school.
So, you know Dr. Buluru forged all the documents that transferred the property to him.
What does this mean?
UNDER NEW MANAGEMENT
Welcome ALL LIVING CREATURES
Well, because my papi willed everything to me, Sky Island is now mine. I can do what I want with it.

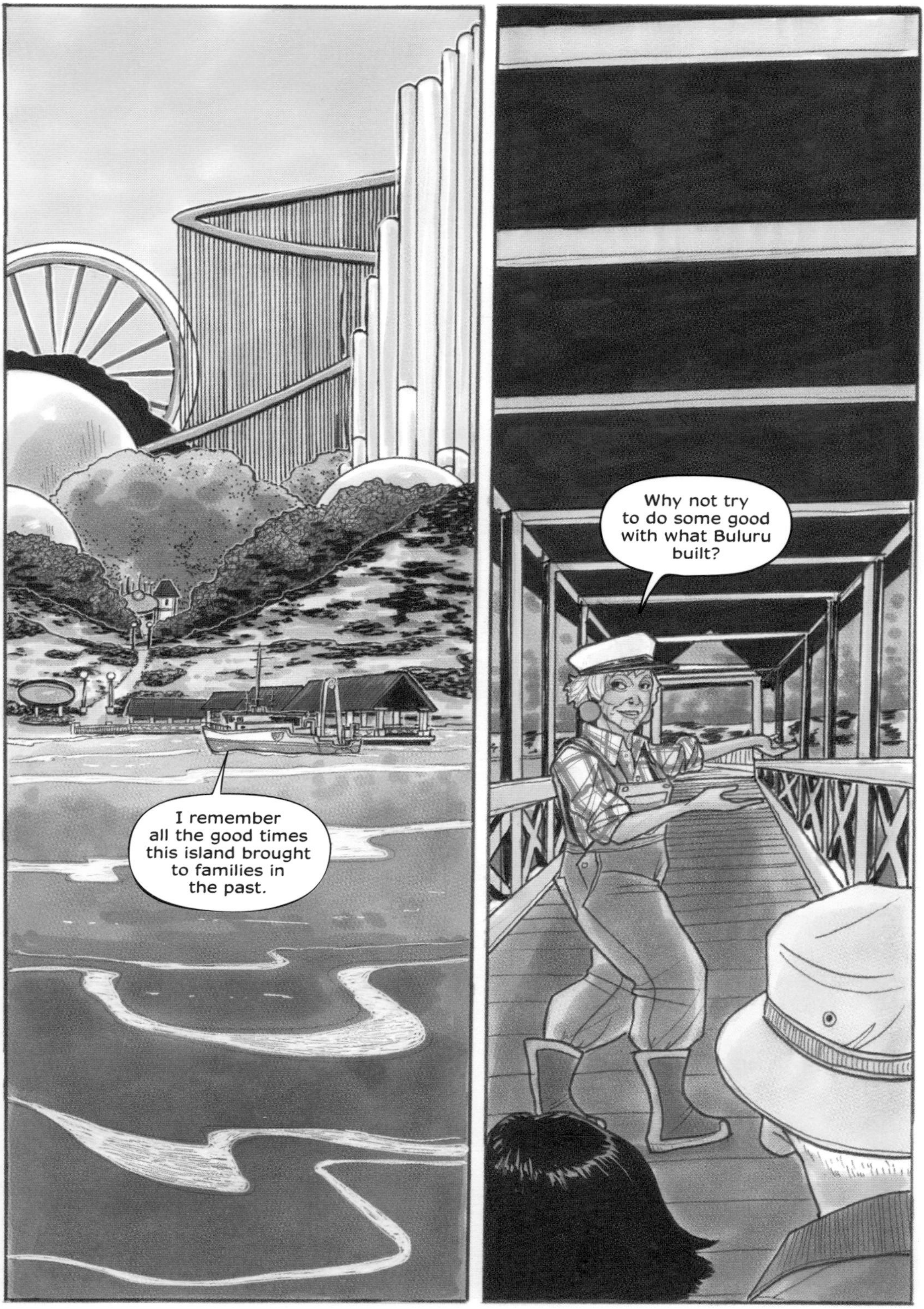
I remember all the good times this island brought to families in the past.
Why not try to do some good with what Buluru built?

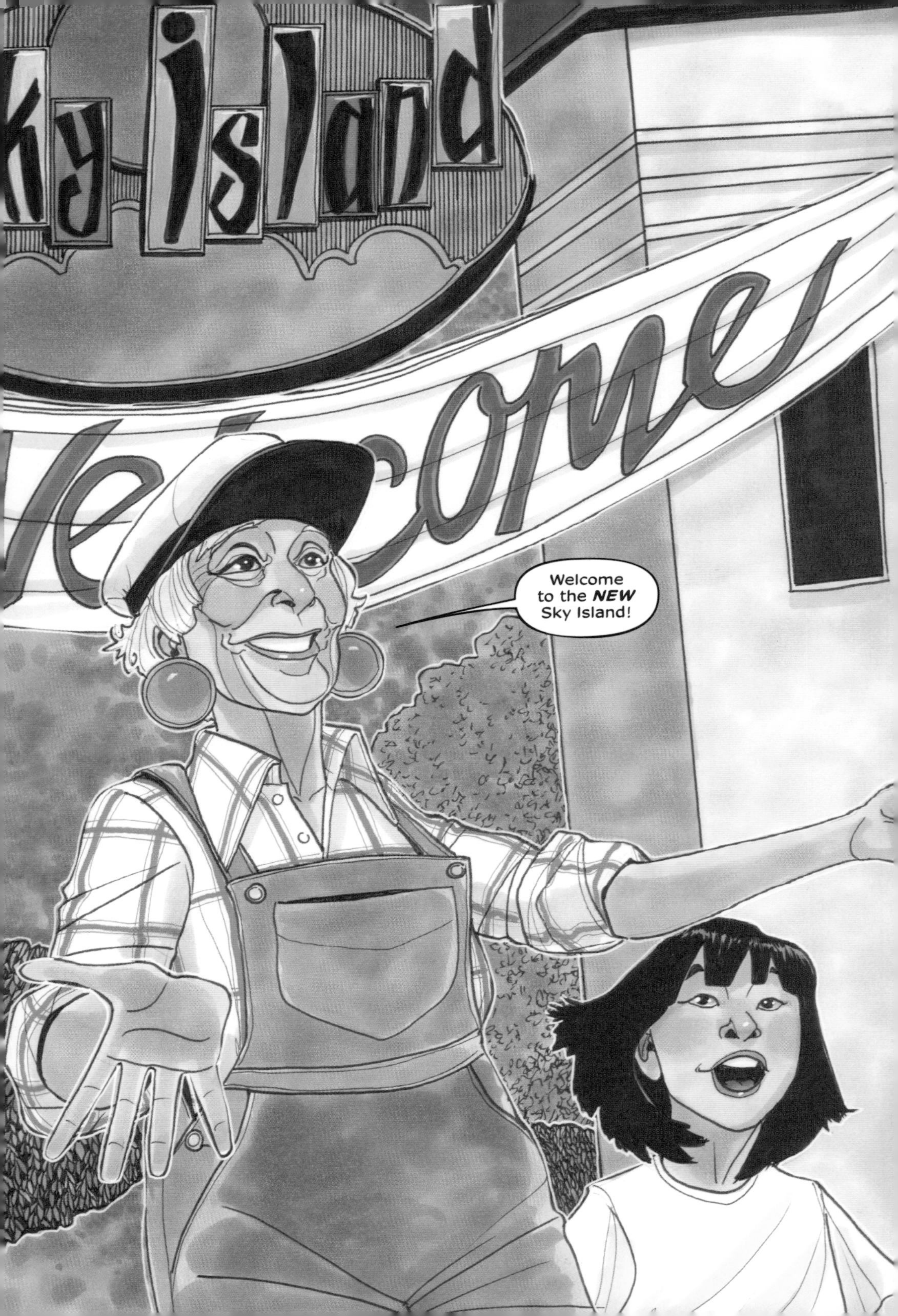
ky island
welcome
Welcome to the ***NEW*** Sky Island!

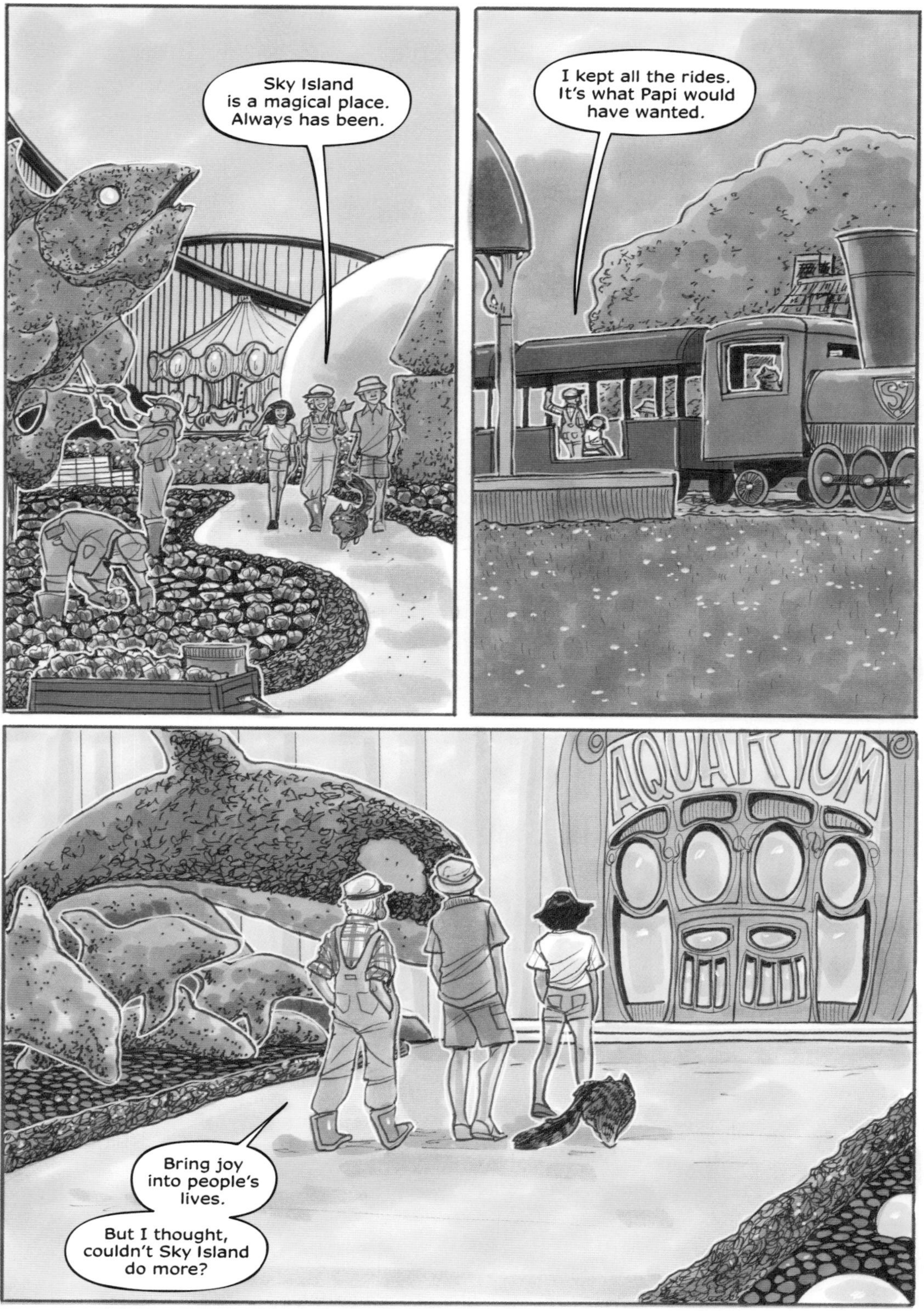

Sky Island is a magical place. Always has been.
I kept all the rides. It's what Papi would have wanted.
AQUARIUM
Bring joy into people's lives.
But I thought, couldn't Sky Island do more?

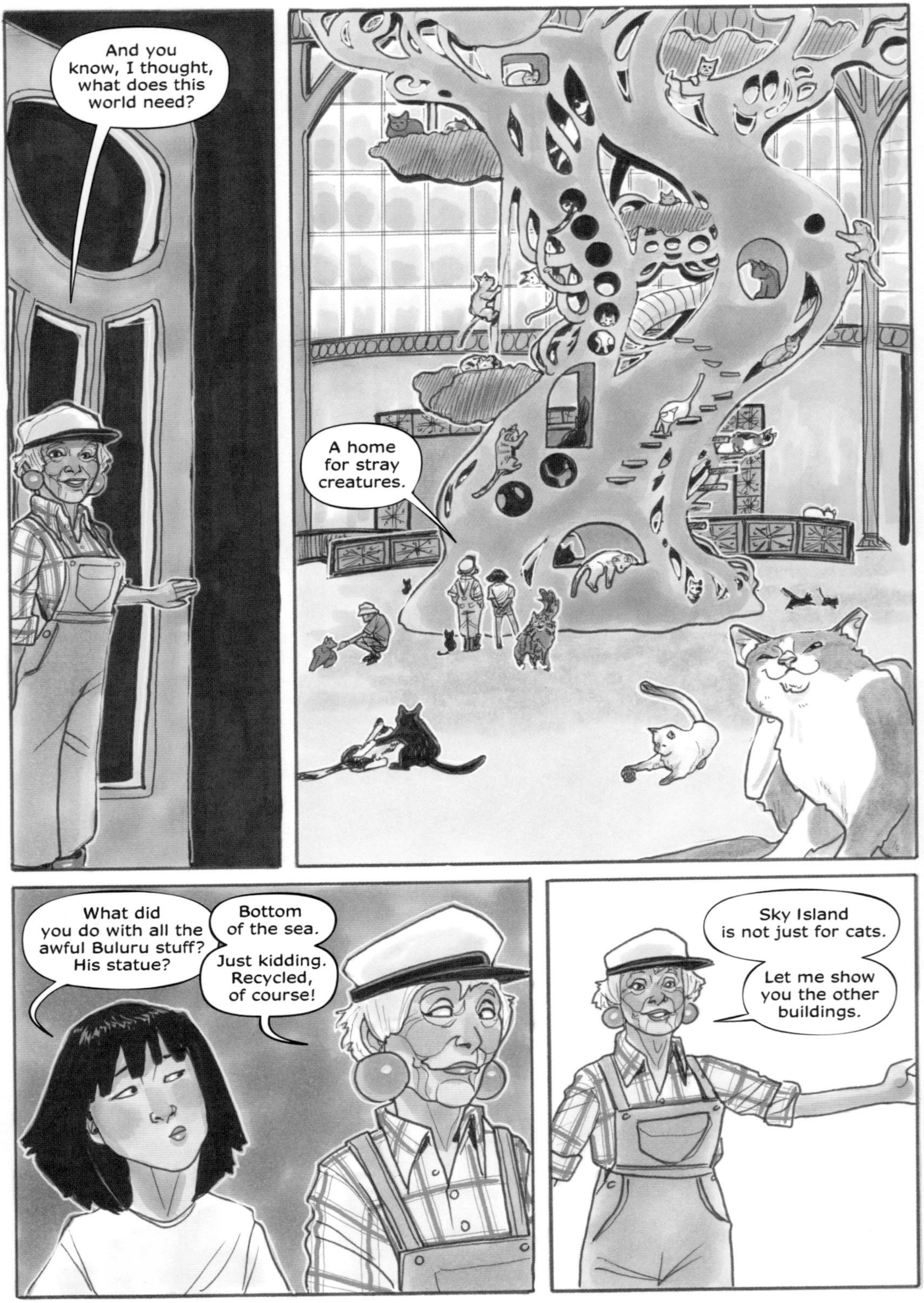

And you know, I thought, what does this world need?
A home for stray creatures.
What did you do with all the awful Buluru stuff? His statue?
Bottom of the sea.
Just kidding. Recycled, of course!
Sky Island is not just for cats.
Let me show you the other buildings.

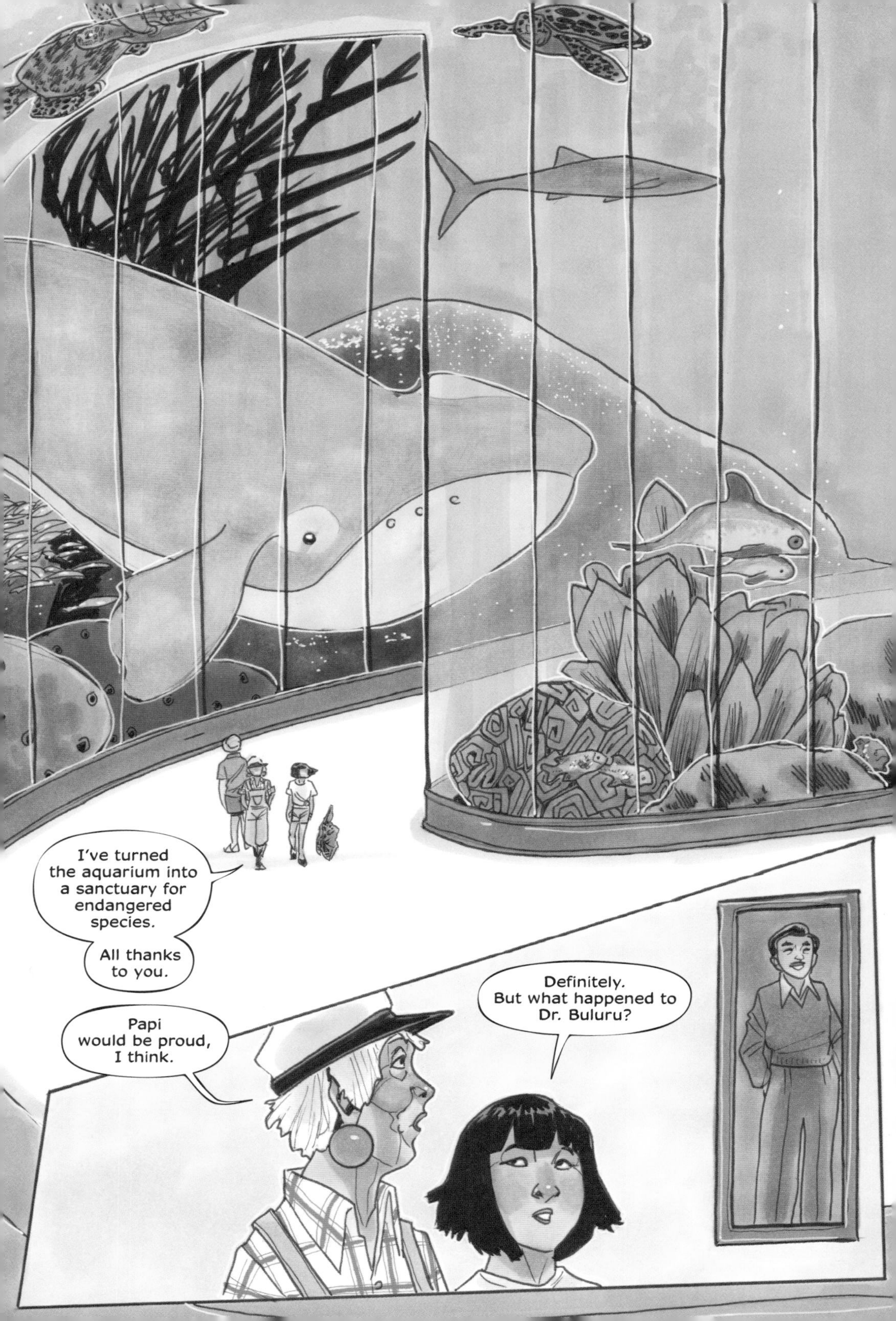
I've turned the aquarium into a sanctuary for endangered species.
All thanks to you.
Papi would be proud, I think.
Definitely. But what happened to Dr. Buluru?

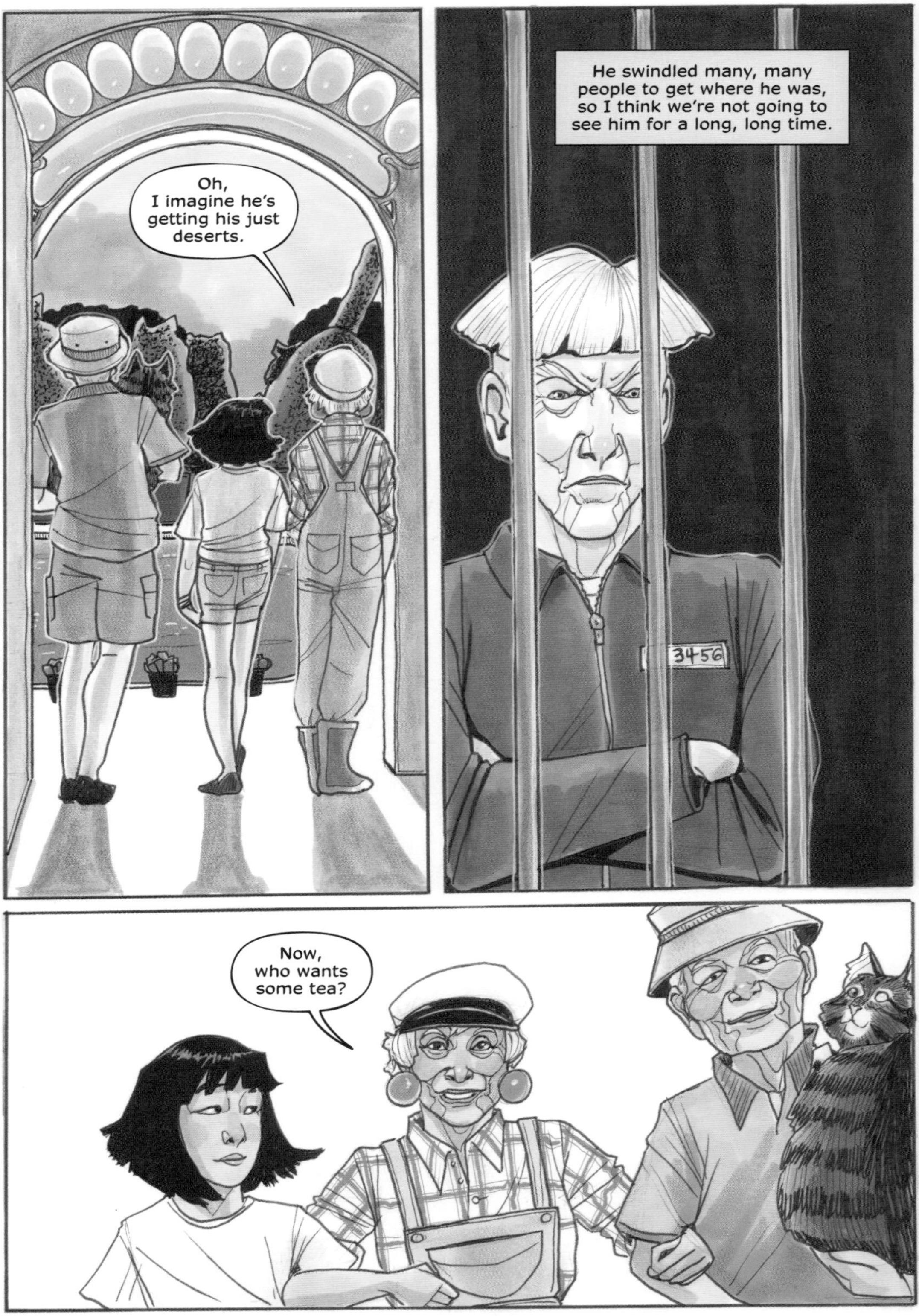
Oh, I imagine he's getting his just deserts.
He swindled many, many people to get where he was, so I think we're not going to see him for a long, long time.
3456
Now, who wants some tea?

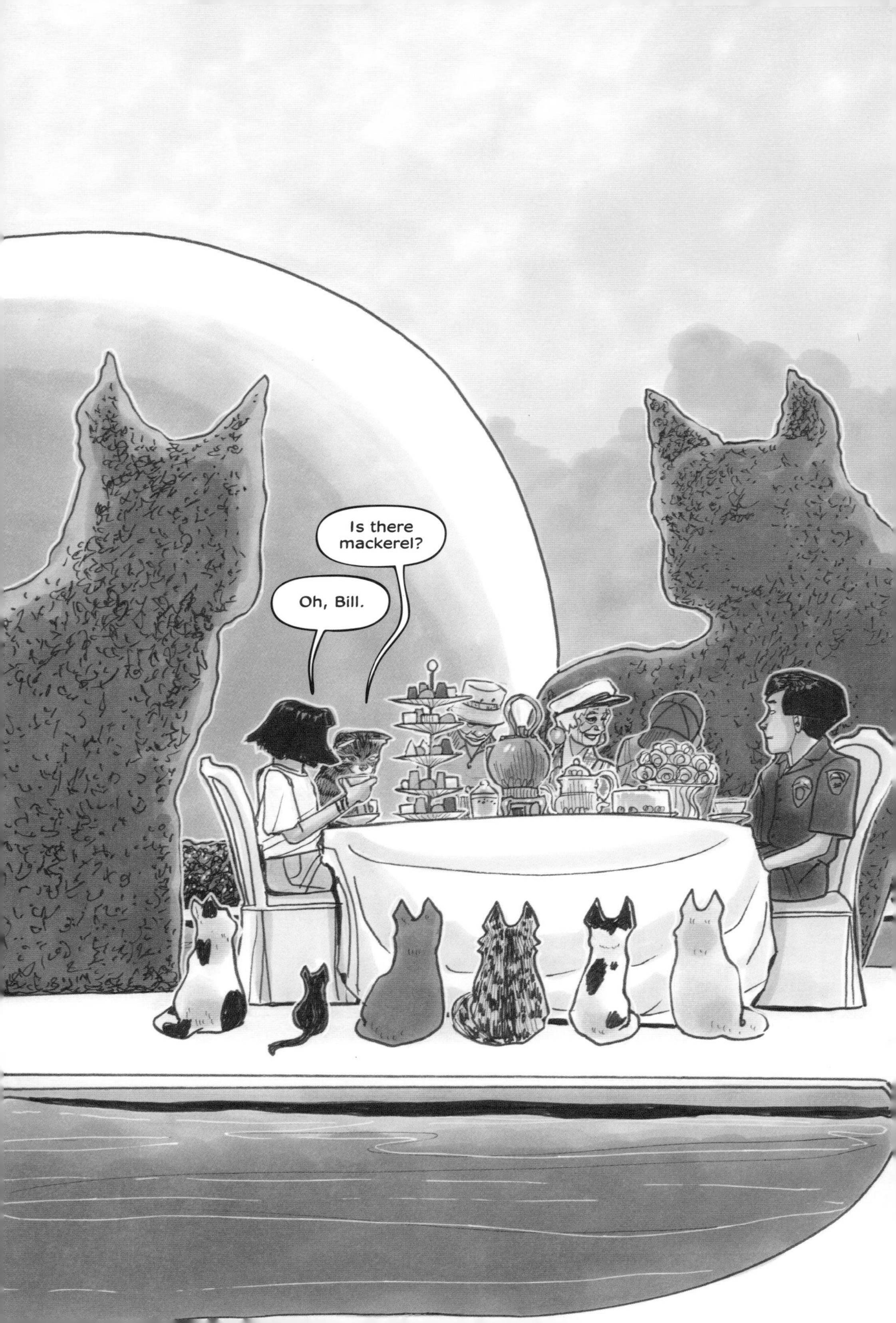

Oh, Bill.
Is there mackerel?

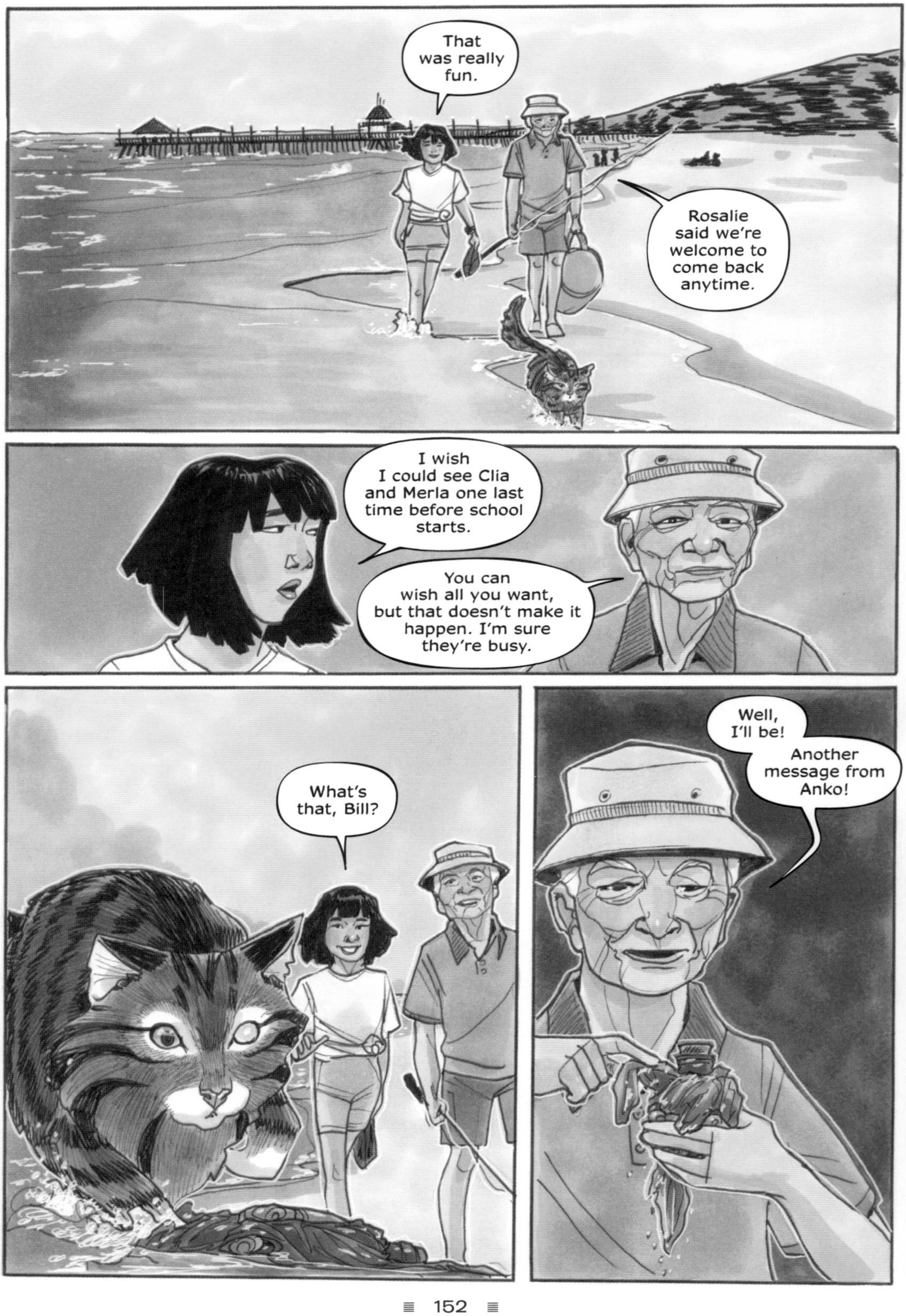
That was really fun.
Rosalie said we're welcome to come back anytime.
I wish I could see Clia and Merla one last time before school starts.
You can wish all you want, but that doesn't make it happen. I'm sure they're busy.
What's that, Bill?
Well, I'll be!
Another message from Anko!

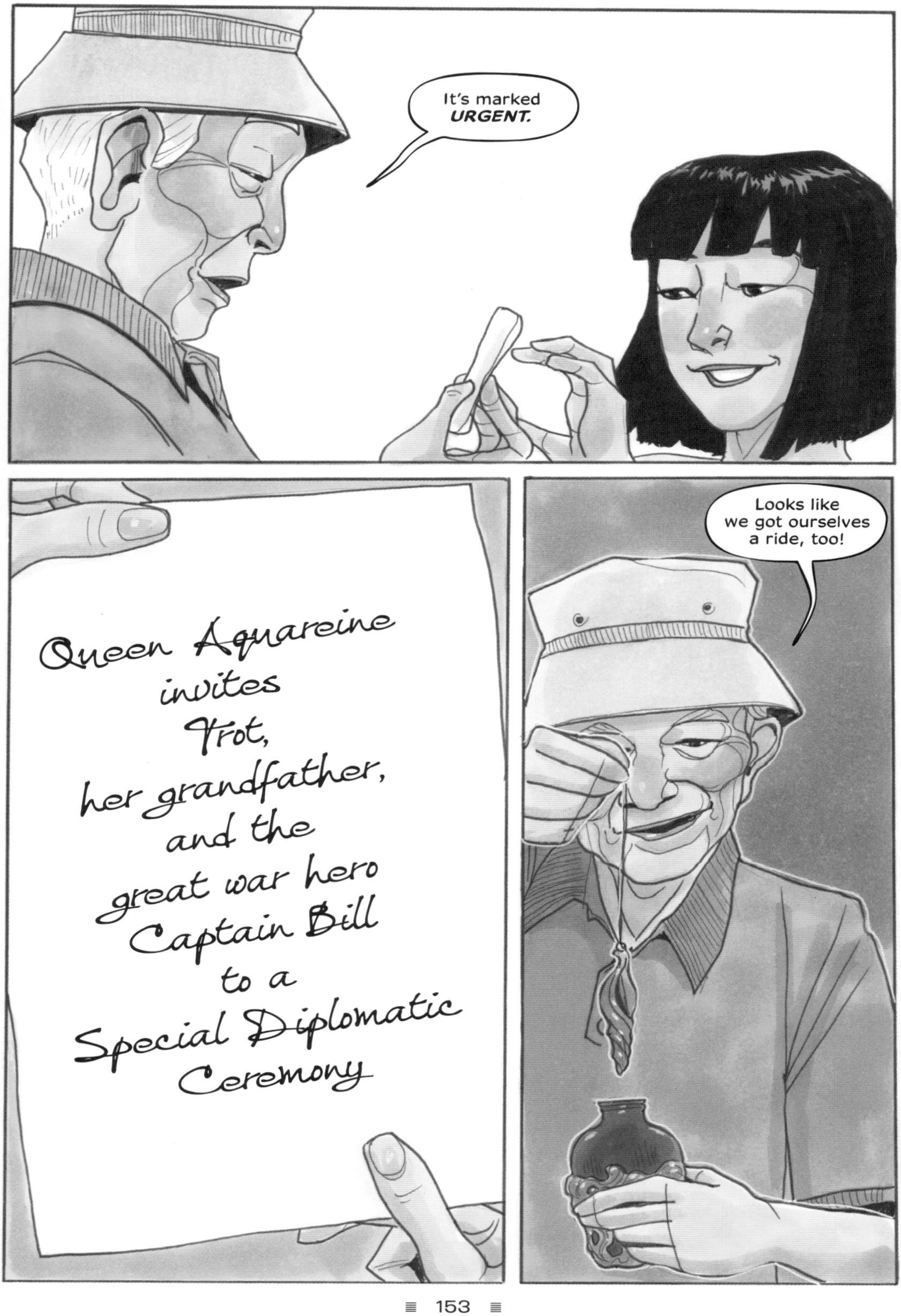
It's marked URGENT.
Queen Aquareine invites Trot, her grandfather, and the great war hero Captain Bill to a Special Diplomatic Ceremony
Looks like we got ourselves a ride, too!

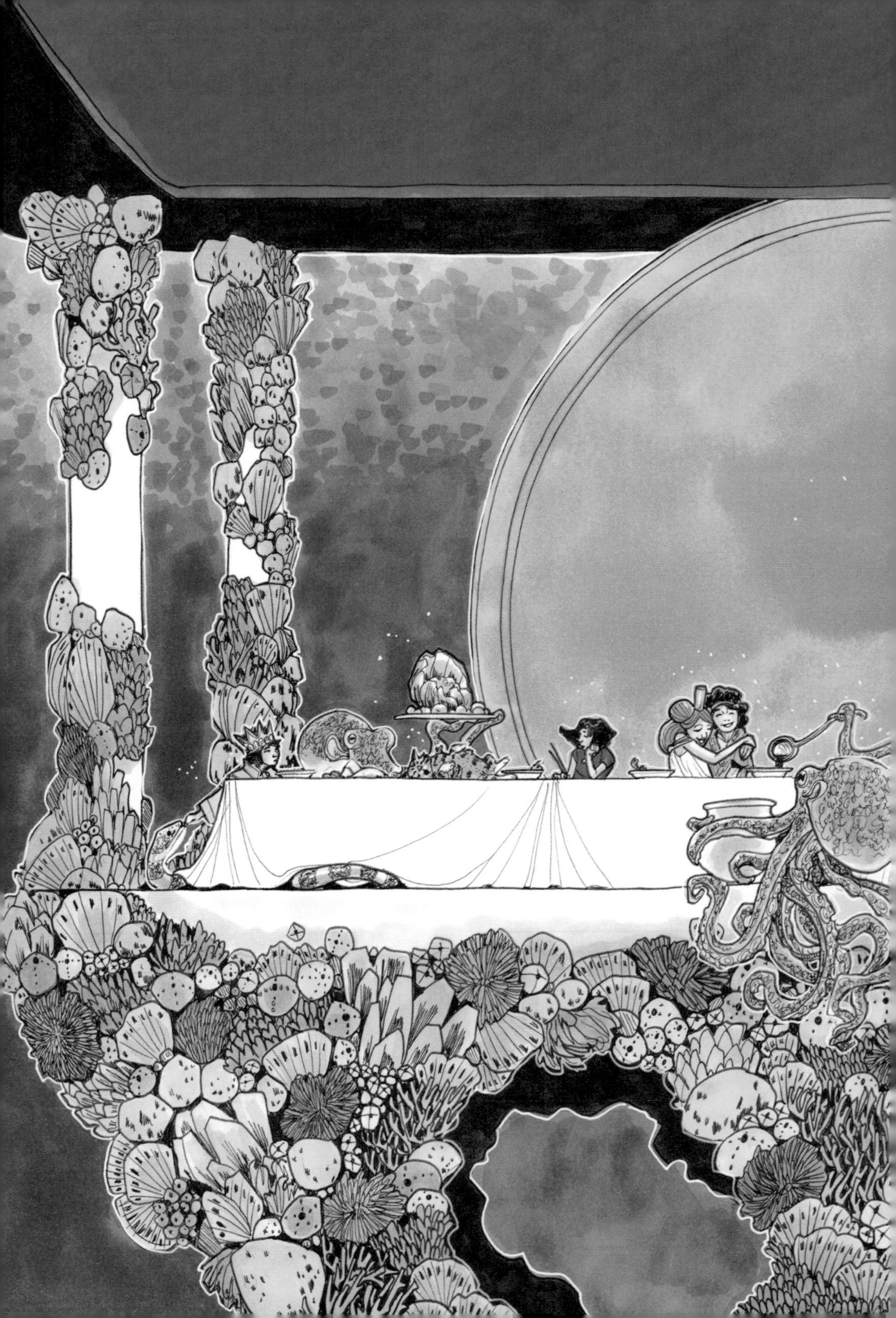

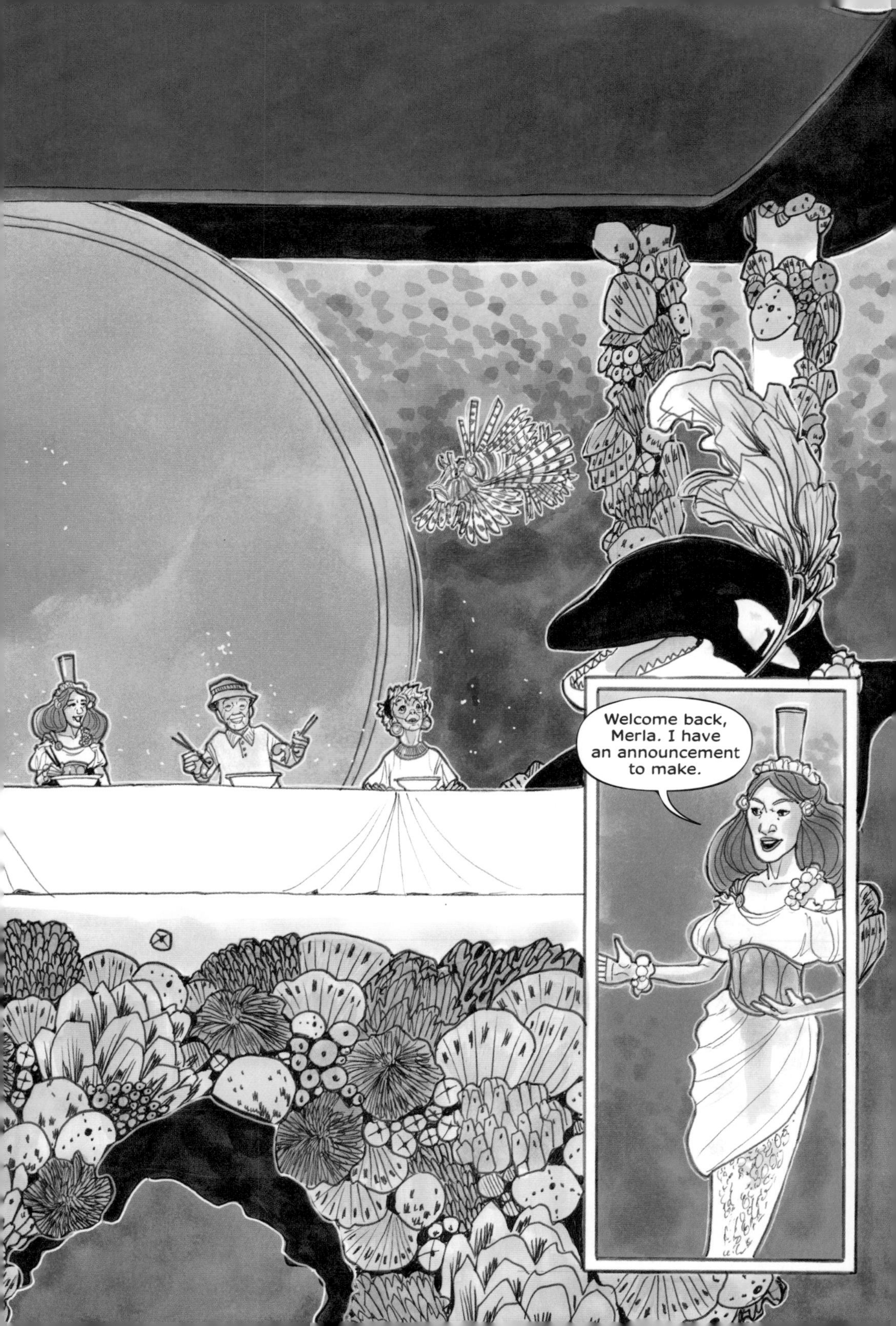
Welcome back, Merla. I have an announcement to make.

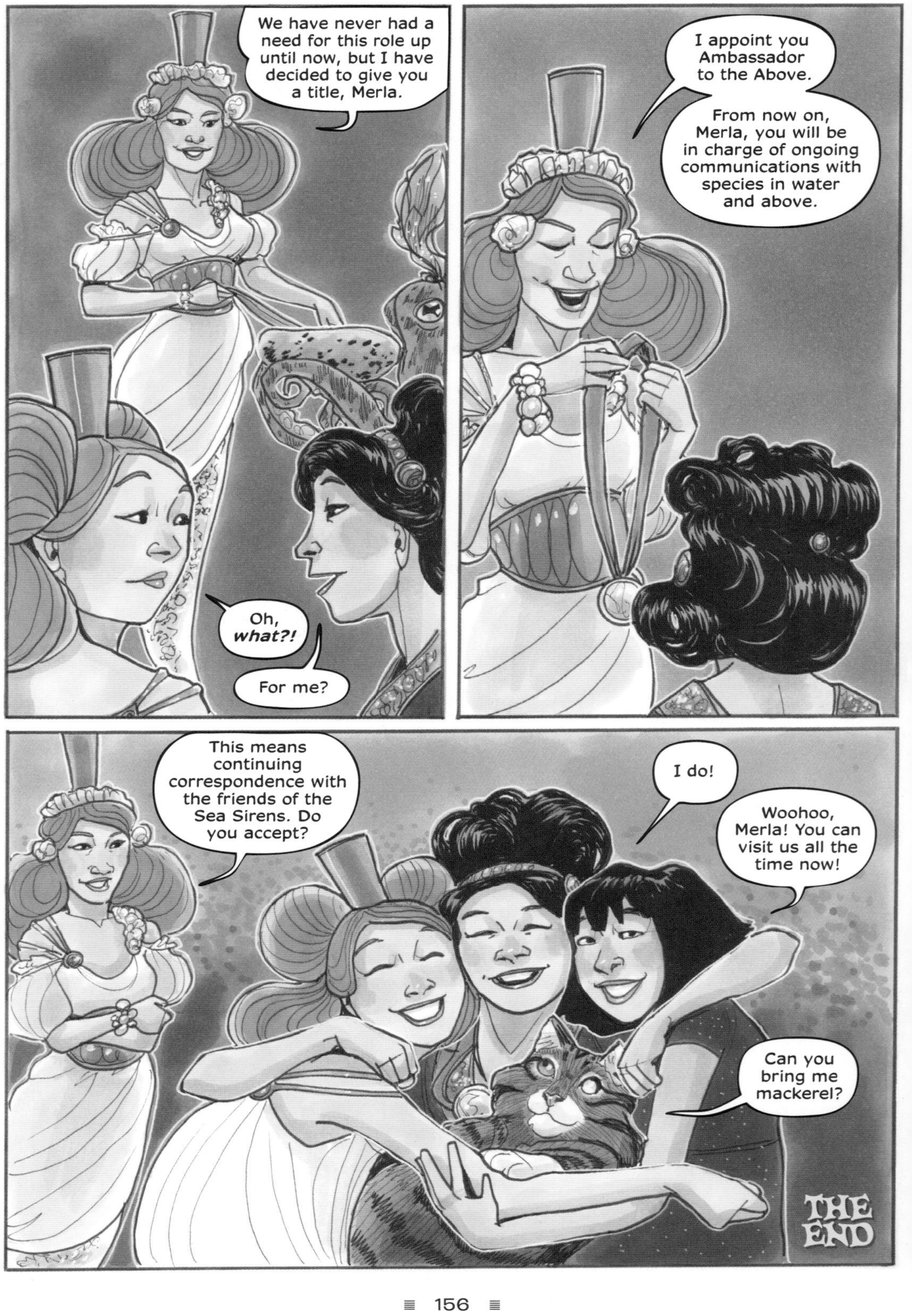
We have never had a need for this role up until now, but I have decided to give you a title, Merla.
Oh, *what?!*
For me?
I appoint you Ambassador to the Above.
From now on, Merla, you will be in charge of ongoing communications with species in water and above.
This means continuing correspondence with the friends of the Sea Sirens. Do you accept?
I do!
Woohoo, Merla! You can visit us all the time now!
Can you bring me mackerel?
THE END

About the Artist

JANET K. LEE moved from Palo Alto, California, to Nashville, Tennessee, when she was eight years old and has been there ever since. Living so far away from an ocean, she never learned to surf like Trot, but she did have a kitten, Genie, as her first pet, rode a skateboard almost everywhere, and loved to draw. So she created her own newspaper, which featured her first comic strips, and passed that out to friends at school.

Fast-forward to adulthood when Janet won an Eisner Award for her first graphic novel, *Return of the Dapper Men*. Now she illustrates comics full-time in a studio surrounded by four cats, one of which bears an uncanny resemblance to Cap'n Bill.

About the Writer

At age eleven, **AMY CHU** wrote her first book. It was about a princess and a magic poodle and went on to win the Best Book Prize in Mrs. Millard's sixth grade class.

Amy is now a professional comic book writer, creating stories for popular Marvel and DC characters such as Wonder Woman, Ant-Man, Deadpool, and Poison Ivy, as well as Green Hornet, Red Sonja, and the Princess of Mars.

Amy was born in Boston, Massachusetts, and has lived in New York, California, Iowa, Oklahoma, and Hong Kong. She now lives in Princeton, New Jersey, with her family and her extensive LEGO collection.

About the Story

Like our first book, *Sea Sirens*, **SKY ISLAND** was inspired in equal parts by the old and the new around us. It is the culmination of our mutual love for the original source material published in 1912, written by L. Frank Baum, the writer of the Oz books, and beautifully illustrated by John R. Neill.

The challenge for Janet and myself was to pay tribute to the original material, while adapting it in a fresh way for a new generation of children to enjoy and remember. So this is a new adventure starring the classic characters of Trot and Cap'n Bill reimagined as a Vietnamese American surfer girl and her cat living in Southern California. But unlike our first book, where *Sea Sirens* took place underwater, *Sky Island* takes place mostly on land. We hope you enjoy the nostalgic exploration of amusement parks from our childhood, most now long gone. We certainly did.

P.S. No cats were harmed in the making of this book.

Acknowledgments

Thanks to Sheila and the extraordinary team at Viking for their expertise and making sure the trains run on time, the indomitable Dave Lanphear for his impressive lettering skills, and Tabitha for all her hard work behind the scenes. Deep gratitude to Mike, who helped carry the ball when the going got tough.